Karin Baine lives in Northern Ireland with her husband, two sons and her out-of-control notebook collection. Her mother and her grandmother's vast collection of books inspired her love of reading and her dream of becoming a Mills & Boon author. Now she can tell people she has a *proper* job! You can follow Karin on Twitter, @karinbaine1, or visit her website for the latest news—karinbaine.com.

SURGEON PRINCE'S FAKE FIANCÉE

KARIN BAINE

A MOTHER FOR HIS LITTLE PRINCESS

KARIN BAINE

MILLS & BOON

First published in Great Britain 2023
by Mills & Boon, an imprint of HarperCollins*Publishers* Ltd,
1 London Bridge Street, London, SE1 9GF

www.harpercollins.co.uk

HarperCollins*Publishers* Macken House, 39/40 Mayor Street Upper, Dublin 1, D01 C9W8, Ireland

Surgeon Prince's Fake Fiancée © 2023 Karin Baine

A Mother for His Little Princess © 2023 Karin Baine

ISBN: 978-0-263-30626-2

12/23

SURGEON PRINCE'S
FAKE FIANCÉE

KARIN BAINE

MILLS & BOON

For my prince. xx

CHAPTER ONE

'What the…? What, now?'

Soraya's head was spinning, partly from the information that had just been launched at her, but mostly from being ushered into a small office at top speed by someone who usually didn't have two words to say to her. At least not pleasant ones.

'I need you to operate on my father.'

Raed Ayad, a neurosurgeon who worked at the hospital, and someone she'd had the misfortune to run into on occasion, sighed as he repeated his demand.

He was slightly less frantic now than when he'd first accosted her in the corridor, asked her for 'a quick word', then corralled her into this room. After the rambling about a country in need and his responsibility, at least now he was clarifying what he wanted from her. She just didn't know why.

It was an open secret that Raed, super surgeon, was also a prince in his own country. An island in the Persian Gulf somewhere that apparently wasn't missing him. Although his royal status was something she could have guessed by the regal way he glided through the hospital corridors. Goodness knew why he was working in a busy London hospital if he had a luxurious palace somewhere to lounge around in. Some people didn't have a choice but to work day and night to pay the bills, but at least she only had herself to support now the divorce had come through. Still, she had a lot on her mind, what with the debt her cheating ex-husband had run up, moving into her sister's tiny flat, and transferring to the London Central Hospital. Getting involved in Raed's family drama wasn't something she needed on top of that.

Especially when he'd been so rude to her when she'd asked him for his help not so long ago. She'd been trying to raise funds for a young local carers' charity to provide a centre where they could go for respite. Something that was close to her heart as she'd cared for her elderly, ailing parents and taken on the responsibility of her younger sister, Isolde, in her teens. New to the hospital, and the area, she'd targeted her fellow surgeons during her fundraising, knowing they had a bigger income than most of the medical staff. When she had approached Raed during the fundraising day, dressed in her pyjamas, her hair tied in pigtails and her front tooth blacked out, he'd snapped, 'Not now,' and stomped off down the corridor. For a prince, he'd been sadly lacking in manners.

'Tell me again what's going on. Slowly.'

His breath of frustration and clenched jaw did little to win Soraya's sympathy.

'My father's in the hospital. He's had a heart attack and needs a bypass operation.'

'Okay, but what does that have to do with me?' Apart from his complete dismissal of her charity fundraising, she was pretty sure this was the first time he'd actually spoken to her directly. Usually he swept into the hospital, worked his magic in the operating theatre, then swept out again, leaving everyone in awe behind him. His reputation was second to none, at least professionally speaking.

He wasn't known for being personable. Cool, precise and controlled were usually the words used to describe him. The nicer ones at least.

Raed was tugging at his hair now, mussing the usually sleek raven locks. Even the carefully groomed beard he sported seemed a little unruly today. 'My father is the King. If anything happens to him, our country will be in uproar. We need to keep this quiet until we know he's going to be all right. You're the best cardiac surgeon the trust has.'

She couldn't argue with that, yet she held a little resentment that he'd clearly had privileges to get where he was in his career, when she'd had to struggle every day. A prince wouldn't have had to work menial jobs to pay for schooling, or raise a sister alone after their parents died, or sell a home to pay off a cheating ex's debts.

Okay, so none of that was Raed's fault, but if he weren't so arrogant she wouldn't have taken such a dislike to him. Not that she would let her personal feelings get in the way of her doing her job.

'I'll check my schedule.'

'You don't understand, there is no time.' He was pacing the room now, which brought back memories for her. She'd been equally worried when both of her parents had been ill. Although a patient still had a chance if they received a heart bypass. Terminal lung cancer was somewhat more difficult to reconcile. Especially when both of her parents had succumbed to it within a year of each other.

'I know you're upset, Raed. Why don't you sit down and we can talk about this?' She tried to direct him towards a seat but he simply resumed pacing.

'Don't you see? I'm the next in line to the throne. If he dies I have to go back.'

This was the first time she'd seen Raed anything other than cool and in control and it was clear he was in a crisis. Not least because he'd chosen her to confide in.

'Surely, that's not news to you? I mean, I don't know much about your country but if you're next in line to the throne…'

'It was supposed to be Amir but I can't expect him to go back now.'

'Ah, yes, your brother? I was sorry to hear about the accident and the loss of your sister-in-law. My sister, Isolde, is working with your niece on her mobility issues.' Soraya remembered the story about the car crash being on the news, back before Raed had been in her orbit. Isolde had recently been working with Farah, his nine-year-old niece, who was still struggling to walk six months on. It was clear the family had been through a lot recently.

'So you know he can't go back. He's not in the right head space to run a country and he's needed here. I—I just need some more time.' He finally dropped into the chair, seemingly defeated by his circumstances, and Soraya couldn't help but feel sorry for him.

'Forgive me, but aren't you the eldest? *Shouldn't* it be you?' Surely he'd had a lifetime to prepare for this role? Soraya didn't understand why it seemed to come as such a surprise now.

'Amir was going to take my position as rightful heir. We were about to make an official announcement to surrender my right to be next in line to the throne when the accident happened. Of course we've had to delay that because he has to focus on Farah, but, with my father ill now, someone will have to go back to Zaki. I guess that's going to be me.' The reluctance was there in every word, but also an acceptance that this was his fate as the eldest son.

Although she wasn't royalty, Soraya knew how it was to be so burdened by responsibility, given she'd spent most of her life looking after her younger sister. Their parents had had them late in life, their health gradually declining when Soraya was a teenager, so she'd parented Isolde even before they'd been orphaned, putting her sister's needs before her own. It was clear Raed had a life here in London, including a successful career, that he didn't want to leave behind, but it appeared he had no choice. That familiar pressure awakened a new empathy towards him.

'Okay, okay. I'll go and see your father and talk to his consultant.'

'Thank you, Soraya.'

She didn't know if it was the unfamiliar sound of her name on his tongue or the look of gratitude in those deep brown eyes that made her legs wobble beneath her jade-green wrap dress as she left the room. Not a development she was excited about when she was still getting over her marriage break-up.

It had been only fourteen months since her whole world had come crashing down, when she found out, not only that Frank had cheated on her, but also that he'd funded it with her money. Romance had been the last thing on her mind when she'd been busy with work and raising Isolde, and though there'd been a few dates and disasters in medical school her priorities had lain elsewhere, so it wasn't until Isolde had grown up and moved out that she'd been open to the idea of sharing her life with someone else. Frank had been her first real relationship.

He was a lawyer who specialised in helping charitable causes, and she'd thought him a man she could trust, who would put her before anything else as he clearly had such a big heart. Wrong.

She'd thought, because he was so generously giving his time and effort to good causes, it was only right that they would live off her earnings. What she'd been unaware of was the fact that he was giving a lot more to one of his administrators than paperwork, and running up credit in both their names to fund his affair.

Isolde had wanted her to go to the police and have him charged with fraud for forging her signature on loans and credit agreements, which she'd later found out paid for luxury holidays and expensive hotels. When she'd believed he was away fighting for funding and debating issues with parliament, he'd actually been living it up with his mistress. Despite all that she didn't want a long, drawn-out court case where she'd have to face Frank and his lies all over again. It was more important to her to cut her losses and walk away. Even if that meant selling her home to do so and taking up residence in her little sister's box room in the meantime.

All that trauma and upset meant she wasn't in any hurry to even think about another man. If and when she was ready to get close to someone else, it would be with a man who would put her first for a change. Certainly not one who had the weight of an entire country on his shoulders.

Royalty was a world away from the life she led, but when she operated on his father she would treat him as every other patient. And Raed? He was just another attractive, successful, concerned family member she would probably never have to deal with again.

Raed stayed in the chair long after the blaze of Soraya's red hair had disappeared out of sight. There was a definite sense of relief easing the tension from his body now that she'd agreed to perform his father's surgery, but it was mixed with the shame of his emotional outburst. In their line of work it was nothing new to have relatives breaking down on them, but Soraya was a colleague, one he didn't know particularly well. That hadn't stopped him blabbing some very personal details he'd clearly been bottling up for too long though.

It had been a long couple of days, watching his father fighting for his life, and inwardly dealing with all the consequences of that. At least he'd been stabilised now, even if he needed that all-important heart bypass. In the meantime, it was down to Raed how they publicly dealt with the situation.

He'd been under pressure to return to the family fold ever since the car crash that had devastated his brother Amir's life. Responsibility to his family and his country had already cost him his relationship, but he wasn't ready to leave his whole life behind here in England just yet. And he knew if they revealed his father's serious health woes his countrymen would expect him to immediately go home and take up the reins, which would be no mean feat. It was something Amir had been preparing for, not Raed.

He took his phone out of his pocket and called his brother.

'How did it go?' Amir knew his plan to get Soraya on-side to give their father the best chance of surviving.

'She's on board, though it took a little grovelling.'

His brother gave a brittle laugh. Raed didn't think he'd heard him truly laugh since his wife had died. 'Now *that* I would like to have seen.'

'It wasn't my finest moment.' He cringed, thinking about the display he'd put on. Usually he was able to keep a lid on his feelings. Even when Zara had left him, unable to deal with the idea of potentially having to move back home with him and become part of the royal family, he hadn't made a scene like that. His emotions were usually the one thing in his life he could keep control over.

From a very young age his whole life had been dictated by his royal role—until he'd rebelled against his position and decided to go into medicine, making his own path. He'd worked hard to be a success, but this just proved he still had no control of his own life. And now he'd loosened his grip on those emotions he usually tried so hard to keep to himself in front of a colleague, it felt as though everything was slipping away from him again.

He supposed it was the culmination of everything hitting him all at once, plus lack of sleep. Add to that the initial hostility towards him from the one person who might have been able to help them get through this nightmare, and he'd lost his usual composure. In that moment when it had seemed as though she wasn't going to make things easy for him, he'd seen himself on the first private jet home. Alone. Leaving his family and all their problems here without him. Despite Soraya's help there was no knowing if his father would survive, his mother was in bits, and Amir and Farah needed his support. Even if he could walk away from his career and the independent life he'd made for himself here, he was torn between the responsibility he felt towards his family, and that for his country. His life was never going to be his own again.

'Well, we're all struggling, Raed.'

'How is Mother? Sorry I had to leave but I wanted to catch Dr Yarrow.'

'I know, don't worry. I've sent her back to the hotel to rest.'

'Good idea. A five-star suite with an entourage to take care of her is a lot better than sitting in a tiny family room with a cup of cold coffee waiting for news. Something Mother is not used to, even if the two of us spend a lot of time in those situations. Albeit on the other end of the conversations that tend to happen in the family room.' His brother was a thoracic surgeon who often worked in life-or-death situations too. Both he and Amir had gone to England for medical school and were working in the same hospital. For now. Neither of them knew what the future held.

'We all need some rest or we won't be any use to Father at all. Listen, I'll be in with Farah for her physiotherapy appointment tomorrow. Why don't you get some sleep tonight and come and say hello tomorrow?'

'I might just do that,' Raed said and ended the call.

Before that he'd check in with his mother to make sure she was all right, and get an update on his father from his consultant. He needed to be with his family. After all, he didn't know how much longer he'd have left with them.

'Hey, Fa-Fa.' Raed greeted his young niece with the nickname he knew she secretly loved even when she pulled that face at him. He hadn't slept any better last night than he had by his father's bedside when he'd been first admitted to the cardiac unit, but he put on a brave face for Farah so she didn't unduly worry. He supposed his brother and mother were also trying to shield her from the possibility of losing another loved one. She knew her grandfather was ill, but they hadn't shared any critical details in the hope he would recover before she realised how sick he really was.

'Hi, Uncle Raed.' Farah smiled, though these days there was a sadness in it that broke his heart.

He kissed her on the cheek. 'So, how's it going?'

She screwed up her nose. 'It's not fun.'

'I know, sweetheart, but these exercises are all to try and make your legs stronger.'

'What's the point if I'm never going to walk again?' It was tough to see her so despondent in the wheelchair, as though she'd given up. She wasn't the same energetic child who used to dance on his feet while holding his hands, giggling and singing. Even though there was a chance she could regain full use of her limbs, he wasn't so sure he'd get that fun-loving niece back again. That crash had stolen so much from her—and Amir—and Raed wished he could do something to make them happy again. Something he wouldn't be able to do if he was on the other side of the world from them.

'We're working on it, Farah, aren't we?' a perky young blonde said as she came into the room. She clearly knew his niece and, judging by the uniform, he assumed it must be the physiotherapist helping her with her rehabilitation.

'Raed, this is Isolde.' It was Amir who introduced her and Raed didn't miss the smile on his face as he did so.

'Isolde? That's not a name I've heard before, yet I think that's the second time in a couple of days… Is Dr Yarrow your sister?' It slowly dawned on him as he saw the family resemblance that Soraya had mentioned something about her sister working with Farah.

'Yes. I'm supposed to be meeting her for lunch once I'm finished up here. Speak of the devil…' Isolde turned her head and Raed followed her gaze to see Soraya waving from the door.

'We'll let you go. I'm sure you have a lot to catch up on.' The sight of her immediately made him cringe at the thought of their conversation yesterday. She'd witnessed him at his worst, his most vulnerable, a side of him neither his patients nor his family had ever seen. It had been

a moment of weakness he hoped never to repeat, or be reminded of again.

'Can Isolde come to lunch with us, Papa?' Farah, who'd
been quiet during the exchange around her, now spoke up
to torpedo Raed's plan to try and avoid the Yarrow sisters
as much as possible.

'Ms Yarrow just said she already has plans with her
sister,' Amir countered, clearly as uncomfortable with the
idea as he was.

'Soraya moved into my tiny flat with me last year so
we're sick of the sight of each other. Only joking. It would
be nice to have some company other than my bossy big
sister and it makes sense for us all to have lunch together.'
Isolde looked as thrilled with the idea as his niece, and
Raed knew they were fighting a losing battle.

Both he and Amir would do anything to make Farah
smile again. Even if it meant asking Soraya to join them
too. Sitting through a lunch with a colleague he'd embarrassed himself in front of seemed a small price to pay for
his niece's happiness.

'We're having afternoon tea at Grandmother's hotel
with scones and tiny sandwiches and macarons.'

'Sounds lovely.' Isolde was grinning at Farah's unexpected excitement over such a simple thing as lunch.

It was clear to see the pair had quickly built up a rap-
port and, though his brother probably wasn't ready to so-
cialise just yet, Raed thought it would be worth both their
personal discomfort to keep that smile on Farah's little
face a while longer.

'Of course you and your sister should join us for lunch.
As a thank you for helping us, and we are all work colleagues after all.' He took the initiative, realising he would

have to face Soraya again sooner or later as they'd probably be seeing more of each other because of his father.

Isolde rushed over to offer the lunch invitation to her
sister and he watched the puzzled look on her face turn
into one of irritation. Then she saw he was watching and
forced a smile as she waved over.

With a little prompting from Isolde, Soraya came into
the room to join them. 'Thank you so much for the invite
but—'

'But nothing,' Isolde interrupted her sister. 'We are
going for afternoon tea with the lovely royal family,
Soraya.'

The pointed look Isolde gave her almost made Raed
laugh out loud and he had to turn away so they wouldn't
see the smirk on his face. It was clear who really called
the shots in this sibling relationship and it made him feel
better to see her on the back foot this time.

'We would have to go and get changed first, Isolde, and
I don't really have time to take out of my day,' Soraya insisted through gritted teeth.

'You look absolutely fine, and it'll be a private affair.
We won't be expected to dine with the public, don't worry.
There is a car waiting to take us there and it can bring you
straight back after lunch so you don't miss any work. You
are allowed a lunch break, Soraya.' Despite previously
embarrassing himself, and not wishing to revisit it in her
presence, there was a greater part of Raed that was enjoying seeing her discomfort. It proved the great Dr Yarrow
was human too.

Soraya Yarrow had an excellent reputation for her surgery skills and for working well in a crisis. Which was
partly why he was cringing at the memory of his mini

emotional breakdown when it had looked as though he couldn't hold it together.

'Thank you. That's very kind.' She smiled graciously but there was a tension in her body that couldn't disguise her annoyance.

It was obvious she didn't want to have lunch with him and Amir, but here she was, trapped by her loyalty to her sibling. He knew something about that. Hopefully her unease would go some way to cancelling his out, then they might even be able to enjoy their meal. Although he did enjoy seeing her lose her cool, proving he wasn't the only one who could have an off day.

Dr Yarrow had a good reputation in the hospital. He'd asked around, and apparently she had joined the staff around the same time he'd split with Zara. He didn't recall meeting her before, but he hadn't been in the mood for much conversation with anyone at that time. His mind had been full of worries about his future, where he was going to end up, and how he was going to get through it all without any support. As usual he'd simply had to push his emotions to one side and get on with things. The same thing he'd been doing from a young age when it came to public appearances, or when he was sent to boarding school away from his family. He hadn't been allowed to say he was unhappy, and had been expected to carry on regardless.

So when Zara had called it quits on their relationship and moved out, he'd gone back to work and helped those who still needed him. It hadn't meant he wasn't hurting on the inside. Just like now.

He would try and make friends, share a meal with the

woman who would hopefully save his father's life, but he was still frightened half to death about what was coming next for him too.

CHAPTER TWO

'THE ONLY THING more intimidating than having to perform heart surgery on a king is probably having afternoon tea with the rest of his family,' Soraya grumbled to her sister.

'It'll be fine. Amir and Farah are sweethearts,' Isolde replied, trying to reassure her this wasn't going to be the awkward, forced meal she was expecting.

'It's not Amir or Farah I'm worried about. Raed has that air of superiority about him at the hospital at the best of times, but this is about his royal status today. We're going to be in the presence of his mother, the Queen. I'm sure he'll use the opportunity to lord it over us peasants.'

Soraya was sure he'd want to claw back some dignity after his emotional outburst yesterday. Men like him usually did that by lashing out at those lesser mortals around them. Since she'd been the one to witness his moment of vulnerability, it stood to reason she'd be the one in the firing line. Not that she could explain that to Isolde when Raed had come to her in confidence.

'You worry too much. Just enjoy the ride, sis,' Isolde told her as they followed the Ayad family out of the hospital and into the back of the luxury car sent to pick them up.

Raed, back to his usual self, barely acknowledged her presence. That was why his emotional plea for her to help his family had been unexpected, as was discovering he did indeed hold her work in high regard. Though she would never have guessed he even knew her name until today. It was clear events with his father had shaken him, unravelling that usual cool façade.

She understood that; she'd been through the deaths of both of her parents, and that feeling of helplessness had helped spur her on to work in the medical profession. The frustration of his father's fate being completely out of his control was understandable. Especially when it was obviously going to impact on his life too. Though she sympathised, there was little she could do to help, other than perform the surgery and hope everything turned out the way he wanted.

She supposed he hadn't intended to share such deeply personal information with her during their short meeting yesterday, but it was also something he'd apparently needed to get off his chest. When she'd turned up to meet Isolde for lunch, she'd seen the way he'd flinched at the sight of her again. Something she was trying not to take personally, aware that he was probably embarrassed by what he had shared with her, and appearing vulnerable to a colleague he barely knew.

So it was baffling why he'd pushed her into coming for this meal. Unless he just wanted to see her squirm too.

'It looks as though it might rain this afternoon,' Raed finally said, breaking the silence in the car.

'Yes. Thank goodness we didn't decide on an al fresco lunch.' Soraya gave a fake laugh at her own lame joke.

'It could have ended up a complete washout,' Amir offered into the small talk.

The short car journey to the hotel should have been something to crow about for the rest of her days, speeding through the streets of London like VIPs in a swanky limo. Yet even with the five of them spread out across the luxurious black leather interior, conversation was stilted, the atmosphere awkwardly tense, because most of those in the car had no desire to be there. With the exception of Farah and Isolde, who were chatting like old friends, oblivious to everyone else now staring out of the windows and avoiding eye contact with nothing left to say to one another.

It was typical of Isolde to drag her along to something she had no interest in, yet she didn't have the heart to refuse her sister. Isolde was something of a free spirit and prone to acting impulsively, causing no end of worry to Soraya. Probably because Isolde had grown up without the burden of household bills, schooling, and learning to parent when she was barely an adult herself. Whereas Soraya had had all that worry and anxiety that came with raising a child without ever having had a choice in the matter.

She wasn't jealous of the freedom her younger sister had without that burden of guilt and responsibility. If anything she was glad it hadn't continued down the family line and ended with her. Isolde got to live the life they both should have been afforded, though ultimately Soraya had been forced to sacrifice her freedom for her sibling to have it. From time to time she did wonder what it would feel like to live without a care in the world. Like now, afternoon tea was such a small thing, albeit with some influential people. And, while Isolde was relishing every moment, Soraya was the one worrying about the impression they would make. If they would measure up. Or if Raed and his family would see them for the commoners they were.

'Isn't this amazing?' Isolde exclaimed as they walked into the hotel, clearly dazzled by the opulence around them.

'It's a sickening display of wealth and privilege.' It

wasn't as easy for Soraya to relax and enjoy the luxury the way Isolde could. Not when she'd spent most of her early adult years counting every penny and thinking they were lucky if they had a roof over their heads for the night. Perhaps it was jealousy, but seeing this display of wealth didn't sit well with Soraya. She just didn't want Raed thinking she could be bought, or, worse, that she somehow belonged to him simply because she'd agreed to come out here. If he wanted someone who would be impressed by this kind of thing and fall in line, he'd certainly picked the wrong woman.

'You deserve to be spoiled for once. You've spent your whole life looking after me and you deserve someone who will do the same for you. That definitely wasn't Frank.' They shared an anxious giggle at the thought of Soraya's ex-husband ever showering her with expensive gifts.

'I should have known from our first date when he divided the bill at the end of the meal according to what we'd eaten and made me pay for my drinks because he'd only sipped tap water. That pretty much set the precedent for our entire marriage. That was the real Frank: selfish and petty. The rest—the apparent altruism and passion— were all for show.' Soraya did deserve someone better, but it had taken her long enough to find Frank and figure out the real man behind the façade—she didn't think she had it in her to go searching again.

'Well, maybe Raed is interested in more than your surgical skills.' Isolde waggled her eyebrows and Soraya hoped no one else could hear this conversation as they followed the royal entourage into a private function room.

'I don't think so.' Soraya tried to shut down the discussion. She didn't want to break his confidence by explaining why he might've felt indebted to her, other than trying to get her to operate on his father.

'Why else would Prince Raed have invited us?'

'Because you didn't leave him any choice?'

Isolde pouted.

'You're so cynical. Why can't you just enjoy yourself for once?' Isolde grabbed her by the shoulders and gave her a playful shake.

'Why do you think?'

'Not everyone is Frank and not all men are out to deceive you. Now, can we go and have afternoon tea with the royal family like any other normal women and stop worrying?' Isolde was grinning as she linked her arm through her sister's and they made their way over to the large table.

An older woman, dressed in the most beautiful purple silk dress embellished with gold threads, walked into the room and Raed immediately went to greet her.

'I'm glad you had some rest, Mother.' He kissed her on the cheek, as did Amir.

It was clear to Soraya that they were in the presence of the Queen, looking like the lowly commoners they were.

'I couldn't resist afternoon tea with my favourite people in the world, now, could I?' She bent down to hug Farah and Soraya felt even more as though she was intruding on private family time.

'This is Dr Soraya Yarrow, who has kindly agreed to operate on Father, and her sister, Isolde, the physiotherapist who is working with Farah.'

'Ah, ladies, my sincere gratitude for everything you're doing for my family.' She clasped her hands together and bowed her head in thanks.

'Your Majesty.' Soraya curtseyed, glad the smart cream

trouser suit she was wearing today wasn't skintight and had some give in it.

It occurred to her that she hadn't shown Raed or Amir similar respect, but she didn't recall anyone else bowing or scraping to them at work, at least not physically. There were a few members of the hospital trust she was sure did their fair share of kowtowing because they were in the presence of royalty, though Raed at least didn't seem to expect it. Guessing by their previous conversation, he probably preferred not to be reminded of his status.

Isolde attempted a curtsey too in her less forgiving leather mini dress, but the Queen gestured for her to stop. 'There's no need for formalities. You're friends of the family now, so just Djamila from now on.'

'It's so nice to meet you, Djamila.' Isolde, unrestrained by social graces now, went in for the full hug, leaving Raed's mother bemused.

'You too. Now, shall we eat?' The Queen graciously extracted herself from Isolde and gestured for her to take a seat between Farah and Amir. She sat at the head of the table, leaving Soraya to sit next to Raed.

'Thank you for the invitation.' Since they were going to be forced together during the meal, she thought it wise to attempt some sort of social niceties.

'I don't think either of us were left much option.' Although stony-faced, Raed still pulled her chair out and waited for her to be seated before he sat down.

'Thank you. You do have manners after all,' she said, the corner of her mouth tilting up into a half-smile.

Raed cocked his head to one side, a dark frown rippling across his forehead. 'Pardon me?'

Soraya flushed, knowing she'd spoken in haste. He clearly had no recollection of their previous encounter during her fundraising attempts when he'd been so rude to her. The comment had slipped out in the moment when he was being so chivalrous. A very different attitude from the one she was used to from him. Though perhaps he was on his best behaviour around his mother and it had nothing to do with her.

'You probably don't remember but we met a while ago. You…er…weren't the most welcoming colleague I had when I transferred here.' She kept her voice low as they took their seats, not wishing to embarrass him in front of his family. Everyone had their bad days when things didn't go their way work-wise, or at home. However, their line of work involved life-or-death situations, and it wasn't always easy to bounce back when things didn't go to plan.

'I'm sure I would've remembered,' he insisted.

'I was fundraising for a young carers' centre dressed in pyjamas.'

Soraya watched his memory of the incident play out across his features. His forehead evened out briefly, before furrowing again.

'Ah. Pigtails? I do remember. I was, er, going through a bad time. Another one. But that doesn't excuse my being rude to you. Sorry.' His apparent remorse over the incident redeemed him a little.

'That's okay. We all have our own troubles.' Despite her curiosity Soraya held back from asking any questions. As much as she tried to prevent her personal life leaking into her working one, it wasn't always possible. She supposed it went to prove that Raed wasn't just a surgeon born in a laboratory, he had emotions like everyone else. It was just unlucky that she'd caught him that day, and, judging by his recent behaviour, she was beginning to think he wasn't as cold-hearted as she'd assumed on first impressions.

They fell into silence as the waiters poured their tea through silver strainers into dainty china cups and brought fancy cake stands laden with goodies for them to enjoy. Once the staff left they all helped themselves to the elegant salmon-filled triangular sandwiches. Soraya had just bitten into hers when Raed shifted in his seat and leaned in to her.

'I was going through a break-up. It wasn't anything personal and I shouldn't have taken my bad mood out on you. Again, my apologies.'

She could hear the remorse in his voice, see that he meant it in those big brown eyes locked onto hers. Yet she also recognised the lingering pain behind it. Every time she spoke of her marriage breakdown it felt like a knife jabbing at her heart, reminding her that loving someone had brought her pain. It didn't matter that Frank had cheated on her, that she was better off without him, it still hurt. Though Raed seemed to have the perfect life on the outside, it was clear he was going through something similar, that someone had broken his heart too.

'It's fine.' She reached out and patted his leg in solidarity but the second she did, regret and shame flooded her entire body. It was one thing ignoring social etiquette on curtseying to a colleague, but she was pretty sure she wasn't supposed to cop a feel of his thigh muscles under the table under any circumstances.

She stopped breathing. Her face was flaming, her stomach lurching in disgust at the situation she'd put herself in. It didn't help that she'd felt him tense under her touch and they were both now staring straight ahead not knowing what to say to each other.

He almost swallowed a sandwich in one bite while studiously ignoring her. Soraya sipped her tea, wondering how the hell she was going to get out of this one, and if the fire alarm was within arm's reach. In the end she decided ignoring the incident altogether was the way to go.

She choked down part of a sandwich in an attempt to look normal and washed it down with more tea.

'I'd just been through a break-up myself so I was probably a little sensitive at the time too. We're divorced now.' Any time she said those words she cringed a little. Oversharing perhaps, but with every reinforcement of what was happening she hoped she'd come to terms with the end of her marriage.

'I'm sorry to hear that. It's never fun going through the end of a relationship. Zara and I weren't even married but it's still hard to come to terms with such a big life change. Although if we had married she might have been more inclined to stick around and support me.' He popped a whole pistachio macaron in his mouth, chewed, and swallowed it before clarifying the situation and satisfying Soraya's curiosity to some extent.

'I'm so sorry.' She resisted the urge to touch him again, even though she'd enjoyed the warm feel of his body at her fingertips. It wasn't appropriate the first time, to do it again would just be plain weird.

'Dr Yarrow, I'm sure you must be finding it surreal that we're sitting here enjoying our tea while my husband is so ill.' The Queen broke through the chatter around the table to address her directly.

'Not at all. Every family has a different way of dealing with things. It's better to carry on as normal and hope for the best, rather than congregating round his bedside night and day running yourselves into the ground waiting for news.' It was easier for the staff in that situation to get on with their jobs too, instead of having to navigate around a prematurely grieving family. There were also extra factors involved when it came to a royal family when they came with an entourage of staff and security.

'We did that the night he was admitted,' Amir added. Although he'd been relatively quiet on the journey to the hotel, Soraya had noticed he'd been engaged with Isolde as well as Farah since they'd sat down. She hoped her bubbly little sister was coaxing him out of his shell, and not overwhelming him with her personality as she was sometimes prone to do.

'Well, I saw your father this morning and, though he's not out of the woods just yet, he's holding his own. As soon as he's stable enough, I'll perform his bypass, which should get his heart back pumping as normal. He'll be in for some physical rehab after that, but I'm sure Raed and Amir have told you all of this already,' she added, addressing the Queen. These were extraordinary circumstances, not least because she was dealing with a patient whose family members were medical colleagues. Soraya couldn't help but feel under pressure to succeed under ever watchful eyes. It gave her some indication of the burden of responsibility weighing heavily on Raed's shoulders. All while dealing with the end of his relationship, and his father's ill health.

She had a new-found respect for him outside the workplace, and had never expected them to have so much in common given their very different backgrounds. Although money wasn't a factor in his struggle, she did recognise that commitment to his family, and need to protect them. No one here would ever have guessed how he'd really felt about his father's condition, or his fears about the future. She wondered if subconsciously he'd realised he'd found a kindred spirit in her and that was why he'd felt safe to express his emotions. It made a change from a man who'd kept so many things hidden from her, and it was a privilege that Raed had been able to confide in her. Perhaps not all men were only out for themselves, disregarding other people's feelings in the process, after all.

'We'll follow your advice on this one. You're in charge,' Raed said, letting Soraya know he wasn't going to give her any trouble, or interfere in his father's treatment. He trusted her judgement, and a lot more besides.

She'd been very discreet about his emotional outburst in her office, as well as understanding. He didn't know much about their family dynamics, but he was sure as the eldest sister Soraya could relate to his need to protect his family and do what was best for them. There was an inherent responsibility that a firstborn took upon their shoulders and he could see in the interactions between Soraya and Isolde that she looked out for her little sister, the way he did for his little brother.

She would've understood his need to do the right thing by stepping up to take over when it became apparent Amir couldn't, in a way Zara, an only child, never had. They both wanted what was best for their families, and would do whatever it took to make them happy. Including agreeing to this lunch. He knew Soraya didn't want to be here any more than he did but she was right, it was best to keep some sort of normality in their lives, at least for Farah, who had already suffered so much.

'Can I get that in writing?' she said, her mouth turned up at the corners.

He liked her sense of humour, and the fact she wasn't intimidated by him or his family as a whole. There were a lot of things about Soraya he apparently liked. His body had responded unexpectedly when she'd touched him earlier. The squeeze she'd given him had been an act of solidarity, he'd known that, but that awareness of her touch had wakened his weary body.

It had been a while since Zara had left and he hadn't dated since, his days too consumed by work and family issues to give space for a personal life. Perhaps this was a reminder that, despite his roles as surgeon, brother, son, and prince, he was still a man. Being alone might prevent further heartbreak, but it didn't stop that craving of a loving touch, of having someone in his life who he could just be himself with behind closed doors.

He'd noticed Soraya didn't observe royal protocol around him the way she had with his mother, especially when she'd touched him like that earlier. It was nice to think she'd forgotten his status so quickly in her hurry to comfort him, or that it had never mattered to her in the first place. She accepted who he was both in the hospital, and here with his family without judgement. Despite his prickly demeanour, which frightened most people off.

'You have my word.' He leaned in, his voice surprisingly husky, and he was sure he saw a little shiver dance across the back of her neck. It did nothing to relieve this sudden build-up of tension between them. Something that had nothing to do with their past less-than-ideal encounters, and everything to do with this new awareness of each other.

In different circumstances he might have pursued the connection they seemed to have, but there would be no room in his life for any romantic notions, even if she didn't have cause to despise him. His future was uncertain, his life here on a knife edge, and he didn't need the complication of getting attached to someone else if he had to leave.

'We do have to decide what we're going to do if the

news gets out about your father. In the meantime, I think as next in line to the throne, Raed, we need to look after your security. We can't be too careful, so I've asked the security team to assign you a personal protection officer.' Raed's mother waited until everyone had enjoyed their bite-sized pastries before she tackled the issue he'd been trying to avoid for too long.

He'd been living in England for so long he hadn't had to worry about his personal security but he supposed they couldn't take the risk of something happening to him too. The prospect of having a permanent shadow didn't appeal to him, but nothing about his new position did.

'There are also some rumblings about why you and Father are spending so long here. I guess compassion has a time limit. Sorry.' Amir knocked back the rest of his tea as though it were hard liquor. Clearly he was feeling the strain of everything too.

'I think people forget we're human too. They expect we should just pack away our emotions and troubles into a neat pile and get on with our public duties. It doesn't mean we have to. None of this is on you, Amir. You and Farah concentrate on yourselves. I'll sort something out.'

He had no idea what that would be, but he didn't want Amir fretting over that too. The whole point of Raed taking over was to give his brother less to worry about. It was just another problem to add to his list of things keeping him awake at night.

It had been a rough year for all of them, but particularly for his little brother. Sometimes Raed forgot about his feelings in all this too.

It was his father's life on the line, so soon after losing his wife, and Raed knew, even though there was no expectation for him to go home now, Amir wouldn't have simply

---

forgotten the matter. He was someone who took his responsibilities seriously, even more than Raed. After all, he was the son who'd always towed the line and stayed out of trouble. Amir had embraced his position in the royal family, done his duty better than the eldest son who couldn't wait to spread his wings and fly away from his heritage. Not being able to fulfil his role properly now was likely eating away at Amir's conscience as much as it was Raed's.

Amir's phone buzzed, and his thunderous face when he checked the incoming message suggested it wasn't welcome news.

He held the screen up so Raed could see. 'I have an alert set up so any mention of the family online will flag up.'

'Why are our royal family living in another country?' Raed read the headline out loud and skimmed through the newspaper article, which raised the question about why the taxpayers were funding the running of the royal palace when none of the family were currently in situ. A valid concern for people who were struggling with the current cost-of-living crisis, but another potential headache for Raed.

'We're going to have to put out a statement about your father,' his mother said, her voice cracking with emotion. They all knew to be seen as fragile and vulnerable was the last thing he would want.

'Let's not rush into that just yet. At least not until he's had his operation and we know better what the situation is.' Raed wanted to put it off as long as possible to delay his return, when he'd be walking into a veritable media storm. That was something he'd rather do once he knew his family were going to be okay and he'd adapted to the idea of returning to his royal role, leaving his life in England behind for ever.

'I think it's the least we should do. We can't announce your plan to give up your right to the throne now, when there's no one else to take the reins at present. The monarchy will look more unstable than ever. I know it's not what any of us had planned but one of us has to go back to Zaki and it's going to have to be you, Raed. I have to be here for Farah.'

'I know that. I'm just asking for some more time.'

Perhaps it was selfish, people had the right to know what was going on, but he was the one who would have to deal with whatever was in store for them on their return, and it was only natural that he'd be a tad reticent about the idea of going back.

'We have to do something, Raed. The longer we leave things to fester, the harder it is going to be to recover. I still intend to go home to take up my royal duties again at some point, but in the meantime we need to give a reason for father's extended stay before there's real unrest. At the minute it's just one of the tabloids stirring up trouble. Surely there's a way to shut this down before they start speculating? Even if we're not ready to share an update on father's health, perhaps we could offer them something?' Amir tucked his phone away once everyone had had a chance to look at the article, but the reality of the situation wouldn't be as easily dismissed.

'A distraction, you mean?' In normal circumstances Raed knew they'd all be appalled by the idea of manipulating the press for their own gain, but these were extraordinary times. If it bought them some time—and whatever spin they put on the story was believed—he was all for it. Hopefully it would only be for a short while until their father was well on his way to recovery, because there was no way of knowing how long Amir and Farah were going to remain in England.

'I don't know about that...' His mother was understandably wary about any potential deception but this was to protect her too. With his father incapacitated for the foreseeable future, and Amir caring for Farah, there would be no one to look out for the Queen if Raed had to return home. And what if the worst did happen to his father and he wasn't here? For everyone's sake it would be better if they could find a way for him to stay.

'A scandal?' Isolde's eyes were wide with excitement as she clapped her hands together in glee, earning her a dirty look from her sister.

'Nothing that will damage our reputation. That's exactly what we're trying to avoid,' he reminded her. 'If the country thinks the monarchy is at risk of collapse it will have all sorts of consequences. Although we don't solely rule Zaki, and the government operates in the King's name, we are seen as a stable institution. To jeopardise that could have political implications, weaken us economically, not to mention decimate the tourist industry. We can't afford to show any sign of weakness.'

Exactly why they needed someone in situ soon.

'I do think breaking another story would buy us some time, but I'm afraid Farah and I have had more than our fair share of press coverage.' Although this was all Amir's bright idea, he was making it clear he didn't want to be the focus of 'the distraction', which came as no surprise given everything he and his daughter had been through already.

The public interest after the car accident, though understandable, had intruded on their privacy at a time when they were grieving and in pain. Raed didn't want anything to jeopardise Farah's recovery any further. Whatever plan they came up with, he knew it was going to have to be centred around him. As ever, he'd simply have to shoulder the burden for the sake of the family.

'What about a love affair?' Isolde piped up, clearly relishing being a part of this salacious discussion. Something they should really have done in private behind closed doors, but he supposed this hadn't been planned. Besides, he'd trusted Soraya not to say anything when she'd kept their earlier meeting to herself, and she'd kept his secret. He was also sure that, as the eldest sister, she'd keep Isolde in line.

'I don't think it's appropriate for us to get involved, Isolde.' As he'd predicted, Soraya took her sister to task over crossing the line and speaking out. It wasn't necessary as he doubted anyone was offended by her input, but he knew he'd have done the same thing in her position. It was the lot of older children to try and keep their siblings in check.

'It's fine, but I don't think that's going to work, Isolde. I'm just out of a relationship and I don't think me dating again would be a big enough news story to detract from my father's whereabouts.' Even if he thought it would work, if he found someone to go along with it, he didn't think he had the energy for a romance. Fake or otherwise.

'What about a royal wedding? That would certainly grab the headlines.' Undeterred, Isolde went a step further with her romance fantasy, causing Soraya to roll her eyes in frustration.

Raed couldn't hold back this time. 'I'm not getting married just for the headlines.'

'It's not a bad idea...' Amir broke the bro code and threw him under the bus. 'You wouldn't have to actually get married, but the promise of a royal wedding and your return home to have the ceremony would certainly divert attention from Father's absence.'

'Who on earth would I even get to agree to this charade? I mean, I can't just pick a random woman off a dating site and ask her if she'd pretend to be my fiancée. Nor would I be able to trust a stranger not to go straight to the papers with the story. Even if I was up to the task, it's too much to ask of any sane person.'

'Isolde could do it!' Farah, who had been quietly taking in the adult conversation around her, was now siding with everyone else.

He could already see Isolde running through the scenario in her head, but before he could object, Amir got there first.

'No. I mean, it wouldn't be fair to ask you to do that, Isolde. You're already doing so much for our family.'

Raed didn't know if it was his imagination, or a yearning for his little brother to move on with his life after losing his wife, but he thought there was something more than a desire to keep Isolde's best interests in mind going on. Amir had been so quick to shoot down the idea, and there was the way he kept looking at her… A surge of love and optimism for his brother's future swelled in his chest, though if Amir was interested in Isolde in any way it completely ruled her out as a potential candidate for the position. Even if he was seriously considering this crazy scenario as a viable option over relocating permanently to his home country.

'No offence, Isolde, but I think you're a little on the young side. If I was looking for a bride it would be someone more my age. Someone I had things in common with. Someone like Soraya.' The room went silent as everyone turned to look at her, including Raed.

Soraya blinked in the spotlight. 'Absolutely not.'

'You'd be perfect, sis! You don't have any skeletons in your closet…well, except for an ex-husband. But you're already aware of the family circumstances,' she said to Raed. 'And it just so happens you're smart and smoking hot,' she declared, turning back to Soraya.

'It would make sense for you two to have got together, given you're work colleagues.'

Raed didn't know if Amir's endorsement of Isolde's reasoning was because he genuinely believed it was a good idea, or to get Isolde off the hook from being his prospective fake fiancée. Whatever it was, his idea to get Soraya involved was gaining traction. With him too. Although she was doing as much for his family as Isolde, she wasn't as much of a loose cannon, and she was already keeping his secrets.

It was becoming clear the family were looking to him to be the scapegoat. Expecting him to sacrifice his privacy to cover up what was really going on. Something he would willingly do to protect them, but circumstances were spiralling out of his control. Again.

It reminded him of those childhood days when everyone made decisions on his future for him, telling him how to behave, sending him to boarding school to mould him into the kind of person they needed him to be. He'd run away to England so he could regain that control over his own life and be the man he wanted to be. These past months had destroyed the progress he'd made, and losing Zara had made him feel like that powerless pawn again, manipulated by the royal establishment to do the right thing regardless of what he wanted.

Yet, at this present moment he didn't know how else they could get out of this mess. At least if he was faking an engagement with a fully versed participant, no one would get hurt, and once his father had recovered they could break up. No big deal. It wasn't what he had planned for his future, or something he particularly wanted to be involved in, but it would be a distraction.

If he could get Soraya to agree he would be regaining some control. It would be better to have her on side than have to fake a relationship with a stranger he'd probably have to pay for the privilege. Of course Soraya would be well compensated for her time and co-operation, but there was something less sordid about her being involved rather than an actress or stunt fiancée. They had a real connection. Okay, mostly one that had been forged over the course of twenty-four hours, but that was what made it special.

He didn't usually open himself up to anyone, trying to keep his lives as a prince and a surgeon separate, but Soraya had been different. He'd told her everything. She would understand why he had to do this, and, since she had just gone through a divorce, there'd be no risk of anyone actually developing feelings for the other. No complications, which could be a factor if they did draft in someone else and they got notions for real about becoming a princess. Until today Soraya didn't seem to have too high an opinion of him, so he doubted she was going to get carried away with some romantic fantasy of them being together. If anything, he was going to have to persuade her this was a good idea. He might even have to come with more incentive than to save his family name.

'Soraya? What do you think?'

'I think this…is crazy.' Soraya was sure the walls had begun to close in, making the room smaller and stealing the oxygen, as everyone stared at her expecting her to agree to this crazy scheme. Including her own sister, who seemed pumped up by the idea of her getting involved in something so exciting.

Pretending to be a fake fiancée to a prince would have been right up Isolde's street. She would love the games with the press and playing up to the cameras. Isolde was the one who could pull this off, and would revel in doing so. Not that Soraya would ever have condoned it.

Soraya could see what everyone would get out of this little charade except her. Cosying up to Raed, pretending to get engaged in the eyes of the world's press, would be nothing more than a headache to her.

She wished they would all stop staring at her, hanging the weight of their expectations on her shoulders, before there was a pastel-coloured pool of vomit on the floor. The last time she'd felt this ill, as though someone were repeatedly squeezing her stomach in their fist, was when she'd discovered Frank's affair. It was the feeling of knowing her whole life was about to be upended. She'd had to make the change then for her own sake, so she didn't spend the rest of her days living with a liar and a cheat, or funding his double life. Here, she had a choice, and she was sick of always putting other people's needs before her own.

'Yes, it is, but I really don't know what else I can do other than go home and face whatever's waiting there for me. I mean, we have people running interference for us, but I'm going to have some explaining to do. It means I'll have to start getting my affairs in order here if I'm going to be leaving.'

Raed's big puppy-dog eyes weren't needed for her to feel guilty about saying no. She knew his circumstances, that he didn't want to go back, and that his family needed him here. It shouldn't be her problem.

'Is there anyone else could do this for you, Raed? If you go back now and something happens to your father—' The Queen couldn't finish the sentence, her voice breaking with emotion, clearly upset at the thought of losing her eldest's son's support.

'I don't think so, Mother. It's asking a lot from anyone who doesn't know us, or our circumstances. I—I don't even know where we would begin to set something like that up. At least with someone we trust.' He didn't look directly at Soraya, but she knew they were all thinking she was selfish in not stepping up.

The pressure to bow to everyone else's wishes was overwhelming. After Frank she'd sworn to look after only herself, and Isolde because she was an intrinsic part of who she was. This guilt, this need in her to help even when it would be detrimental to herself, was something she was still working to overcome.

'If you'll excuse me, I need to get some air.' She pushed her chair back so quickly as she stood to leave, it toppled over.

Raed got up and repositioned her chair.

'Soraya, are you all right?' Isolde's concern was too much, bringing tears to her eyes as she tried to flee the scene.

Behind her she heard Raed say, 'I'll make sure she's okay.'

If she hadn't been so desperate to get away she would have told him not to bother coming after her. She wanted space to breathe, not have the origin of her guilt stalk her until she passed out from the pressure.

It took her a minute to navigate her way through the corridors and doors to reach the hotel lobby, and then wait impatiently for the revolving door to spit her out onto the

pavement so she could actually breathe again. The sight
and sounds of the busy London traffic and the smell of
diesel in the air were strangely comforting, bringing her
back to real life. Away from the fantasy world of fake royal
romances and princes who needed rescue.

She dodged around the doorman decked out in his top
hat and maroon and gold livery who'd admitted her with
the family not too long ago, and walked around the corner
of the hotel where she wouldn't be on display for passers-
by to witness her panic attack. Bent over with her hands
on her knees, she inhaled great lungsful of air.

'I'm sorry, Soraya. I know this isn't fair on you.'

She felt a hand on her back before she heard Raed's
voice trying to comfort her. If she weren't so strung out
from the pressure he was putting her under, she would've
been touched by the concern.

'I'm your father's heart surgeon. Why is it suddenly on
me to play make-believe in a royal romance to save your
backside?' She knew why, she was just venting because
she was cornered and needed to lash out at someone.

'I know, I know, it's ridiculous. That we're even asking you to do it shows how desperate we are. Maybe I
should take Isolde up on her offer...' Hands in his pock-
ets and staring down at his shoes, he looked dejected, but
she had to remain strong. Folding at the first sign of vulnerability was not how the new Soraya was going to be
able to move on with her life. Away from men who took
advantage of her.

Yet she didn't want Isolde to be in the line of fire either.
She'd just gone through a messy break-up and didn't need
another complication in her life right now. Isolde was im-
petuous, jumping into relationships, and situations, that
weren't always good for her. All that attention and pres-

sure wouldn't be good for her mental health at a time when she was particularly vulnerable. Soraya knew herself the effect a break-up could have and didn't want her little sister to get hurt all over again if all of this was to fall apart and her life got picked over in the press. Sometimes Isolde didn't know what was best for her.

'No. Leave her out of this.'

'She volunteered, Soraya, and I'm all out of options if you won't help.'

'She's been through enough and there isn't anything in it for her, or me, that would justify opening up our private lives to be scrutinised by the whole world. We both know that's what will happen for any future wife of a prince.'

'So, you want money, is that what you're saying?' Raed's face was dark, his pleading eyes now filled with contempt that Soraya knew she didn't deserve.

'No. I'm saying I see the benefits for you and your family in all of this, but for me or Isolde it's asking for trouble. Especially if anyone finds out it's all an act.' She could only imagine the fallout if it was discovered the 'engagement' had been a cover for his father's illness, and an excuse to keep Raed from taking up his rightful place at home. There was a lot at stake for them all, but more for the royal family to gain than for her and Isolde.

Raed nodded, as though he was giving serious consideration to what she was saying. 'We're all hoping it won't come to that, but I understand that you'd be taking all the risk for no reward in this scenario.'

'That's not what—'

'What if we made a considerable donation to your charity? Enough to fund that centre you wanted to set up.' Raed interrupted her denial that she was in this for any kind of payoff with an incentive that made her reconsider that notion.

She'd struggled to raise the money she'd wanted for the charity, to give young carers a place to hang out to get a reprieve from the intense home life she'd had to endure as a young teen. With some extra funding she hoped to have enough to even pay for a counsellor who could provide a listening ear to those children forced to grow up too quickly under the burden of responsibility.

'I...er...' It was tempting. Although she would be putting the needs of others over her own comfort once more, it would be for a good cause. It would be giving young carers somewhere they could be with other children their own age, who understood what they were going through, a safe space where they could simply be kids. If she could give other families that respite, that comfort of knowing they weren't alone, that she'd never known, it would be worth it.

'Please, Soraya. We need your help.' Raed's plea, coupled with the chance to make a real difference to children weighed down by responsibility of caring for their families, wore away the last of her resolve.

'Okay, okay. I'll do it,' she huffed out on a sigh. 'I guess I'm going to have to pucker up and play nice with my beloved Prince Raed.' She clasped her hands to her heart in an exaggerated swoon, while inside it really was beating a tattoo fast enough to make her faint at the thought of being Raed's pretend lover.

Raed gathered her in an uncharacteristically enthusiastic hug. 'Thank you, so much.'

Soraya let herself be swept up into his strong arms. She'd forgotten how nice it was to be pressed close to a warm, male body. That solid reassurance of a wall of muscle against her was something she missed, along with that feeling of security. Even if none of it had been real with Frank.

She inhaled the masculine scent of him and sighed. The smile on her face as she let him hold her for a fraction longer than a celebratory hug would normally necessitate told Soraya she was doomed.

CHAPTER THREE

'I'LL HAVE HIM back to you as soon as possible,' Soraya promised as they wheeled Raed's father away to prep for surgery.

'He's in the best hands, Mother.' Raed comforted Djamila, who was crying into his shoulder. He gave Soraya a smile and a nod, as if to say, 'I know you've got this.'

She swallowed hard, hoping for all their sakes that she had.

The family, including the King, knew exactly what was going to happen. She'd talked them through the entire procedure so there wouldn't be any surprises; hopefully that went for her too. Surgery, and heart surgery in particular, always carried risks. Even the general anaesthetic used to put the King to sleep came with warnings. As heart operations went, it was a standard procedure she carried out regularly, but that didn't mean there wasn't the possibility of complications. The surgical team always had to be ready in case everything didn't go to plan, but her patient seemed in good overall health, apart from his heart, so it should go smoothly.

She would be lying if she said she wasn't nervous as she made the first incision. The responsibility of having his life in her hands wasn't lost on her.

'Okay, let's do this,' she said to herself as much as to the rest of the team.

It was more pressure than usual knowing they had a king under the knife, even though they were using off-pump coronary bypass surgery. A relatively new procedure, which, although it took less time than the conventional methods, meant less chance of bleeding during surgery. It also had increased recovery times, and was more technically demanding. She had to graft vessels while the heart was still beating. With two coronary blood vessels narrowed, Soraya had to attach two new grafts to divert the blood supply around the blocked artery. Something that always had her holding her breath until they knew everything was working as it should. Not every heart surgeon had the training to use this method and she supposed it was part of the reason Raed had chosen her to perform the surgery on his father.

Today in particular she was relieved to see and hear the heart beating of its own accord. As she fixed the breastbone back together using metal wires, and sewed the skin on the chest back together, all she could think of was Raed and the relief he would feel.

The hours waiting for his father to come out of surgery seemed to drag on, every second ticking by noted by the loud wall clock in the family waiting room.

'Raed, you're making a mess.' Despite all attempts to get his mother to leave, she'd insisted on waiting with him and Amir until they knew his father was out of surgery and safe.

He looked down and noticed the pile of paper snow at his feet where he'd been subconsciously shredding the takeaway cup in his hands.

'Sorry.' He scooped up the debris from his anxious wait and dumped it in the recycling bin.

Although Soraya would be feeling under pressure performing the life-or-death operation, time seemed to go quicker inside that operating theatre. It was so much harder, emotionally, to be on this side of the patient-surgeon divide.

Lately he felt as though he were falling apart just like that cup he'd decimated. For years he'd done his own thing, been in charge of his own life, and within a few months it had all been ripped away. That loss of control had clearly impacted him when he was finding it so much more difficult to keep a lid on his feelings. Especially around Soraya.

Even yesterday, hugging her out of relief for agreeing to help was out of character for him. Something he regretted, not only because it represented another display of emotion he should have kept at bay, but also because now he had the memory of holding her in his arms to contend with. Remembering the warmth of her body pressed against his wasn't going to help matters when they were going to be forced together for this fake engagement debacle. It needed to be a clinical transaction with no further emotional complications if he was going to get through it. He did not have time or room in his life for anything more at present.

When the door opened, his own heart felt as though it had stopped, ready to hear the news that could affect the rest of his life. He'd never been so pleased to see Soraya as she walked in with a smile.

'Mr Ayad is out of surgery and on the recovery ward. Everything went as planned but we'll have to keep him under close observation for the next forty-eight hours in intensive care just to make sure there are no complications.

He should be able to be discharged in about a week or so, with full recovery usually taking about twelve weeks.'

Raed knew there was a risk of stroke after a heart operation like this, but he was also aware his father had survived the surgery and was in the best place should anything untoward arise.

'Thank you so much, Dr Yarrow.' His mother let out a sob, probably the same relief they were all feeling.

'You're welcome,' Soraya said, and he could see her eyes welling up, as though the enormity of the situation had finally hit her too. After all, she'd been dragged into their family drama beyond his father's medical needs, and she would likely be glad when her role in all of this was over.

Amir shook her hand first and it looked to Raed as though he was fighting to hold back the tears too. Raed still felt a little too numb but he was sure it would hit him later, in private. He'd already shown too much of himself in front of Soraya. It had surprised him as much as her that he'd opened himself up to her about his personal turmoil, begging for her help twice in the space of a couple of days.

Soraya had just happened to be in the wrong place at the wrong time, twice, to witness him fall apart. Or perhaps he recognised something in her that made him feel safe sharing his fears and asking for her help. Whatever the cause, he knew he had to stop doing it.

'Thank you, Soraya, for everything.' He moved in for a handshake next, but it seemed so inadequate given everything she'd done for them. With a tug of her hand, he pulled her in closer for a hug.

Okay, so maybe one more display would be forgiven in the circumstances.

If this were any other surgeon it might have been inappropriate, but as she hugged him back he knew they'd both needed this. In a way, she'd been under as much pressure as he had to save the family and his country.

The soft comfort of her body pressed against his was something he could have luxuriated in if they'd been in private, and she'd let him; he needed it. But he was aware they weren't alone. He reluctantly let go.

'You don't know how much this means.'

'I do,' she replied, and the flush of pink in her cheeks and her dilated pupils said she wasn't just talking about his father's successful surgery.

A surge of awareness reinvigorated his weary body as he looked into those beautiful big blue eyes, and a sudden need to kiss her came from nowhere.

Raed took a step back. He knew this had to be a reaction to her saving his father's life, saving him from having his own turned upside down in the blink of an eye. Because he wasn't ready for anything more.

Soraya rang the buzzer for Raed's apartment. It was on the top floor, of course, part of a swanky new complex down by the Thames with river views and transport links on the doorstep. All angles and glass, it wasn't exactly what she would describe as pretty but was certainly expensive.

'Come up,' he commanded over the intercom as the door slowly swung open.

The air-conditioned lobby and bank of elevators wildly contrasted with the graffiti-decorated hallway of Isolde's building, which often smelled so bad Soraya had to cover her nose until she reached the flat.

As the lift rose, her stomach dropped. She had no reason to be nervous. This wasn't a booty call or anything untoward at all. Unless you included conspiring to defraud the public over an alleged romance in that bracket. Raed had simply suggested she come to his place to talk about the terms of their arrangement in private, away from listening ears at the hospital.

Perhaps it was the prospect of being truly alone with him that was making her palms sweat and her pulse race. Although that didn't explain why, when he'd hugged her at the hospital, her body had gone into meltdown. She'd put it down to exhaustion at the time after the stress of performing a successful surgery on the King. That was the only reason she'd agreed to come here tonight, telling herself it had simply been a momentary need for some comfort of her own.

After everything she'd been through with Frank there was no room in her life for silly crushes, especially on a man so burdened with his own problems and responsibilities. If she ever intended to share her life with another man, it would have to be with someone who put her needs first for a change. She was done being a doormat and the only reason she'd agreed to partake in this charade was because she felt sorry for him.

Although when Soraya saw Raed leaning in his doorway and her heart gave an extra beat, she considered for a moment that this was more than sympathy.

'Thanks for coming,' he said, pushing the door open further so she could step inside.

'Well, we have a few things to sort out.' She took a deep breath before entering, feeling as though she were walking into the lion's den.

The apartment was spacious, sleek and masculine, just like Raed. The pristine leather sofa looked as though it had never been sat on, the chrome in the kitchen area shining so bright she doubted it had ever been used. The place had all the hallmarks of a busy surgeon, and warning signs of a man who had no time for a personal life. Probably why his girlfriend had left him when it had become clear he'd have more responsibilities in his home country too.

'Take a seat,' he instructed. 'Can I get you a drink?'

'No, thanks. This isn't a social call, remember?' The reminder was as much for her as for Raed. As soon as they'd discussed the terms, she was out of here.

His face darkened, the smile fading as he took a seat opposite her. 'Of course. Now my father is successfully through surgery—thanks to you—I hope it won't be long before he can return to the throne. However, we will still have to distract the press in the meantime.'

'That's where I come in.' It wasn't a position she'd ever imagined herself in, as a decoy for a royal family to avoid scandal. Nor was it one she relished, but she'd agreed to do it to help the family and get funding for the centre so she had to go along with whatever Raed had planned. Within reason.

'We will have to announce our engagement.' He paused as though waiting for her to react, and, though she baulked inwardly, it wasn't a surprise.

'Okay. Then what?' Soraya was sure it wouldn't be as easy to get rid of the press interest by simply taking out a newspaper ad. She had no idea how invested the English tabloids were in the Zaki royal family in general, or if news would even filter back to his home country to justify the lie.

Raed cleared his throat then studiously stared at his feet and she just knew she wasn't going to like what came next.

'I'm going to have to take a leave of absence from work

and go back to Zaki. Temporarily.' He took a deep breath. 'I need you to come with me.'

Soraya opened her mouth to object, then swallowed the *No!* she wanted to bellow. It was only natural he'd expect a fiancée to return to his home country with him if he was going to announce his betrothal. However, the idea of a trip away with Raed unnerved her when she apparently couldn't even spend an evening in his presence without fretting over the implications.

She sat for a moment before she spoke.

'Is there no other way? I've got work to think about.' It was more than her responsibilities at home that worried her, but she doubted that confiding in Raed about her body's inappropriate responses to being near him was going to do either of them any good.

He shook his head. 'Trust me, I've been going over every scenario in my head. I don't want to spend any longer out there than necessary, but I think if we're going to convince everyone that we're a couple, that the monarchy is as strong as ever, we need to put on a united public front.'

'I'd hate to leave Isolde—'

'She isn't a child, Soraya,' he interrupted, making her bristle.

'I know that, but she is my responsibility. I'm sure you can appreciate I can't just walk away and forget about her. I live with her and pay half the rent so it's only natural that I would have concerns about leaving her to travel halfway across the world.' She didn't like being called out like that. Okay, so she was a tad overprotective but that wasn't such a bad thing when her little sister was the only family she had left. Raed certainly didn't have any right to tell her how to feel when she was doing him a favour.

He raised his eyebrows at her sharp retort, but at least had the sense not to criticise her decision any further. 'It would only be for a few days.'

'What do I have to do?' Now he'd got her back up, her arms were folded, telling him he was going to have to work harder to impress her if he wanted her to play ball.

'There's an event soon that my father usually attends. I thought if we at least made an appearance there, to co-incide with the engagement announcement, perhaps you might only be required to stay for a few days. I'll remain in Zaki until my parents are able to travel, but we can say you have to return home to get your affairs in order before the wedding. I can cover your rent with Isolde and have someone check in on her if you need.'

Okay, he was trying. A few days was as good as she could hope for in the circumstances. Though she doubted it was going to be the most relaxing time off she'd ever had. Apart from her unwanted apparent attraction to Raed, and the stress of faking an engagement to a prince in his home country, there was also the matter of Raed himself. He'd made no attempt to disguise the fact he was ill at ease with this part of his life and she could only imagine his mood to be darker than ever once he was forced to live it indefinitely.

'I don't think that's needed, but thank you. What about you? Weren't you set to announce you relinquish your official position in the royal family?'

He shrugged. 'There's no chance of doing that now. Amir insists he still wants to return some day, but my father's health has given me a wake-up call. I can't hide from my responsibility for ever. Other than my job, I have no real ties in London. It makes sense for me to return on

a more permanent basis instead of Amir when Farah is
making progress here.'

'That's not fair on you.' It was silly, but Soraya had felt
as though she'd been slapped across the face when he'd
said he had nothing to stay in the country for. She had no
claim on Raed, indeed she didn't wish for one. For him
to move abroad indefinitely should relieve her of a lot of
her current stress. Yet seeing him so despondent over a
future he apparently had no control over brought an in-
explicable sadness that she wasn't going to be a part of it.
Even when he sometimes lived up to that cool reputation
that set her on edge.

'Since when is life fair?' His scowl softened into a smile
and Soraya's heart gave another skip of happiness at wit-
nessing the transformation. It was those moments when
he let his defences drop and show a glimpse of the man
behind the carefully groomed exterior that caught her off
guard and gave her reason to like him.

If there were any cause for him to abandon his dark and
brooding façade on their trip away together, she considered
herself in big trouble with no way of avoiding it. At least
tonight she could go back to the flat, put some distance
between them, and talk some sense into herself. Faking
a role as his fiancée in his home country wasn't going to
leave room for an escape from these unwanted feelings
she was beginning to have towards him.

'Well, let me know the arrangements so I can get some
time off.' Soraya rushed to get to her feet, desperate to
get away for now.

Raed saw her to the door despite her protest that she
could let herself out.

'Thanks again for doing this, Soraya. I don't know what
I'd do without you at the minute.'

The last thing she saw before turning away was that beautiful smile again. She might need a drink tonight after all.

'Once we've seen Father and said our goodbyes we can head to the airport.' Raed wasn't in a particular hurry to get on that plane but at least with Soraya by his side he'd have some sense of normalcy. Since his father had pulled through those first critical forty eight hours, the family had agreed it was time for Raed to return to Zaki.

'Yay,' she said, with a distinct lack of enthusiasm.

He was grateful she'd agreed to go with him when she had no real obligation to travel outside the country. It was one thing pretending to be a couple in her home town, but it was a huge favour she was doing him by continuing the pretence overseas. He could probably have fronted it out on his own, made some excuse later as to why his fiancée hadn't accompanied him, but he would be glad of an ally who would treat him as Raed, instead of a prince.

There was no need to hide his true self around Soraya, although he could do with keeping a tighter hold of his emotions around her. At least by bringing her along he felt as though he had some control over what was happening. Despite the burgeoning feelings he was having towards her. He hoped, since they would only be together for a few days and busy with public engagements, he wouldn't have the time or inclination to explore them any further. Given the circumstances it would be pointless anyway. They were going to be living in two different countries, both concentrating on the welfare of their own families, with their personal lives on hold.

'I know it's a hardship being around me, but it won't be for long. I promise.' After her swift exit from his apartment three nights ago it was obvious she didn't want to spend any more time with him than was absolutely necessary. Which made her decision to travel back to Zaki all the more surprising. He supposed that funding meant more to her than he'd realised.

'Well, I've managed this car journey with you so hopefully I'll survive a little longer,' Soraya said with a heavy dose of sarcasm.

'If you could pretend you like me, that would probably help too.' Raed knew that the only quick solution to detract attention away from his father's ill health was to let the press and the public believe they were together, and Soraya was simply a colleague that he had fallen for at the hospital. Except it entailed spending more time with her, something that was already proving detrimental to his health when his sleep had been disrupted since the moment his father had taken ill.

He knew he wasn't her favourite person either, given he'd been unforgivably rude to her on their first meeting, and especially now, after he'd emotionally blackmailed her into helping with this charade.

Although his resolve had considerably weakened when she'd been a listening ear, showing compassion when he'd inadvertently opened up about his struggles, he was too wounded, too raw from the end of his relationship to contemplate another. Even though he was becoming increasingly attracted to the woman tasked with saving his father's life and the country's future.

If Zara, the woman he'd thought he would spend the rest of his life with, couldn't handle the idea of being part of the royal family, it was a wasted exercise expecting anyone else to want that lifestyle either. Especially someone who was only in his life temporarily. Who had a successful career she would never give up for the responsibility his family demanded. He knew, not only because Zara hadn't wanted to do it, but also because neither did he. Once his father was out of the woods they would end things because Soraya Yarrow was not a woman he should be getting close to. At least not emotionally. He no longer had a choice over the physical distance when their closeness was a necessity to maintain their cover.

'We're going to have to put on a bit of a show when we get out of this car,' he reminded her as they pulled up outside the hospital.

'I know.' Her grimace didn't do much for his ego.

'I don't want to do this any more than you do, Soraya. Trust me. I have more important things to concentrate on than this ridiculous farce.'

'I think you might need to take some acting classes if you think calling me a ridiculous farce is going to persuade anyone we're a couple, including me.' Soraya huffed out of the car before he had a chance to apologise and explain it wasn't anything personal.

'Wait, Soraya—' He had to hustle to catch up with her across the car park and when he tried to put his arm around her shoulder she almost shrugged him off.

'Hey, we have to do this,' he reminded her. 'You can shower straight after if you need to, but for now we need to convince everyone that this is real.'

Raed saw the resistance in her eyes, felt it in the tension of her body, but at least she let him touch her without punching him in the face.

'How do we even know there's anyone watching?' she asked, looking around as though expecting to see long-lens cameras pointing at her from every direction.

'There might have been a tip-off that the Prince drops

off his new girlfriend at work every morning. We thought it would make it more believable to see us together before we make our surprise announcement.'

'You actually set this up?' She stopped walking and turned to look at him, her blue eyes blazing with indignation at the tactics they'd used to set their plan in motion.

'Not personally. We have advisers and press officers who deal with this sort of thing. I know it seems underhanded but public figures and celebrities do it all the time when they want to promote something or get attention. Our circumstances are different, but we need to get this story out there to replace the truth. Time is of the essence.'

He sighed and reached out a hand to take hers. This time she didn't try to pull away from him. 'The lies don't sit well with me either. Goodness knows I've told enough over the years to hide my real identity, and learned my lesson the hard way that the truth always comes out in the end. But in this instance we're just hoping by the time it all comes out Father will be recovered and any crisis averted. Don't hate me for this, Soraya.'

Her features softened as she listened to his explanation of why they were doing this. 'I don't hate you, Raed. Neither of us asked to be in this position. Well, technically you did, but I know that was because you were desperate. I understand. You love your family and your country, just as I love my sister and would do anything for her. It's a cross eldest children have to bear, I guess.'

In an act of what he assumed was solidarity, and perhaps for the cameras, Soraya laced her fingers through his and leaned into him as they walked into the hospital. For a brief moment Raed wished it weren't just an act, that he'd met someone who understood his position and was reconciled with it. Who loved him enough that they would want to be with him whatever happened. Something he'd never had in his life from his parents or a partner.

He wished that Soraya weren't someone else who would walk away when the going got tough and leave him to pick up the pieces of his broken heart again.

But the only thing more dangerous than getting caught in a lie was believing it himself.

'How are you feeling today, Your Majesty?' Although Soraya and Raed were leaving for the airport, they'd both wanted to check in on her patient first. After a meeting with the night staff, it seemed he was recovering as well as could be expected, even if he still looked fragile lying on the hospital bed, plugged into all the machines monitoring his vital signs.

'As though I've been trampled by a herd of wild horses,' he said weakly.

Soraya didn't know the man that well beyond their doctor-patient relationship, but she appreciated his sense of humour. It showed a strength of character. His son displayed a similar stubbornness when it came to survival.

'It's not surprising after what you've gone through, Father, but you're here and that's all that matters.' This was a softer side of Raed she was seeing as he moved to his father's bedside.

Soraya wondered how long it would be before the shutters came down again. There were flashes of kindness and compassion in Raed, but they were quickly overshadowed by the dark brooding introspection he seemed to lose himself in occasionally too. It was little wonder when his life was so complicated, but it made it difficult to get to know the real Raed, which was probably just as well when her body betrayed her every time he touched her. She knew it was all for the cameras, but the goosebumps along her skin were proof she was refusing to believe it deep down.

'I know you're still in some discomfort and we'll give you some painkillers to help with that, but we will have to get you mobile as soon as possible. Tomorrow we will look at moving you from the bed into a chair at least. The physiotherapist will also work with you on some exercises to keep your muscles supple and an occupational thera- pist can help prepare you to undertake daily tasks again.'

'No rest for the wicked, eh?' he joked to a stony-faced Raed.

'It's all for your own benefit, Father.'

The King tutted. 'For yours too. The sooner I take my place again, the quicker you're off the hook.'

'I'm going back to Zaki now until you're better.'

'You can't blame me for that, Raed. It's not my fault you were living a lie. If you'd just stayed at home and done your duty in the first place—'

'Okay, I don't think this is the right time or place to de- bate that. Your father needs to rest, he doesn't need any stress right now.' She didn't know anything about their relationship but from this brief interaction it was obvi- ous things were strained between them. Although, given everything Raed had done to try and protect his family, it was clear he loved his father, even if he didn't like to show it. It was safe to say those shutters had slammed down again as soon as he knew his father was out of im- mediate danger.

'It's probably better if I go, in that case. I'm glad you're on the way to recovery, Father. It's all any of us want.' To his credit Raed didn't relay the details of their newly formed fake romance, or indeed the fact that the paparazzi were sniffing around looking for a story. That would have given the King a lot to worry about and might have hindered his recovery. Yet another sign that Raed cared about his father more than he probably even realised.

She recognised well that need to keep problems secret so as not to upset family members, given she'd been doing it her whole life. The trouble was that the person holding the secrets, dealing with the problems, was often the one who needed the most support, and no one knew it.

'We'll let you get some rest for now, Your Majesty. I just need to need to see Isolde, then we can go, Raed.' The majority of her work had been done in the operating theatre and her colleagues would be on hand should any complications arise, making sure her royal patient progressed as well as he should.

'Can I have visitors? I would like to see my wife.' The King looked small as he made the plea and it was hard for Soraya to picture him in all of his regal finery ruling a country. She could only imagine how difficult it was for Raed to see him in this light. Perhaps that unstable mood had something to do with the uncertainty still remaining around his parent's health, and therefore his own future.

'Of course. I know the Queen is keen to see you, too.' It was nice to see a smile on the elderly man's face. He was no doubt afraid about what was going to happen to him and needed the comfort and support of his wife. It was a refreshing change to see a couple who still genuinely cared for one another, given that Frank had turned to someone else for that and ended their marriage.

In the past few days she'd got to know them a little, and liked them a lot. She wanted to protect them from any further heartache, but for that to happen she was going to have to keep this charade with Raed going for a while longer at least. It was one more sacrifice on her part in order to fulfil someone else's needs—and an ongoing battle to maintain her peace of mind. That need for self-preservation since her marriage break-up was screaming so loud for her to find something else to do, somewhere else to be, it was deafening.

For now she had to stick her fingers in her ears and pretend she couldn't hear it.

CHAPTER FOUR

'THIS COULD BE part of a ransom plot, you know.'

'Hmm?' Raed barely registered Soraya's murmurings, his head buried in his phone, while she watched the world beneath them come to life.

After saying goodbye to Isolde, making sure the freezer was full of home-cooked dinners, and there was no washing left in the machine to go mouldy in her absence, Soraya had joined Raed and flown out overnight. Though her travelling companion seemed to have spent most of their journey arranging his schedule. Eventually she'd given up trying to hold a conversation with him and dozed as long as the mid-air turbulence had let her. Shaken violently awake, fear gripping her heart, she'd decided this stunt was more like something Isolde would have done—spontaneous and exciting. Unlike her, who had been the responsible, sensible one of the pair her whole life. She wasn't enjoying the experience so far, despite their attentive steward.

'Flying out on a private jet with a prince sounds like the elaborate plot of a Liam Neeson movie, or an Isolde whim. It does not seem the sort of rational decision an older, more responsible sister would usually make,' she mused aloud for Raed's benefit, not that he seemed to be listening.

With her head pressed up against the aeroplane window, the small island kingdom that was about to become her temporary new home gradually came into view. The palm trees and turquoise seas were a far cry from the bustling city of London she was used to. Slowly, signs of life filtered through the gloomy morning mist. The coloured lights from moving vehicles snaked their way through the hills, like arteries pumping life into the city that was splayed out before them now. The lights and movement of the traffic heralding the start of the day as the sun rose in the sky outside the window, burning away the darkness to replace it with the bright display of dawn emerging.

Now, as they came in to land in this unknown terrain, Soraya was experiencing a flurry of doubts suddenly bombarding her about what she was doing. They were in a foreign country, at Raed's mercy. The nervous energy that usually fuelled her through tricky life-changing operations was mixed with a sense of foreboding.

'Could you buckle your seat belts in preparation for landing? Thank you.' The lovely steward who had been looking after them on the flight, supplying a seemingly endless supply of drinks, snacks, blankets and pyjamas, supervised their compliance before taking his own seat.

As they touched down Soraya was afraid that bump when they hit the tarmac was the same moment she'd come back to earth and realise she'd been lured out into the middle of the ocean under false pretences. Any second now she'd be bundled into a waiting car and trafficked over the border never to be heard from again. Except Raed stood to gain more from her as a fake fiancée than a kidnap victim.

The door opened but Soraya remained in her seat just a fraction longer, waiting for masked strangers to burst onboard and prove her fears right. It didn't happen.

As they climbed down the steps she could see several

suited men waiting below with a black limousine to collect them. She almost turned back.

'Good morning, Your Royal Highness. It's good to have you home.'

Raed nodded an acknowledgement to the smallest of the men who'd stepped forward to greet them. Soraya wondered if the other silent, intimidating members of the group were security detail. It was a little unnerving to think they needed this level of protection when they'd just set foot in the country, but she supposed no one wanted to take any chances with their safety and for that she was grateful. If there was a risk that someone thought them potential targets, whether for political or financial gain, it was preferable to have multiple bodyguards whose bodies were so pumped up they looked as though they would burst out of those tailored black suits at any moment.

'What about our bags?' She didn't have much in the world but what she did have was packed into her luggage and she wasn't mentally prepared to lose anything else.

One of the burly squad stepped forward. 'We'll take care of it.'

She didn't dare argue with him and climbed into the back seat of the limo with Raed, phone in hand to text Isolde the second she had a signal.

Landed safely. On way to the palace. Don't forget to leave the bins out. x

'It's only been a matter of hours.' Raed was peering over her shoulder at the text.

Soraya hastily shoved her phone back in her bag. 'Yes, well, she's not used to doing everything herself.'

'What did she do when you were married and living

in a different house?' He grinned at her, and though she was glad to see he was relaxing a bit more, he was highlighting the part of her personality that both she and Isolde were struggling with.

'She had a partner then too to help with things.' Since leaving Frank she'd busied herself in her sister's life, taking up where she'd left off before she got married. Perhaps it was because she needed to be needed again, she'd replaced caring for her husband for looking after Isolde. There were times that Isolde got exasperated by her constant cleaning and fussing, but Soraya had to keep busy, make herself useful around the place. She was lucky her sister had agreed to let her stay in the flat, because, without her, Soraya had nothing and no place to go.

'You do too much,' he said gently.

'Says you,' she childishly bit back, knowing everything he said was true.

They sat in silence for the remainder of the journey but thankfully they seemed to fly through the traffic, the driver expertly weaving in and out of lanes, all the while being followed by another car containing the security team. It wasn't long before they were driving up the impressive mall towards the palace. Once they'd entered the grounds through the large ornate golden gates, Soraya wound down the window to take it all in.

The air was warm on her face, the sun now making its presence known, the golden spires of the palace glinting in the light. The white, gold and cobalt-blue columns and arches were imposing in the vast green landscape, and the opulent, extravagant exterior of the sprawling palace couldn't have contrasted more with her humble upbringing. She wondered which part of the building housed the dungeon for stupid Englishwomen who agreed to fake a relationship with the Prince.

Before she had time to panic any more, the door opened and a hand came in to help her out of the car. The guard walked them into the palace then seemed to disappear, leaving her to marvel at the décor in the massive hall.

Soraya spun around on the white marble floor, staring at the ceiling. 'Wow. It's like something out of a fantasy novel.'

She was captivated by the bright colour of the rich royal-blue mosaic inlays covering every inch of the walls and the ornate stained-glass windows above multiple archways. It was all too much, yet breathtaking at the same time.

'I'm glad my home meets with your approval.' Raed's deep, authoritative voice echoed around the walls.

'It's stunning.'

'I'll have someone show you to your room. I have some business to attend to, if you'd like to freshen up before our outing.' This efficient, closed Raed, checking his watch and effectively abandoning her in a foreign country, was completely different from the man who'd begged for help in her office less than a week ago. It was probably her fault he'd reverted after she'd called him out for taking on too much in the name of his family too.

She decided she preferred the man who hadn't been afraid to take her into his confidence, sharing his fears, instead of blocking her out.

'I'm not sure I have anything suitable to wear to this… event,' she whispered, feeling even more out of place now she could see the luxury he'd grown up in. Although she'd brought her best clothes, she didn't want to make a spectacle of herself if she didn't measure up as a suitable match for Zaki's prince.

'It doesn't matter. You're here to do a job, not to impress anyone with your wardrobe.'

'Just wave, smile, and hang on your arm,' she said with sickly sweet sarcasm.

'Exactly,' he confirmed before turning away, oblivious to her obvious discomfort. Or perhaps he simply didn't care.

The thought that she really was nothing more to him than a convenient cover story stung more than it should.

'My generous benefactor.' Soraya curtseyed as Raed met her in the magnificent hallway, wearing the beautiful outfit that had mysteriously appeared in her room not long after she'd voiced her anxiety about her wardrobe.

When she'd finally emerged from the sumptuous tub in her bathroom, the air thick with steam and essential oils, an extravagant red and gold gown had been laid out across her bed. Clearly, Raed had been listening after all.

'I didn't want you to feel uncomfortable.'

'Or perhaps you were afraid I'd embarrass you by turning up in my civvies?' she suggested.

Raed laughed. 'So sceptical.'

The only reason she held onto her cynicism was she was pretty sure he could coerce her into doing anything with one hangdog look. Soraya shuddered, realising the situation she'd put herself in, where she was at his mercy because she didn't want to let anyone down. Since Frank she'd learned to be more cautious about giving her trust so easily.

'I've had to be. My ex-husband lied to me and ruined my life. Remember I'm only doing this because there are people relying on me.' She hadn't meant to share such deeply personal information—it was humiliating—but she needed him to understand she couldn't simply blindly follow wherever he led. Frank had left her with serious scars and she'd been married to him for a decade. She'd be a fool to trust a man who clearly had an agenda other than her welfare.

'I'm sorry. Although I had convinced myself it was my stunning personality that had been the enticement.'

She rolled her eyes at his attempt to lighten the mood, although she was glad to have another glimpse of the Raed she'd come to know. 'Obviously it was the idea of faking a relationship with the Crown Prince that I couldn't resist.'

'Obviously.' He was grinning at her and she couldn't help but return it, regardless that she was still a little mad at him for hijacking her. She liked that she could make him crack that ever-present frown and smile once in a while.

'You haven't told me where we're going. I would like to know so I can stop fretting about what it is I'm getting into, or, you know, worry more that I'm not up to whatever task is expected of me.' The more she talked about her anxiety, the quicker her breathing became, until she was making herself dizzy with the lack of oxygen.

'Of course. I didn't mean to panic you. For this story to work we need to raise our profile, so I thought we needed a more public setting.'

Soraya appreciated the explanation, but he still hadn't told her where, or what they'd be doing.

As if reading her mind, Raed continued. 'It's nothing to worry about, honest. We will be merely spectating. It's a horse show with international participants competing in different equestrian disciplines. Father is well known for his love of horses and was invited as a guest of honour. I'm going to be taking his place awarding the prizes at the end, but you don't have to take part in that. I simply need you to sit next to me and, when you're not watching the horses, look at me adoringly.'

'Raed, I know nothing about horses.'

'Soraya, neither do I.'

At least by the time they arrived at the arena, they'd forged a new bond other than their resentment of being forced together, and their newly single relationship status.

'Oh, yeah, I hope red's your colour,' Raed whispered into her ear as they exited the car onto the carpeted walkway rolled out specially to welcome their visit.

Soraya wasn't prepared for the rush of noise that greeted her outside. She stumbled back as a crowd gathered near the entrance surged forward, cameras snapping and people shouting for their attention.

'You're okay, I've got you.' Raed put his arm around her waist, steadying her on her feet and guiding her towards the building.

Once she was safe in the knowledge that he would keep her upright, and with the security team pushing the crowd back, Soraya could breathe again. They were whipped through the building into a private lift away from the general public and taken to a private box to view the event from on high.

'I didn't realise you're so popular.'

'Not usually, but I think my return has stirred up interest.'

'It's like having a fast pass at an amusement park, except you're able to bypass people everywhere to get to the head of the queue.' Soraya marvelled at the perks that came with this privileged lifestyle. After spending a lifetime working to support her younger sister and doing all the worrying for two, it would be nice to have people who did things for her for once.

Raed fixed her with his dark stare, but this time he had a twinkle in his eye. 'We don't have to queue.'

He broke into a big cheesy grin that couldn't fail to make her laugh, just as the catering staff came in to offer them trays of champagne and canapés. She helped herself to a glass of bubbles and some smoked salmon.

'Sorry, I was hungry.' She wasn't sure why she felt the absurd need to apologise. Perhaps because often, when at fancy medical functions laden with lavish spreads, she'd been given the impression it was bad etiquette to actually eat the food.

'Can I get you anything else? I'm sure the chef would be happy to accommodate you. Some beans on toast or a full English breakfast, perhaps?' He was teasing but Soraya's stomach was grumbling and, as lovely as the food seemed, it was rich compared to the plain meals she was used to cooking at home.

'Thank you, but I'm sure this will suffice for now.' She said it as much to the waiter as Raed—he was hovering beside her as though he was expecting her to plant herself face first into the serving platter to scoff the lot.

Raed whispered something to him before he left. Likely an apology for bringing an unexpected plus one to gate-crash the party.

She wandered out onto the balcony to see what the view was like, only to be met with cheers and a wall of camera phones facing towards her. A hand grabbed her and pulled her back inside.

'I should have warned you about that,' Raed said, too late.

'I just… I'm sorry.' Soraya didn't know if she'd broken some kind of protocol by stepping out there first without Raed.

'I guess there's more interest in me coming out of the wilderness than I thought too. Rumours will no doubt be circulating already that I'm ready to take up my rightful position at home, and settle down with a new bride.' He sighed.

It was part of the plan, of course, for them to be seen together, but for a moment she'd forgotten where she was and what she was supposed to be doing. As if she and Raed really were here on some kind of date instead of a royal engagement. This was everything she'd worried about and they'd only been a 'couple' for a short while. It was easy to forget he was heir to the throne when he dropped his surly façade to be nice to her. If he would go back to that arrogant, curt prince who'd met her at first, she might be able to hold onto her heart instead of clinging to him now like a lifeline.

'It's okay.' He rested his chin on top of her head but she could hear the smile in his voice. 'But you don't have to do this alone. I know it can all be a bit overwhelming but we're in this together, okay?'

He tilted her chin up so she would look at him and believe he wasn't going to let her face the crowd alone again. Not knowing it wasn't their public relationship that was giving her palpitations.

She swallowed hard. 'Okay.'

'You ready?'

No.

'Yes.'

Raed took her hand. 'Then let's get this over with.'

They walked out onto the balcony and she clung to his arm as though her life depended on it, relying on him to guide her through this charade. A wall of cheers and whoops went up as they announced their relationship to the waiting crowd with a smile and a wave. Once the noise began to subside, and people got used to the idea, they retreated back inside.

'That should give them what they wanted. Thank you, Soraya, for doing this, and for saving my father's life, if I haven't already said it.'

'You're welcome, although I have to say this is scarier than performing a life-saving operation on a king.'

Raed sighed. 'I know. Zara hated the idea of it too. Not everyone is cut out for this world, myself included, but I guess I don't have a choice any more. I tried the anonymous life but family duty comes first, right?'

She nodded. Like her, Raed had to put his family's needs above his own. Although there would have been greater consequences involved if he hadn't stepped up and worked so hard to provide some stability at a vulnerable time for his family and the country.

'I guess it would have been too much of a culture shock for her.'

He grimaced. 'It wasn't only that. I don't think she loved me enough to give up life in London and venture out here with me when the time came.'

'I'm sorry. It's not nice having someone you love let you down like that.'

His shrug didn't convince Soraya that he was able to dismiss what had happened so easily. 'Perhaps I didn't give her reason enough to want to follow me. It's not easy for me to open up to people. In hindsight maybe she thought I didn't love her enough to make it work.'

Raed's admission made her heart ache for him but also made her feel privileged that he had confided in her about some of his very personal struggles. 'You do have a reputation for being very...closed off.'

Her carefully chosen words earned her a grin and the relief of not having offended him. 'The result of my up-bringing, I'm afraid. The royal family aren't supposed to show emotion in public. And when you're schooled in hiding them it becomes very difficult to express yourself in private too. I guess they're the one thing I was able to control when everything else was decided for me—school, where I lived, what I did, what I was going to do. I guess going into medicine was my way of breaking out of that, but we both know that didn't work out when I'm back here. My emotions are the last thing I'm able to have for myself. Often to my detriment. It doesn't mean I don't feel any-thing, just that I don't like to give away that part of me.'

It was a revealing insight as to why he appeared so cut off at times. Soraya had some experience of not showing her emotions in front of Isolde in order to protect her, and also to prevent herself from losing control. Growing up, with her little sister relying on her, they couldn't have af-forded for Soraya to fall apart. She began to wonder if, like Raed, she'd also been guilty of holding back a part of herself from Frank too. Not giving herself completely to him, so she could maintain a little control. It was possible he'd picked up on that and gone searching for that missing part of their marriage in someone else.

'I can relate to that. Though you've been very honest with me about everything that's going on in your life.' She had to wonder why.

'True. And I haven't always been proud of the way I acted in front of you. It's a big deal for me and I'm thank-ful that you've been very gracious in helping me out.'

Given his reputation and the way he'd sometimes been around her after one of his emotional displays, Soraya knew he'd struggle to come to terms with showing her that part of him. She was grateful, if baffled, that he'd felt able to be honest with her but not someone he'd been in an actual relationship with.

'I don't imagine any of this is easy for you. Especially coming home after such a long time away.'

It occurred to her that Raed would have had to adjust several times over. First in leaving his royal status behind to train as a surgeon in England, and learning to become a mere civilian again. Only to have to adapt again by coming back and giving up that person he'd become. He had responsibilities and duties to carry out, but it would never be the same as the job he'd done here. Swapping the life of a busy surgeon, working in exhilarating, highly dramatic and emotional circumstances, to wave and hand out prizes would be something of an anticlimax. All that hard work training for the specialised role seemed wasted, traded in to be a spectator at a horse show.

He stared at her for what felt like a long time, before answering. 'Sorry. I don't recall anyone asking me how I felt about coming back. My family just expected me to do it and Zara blamed me for ruining our life together by even considering it. No one seemed to care what I was going through, torn between two worlds, having to decide whether to go with my head or my heart. Either way it meant losing someone I cared about, and in the end I had to think about the bigger picture. About what Amir and Farah were going through, and what would happen if Father died. I'd spent years pretending to be someone I wasn't and reality eventually caught up with me that I can't have it all.'

'You wanted a different life. I think most of us have at some point, and there's nothing wrong with that. The fact that you're doing this for your family's sake is honourable and I know things didn't work out with Zara, but at least you tried.'

That burden of responsibility to make the right decision had weighed heavily on her shoulders at times too when she and Isolde had been growing up. She was sure she hadn't always got it right but everything she'd done had been with the best of intentions for her little sister. It was clear Raed had made his choice to give up everything he had here with the welfare of his loved ones uppermost in his mind.

'I tried… Do you think I could use that as a defence when this all comes crumbling down around me again?' His half-smile and the slump in his shoulders gave Soraya an insight into how the real Raed was struggling with the pressure and she wished she could help.

'Hey, you're doing your best. That's all anyone can ask of you.'

'I'm not so sure I did my best for Zara. I don't know if I fought hard enough for our relationship, or thought enough about her feelings. I certainly should have been honest with her about the possibility I'd have to take up my royal duties again instead of dropping her into the midst of the storm.' He raked his hand through his hair, making Soraya itch to comb the few errant strands he'd mussed back into place.

'Perhaps, though it sounds to me like you both could have communicated better. Not that I'm an expert. My husband was cheating on me, spending every penny we had on another woman, and I had no clue. Clearly he wasn't happy in our marriage and I was completely oblivious, believing I was married to a wonderful man who was never home because he was spending all of his time fighting for worthwhile causes. He was a lawyer who worked with charities and organisations for disadvantaged minorities in the community. But he was also a liar, a cheat, and a terrible husband as it turned out.'

'I'm sorry. You deserve better than that.'

She shrugged, having done enough crying and soul-searching over why her marriage had failed. 'Perhaps I was guilty of neglecting Frank's feelings in some ways too, keeping too close an eye on Isolde and how her life was going to pay enough attention to my own.'

'It sounds to me as though you're a great big sister and he should have supported all of you, as a family.'

'Ditto with Zara,' she said, offering him a consolatory smile, astounded that they had dysfunctional families in common. Albeit on opposite sides of the class system.

'You don't have any other family to turn to for help when you need it?'

She shook her head. 'Our parents had us quite late in life and they died within a year of one another from lung cancer when we were young. I did a lot of the parenting, along with caring for Mum and Dad, then became her legal guardian at eighteen. I guess I've never stopped looking out for her.'

'It's understandable.'

'We've both been through a lot. That's why this charity means so much to me. With your financial aid I'm hoping we can get a centre built for young carers, and their families, where they can get the support we never had.'

'I'm sorry you've been dragged into our mess in order to get that funding.'

'Yeah, it's so inconvenient being here in a private box with the most eligible man in the country drinking champagne and waiting for a show in his honour.' If they could keep this level of light-hearted teasing going, instead of counselling each other over the heavy emotional baggage they shared, she might just survive this fake relationship.

There was a light rap on the door and their waiter came bustling in, followed by a slew of other catering staff all carrying trays.

'If I'd known champagne was all that was needed to keep you happy here, I wouldn't have bothered with this,' he said, directing the staff to leave their assortment of platters and delights.

'What is all this?' She moved closer to the now full table to marvel at the food laid out for them.

Raed set out two small china cups and saucers and began to pour from the silver teapot that had been provided. 'Some good old fish, chips and mushy peas.'

Soraya wanted to protest, tell him it was too much, when the gesture went beyond a mere token to satisfy her hunger. This was a kind attempt to put her at ease, and provide the plain food she had been craving.

'I love a chippy tea, but you really shouldn't have done all this for me.' She took a seat at the table, letting Raed serve her.

'It's my pleasure. My way of thanking you for helping my family and understanding our predicament.' He offered her the plate of buttered white bread that proved he was very much a local.

'I think you're going to have to hire a crane to lift me out of here after I eat all this.'

'Don't worry, you're not going into this alone. I've got your back,' Raed said, with a serious scowl he was clearly struggling to maintain.

Then he smiled that brilliant white smile as he made himself a chip butty, and Soraya realised there was no hope for her poor heart after all.

* * *

Raed took a bite from his chip sandwich before he said anything else he'd come to regret. From the moment he had proposed this idea he'd known it was a mistake, yet they hadn't been able to come up with an alternative plan to cover up what was happening with his father. Now Soraya was hopefully going to save the day for them, he'd become protective of her. Perhaps even more so than with Zara.

He'd been so caught up in his own feelings about having to go and be part of the family he'd been born into that he'd failed to recognise Zara's struggles in time and he didn't want to make the same mistake with Soraya. If she was overwhelmed by the crowds and attention, he would do his utmost to make her more comfortable.

The only drawback to that was the look of gratitude she gave him every time he did something nice for her. Those big blue eyes could persuade him to do anything. Not ideal when he was supposed to be keeping his distance. Something that was becoming increasingly hard to do when they appeared to have so much in common. She was the only person in his life to date who seemed to understand his struggle with family responsibility and it was difficult to walk away from someone who listened, who empathised with him, and sacrificed her own happiness for others too.

'Thank you again,' she said, pouring herself another cup of tea.

'You're welcome.'

Soraya took another bite of her butty, leaving her top lip smeared with butter.

'You've got something on your lip.' He pointed towards the butter rather than risk touching her himself and experiencing another one of those shock waves through his body that seemed to happen every time he laid a hand on her.

'Oops.' She attempted to wipe it away with a napkin, completely missing the spot.

'It's still there.' He tried again, only to put himself through agony watching her tongue search around her mouth instead.

'Here, let me,' he said in the end, somewhat abruptly, and leaned in to sweep it away with his thumb.

'Thanks.'

He was aware of the breathy tone in her voice, of her eyes watching him intently as he came closer, and when he licked the butter off his thumb, he saw her pupils dilate. And knew he had to get the hell out of there.

'I think it's starting. We should go and show our faces, put on an act of unity.' Raed scrambled to his feet, knocking the table and spilling his tea in the process.

'I'll clear this up first.' Soraya began to dab at the spilt tea with a napkin but Raed needed out of this enclosed space. It sounded ridiculous even to him but he thought he would breathe better outside with the crowd of thousands, rather than in here with just Soraya sharing the oxygen.

'No. Someone else will do it. We can't miss the opening ceremony.' He would have gone out by himself except that would have defeated the whole purpose of bringing her here in the first place.

After several deep breaths she took his hand and they walked out. The crowd went wild as they waved and bathed in the attention their relationship received. As the national anthem played they remained standing, paying respect to the country. Raed thought of his country and became a little choked up realising how close they had come to losing his father, and how this could all be for him at home some day. It was overwhelming and he was glad when they were finally able to take their seats again.

'Are you okay?' As perceptive as ever, Soraya leaned across to check on him.

'Yes. I think the moment just got to me. I've been so busy trying to cover everything up, holding things together, it's only now I'm realising what might have happened if my father had died. We'd be a country in mourning, in turmoil, with my life in even more disarray than it already is. I don't even know if they would want me to be King, or if that's what I want. At least we've got more time before we have to deal with all of that and we've got you to thank for that.'

He'd treated her as an inconvenience when they'd first met, but Soraya had become an asset to the whole family. The only good thing to happen to him in a year.

'Just doing my job,' she nonchalantly responded to him pouring his heart out. But they both knew she'd done much more than that.

CHAPTER FIVE

ONCE THE INTEREST in them had died down and the event started, Soraya was able to relax and forget about being on show herself with the focus on the horses and riders. The dressage event had Soraya mesmerised. The riders had such control over the horses' every movement she knew it must have taken years of dedication and hard work to gain the animals' trust.

'Do you ride?' she asked Raed, curious if he could wield the same power over these huge beasts as he did with humans.

'I used to. It's expected of the royal family to have some level of ability. Not as much for going into battle any more, but at least for ceremonial purposes. It's been a while for me though. There wasn't much opportunity for me to ride in the city.' With another insight into Raed's life came a sadness in his eyes. One that she recognised, which told of personal sacrifice and a wish for more in life. It seemed wealth and privilege couldn't free an eldest child of responsibilities either.

'Yeah, I can't say it was practical for us in London either. Or financially viable.'

'It must have been tough, raising your sister alone and putting yourself through medical school. I know I rebelled against my family, but I wasn't against taking their money to pay for my schooling.' It was clear he thought himself a hypocrite in doing so, but Soraya knew she would've done the same thing.

'Listen, I've done the scrimping and saving and scrabbling to pay the bills. There's no shame in accepting a helping hand, and no gold medals handed out for struggling alone.' It would have made her life so much easier if she'd had financial support at least trying to raise Isolde and manage her studies at the same time. Then she wouldn't have had to add the stress of a waitressing job on top of it all.

'Maybe we should start giving them out.'

'To be honest, I think any families who are going through what we did would appreciate financial aid rather than a symbolic gesture.' It was too late for her and Isolde, and, even though Raed was probably joking, the memory of that time was still raw for her. When Frank had come into her life, seemingly fighting for disadvantaged families like hers, she'd been blinded by his goodness. She hadn't discovered what lurked behind that altruism until it was too late.

Raed's sudden lapse into silence made her wonder if she'd overstepped the mark by speaking her mind so bluntly. When he was chatting so casually to her it was easy to forget it was royalty she was talking to. Despite the years he'd spent out of the country, he had no real concept what it was like to struggle to pay for basic amenities when, by his own admission, his family had continued to pay all of his bills when he'd left home.

It wasn't his fault any more than her circumstances had been something she'd had any control over, but trying to survive on very little money, counting every penny, left scars. She had a different life now but those memories were the very reason she found it hard to shake off that imposter syndrome. Especially here, pretending to be part of Raed's world, where food could be demanded on a whim and people made horses dance for your entertainment.

'Perhaps it is about time we did something for disadvantaged families. As you say, meaningless gestures might salve our social conscience, but they don't put food on the table.'

'I'm sorry, I didn't mean to be so rude. It's just a touchy subject, that's all.'

'No, you're right. If I'm fated to be in this position I should do something more than complain. I could make a difference and give the royal family some meaning rather than simply being a meaningless symbol. When I'm in charge I could make changes that benefit the people of our country. We could give scholarships to some of the families that wouldn't otherwise be able to afford a university education, or run schemes to help with childcare for single-parent families.'

'That's a great idea, Raed. I'm sure you could make such a difference.'

'You know what, I think it'd give me a real sense of purpose too. There are so many areas of social deprivation that need attention and I think my family have been blind, sitting up there on our jewelled thrones. I have you to thank for opening my eyes. Maybe I'll name the scholarship after you.'

He was so animated about the whole thing, so enthused about making a difference it was difficult to tell if he was serious about that last part. Soraya didn't care as long as it meant there would be help available for families who couldn't see an end in sight to their struggle.

This decision to better himself, to use his position to

help others, only made Raed seem more attractive. With every second she spent getting to know him, that tough outer exterior fell away. The cool, efficient surgeon showing the warm, kind man he was at heart. Soraya really should have learned her lesson about falling for men who championed passionately for others.

Unfortunately, it seemed as though she was a lost cause.

CHAPTER SIX

RAED COULD BARELY focus on the rest of the events, even though Soraya was beside him clapping at every horse jump and wincing at those who didn't manage to clear the bars. His mind was buzzing with ideas of how the family could contribute to society beyond being merely decorative. Part of what made his job as a surgeon so rewarding was being able to make a difference to people's lives, and knowing that his life had meaning too. To have that taken away from him had made him question his own worth. Especially when Zara hadn't found sufficient reason to stay with him.

Due to her impoverished and difficult background, Soraya was clearly finding some aspects of his lifestyle challenging too, but with one huge difference. Instead of simply shutting down and rejecting it, she'd been able to make him see how he could turn things to everyone's advantage. She was offering him solutions to his problem, using his position to do good and giving him a reason to carry on. They'd communicated more in the space of a few days than he had in seven years with Zara.

If he was honest though, it was his fault she hadn't been prepared to deal with the idea of his real identity, his duty to his country. In pretending that part of his life wasn't happening, that he would never have to return to it, he'd been lying to himself and Zara.

It would always have fallen to him to return home—it was his birthright, his responsibility. Trying to run away from it had been stupid and naïve, but also damaging to his relationship. It had proved the lack of real trust between them when he'd kept that information from her, and he knew Zara had felt betrayed. Raed couldn't keep blaming her for everything that had gone wrong when he'd played a huge part in the breakdown of the relationship.

It had taken being with Soraya to see how much he had kept hidden from Zara. Not only did Soraya know about all the skeletons in his closet, she had helped to keep the door shut on them.

If he and Zara had talked the way he and Soraya had, been honest about what they wanted, or what they were struggling with, they might have been able to salvage their relationship. The fact that they hadn't even tried suggested it was over long before his father's health issues had forced him to think about going home.

The only problem with that realisation was the thought he should have been with someone like Soraya from the start. There was more than her beauty that drew Raed to her, and they were getting closer by the minute. However, it wasn't going to do him any good to start believing Soraya could be the woman he needed, who would be there for him the way Zara hadn't been, when she'd be out of his life as soon as his father was well on the way to recovery.

'I should probably go down there and meet some of the riders, shake a few hands and hooves.' Near the end of the event he made a move to leave and put some space between him and Soraya. They'd played the role of love-struck couple and he didn't want to get too carried away with the idea. Some time refocusing as a VIP here would remind him that there were more important issues at stake other than his love life. He was here representing his father, the King, not Raed the lonely surgeon who was apparently still hoping he'd find his soulmate.

'Should I come down with you?' Soraya rose hesitantly from her chair and he was tempted to tell her to stay where she was, but it wouldn't have been fair to leave her here on her own. She didn't know anyone here, or what was expected of her. He'd simply dropped her in the middle of his world and expected her to adapt. A mistake he'd made once before.

'Sure. You can stay in the background if you don't want to get involved but you can come down behind the scenes at least.' He let the security team know of their plans so they could escort them down.

At least when they were being taken through private exits and secret corridors they didn't have to keep up the pretence with physical contact. Holding hands or placing an arm around Soraya's waist might seem innocuous in itself, but, in tandem with his growing emotional connection to her, the slightest touch was becoming so much more. With every interaction and shared secret their connection grew stronger and he couldn't afford to form another attachment with someone who was ultimately going to leave him to deal with everything on his own again here.

'It's true what they say about royalty.' Soraya waited until they were in the elevator before she spoke.

'What's that?'

'That you must think the whole world smells of fresh paint.' She grinned and pointed at the expensive wallpaper that lined the back of the lift, clearly added recently to give it more of a regal feel for his benefit.

He hadn't noticed until she'd pointed it out to him. Something else he'd taken for granted and he thought of all the extra work that had undoubtedly gone on in the background to prepare for his visit. Yet another example of his obliviousness when it came to people around him. It was about time he appreciated his status and the effort others went to in order to make him comfortable. He made a note to give his thanks to the venue staff for their contribution to his visit, as it was the least he could do here. Once he was back at the palace he was going to make enquiries about how to make a greater difference to the people of their country.

The competitors lined up with their horses for the meet and greet and Soraya stood at the perimeter of the jumping ground while Raed went along the line.

'Well done.'

'Great show.'

'Congratulations.'

He smiled, shook hands and took an interest in every one of the people he was introduced to, all the time aware that Soraya was close by and wanting to show her that he wasn't some spoiled rich brat who didn't appreciate his privileged position.

'Thank you for coming, Your Royal Highness.' The organiser stepped forward and introduced himself as Ranj Abdallah.

'My pleasure. You put on an excellent show and I'm sure it's done a lot for the tourist industry here.' The international competitors would be a boost to the local economy by staying in local hotels and availing themselves of the hospitality services nearby. It was something they should capitalise on in the future and work to make bigger and better to attract more foreign interest.

'Well, thank you, sir. It's nice to be appreciated.' Ranj's smile and the proud puffing out of his chest told Raed praise wasn't something often dished out by his father at such occasions. He thought it was about time that changed. If the royal family wanted more respect they had to earn it by showing that they appreciated people and becoming more of an asset to those around them at home, rather than simply living off their taxes.

'I'd like to talk to you some time about perhaps setting up a charity event to raise funds for disadvantaged members of our society. In return you can count on my patronage and whatever influential connections I can bring to the table.'

'I—I'd like that very much, sir.' Forgetting himself for a moment, and royal protocol, Ranj shook Raed's hand enthusiastically.

It wasn't a fully-fledged plan but at least by voicing his intentions out loud he was committing to the new project. The details could be fleshed out later, hopefully with his parents' approval and co-operation too.

'Great. We'll get something in the diary.' Raed handed him his business card. He knew he was taking a risk arranging this without running it past the official channels first, but he was keen to start making decisions, and a difference, as soon as possible. Along with telling Soraya the news of his plans. He wanted to impress her, show her that he could use his position to help others, and there was also a futile hope that she could somehow be a part of it all. Nonsense, of course, when she had a life in England, but in an ideal world he'd have someone like Soraya supporting him and working with him instead of only seeing the negatives in this way of life.

Just as he turned to walk back towards Soraya there

was a loud bang, which echoed around the arena, causing screams and panic and his security team to rush at him. Raed's first thought was for Soraya, who looked scared to death. His personal bodyguard was trying to bundle him out of the arena altogether, but he wouldn't leave her. If this was some sort of terrorist attack or attempted assassination, she was as much of a target as he was, if not more when he'd left her unprotected.

All hell had broken loose around them with people rushing towards the exits and onto the showground. Horses that had been spooked by the bang were running amok around the arena, some trailing their trainers, others blinded by panic taking the jumps on their own. Raed's instinct was to wrap his arms around Soraya to protect her body with his and in that moment he came to realise how important she'd become to him, given he was willing to put his own life on the line for hers.

He brushed away the usual protocol to get him out of harm's way as soon as possible, concerned only with Soraya's well-being. 'Are you okay?'

'Yeah, just a little shaken.' There was a tremor in her voice, her eyes wide with fear, but no visible signs that she'd been hurt.

The relief that washed over Raed was akin to that he'd experienced after his father's heart bypass when he knew he was out of immediate danger. But Soraya wasn't family and it was strange that he should feel so strongly about keeping her safe. Of course, as a medic he always did his best to save people, but his urge to protect Soraya in that moment was something more, came from somewhere deeper than a sense of duty and compassion for another human being. It spoke volumes about the bond they'd forged over such a short time, but was also going to make saying goodbye harder than he'd ever imagined when the time came.

'We really need to get you out of here, sir.' Now he knew Soraya was safe he was willing for them both to be transferred somewhere by the security team.

The Tannoy crackled to life. 'Ladies and gentlemen, please do not panic. We have confirmation that the blast you heard was caused by an electrical surge. There is no threat to life but we need to evacuate the building. Please make your way quickly and calmly to the exit.'

Raed turned to look back at the scenes unfolding in the wake of the unexpected incident. Now he knew there was no immediate threat, that they weren't under attack, the urgency to run lessened, even though he still wanted to get Soraya away from any potential danger.

'Take Ms Yarrow back to the palace. I want to make sure everyone here is okay first.'

His decision to see if he could be of any assistance was met with protests all around.

'I don't think that's a good idea, sir.'

'I'm not leaving without you. I can help too.' Soraya brushed off any suggestion that she should be taken to safety and leave him to deal with matters here alone.

He briefly considered using his influence to insist the team take her out of harm's way but, apart from the determined look in her eyes and the stubborn folded-arms stance, he wanted her to stay with him. She was capable and courageous, and exactly who he needed to help him with this crisis.

'In that case it looks as though we're all here for the foreseeable future.' Raed ventured back out onto the arena floor to see the aftermath with the entourage in tow.

The trainers and riders were trying to rein in the horses,

the spectators had thinned out and were now moving towards the exits in a calmer manner, assisted by stewards and security. However, there were a few casualties on the ground being attended to, including Ranj, the event organiser, who was stretched out and seemingly unconscious.

Raed bent down to speak to the first aider by his side who was tending to a nasty wound on the man's head.

'What happened?'

'One of the horses got spooked, kicked out and struck Ranj on the head. He's breathing but hasn't responded to me. I've phoned for an ambulance but I'm worried about his head injury.'

'I'm a doctor, let me take a look.' Raed pulled off his jacket to cover Ranj's body and keep him warm, and rolled up his own shirt sleeves. All thoughts of his ceremonial role were forgotten as his medical instincts kicked in.

'Why don't you go and tend to some of the others needing help? We're both doctors, we can handle him until the paramedics arrive.' Soraya rested a hand gently on the man's shoulder, relieving him of his responsibility here. Although there were people at these events trained in first aid, Ranj had two experienced surgeons more than capable of taking care of his injuries.

'If you're sure.' The man looked towards Raed for confirmation it was okay to leave his post.

'Soraya's a doctor too. Thanks for your help but we can take it from here.' It was important to him that her capabilities be recognised too. That she wasn't just here as his fiancée, or someone to hand-hold the injured, and they were lucky to have someone with her skills in attendance. While 'doctor' couldn't adequately describe her talents in the medical field, it did justify her place here in as few words as necessary.

It was sufficient explanation for the man to leave them.

'But leave us some of your first-aid supplies before you go, please,' Soraya added, taking possession of some dressings and bandages.

Ranj had been moved into the recovery position and, though he was breathing, a serious injury like a kick to the head meant his condition could change at any time.

'Ranj, can you hear me? It's Raed. You've had a blow to the head. The ambulance will be here soon but I need you to squeeze my hand if you can hear me.' There was no response.

Soraya knelt down and began to dab the wound at his temple, cleaning the area so they could see how bad the injury was beneath all the blood. 'Raed, there's clear fluid leaking from his ears and nose.'

It was bad news. Raed knew that this was a sign that Ranj's head trauma had caused a leak of cerebrospinal fluid from around the brain. An indicator that there might be a fracture of the skull, or a subdural haematoma where blood had collected causing pressure inside the skull. If left untreated it could lead to meningitis or seizures, but, with Ranj remaining unresponsive, they had no way to gauge his symptoms.

'We need to get him to hospital for MRI and CT scans to see exactly what is going on in there. The sooner he gets treatment, the quicker he will recover.' Raed was tempted to get him into the back of the limo and take him to the hospital himself until he heard the sirens and knew help was on the way.

'Medic! We need a medic over here,' someone shouted from across the arena.

When they looked over to the source it was to see a

man cradling a woman in his lap, clearly distressed and in desperate need of attention.

'You go, Soraya. I'll stay here with Ranj.' He didn't think twice about enlisting her help and she certainly didn't need him to supervise when she'd just successfully operated on a king.

Soraya grabbed some medical supplies, kicked off her shoes, hitched up her dress, and sprinted barefoot over to the couple. She wasn't someone afraid to get her hands, or feet, dirty, and always put others before herself. A flaw they both suffered from.

'Ranj, if you can hear me, please open your eyes.' There was no response. 'An ambulance is on the way. Hopefully it will be here soon.'

While Raed tried again to rouse his patient he could see Soraya setting to work on the woman across the way. She appeared to be making a tourniquet around the woman's leg, and commandeering people's jackets to cover the woman's body, probably in an attempt to keep her warm and prevent shock from setting in. When she began dismantling the horse jumps and using them to prop the leg, stabilising it so as not to exacerbate the injury, he figured it was a fracture she was dealing with. Likely caused in the crush.

Raed smiled at her ingenuity. Soraya wasn't prone to panic and simply got on with the task at hand, something that stood her in good stead in her career, but also a quality he admired in her in general. He'd asked a lot of her lately, and though she hadn't always been happy to oblige, she'd done so to the best of her abilities. At times he felt as though she was the only one he had on his side helping him navigate the new direction his life had taken and he was grateful to have her.

They both sat with their respective patients until the ambulances arrived to transport the casualties to hospital. As the most serious of the casualties, Ranj was lifted into the ambulance first.

'I'll come with him. I'm a neurosurgeon. I might be needed to assist at the hospital.'

'Your Royal Highness, we can't possibly let you travel alone in the ambulance,' his bodyguard reminded him, putting him firmly back into his princely role.

'Then we can follow in the limo.' Undeterred, Raed insisted that they continue to the hospital, though he drew the line at the whole team waiting with him for news.

'Soraya? Would you like to come with us?' He caught up with her as she loaded her patient onto the ambulance. This time he knew better than to try and send her back to the palace when he knew her work ethic was just as strong as his.

'Yes. I think it's a clean break but I'd like to make sure. How's Ranj?'

'The same. Unresponsive. That's why I'd like to go and see if I can be of any assistance.'

Once the ambulances were safely loaded and on their way to the hospital, sirens blaring, Raed and Soraya got into the limo.

'Thank you for your help back there.' Sitting close on the back seat of the car, he could see her dress was torn and dirty now, her make-up all but gone, and her hair in disarray around her shoulders. She'd never looked so beautiful.

'It's my job. My real job, not the pretend one.' Soraya smiled as she teased.

'You've certainly made an impression today.' Raed was sure if there had been any opposition to his new romantic interest, her skills and compassion today would have won everyone over, just as they had him.

'Can I go home, then?' She laughed, but, even in jest, the words struck Raed hard.

He wasn't ready for her to leave him. It was the first time he'd really felt as though he had support, emotionally and physically. Soraya had been there for him when he'd been going through a difficult personal time, and now she was here assisting him in a medical capacity too. It was the crossover between his two worlds that he'd thought he'd never achieve with anyone else. And now he'd found a certain acceptance of his royal role again, aided by Soraya, he wasn't sure he'd ever be ready for her to leave.

Soraya was exhausted, and she was sure Raed was drained. It was a lot to cope with between his father's health, coming back home as part of a lie, and then getting caught up in an emergency medical incident. In a way she was glad she'd come to Zaki with him so he didn't have to deal with everything on his own. She knew how that isolation felt, having to shoulder all the responsibility of the family.

Today had also given her an insight into his professional manner. He had a reputation as being stern and efficient but she could see that was simply because he was so focused on his job. She would even forgive him for telling her what to do earlier because she understood his need to take charge in that scenario. A medical situation was one thing he could control, unlike the rest of his life.

Soraya felt bad for him that he'd been put in this position. She'd be able to walk away from it eventually but he never could, as events had proven. Despite his efforts to hide it, she knew there was a vulnerable side to him that struggled with his burden. She'd seen it, recognised herself in it, along with that feeling of loneliness. Although she had Isolde and her career back in England, it wasn't going to be easy to leave him here dealing with everything on his own when the time came.

Not least because of the way he'd looked after her today. The gesture of ordering familiar cuisine for her so she didn't feel so out of place had been sweet, and she would have put it down to a simple act of hospitality if it weren't for his behaviour during the scare at the arena. Soraya didn't think his concern for her had merely been a polite display of chivalry.

The way he'd dived upon her, covering her, had been a natural instinct to protect her. A real concern for her welfare when he'd put his own at risk, going against the advice of his security team to save her, and the injured they'd later discovered.

It spoke of a bond between them that came from more than circumstances. There were some emotions involved. And they weren't all hers. They were growing closer all the time, and though she knew it was impossible for them to be together, there was a part of her still leaning towards the notion. As well as being handsome and successful, Raed was loyal and compassionate. Qualities that had sadly been lacking in her husband. She knew expecting anything to happen between them was heartache in waiting when they came from two different worlds, both bound by responsibility. Yet Soraya found herself spinning wildly into the abyss.

Once Soraya had been assured her patient hadn't suffered anything more than a broken leg at the hospital, she came to join Raed waiting for news on Ranj. With no one brave enough to tell him he wasn't needed, he and Soraya were

ushered into a private family room with his bodyguard on
sentry outside the door.

'I hope he's going to be okay,' Soraya said, worrying
her bottom lip with her teeth.

'Me too. We were talking about setting up a charity
event to raise money for our poorer members of society.'

'That sounds really positive, Raed. I'm sure you'll come
up with an amazing plan once Ranj has recovered.'

There was something about Soraya's genuine interest,
her praise for him, that made him crave more. Talking to
her today had really fired him up to generally *be* more.
Although the day's events had been shocking and unset-
tling for all involved, that drama and adrenaline rush of
getting involved took him back to his time working in the
hospital environment and he knew he wasn't done with
that part of his life just yet either.

With the permission of Ranj's family, who were en-
sconced in another room waiting for news, and Raed's
request to be updated about his condition, the A & E consultant came back to see them with the results of the scans
and blood tests they'd run on his patient's admission to the
emergency department.

'Mr Abdallah's apparent head trauma this afternoon has
indeed caused a subdural haematoma, as you'd suspected,
Your Royal Highness.'

'Please, just call me Raed.' He knew no one here would
but this occasion wasn't about him or his family. Here he
was simply asking to be treated as another medical colleague with a professional and personal interest in the
patient.

'Mr Abdallah is going to require surgery to relieve the
pressure on his brain. He still hasn't gained conscious-

ness so we are hoping to get the surgeon here as soon as possible.'

'You don't have someone available now?'

The consultant went red in the face. 'I'm afraid not. We don't have the budget to keep a specialist permanently on call here. It will be a while before the one in the city hospital can get here.'

It appeared their health service was one more area that had been neglected lately and he knew it was because the family had been too distracted by their own personal problems to focus on any fundraisers or personal appearances, which could have helped to boost the hospital coffers. They had their own private team of highly skilled professionals to call on when they were sick and it didn't seem fair to expect those born into less wealthy families not to have access to the same levels of care.

'I'll do it.'

'But, sir—'

'Raed, are you sure?'

He understood the consultant and Soraya's concerns but this wasn't simply a knee-jerk reaction because he was invested in this patient now. 'I'm a highly qualified, respected brain surgeon. I've performed this procedure hundreds of times. You can wait until your own surgeon arrives but I'm here and time is of the essence. The longer we wait to relieve that pressure on Ranj's brain, the more we risk serious long-term effects.'

'I'll talk to the family.' The consultant left and Raed knew he'd be scrubbing in again for perhaps the last time.

'Raed, are you sure about this?' Soraya asked, her brow creased with concern he knew was for him just as much as it was for Ranj.

'I've never been more sure about anything in my life.

Life-saving brain surgery I can do. I'm infinitely more comfortable in an operating theatre than a royal box, and certainly more useful.' That seemed enough to convince Soraya that he knew what he was doing, although guaranteed success would be the only way his father would ever have agreed to such extreme measures. Something a surgeon could never truly offer when surgery always came with risks of complication, but Raed was confident enough in his abilities and himself to undertake the procedure, anticipating a positive outcome.

'In that case, could I assist you? Two surgeons are better than one, right? I mean, you'd obviously take the lead on this but I would like to help.'

Sometimes having two surgeons working alongside one another caused a clash of egos, but Raed knew that wouldn't happen with Soraya because, just like today, his overwhelming want to be with her overruled his head.

CHAPTER SEVEN

RAED NEVER CEASED to amaze her. Not only was he preparing to give up the life he'd built for himself in England
to aid his family, but he was also still working to help everyone who crossed his path. He seemed really excited
about the charity event he'd been talking to Ranj about
hosting and Soraya had a feeling it would be the first of
many fund-raising projects he'd undertake now he was
getting used to his position back in the family again. If
only she'd had someone like Raed to help her and Isolde
growing up they might not have struggled so much. She
was proud of him and the work he was doing. Including
now, performing this craniotomy on Ranj.

'Scalpel,' Raed demanded before making an incision
into Ranj's scalp to make a window flap of skin where he
could access the skull easily.

Although Soraya was every bit as capable a surgeon
as Raed, she had her own area of expertise and respected
that he was the expert in this field. On this occasion, she
was content to merely assist.

'Drill, please.' He cut away a section of the skull to reveal the bleed beneath.

'I need someone to suction and irrigate.'

'I've got it.' Soraya was glad to have something to do,

though the other theatre staff were probably capable of doing the task without her.

She suctioned away the blood so Raed could see where he was working and cleaned the area with water. It was clear why he had such a stellar, if not warm, reputation. He was completely focused on the task at hand, as a good surgeon should be. Okay, so he didn't hold full conversations or like to listen to music as he worked like some other surgeons, but that just proved how invested he was in his patient.

Surgery was nothing new to Soraya but she still marvelled as he removed the subdural haematoma, relieving the pressure on the brain. It seemed second nature to him as he replaced the piece of bone and sewed the skin back over the site. Saving someone's life had been commonplace for him once upon a time, and it was a shame for Raed and those who needed his sort of skills that he would no longer be allowed to work in this field.

She could only imagine the uproar at the palace once they found out about this little venture so soon after his public reappearance as the Crown Prince. Still, it might take the heat off her if the focus moved from his new girlfriend to his inability to leave all of his old life behind for good. The strain of faking a relationship for the cameras, all the while yearning for it to be real, was taking a serious toll on her mental health.

Today had shown her how much Raed changed when he was around her. Here in the operating theatre he was precise, exact, almost emotionless. Yet she'd seen quite a different side to him, one that he'd admitted he tried to keep to himself. While she appreciated his cool, calm demeanour was what was needed in surgery, she could understand why it would have caused problems in his personal life. She considered herself fortunate to have seen the real Raed, who'd come to her for help, who got excited about future projects and whose smile made her go weak at the knees. It also made her worry about what they were letting themselves in for by getting so close.

'That was something different,' she commented as they exited the hospital.

'Perhaps it'll make you think about expanding your surgical repertoire,' Raed teased.

'No, thanks, I have plenty of work to keep me busy in cardiology.'

'I'm going to miss it,' he said with a sigh. 'I think that operation was as much for my benefit as Mr Abdallah's. One last hurrah.'

'It would be a shame if you have to give up a job you love when you could help so many families, just because of your position in society.' It was obvious how much he enjoyed his work as a surgeon. She hoped, given some of the changes he was already bringing into effect, he might also be able to find some way of continuing his work at the hospital.

'If there was some way to continue working as well as carrying out my royal duties, I would happily do both. Perhaps you could even join me. I'm sure your skills would be greatly appreciated in the hospital too.'

Even though said in jest, the idea was tempting. Though it wasn't the luxury, or the thought of a new start, that proved the greatest draw. Spending more time with Raed seemed to be something she couldn't resist, despite the issues that would surely bring into her life.

'I'm not sure that's an option,' she said, willing him not to push it any further.

Every second she spent getting to know this man pushed her deeper and dangerously closer to him. Although she didn't want to admit it to herself she liked him, and more than in a professional or friendly capacity. What she was beginning to feel towards him was bringing emotions to the fore that terrified her. He was attractive, yes, rich and powerful, but that paled in significance in the face of his utter kindness. It had always been her weakness, and her undoing.

She'd fallen for that generous spirit once before and it had left her broken-hearted and homeless. Although Raed wasn't likely to leave her paying off his debt, there was a chance she'd find herself a low priority in his life too. Even if he did reciprocate her growing feelings, it was clear today how much other stuff he had going on in his life. All of which he would have to put before a woman. Especially when he'd already lost a relationship because of his dedication to his family and royal duties.

Why should she think she was any different? She wasn't special and certainly not worth him giving up his position in the royal family so she would be number one in his life, nor would she ever ask him to even if he did show any romantic interest in her. However, that was the level of commitment she would need from a man if she was ever to entertain another relationship in the future.

Even if she took the idea of getting involved with Raed off the cards, she doubted her attraction to him would simply cease because it was inconvenient. If anything, she feared watching him every day proving what a great man he was would make her fall for him harder. It seemed she was doomed to get hurt no matter where she was, but at least if she was in a different country she wouldn't have to see him every day.

'That's a shame. I'm getting used to having you around.' It wasn't the declaration of undying love it would take for her to take a chance on a new relationship, but as he paused to look at her she could see in his eyes he meant every word. But that was what was causing the trouble, wasn't it? She was getting too comfortable with the arrangement too and it wouldn't be long before she believed their fake relationship was real.

'Thanks for your help in theatre today,' Raed said as they made their way back to the car. It had been a long, difficult day for them both and he wasn't sure he would have got through it without Soraya.

'I'm not sure I did anything a theatre nurse couldn't have done.'

'I disagree. My offer still stands. We could use you out here.' Although the initial invitation to stay had been a spur-of-the-moment suggestion, he didn't regret it. They needed someone with her expertise in the hospital. In another time or place he might've decided to set up his own consultancy, with Soraya on board for all matters of the heart. It was ironic that was what was fuelling these incentives to get her to stay with him too. His heart was making decisions his head knew would hurt them both.

By her own admission Soraya was scarred by the end of her relationship, as he was, and he couldn't offer her any more of himself than he was able to give to Zara. Same problem, different woman. Soraya needed someone to put her feelings first, to treat her like the queen she was, but it couldn't be him when he already had an entire royal family to think about, not to mention a country. That didn't stop him wanting her around though. She was a steadying influence on him, a support he desperately needed.

'You were a big part of the process in getting me in that theatre again, doing the job I love.' It was Soraya passionately extolling the need for something more than awards for poorer families that had got him thinking about the things he could do rather than those he couldn't. That newfound belief in his abilities had re-emerged when Ranj had been hurt. In the future he might not be able to perform surgery every day the way he used to, but he had been able to do it today. The bonus was having Soraya there with him through it all.

'I don't think you needed much persuading.' She grinned.

'No, but apparently you do.' He stopped walking, afraid once they reached the car and got back to real life they wouldn't have a chance to talk like this again.

'Raed, please don't do this.' She seemed to anticipate what he was going to say, as though she'd been dreading the moment since he'd first suggested staying with him.

'I need you, Soraya.' He wasn't usually one to resort to emotional blackmail but he was a desperate man in need of an ally.

'The longer I'm in your life, the more we'll have to keep up this pretence between us. I don't like lying to people and I don't think I can do it much longer.'

Before Raed could attempt to placate her he heard a rustle in the nearby bushes and spotted a camera lens glinting in the undergrowth. If the press were here there was no way of knowing how much they'd heard, or what would be printed in tomorrow's papers. Even though his father was through his surgery, he was a long way off full recovery and the country was in Raed's hands until then. The last thing he could afford now was a scandal to break about his fake romance and how it had been a cover for the instability of the current monarchy. He had to act quickly and do something to negate what they already might have overheard.

'In that case, we'll announce the engagement as soon as possible. I know you want time to let your family know what's happening, but I think the truth is going to come out sooner or later.'

He watched Soraya's face contort into a puzzled frown as none of that would have made any sense to her whatsoever.

'What on earth—?'

The second she made it obvious she had no idea what he was talking about the game was over. He would never recover if he was exposed as a liar in the press even if it had been done with the best of intentions. There was only one way he could think of temporarily stopping her from breaking their cover, and, though it might earn him a slap, he had to take the chance. It would be easier to explain things to her later than to the entire country.

Raed grabbed her face in his hands and kissed her hard. He expected the resistance, her attempt to push him away. What he hadn't been prepared for was the way she began to lean into him, her body pressed against his, her mouth softening and accepting his kiss. All notions of the press and what had or hadn't been captured seemed to float out of his brain, replaced only with thoughts about Soraya and how good it felt to have his lips on hers.

She tasted exactly how he'd imagined, sweet and spicy, and infinitely moreish. He couldn't get enough. Soraya's hands, which had been a barrier between their bodies at first, were now wrapped around his neck, her soft breasts cushioned against his chest in the embrace. Every part of him wanted more of her and if they'd been anywhere but in the middle of a car park he might have been tempted to act on that need. It had been a long time since he'd felt this fire in his veins, this passion capable of obliterating all common sense.

He knew this had gone beyond a distraction for any nearby journalists but he didn't want to stop kissing her, touching her, tasting her. Once this stopped and reality came rushing in, he knew he'd never get to do this again.

'Ahem.'

Soraya vaguely acknowledged someone clearing their throat nearby, too deep into the moment to pay it much attention. Raed was kissing her. She didn't know why or what on earth he'd been talking about before launching himself at her, but she could overanalyse that later. Once the kissing was done.

There was another exaggerated cough. 'Your Royal Highness, I really think we should move somewhere more private.'

The warning from Raed's personal protection officer was enough to end the fantasy. There was no way of avoiding the real world with a burly security guard pointing out how indiscreet they were being.

The moment they broke off the kiss, leaving Soraya's head spinning and her lips swollen, she realised there was more behind it than his desperate urge to snog her senseless. Raed was looking around as though watching for someone, waiting for them to be discovered, and his security were trying to bundle them both into the car out of the way.

'What was all that about?'

'I'm so sorry. I spotted a paparazzo hiding in the bushes

and panicked. He was bound to have heard our conversation and I just did the first thing that came into my head.'

Through the fog of her kiss-addled brain she recalled a mention of their engagement. 'You knew they were there the whole time?'

He had the decency to look ashamed of himself. 'I needed to give them something more newsworthy. I know it's not the way we had planned for this to come out, but it's more of a story if they think they've discovered it first. If they think we've been hiding the true nature of our relationship from the public. A secret engagement might just about save our backsides.'

'Your backside. It's not going to do much to uncomplicate my life,' she grumbled, trying not to think about his backside and wondering if she'd grabbed hold of it in the heat of the moment. Her cheeks flushed hot enough to rival the passion of that kiss as she thought about the display they'd just put on in front of witnesses, and wondered if it had been captured on camera, ready for the rest of the world to see too.

'I know and I am sorry, but I can't risk this all being revealed as a charade. I'd lose all respect to be caught out in the lies and it wouldn't look favourable for us as a family if the press realised it was all a ruse to cover up news of Father's health.' Although Raed seemed ruffled by the exchange, Soraya was sure it was more to do with what was going to be in tomorrow's headlines than the kiss itself. While she'd been left shaken and stirred by the whole incident.

It was everything she'd been trying to avoid, and apparently with good reason. She resisted the urge to trace her fingers over her lips where Raed had so thoroughly ravished her, still tingling from his touch. Despite the knowledge it had been nothing but another part of the couple disguise, her body was craving more. Raed had awakened that pulsing need for him she'd been trying to bury deep since that first time she'd touched him. Now she knew the rest of his body could match the promise she'd seen sometimes when he looked at her, as though he was ready to devour her, one kiss was never going to be enough. Yet she knew it was all they'd have when she was nothing more than a convenient explanation for his version of the truth.

'And how are we supposed to proceed now? I assume a royal engagement isn't going to stay as a rumour only, if you want to keep your father buried under the headlines until he's ready to take back his throne.' Soraya tried to get them back on track but she was mad at herself for getting swept up in it all. Her reaction to the kiss had been real, those feelings she'd desperately been holding back suddenly surging forward because in that moment she'd believed they were reciprocated.

To find out it had all been a ploy to throw reporters off the scent of the real story going on behind the scenes was crushing. He had been acting a part while she had thrown caution into gale-force winds and kissed him with abandon. Now there was no going back and she couldn't simply stuff those emotions back inside. She didn't know how she was going to survive the rest of her time here harbouring feelings for him she knew were hopeless. Apart from the fact he obviously saw her only as a decoy for press attention, they were a complete mismatch.

Soraya needed a man who would put her first, and he deserved a partner who would support him unconditionally. They both had too many responsibilities to make those sorts of promises to one another. Even if he ever wanted her for more than an extra pair of hands at the hospital.

She cringed, imagining what had been going through Raed's head as she'd wrapped her body around his, totally invested in them as a couple in that moment. Still, she supposed they'd put on a good show and that had been Raed's aim. Mission accomplished.

Raed grimaced, as though he'd just remembered her throwing herself at him too. 'We are going to have to make the announcement.'

'Okay. I guess that's why I'm here. That's what I agreed to.' She had to remind herself of that. It wasn't Raed's fault he didn't have feelings for her, or that she'd mistaken their arrangement for something more. But it didn't make it any easier to feign enthusiasm for the prospect of their fake engagement.

Something Raed seemed to pick up on. 'You know the position I'm in, Soraya. I'm sorry. I didn't want any of this.'

His words didn't make the current situation any less painful or humiliating. At least the kissing part. The fraudulent relationship, being press fodder, falling for a totally unsuitable prince and throwing herself at him, she could do without.

She watched a lone drop of condensation slip slowly on its sad journey to nowhere down the car window. It was only when it dripped onto her hand that Soraya realised she was watching her own reflection.

Raed's heart should have been full, his morning full of sunshine and rainbows. A check at the hospital had brought the good news that Ranj had had a good night. He had come round some time after the operation, and though surprised by the events relayed to him about how he'd come to be in the hospital, was recovering well.

The first person he'd wanted to share the news with was also the reason he was so blue today, despite everything going to plan so far. Every headline in the morning's papers had been screaming about his romance with Soraya and a write-up about their part in the drama at the horse show, with one paper in particular claiming an exclusive with news of their engagement featured with photographic evidence of their very steamy kiss in the car park. They'd done a good job of convincing their audience that they were a genuine couple judging by the article proclaiming the greatest, most surprising love story of the year. Perhaps too good a job when he'd managed to convince himself it was real too.

The kiss, which should have been a brief interaction solely to give the papers something to talk about, had turned into something much more at his insistence. As soon as his lips had met Soraya's all pretence had vanished, replaced with his very real desire for her. Satisfying his need had come at too high a price now he knew what it was to kiss her, taste her, and want more. Something that could never happen when she was here as a favour, pretending to be his love interest only.

It was unlike him to get carried away the way he had, kissing her so thoroughly, and passionately. But in that moment he'd forgotten all about the donation he'd promised in order to get here, and the whole 'protecting the monarchy' ruse they were engaged in. Selfishly only thinking about what he wanted. Soraya.

When he'd stopped kissing her long enough to think properly, and remembered the reason he'd kissed her in the first place, he could tell it had changed things between them. Soraya was obviously regretting agreeing to this debacle. Even if she had kissed him back, he'd heard it in her voice that she didn't want to go through with the engagement announcement. Despite everything he had on the line, he didn't want to force her into doing something she didn't want to.

Soraya was someone who deserved the world. She'd sacrificed so much in the past to benefit her loved ones it was unfair that people took advantage of her kind nature. Him included. She'd told him she didn't want this fake romance, yet he'd ridden over her wishes at the time because it didn't fit his agenda.

He knocked on her bedroom door. 'Soraya? It's me, Raed. Can we talk?'

He was sure he could hear her moving around in there and the knowledge that she might be avoiding him was a dagger to the heart.

'I don't want to be someone else who takes you for granted and disregards your feelings. If you want to end this now I'll understand. I won't stop you.'

The decision wasn't one he had made easily, because he didn't want to lose her, but that was partly what had caused the problems. He'd put his needs before hers. For now the most important thing for him was to do the right thing, even if that meant letting her go.

Shoulders slumped, he wondered if she'd ever talk to him again as he walked away. She might decide it was easier to jump on a plane and go back to England without another word.

Then the sound of a key turning in a lock echoed along the corridor, followed by the soft pad of footsteps.

By the time Raed had turned around Soraya had already disappeared back into the room, leaving only a scent of roses and a swish of a silk robe in her wake. He followed her like a faithful hound, grateful that she would even give him an audience. Only time would tell if she was simply granting him a last request, or a last-minute reprieve. He crossed his fingers and hoped there was a chance he was enough to make her want to continue.

Soraya was aware she was still in her nightclothes and belted her dressing gown tight around the lacy camisole and knickers she wore. It wasn't an appropriate outfit for dealing with Raed. She didn't need to be at any more of a disadvantage while he was sitting in her bedroom in his power suit. On the same bed she'd lain on all night staring at the ceiling trying to decide what she wanted to do. Now here he was offering her an out, but the very gesture was making her think twice about getting the hell out of here.

'Do you want to end this?' Raed asked again, giving her the choice and complicating everything.

Putting her feelings before her needs was more than anyone else had ever done for her and only made it harder for her to leave. However, her insecurity made her question this sudden turnaround and she wondered if it was because he'd decided she was more trouble than a whole country finding out he'd lied about being in a relationship to hide his father's ill health. If he'd been able to tell she'd put her heart and soul into that kiss and wanted an easy out before he had to let her down gently that he wasn't interested in her.

'No. I said I would go along with it and I will.' She took a seat at the dressing table rather than get cosy next to him on the bed so she could try and keep a clear head. Even the mention of that kiss set her on fire and it wasn't helping seeing him sprawled all over her bed as though he was waiting for her to join him. Apparently it didn't matter to her body that she'd humiliated herself, as she was aching for a repeat performance.

'I've asked and expected too much from you. You did the job I asked you to do and it's not fair to keep expecting more. I never meant to take advantage of your good nature.'

'Why did you kiss me?' The words burst out of her mouth before her filter could catch it. 'You could have shut me down some other way.'

One of the things keeping her awake last night had been the replay of that kiss over and over again and the knowledge that he could have achieved the same outcome with the press without even touching her.

Raed turned over onto his back, hands behind his head as he stared at the same ceiling she now knew intimately. 'I did what came naturally. I acted on my instinct and that was to kiss you.'

A shiver danced along her spine at the thought he might actually have wanted to kiss her, the same way she'd been yearning for it too.

'If I overstepped the mark, I'm sorry.'

He must have mistaken her silence as a sign she was still in need of an apology. The truth was she didn't need it or want it. What she needed was for Raed to have been invested in that kiss as much as she'd been. Although that would have brought a whole set of new problems for her to deal with.

Ending this was the sensible option, removing herself from temptation and the whole tangled mess of lies she'd found herself wrapped up in. Raed was unattainable, and when this whole fake relationship had run its course she would be surplus to requirements. This was exactly what she needed to get out of here guilt free. So why was her heart insisting that she needed to stay and see what came next after a kiss?

'You did what you had to. But tell me, what's the next step in this great plan?' She didn't want to be taken by surprise again.

'I haven't figured all the details out yet, but we can't put off making the official engagement announcement for ever. I'll go make some calls and let you get dressed.'

Soraya stood to see him to the door, her robe falling open to expose her bare legs, and Raed's gaze lingered there long enough to send her temperature rocketing again.

When he was looking at her like that it made her consider joining him on the bed and finally doing what she wanted for once, to hell with the consequences.

Then Raed bounced back up onto his feet and headed straight for the door, leaving her wondering once again if she'd imagined his interest.

'See you later.' And just like that, he rushed out of the room, away from whatever was clearly still simmering between them.

The door slammed shut before she could catch up with him and ask what was wrong. Of course, she knew the answer to that because it was the same reason she'd been freaked out last night too. There was an attraction between them, even more dangerous, a connection, that seemed to keep drawing them back to one another, despite the obvious pitfalls.

Soraya threw herself onto the bed, warm from Raed's body, his cologne still hanging in the air. She grabbed the nearest cushion and screamed her frustration into it.

The choice to leave had never really been hers, but at least Raed had let her pretend for a while.

CHAPTER EIGHT

RAED DIDN'T KNOW what had convinced Soraya to continue with the plan any more than what had prompted him to give her an out. Perhaps he'd realised it would be safer for him if she had called it off. Then he wouldn't have to worry about her abandoning him once he was head over heels in love with her because she'd already be gone, crisis averted. Because he knew he was falling for Soraya deeper every day.

It was going to be tough enough to keep seeing her, that attraction seemingly building every day, and he was beginning to believe that she might feel it too after the way she'd returned his kiss. There were so many obstacles in the way of them being a couple, it would be impossible for them to act on that chemistry between them.

Even when he wasn't with her, he was thinking about her and had spent most of the day working on a surprise for her tonight. He knew it was blurring that line between keeping their cover story alive in the press and a personal need to be with her, but he hoped he could persuade her to go along with his plans.

All he'd told her was that she should dress up for dinner. Now he was standing here in a tux, praying she wouldn't stand him up.

Raed looked at his watch, waiting for the hands to reach

the time he'd suggested they meet. Sweat began to break out on his forehead as it came and went. If she'd had second thoughts about continuing with this pretend romance he'd be back at square one trying to hold the whole country together on his own until his father had recovered.

'Sorry I'm late. I couldn't decide what to wear. Especially when I don't know where we're going.' Soraya eventually appeared, still attaching her earrings, and putting Raed's mind at ease that this might not have been a waste of time after all.

'It's a surprise and you look beautiful.'

'Not too much? I mean, if we're going for street food I can change into my jeans.' She gave a little twirl, letting him appreciate the gold sheath dress clinging to her curves and the matching shawl draped around her shoulders.

'You're perfect.' He held out his arm for her to take as he escorted her outside to where a helicopter was waiting for them on the lawn.

'Raed? Dinner, you said, not a near-death experience,' she said, eyes wide as she took in the sight.

It hadn't occurred to Raed that the method of travel would prove a problem. He'd grown up used to being flown around at the drop of a hat to save time and avoid traffic and assumed Soraya would enjoy the same. Apparently he still had a lot to learn about how to impress her.

'I'm sorry. I didn't realise you would have an issue with flying.'

'A private jet with champagne on tap to soothe my fear of heights is one thing, but flying in one of those hamster balls is quite another ask.'

Raed's mood dipped. He knew he'd screwed up. They needed the chopper to get them to their destination in good time. If he had to change it now all of his plans would be disrupted.

'They're perfectly safe, I promise, and I can offer you all the champagne you wish when we land. But if you really don't want to go, I'll try and arrange something else.' He didn't want her to feel pressured into doing something she wasn't comfortable with when it would only end in disaster.

She looked at the helicopter and back at Raed. 'Is it far? I mean, maybe I could manage if it's not for long and you promise to hold my hand.'

'It's about a twenty-minute ride from here and I promise you can squeeze my hand the whole way there if it makes you feel better, but I don't want to force you into going.'

'No, I can do this. I suppose I'll have to get used to it as the next princess-to-be.' The sparkle in her eyes said Soraya's tongue was firmly in her cheek as she referenced her new royal role. It put a smile on his face. Which, frankly, given his personal circumstances recently, was a miracle.

Soraya took Raed's hand as they made their way to the helicopter. It had taken her a while to come to the decision that dinner was a good idea, but if she was all in with their pretend romance, then she had to play her part too. She assumed dinner would be some grand affair in public for maximum press exposure, given the palpitation-inducing suit he was wearing now.

Though she was dreading this trip with little to save them from plummeting to their deaths, she was already thinking about the feel of his hand in hers. The strength and comfort she drew from him was something she hadn't had for a long time and she wasn't sure she'd ever let go.

They climbed into the helicopter, Raed's bodyguard joining them, and the pilot up front who gave them a thumbs up. She had to remind herself this was the fake Soraya and Raed going to dinner, likely for a photo shoot, and not to be impressed that her rich boyfriend was flying her somewhere just for a meal.

'Are you okay? You can still change your mind if you want.' Raed gave her hand a squeeze as they settled into the seats of the helicopter. She appreciated that he was still giving her the option to back out even though he'd clearly gone to a lot of trouble to set this up.

'I'll be fine,' she lied, believing she could tough it out for twenty minutes if she really tried.

Then the blades started swishing, the sound obliterating any further conversation, and the chopper began to lift off the ground. She screwed her eyes tightly closed as the ground began to get farther and farther away, and clutched Raed's hand tighter.

After a little while, when she hadn't fallen out to her gruesome death, she began to loosen her grip. Raed tapped her on the shoulder and she felt brave enough to open her eyes again. He pointed out of the window, encouraging her to lean across to look out. The coloured lights from moving vehicles snaked their way through the streets, like arteries pumping life into the city now splayed out below them, the lights and movement of the traffic heralding the end of the working day as the sun set on the horizon outside the window, darkness claiming the skies.

For a moment it really began to feel as though they were escaping the pressure cooker their lives had become. She knew they'd be plunged back into the stress and hurly-burly of public life the moment they landed, but she had to accept the cons of this lifestyle if she wanted to enjoy the pros. For now she would take advantage of the respite, her nerves beginning to subside. Though she didn't let go of Raed's hand for the duration of their journey.

Eventually another pocket of tall buildings came into view, and when the helicopter came to rest on the roof of one, and the blades stopped whirring, she was finally able to relax.

'Where are you taking me?' she asked, slightly concerned that she had no idea where on earth they were. If he decided to ditch her now, or her very rational fear of crashing in that tiny flying bubble prevented her from making the return flight, she was in serious trouble in these heels.

'I told you, we're going to dinner.' Raed jumped out of the helicopter and helped her out onto safer ground.

They were met by a small party of men and women in suits and chef outfits.

'Welcome, Your Royal Highness, and thank you for patronising our establishment tonight. Our chefs will prepare for you the very finest food we have to offer.'

The clearly awe-struck hosts bowed and curtseyed until Soraya was almost embarrassed by the display of gratitude. Raed of course took it all in his stride as he thanked the welcoming committee and added that they were ravenous after their journey. She didn't know if it was true or simply a ruse to get them to stop fawning but it did the trick as the party hustled back inside to prepare their food.

'How do you ever get used to that?' she asked Raed quietly as they made their way down into the restaurant via another recently renovated elevator.

'I never did, but it's part of the gig. People tend to lose their minds a bit when members of the royal family turn up, but I'm very lucky anyone still knows who I am in the current climate. I've lived quietly in London for some time but all of that has changed these past couple of days.'

Despite his obvious privilege, Raed somehow managed to stay humble and Soraya liked him even more for that. In her job she'd come across many surgeons at the top of their field who thought that gave them free rein to treat everyone else as though they were beneath them. That superiority complex wasn't attractive, but apparently a man who treated everyone with respect was someone she couldn't resist. It didn't bode well for however long they had to maintain this fake relationship when she was finding more reasons to fall for him.

'Wow.' It was the only thing she could manage to say when they walked into the restaurant, a circular room with full-size windows the whole way around. As it was beginning to get dark, candles were lit on each of the tables, still managing to give the place a cosy atmosphere. A lady dressed in a formal ball gown sat playing the piano with a harp sitting close by. The crystal chandeliers hanging all around were so numerous and heavy Soraya wondered how the ceiling stayed up, and the wall-to-wall white carpet and furnishings were a messy eater's nightmare. Even without the gold gilding on the walls the whole place screamed money. That part of her who'd struggled to buy even basic groceries after her parents had died baulked at the extravagance, but the new Soraya was enjoying this level of luxury. Raed was treating her to this decadent night out and it wouldn't hurt to indulge him when he was going to such lengths to impress her.

'We have reserved the best seat for you over here.' The maître d' bowed and led them over to a table for two at the window with impressive views over the city.

'Reserved? It's not exactly heaving with customers at

the minute,' she whispered discreetly to Raed once they were alone, his security shadow seated at the bar where he could observe the room but wasn't close enough to hear their private conversation.

'I bought it out.'

'Pardon me?' Soraya spluttered on her glass of white wine.

Raed leaned across the table so the candlelight was dancing on his face. 'I covered what they would usually take for a full service tonight so we could be alone. No press, no gawkers, no pressure to be anyone but ourselves.'

Her mouth dropped open at the thought he would go to such lengths to make her feel comfortable. She wasn't sure she deserved it.

'Raed, it's really thoughtful of you but—'

'I know what you're going to say but I've come to an agreement with the restaurant that they will prepare all the meals they would usually cook over the evening and they're going to distribute them to local charities. Any excess produce will go to local foodbanks.' It was a move he knew she couldn't argue with.

'That's, that's, really generous of you.' She struggled to find words to express how grateful she was and was horrified to find tears pricking her eyes. It wouldn't do to launch into a sobbing fit, mascara running down her cheeks, her eyes and nose puffy and red, and ruin this beautiful moment. It was overwhelming.

'Now, what would you like to eat? I'm starving.' He snatched up the menu, scanning the extensive list for something to satisfy his hunger.

Soraya knew now there was only one thing—one man—who could satisfy hers, but unfortunately that wasn't on the menu.

* * *

Raed devoured his meal even though his stomach felt as though it would rebel at any moment with the thought of the next step he was about to take. They'd dined on lobster and mussels infused with saffron, and had lemon chiffon pie for dessert, every mouthful a taste experience.

'What's up, you stuffed too full of food to even talk now?' Soraya teased as she raised another forkful of lemon and cream to her lips.

He loved moments like this when they were just two people having dinner together, without outside pressures making them stressed or uncomfortable. There were no expectations other than enjoying one another's company, and that was easy as he genuinely liked being around Soraya. It was a shame they had all this other stuff circling around them, waiting for an opening to break through their happy bubble and spoil things. Perhaps it could wait a little longer.

'I was just thinking how nice this is. Normal. Well, except for the helicopter and the bodyguard and buying out the restaurant for some privacy.'

Soraya giggled. 'I've had a wonderful time, thank you.'

'If we weren't under so much scrutiny I'd take you to this place I love that makes the best chicken fajitas and margaritas. Mmm-mmm-mmm...' His mouth was watering for Mexican food, or anything that wasn't served up under a silver cloche with more cutlery than any one person could possibly use in one sitting. Since his family's troubles had begun he'd no longer been able to live his anonymous life, and had been absorbed back into the royal lifestyle.

'Like on a date, date? Sounds good to me.'

'It would be nice, wouldn't it? A meal, somewhere anonymous, a few drinks, then stroll home a little bit tipsy, with no need to worry about who's seen us.' As nice as this had been, it wasn't reality and never would be. However, it had been his decision to come back into the family fold, and he'd known what he was walking back into. He guessed now Soraya did too. It didn't make circumstances ideal.

She sighed. 'I don't know the last time I did that. Frank was always too busy with "work" for a date night. At least with me. For all I know, he was out on multiple dates when I stupidly believed he was staying late at the office trying to make a difference in the world. The only thing he managed to do was ruin my life.'

Soraya's playful tone had turned to something bitter and angry as she tossed back more of her wine. It was clear her break-up had been as devastating as his own, both experiencing a betrayal of sorts. Zara might not have cheated on him, or lied to him, but she hadn't stuck by him or even tried to make things work. She'd tossed their relationship away without even attempting to fight for it. He supposed he was guilty of doing the same, which ultimately proved that they hadn't been right for each other. From everything he'd heard about Frank he'd taken Soraya for granted and treated her despicably. Raed didn't want to be guilty of doing the same.

'Do you ever wonder what it would have been like if we'd met somewhere away from all this craziness? If we'd just been two surgeons who happened to cross each other's paths at a medical conference or a Mexican restaurant? When we weren't just getting over the breakdown of our relationships, obviously.' If he hadn't been so consumed with self-pity at the time they'd first met, they might actually have stood a chance.

Soraya thought for a moment before she responded.

'But we didn't, Raed. If there's one thing I've realised it's that there's no point in venturing down the "what if" route. Yeah, we might have met and perhaps there might have been something between us if we didn't have family to think about or a country to run, but that's not what happened. It's as pointless thinking that way as it is wondering how different life would have been if I'd been enough for Frank.' She hiccupped that last part of her monologue, the raw pain of her divorce still evident.

He'd been through that stage as well, blaming himself for how things had ended between him and Zara. It was only since meeting Soraya, having her support, that he'd begun to realise the failure of his relationship hadn't been entirely down to him, or Zara. This lifestyle hadn't been what either of them had signed up for and it simply hadn't been compatible with their relationship. If he'd been able to open his heart fully to her, perhaps she would have seen a future together, wherever that might have been. In Soraya's circumstances maybe if Frank hadn't spent so much time at work he wouldn't have succumbed to temptation. At the end of the day they'd simply been with the wrong people.

'Frank didn't appreciate the amazing woman he had waiting for him at home. That's not your fault. You're right, we shouldn't agonise over how things might have worked out if this or that hadn't happened. It won't change anything. We need to leave it all in the past where it belongs. Neither Zara nor Frank are part of our lives any more and I'm pretty sure neither of them are fretting about us right now. We have to move on.'

'I can't really do that yet though, can I? I mean, how do I move on when I'm here playing make-believe with a prince?' Her laugh had none of the usual warmth in it and Raed knew then that the real world had managed to pierce their illusion of normalcy already.

'I know we haven't made life easy with our ridiculous expectations of you, Soraya, but I do like to think all of this has helped you to move on emotionally at least.'

She eyed him with some scepticism.

'When you're mad at me, there isn't time to wallow in self-pity,' he explained with a grin.

'True, but you're not going to be around for ever, Raed.'

He wasn't sure if he'd imagined the fleeting look of sadness cloud her blue eyes, but he knew the time had come for him to make his next move.

'Then maybe we should make the most of our time together as our alter egos. If we're supposed to be engaged I thought we should make it official.' He felt for the ring box, which had been burning a hole in his pocket all night. While Soraya had been working this morning he'd made a special trip to an exclusive jeweller. Although the engagement wasn't real, what she'd done for his family was priceless and he wanted to show his appreciation to her with more than lip service.

He opened the box and held his breath, waiting for her reaction to the square-cut emerald on a diamond and platinum band. The frown across her forehead wasn't what he'd expected.

'I don't understand,' she said in the end.

'I thought it would complement your red hair.'

'But the engagement isn't real, why get a ring?'

'It'll look good in the photos,' he jested, but she still wasn't smiling. 'Listen, we're going to have to make an official announcement, probably do a photo shoot. It's expected.'

'Oh, okay. It just seems...excessive.'

'I thought once all this is over that you could sell it or donate it to charity, or do anything you want with it.'

Her eyes widened. 'You're really giving this to me?'

'It's a token of my gratitude for everything you've done here. Really it's a two for one: it gets us some publicity and it could set you up with your new life.'

'Still—' She was staring at it as though she couldn't believe what she was seeing or hearing. It was down to Raed to take it out of its velvet cushion.

'Soraya Yarrow, will you do me the honour of becoming my fake fiancée?' It was an odd feeling proposing to someone he knew would never marry him.

After being with Zara for so long he'd felt that marriage would be their next logical step, part of life's plan. Not knowing it would come to an abrupt end a few years down the line. At least there were no expectations after this, only an impending feeling of loneliness once it was all over and Soraya went back to her old life.

'I made sure the stones were ethically sourced too, so we both have a clear conscience over this at least.' He was sure the guilt over everything they were doing to protect his father and the reputation of the family as a whole would haunt him for some time to come. Along with dragging Soraya into the whole sordid affair.

She was admiring the emerald on her finger when the sound of a champagne cork reverberated around the room, followed by another procession of staff emerging from behind the scenes clapping and cheering.

'We're so honoured to have you here to celebrate your engagement.' The manager was beside himself with excitement, having apparently witnessed the royal engagement.

He glanced at Soraya, who was smiling uneasily at the gathered crowd. 'Thank you, but we're not ready to make a public announcement just yet. If you could hold off on telling anyone about this for now, we would be very grateful.'

'Of course, Your Royal Highness. Anything you want.' He gave a bow and while Raed was inclined to believe he was genuine about maintaining his silence on the matter for now, the same might not apply to the other members of staff present.

'If you can guarantee that this will stay between us, we will give details of tonight to the press with our announcement. I'm sure you'll have a rush of love-struck couples wanting to come and have the same experience at your wonderful restaurant,' Soraya said, adding extra incentive for their co-operation, and though the official statement they would have to make was inevitable, this could give them a little longer to get used to the idea of their official relationship status.

'I promise my staff will be very discreet.' The now solemn-looking manager ushered his staff back towards the kitchen and Raed suspected they were going to have a stern talking-to about keeping their jobs to guarantee their silence.

'Very smooth. Perhaps you should take control of our PR from now on,' he suggested, impressed with how she'd handled the situation.

'No, thanks. It's one thing reading rumours and gossip, but I don't think I'm prepared for the press descending en masse once we confirm their suspicions. Still, it's what I signed up for, I guess, so I shouldn't complain.' Soraya stood up and wrapped her shawl around her shoulders, their night apparently at an end.

Even though they'd both decided it was pointless, Raed couldn't help but wish their circumstances had been different.

CHAPTER NINE

THE SHINE OF the evening had worn off for Soraya with the glint of that huge emerald. She knew she was being ungrateful when Raed had gifted it to her, not expecting to get it back when they inevitably called off their fake engagement. It was foolish of her to be upset that this had all been part of the greater PR plan.

Okay, so he'd tried to keep dinner as private as possible, and they'd had a lovely heart-to-heart about the wounds they were still carrying from their relationships. To her though, the reminder that this hadn't been a real date meant it ended on an unhappy note. It felt as if her emotions were being toyed with, especially after Raed had asked the question if they could've had something together if they'd met under different circumstances. Suggesting that he was interested in her, but knowing she would never be a viable option. It didn't help keep her emotions on lockdown believing there might have been more to that kiss between them than a publicity stunt after all. She wasn't an actress, or a celebrity with an alter ego—all of this toing and froing between playing his fiancée, and dealing with her real feelings for him, was causing havoc inside her.

Producing a ring to convince the wider public of their engagement was a reminder that none of this was real.

But she'd made the decision to stay knowing all of this, so it was her own fault she was making herself miserable.

'Is everything all right, Soraya? You've been very quiet.' Raed helped her on with her seat belt before attending to his own.

'Sorry, I'm just tired,' she lied, not in the mood for small talk. At least, not until the helicopter started up again, and the nerves began to flutter in her belly.

'Is this thing okay to fly in the dark? How can he see where he's going?' She hated that she worried so much about things beyond her control, especially in front of Raed, who was so calm and taking everything in his stride, but to her mind these were legitimate concerns.

'Don't worry, he can see. You've flown in planes, right? It's the same principle. He has lights and radar and people to guide him if necessary. We're perfectly safe.' These were all things she knew in her heart but hearing him say them somehow made them more believable. Perhaps that was her problem—when Raed was being her charming fiancé for the cameras she was buying into the fantasy too. If he was able to lie to his country about major issues and pull the wool over their eyes, it wasn't a huge stretch to see why she would believe he was her doting other half even when she knew the stark truth.

She turned her head to look out of the window, away from temptation. Only for him to reach out and take her hand, pre-empting her need for his support. She didn't pull away, but it didn't help her predicament when he insisted on being nice to her away from the watching eyes of the world.

Suddenly, the relatively smooth journey back towards the palace took an unexpected turn. There was a loud bang and the helicopter lurched violently, lifting Soraya out of her seat before she was pulled back down by her restraints. Now, as the helicopter plunged down, taking her stomach with it, alarms were going off, and lights in the cockpit flashing, all as the pilot tried to wrestle some control. Even Raed looked concerned this time and that was reason enough for her to spiral, her pulse racing and heart lodged in her throat as panic set in.

'What's happening?'

'It's a bird strike,' the pilot relayed, though it didn't allay her fears. Especially when she swore she could see a crack in the windshield.

'What does that mean?'

'Usually it means there's been a collision with a bird, or even a flock of them. I'm sure they'll let us know if it's anything serious.' Raed smiled and squeezed her hand, presumably to convince her she was still safe. However, his reassurances couldn't drown out the chaos happening all around them.

'You're going to have to brace yourselves back there. We need to land and we're coming in hard. The damage is too great for us to stay in the air. I've radioed for help but strap yourselves in, this is going to be a bumpy one. I'm going to try and head for some waste ground, away from more populated areas.'

The pilot's update prompted Raed to check their belts again. 'We'll ride this one out together. I'm here for you.' He lifted her hand to his mouth and kissed it.

Soraya closed her eyes as the helicopter descended rapidly, too quickly for her to catch her breath.

There was so much noise her head felt as though it were going to explode. People shouting, the mechanical sound of the helicopter struggling to fly, alarms blaring, and her heart pounding.

'Mayday, mayday.'

That high-pitched squeal she assumed was the helicopter in freefall grew louder as her stomach lurched. Anything not bolted down was being tossed around inside adding to the sense of chaos, and all the time Raed was clutching her hand.

'We're going to die.' Her voice was remarkably calm, as though she'd simply accepted that this was the end for them.

'Not if I can help it,' Raed told her, jaw clenched, fingers tightly wrapped around hers, and Soraya loved him for his determination, no matter how futile.

Suddenly she needed to tell him that. 'I'm not sure you can but thank you for looking after me. If we do die—'

'But we're not going to,' Raed interrupted as the helicopter jolted again, making a mockery of his words.

'If we do...' Soraya had to shout to be heard over the din of their impending crash '... I want you to know I would have done this without the money for the centre. I... I like being with you, Raed. Even though you drive me crazy at times, and I know it could never work out between us, not least because we're about to die in a ball of flames...'

Before she could descend into complete panic, Raed silenced her with a hard kiss. His lips were insistent and demanding on hers, as though he was trying to make up for lost time. Soraya screwed her eyes shut, trying to block out the crisis going on around them and focus on the feel of Raed against her. She gripped him by the lapels of his jacket, and pulled him as close as the seat belt would bring him, kissing him back. Completely in freefall, body and soul.

Eventually they had to break apart as gravity and the intensity of the moment stole away their breath. Soraya tried to brace herself for the inevitable crash but one look at Raed and she was putty again. Those soulful brown eyes were locked onto hers and if it was the last image she ever saw she'd die happy.

'I don't think I'd have had the strength to come back if I hadn't had you by my side,' he said, making her heart melt. 'Just in case I never get to say it again, I'm glad I have you in my life.'

Tears filled Soraya's eyes with the unfairness of it all. She knew they were only saying these things to one another because they were staring death in the face. It was cruel irony to find out now he did reciprocate her feelings when they were never going to get a chance to do anything about it. If they'd been braver, willing to face their demons when they weren't in a life-or-death situation, there could have been more kissing, more Raed, more everything. Now they were facing the end of it all.

The embrace they shared in that moment was an attempt to cling onto life just a little bit longer, holding each other so tightly she never wanted to let go.

They were plummeting, the cacophony of sound around them overwhelming.

'Just hold on,' Raed shouted above the noise, then he covered her body with his like a protective shell as they hit the ground with a deafening crunch.

Soraya's head whipped back and forward with the impact and she lifted out of her seat before being thrust back into it. They seemed to skid along the ground for some time before the interior of the helicopter was filled with dust and dirt. Only then did she open her eyes and try to move, all to no avail. It was pitch black and she had a heavy weight pressing her down. She felt around to try and figure out what had landed on her and her hands found Raed still shielding her body with his.

'Raed,' she croaked, her lips dry, her throat parched.

When he didn't respond she nearly stopped breathing herself, afraid that he mightn't ever wake up again. The thought was so devastating she didn't want to contemplate it for another second. She couldn't lose him when they'd just confessed their feelings for one another.

'Raed, wake up,' she said more urgently, shaking him and praying for signs of life.

He gave a groan and gradually the weight lifted from her body as he sat up. Relief helped to settle her heart back into an almost normal rhythm.

'Soraya? Are you okay?'

She was touched that his first thought was for her even though he was the one who'd struggled to wake up. It spoke of feelings for her that went beyond her being a mere convenience to him, and, though that brought its own problems, for now she needed it. After opening herself up, admitting that she more than liked him, it was reassuring to know that he hadn't simply said those words to her because he thought he was dying. It was an even playing field now they'd both confessed.

'Yeah. A bit banged up but I'll live. Thanks to you. Are you all right?' It was hard to see him in the dark and check for injuries, so she had to rely on him to tell her if he was hurt. He'd been so intent on protecting her she doubted he would even say if he had a leg hanging off, so as not to upset her.

'A few cuts and bruises. I think I got hit by some of the debris. That'll teach me to leave water bottles lying around.' He was still trying to make her smile, even in the wake of a horrible crash that had knocked him unconscious.

Soraya couldn't stop the sob that had bubbled up from nowhere and erupted into the quiet night, the seriousness of what had just happened suddenly catching up with her. Not to mention the thoughts of an alternative, and very final, ending. In the face of death, her life hadn't flashed before her. Her thoughts had been only of Raed and wanting to be with him. A serious development that complicated everything about their fake engagement, but, with no time to overthink, her real feelings had come to the fore. In that moment the fact that they'd be living in two different countries, that he had other priorities than her, wasn't an issue. The only thing that mattered was that he was safe.

'Hey, it's going to be all right. The pilot radioed for help and the emergency services won't be far behind. Everything's going to be okay.' He brushed her hair tenderly away from the stream of tears now flooding down her face. It only made her cry harder.

'You said that before the crash.' She hiccupped.

Raed sighed. 'I know, I'm sorry. The birds must've hit the propeller blades and caused us to spin out of control. It's very rare, especially at this time of night. We were very unlucky, but, hey, we're both alive to tell the tale.'

'I thought you were dead.' Soraya couldn't help the renewed torrent of tears, imagining what could have happened.

'Well, I'm not.'

'So why can't I stop crying?' She was laughing at herself through her tears because Raed made it so easy for her not to be scared even though they were sitting in wreckage goodness knew where in the outskirts of the city. There was no way of knowing what was in store for them next, or if their earlier revelations would come to anything, but she was relieved Raed was still here with her.

'It's shock. We've just been involved in a major trauma. Mine will probably hit later but for now I'm more concerned with getting out of here in case there's a fuel leak somewhere.' Raed was right, they probably had a lot to discuss, but for now they had to concentrate on their safety.

'What about the others?' she asked as he wrestled to get the jammed seat belts off both of them.

'Let me get you to a safe distance, then I'll come back and check on the others.'

Soraya gave him the side eye. 'You know that's not going to happen.'

She heard him take in a breath, as though he was about to argue then he realised it was pointless.

'I just don't want you getting hurt.' He paused the struggle with the belt to rethink his words. 'Sorry. I don't mean to patronise you, you're every bit as capable as I am. All I want is to keep you safe.'

'I know.' How could she be mad at him when his intentions were so honourable? Despite the horrendous situation they'd ended up in, it was nice to have someone to look out for her for a change. Someone who'd protected her with his body, his life, as they'd crashed. She would never forget that.

In the end he had to lift up the fabric of the belt while she wiggled her way out. It was only then she realised she must have been bumped around more than she'd thought, her hip bones aching when she brushed against anything.

They stepped cautiously over the detritus now littering the floor to get into the cockpit where both the pilot and bodyguard were unconscious. The windscreen was shattered, glass and blood covering everything.

'I'll see to Steve. He seems the most badly hurt. Can

you see to Duke?' Raed climbed in beside the pilot, who was slumped against what was left of the blood-smeared window, not hesitating to enlist her medical expertise.

She set to work assessing the bodyguard.

'He's tachycardic. Breathing shallow. Signs of cyanosis. Suspected pneumothorax.' The fast pulse combined with the blue tinge of his skin suggested he'd suffered a collapsed lung, perhaps caused by a fracture of the ribs during impact.

'Steve's breathing and has a steady pulse. Let me go look for some first-aid supplies.'

The sound of Raed banging around in the wreckage gave her some comfort knowing he was close by. It was going to be difficult returning to a life where she was the one who carried everyone else's worries and expectations on her shoulders. At least here she had Raed to turn to, to share her fears, her problems, and emergency medical situations. She hoped she did the same for him when he had the weight of an entire kingdom wearing him down. By agreeing to stay and keep the myth of their relationship alive, she was relieving him of some of that burden. Even if maintaining the pretence and attempting to keep their personal lives separate from their public personas brought different issues.

'There's a good first-aid kit, probably in case of emergencies like this, and some blankets. Along with this because you're shivering.' Raed emerged with an armful of supplies and what was left of her gold wrap. He carefully draped it around her shoulders.

A sudden rush of love at the gesture, that even in the midst of this disaster he was thinking of her, threatened to overwhelm her. She managed to swallow down her emotions to focus on treating their patient because now wasn't the time for that kind of epiphany. If she let herself think about the fact she'd fallen completely for a prince she'd start to catastrophise the situation even more. At least when they'd thought they were going to die they hadn't had time to overthink, only express how they felt about one another, and that wasn't something she was going to forget in a hurry.

'Thank you,' she said, accepting the gesture without spiralling about all the reasons they shouldn't be together.

Later, when they were somewhere safe and private, they could deal with the new emotional development between them, but for now there were other issues at hand. As medics, in this emergency situation, they had to put other people's welfare before their own personal issues.

'We should probably get him out of here,' Raed concluded.

'Yeah, I really don't like his colour. With no sign of the emergency services, I think I'm going to have to do a needle decompression.' Duke's rapid deterioration was likely attributed to chest trauma trapping air in his pleural cavity. If left untreated it could lead to cardiac arrest. They needed to release the trapped air.

Raed manoeuvred himself in behind Duke and lifted him under the arms, leaving Soraya to grab his legs. Between them they managed to carry him out of the cockpit and set him down on the ground outside. Soraya quickly opened Duke's shirt, noted the severe bruising to his chest and listened to his breathing using a stethoscope from the medical bag Raed had salvaged.

'Decreased breath sounds suggesting a partially collapsed lung,' she confirmed.

Without hesitation Raed opened a new needle and handed it to her. It showed his confidence in her and her abilities once again and Soraya liked that he wasn't the kind of arrogant man who tried to take over, or thought he knew best. He trusted her, and she knew that wasn't something he gave away easily when he took on so many responsibilities for himself.

She used a sterile wipe to clean Duke's chest, and felt along for the second intercostal space along the mid-clavicular line.

'Where's Amir when you need him?' she joked, as the implications of getting this wrong hovered in her psyche. As a thoracic surgeon, Raed's brother was the one who performed this procedure on a regular basis, but Soraya was acutely aware in this moment of the things that could go wrong. If she failed to penetrate the wall, or damaged any of the organs, she could make Duke's situation worse.

'You can do this,' Raed assured her, and she knew he was right.

Just above the third rib, she plunged the needle into the chest at a ninety-degree angle and was rewarded with the hissing sound of air escaping. She removed the needle, leaving the catheter to keep the airway open, and taped it in place. Only once she was finished did she take a shaky breath of relief.

'One down, one to go,' she said with a smile, aware that this wasn't over yet. They still had another patient waiting for their assistance.

'I can get Steve…you stay here with Duke. I think you've done your part.' Raed covered both Soraya and Duke with blankets, then dropped a kiss on her forehead before going back to retrieve the pilot.

It was this kind of teamwork, looking out for each other, that she enjoyed, and was going to miss most when their fake romance came to an end. Despite all their differences, he treated her as an equal, not a fool to be duped and used as Frank had done. She was beginning to hope there was some way to continue their relationship, because she didn't want to go back to a life without that support, without Raed.

She watched as Raed grabbed hold of Steve's shoulders and began to drag him from his seat. He managed to get him halfway out of the helicopter and onto the ground, but there was clearly something wedging his feet and preventing him from getting out. Soraya realised it wouldn't be an easy task for him to manage alone. It wasn't in her nature to simply stand back and watch someone struggle so she rushed over and offered another pair of hands.

'I've got him. You see what has trapped him in there.' Soraya bent down and covered him with her blanket. Whatever other injuries he had, she didn't want him going into shock as well. Keeping his body temperature regulated would help prevent that.

'Uh, Soraya, we have a situation here.' Raed motioned her over to where he'd been pulling out bits of mangled machinery in an attempt to dislodge the man's lower half.

When she peeked inside, where Raed was using the torch on his phone to light the interior, she had to cover her mouth to stave off the sudden urge to vomit.

Even though she was a trained, experienced surgeon, the sight that met her was hard to stomach. The foot, still encased in the shoe, was barely attached to the rest of the leg, bone visible and turned the wrong way around.

'Can you get him out?' Preferably without accidentally amputating the foot.

'I can now, but we're going to have to be very careful.

I'm sorry but I'm going to need you to hold the foot in place while I try to manoeuvre him out of here.'

Soraya had to push through the nausea and squeamishness to focus on their patient and saving his foot. It would be career-ending, or at the very least life-altering, for him to lose it. She and Raed were both used to saving lives in difficult circumstances and this shouldn't be any different, even though they didn't have the comfort or the facilities of a modern hospital. The amount of food she had eaten for dinner, however, was coming back to haunt her.

'No problem.' She ducked inside the door and leaned down so she could reach the foot, turning it to where it should have been and holding it firmly in place as Raed gently eased Steve's legs out onto the ground, bringing her with them.

Afraid to set the open wound down and risk infection from dirt and sand getting in there, she rested the foot on her lap. Raed grabbed bandages and dressings from the medical supplies.

'This should keep the foot in place until help arrives.'

'Any word on that?' she grumbled. The longer they were all stuck here, the greater they were at risk of something happening to them too. She would have expected a search party out here the second this precious prince disappeared. Even though it had been mere minutes since they'd crashed it already felt like an eternity.

'They will be here as soon as they can. They're probably just trying to pinpoint exactly where we've come down. The best thing we can do is have him ready to transport the second they get here. Okay?' He nodded towards their injured companion and she knew he was right. If anything they were lucky Raed had been part of this, because they'd pull out all the stops to find him, not write them off as missing presumed dead.

Soraya kept talking to her patient, though he was still unresponsive. Currently it wasn't such a bad thing he was sleeping through the pain, but she hoped he hadn't suffered any head injuries she hadn't spotted, or internal bleeding that could cause complications to his recovery.

'Okay, we need to get that bone in place again, then we'll strap it up. Hopefully at the hospital they can operate and repair the damaged muscle and tendons so he can maintain mobility.' It was all they could do on this end as well as try to keep the blood circulation going for now.

Soraya tried again to rouse their patient, or at least find out if he was awake, while they attempted to push the bone back in place. The last thing she wanted was for him to suddenly kick out in pain and damage himself or them.

When there was no response they agreed to forge ahead. She gently lifted the foot from her lap and Raed held the end of the leg securely.

'One, two, three—' They counted together and on three she forced the two pieces of exposed bone back together.

Raed began strapping the foot and leg to keep it in place. He spread one blanket on the ground and covered the patient with another. Once she was sure the foot had been stabilised Soraya was able to rest the whole leg on the blanket so she could stand up and stretch hers.

'Good job.' He high-fived her and it made her smile after the stress and tension of the last few minutes.

In an operating theatre she had some control over what happened, was able to work with the benefit of X-rays and cameras to assist her. Here in the dark, working solely on their instincts, with these men's lives at stake, there was a question mark hanging over what they were doing. And if it was good enough. That uncertainty wasn't something she could shake off easily.

It was only when she looked back at the crash site Soraya realised how lucky they had been to be able to walk away. The tail was completely severed from the rest of the helicopter, taking the brunt of the hit, she supposed, as the pilot did his best to land in the field. If they had hit anything other than this grassy oasis she was sure none of them would have survived the impact.

Thankfully the sound of rotor blades were heard in the skies above them, followed by a bright search light from the rescue helicopter scanning the area around them.

'We're down here.' Regardless that they probably couldn't hear her, Soraya was yelling at the search party and waving her wrap high above her head in an attempt to catch their attention.

It was such a relief that help had arrived, but there was still that fragment of doubt lingering in her anxious thoughts that they would somehow be missed. Even the regal Raed was flagging them down with both hands high in the air, yelling at them like any other stranded, trauma-tised civilian desperate to be saved.

They waited impatiently until the helicopter found somewhere to land, followed by the arrival of an ambu-lance a few minutes later. A team of paramedics rushed straight to Raed, but he dismissed their concerns and di-rected them towards Soraya and the two men.

'I'm fine,' she insisted as one of the medical crew veered over to see her.

'You should really get checked out at the hospital. We've been running on adrenaline since the crash and who knows what injuries might be hiding?' Raed said as he came to join her.

'I will if you will,' she said, more concerned with the possible injuries Raed could have sustained while he'd been shielding her. It would also give her a chance to get an update on their patients and their future prognosis.

There was little else they could do at this point, but it didn't make it any easier to walk away. They were chivvied into an ambulance and Raed took her hand.

'I know it's tough. It's not in our nature to walk away from our patients, but we will be diverting to the hospital where they're being transferred.'

The farther they left the scene behind, the more Soraya noticed her breath was becoming shallower by the second. She closed her eyes and tried to regulate it, squeezing Raed's hand so tightly it was even hurting her. Whatever it took to get her mind off the accident.

'Next time we'll get the driver to take us somewhere local for dinner.' Raed's lame attempt at humour at least managed to distract her from the vision in her head of the ground rushing up to meet them again long enough to roll her eyes at him.

'I'll settle for a takeaway, thanks.' She almost managed a smile, then she looked into his eyes and saw the same ghost of the horror they'd just experienced haunting him too. Without thinking about anything other than the need to comfort him, and feel his warmth against her, Soraya launched herself at him and swamped Raed in a hug.

She could feel the initial surprise in the tension of his body, then he relaxed, tightened his hold around her and buried his head in her neck. They sat that way for some time, oblivious to the others around them, concerned only with the comfort they were drawing from one another, it seemed.

'You smell of diesel and dirt,' he whispered into her ear to make her laugh even when all she wanted to do was cry.

'You say the sweetest things,' she mumbled back, even though it was exactly the right thing to say in the moment. If he'd apologised for the events that had been out of everyone's control, or said anything remotely nice, it would have made her over-emotional. She was barely holding it together.

'We'll be at the hospital soon.'

She didn't know who'd said it, but it was the reason Raed had moved away from her. He sat back in his seat and before that bereft feeling chilled her again, he pulled her into his chest. She nestled against him with a sigh, in too great a need for his support to concern herself with the consequences of being so close to him. There would be time for self-recrimination later, but for now she needed this, needed Raed.

CHAPTER TEN

RAED AND SORAYA barely made it through the palace doors before their phones were ringing.

'We were so afraid you'd been hurt when they said your helicopter had gone down, Raed.'

'Don't ever do that to me again, sis.'

It seemed their families had joined together upon hearing the news. On speaker phone, his mother and Soraya's sister immediately let them know how worried they'd been about them even though he knew they'd been informed they were safe the second the search party had found them. He understood. There'd been times when he'd thought they mightn't make it too. His first and only thought when it was apparent the helicopter was going down had been to protect Soraya.

Protocol and common sense, when his father wasn't in good health and he was next in line to the throne, should have dictated he got himself to safety at all costs. However, his heart had reacted first, and he would have willingly given his life to save hers.

It was only the luck of his birth that had bestowed this status and wealth upon him, Soraya was a better person than he could ever hope to be. She'd never lied to anyone or shunned her family even when she'd been left in the most difficult circumstances. But above all of that, deep down he knew it was his feelings for her that had made him act so recklessly.

Soraya's welfare had suddenly become more important to him than his other responsibilities and that was remarkable given the task he currently had keeping the country running in his father's absence.

Even now, as they were having their ears assaulted by well-meaning family members, his instinct was to carry her off somewhere private to give her some space to decompress.

They'd both been through a lot tonight and if she was feeling anywhere near what he was experiencing, she needed time out too.

'Did you get checked out at the hospital?' Amir asked, the concern evident in his tone.

'We're fine, brother. Just a few cuts and bruises. Duke and Steve are both in surgery, but it looks as though they're going to be all right. If you don't mind we'll talk you all through it tomorrow.' Their families had been understandably worried and upset but he thought it was too much to deal with their feelings on top of their own. They had a lot to process.

'Raed's right. We're fine, everybody. I really just want to have a shower and go to bed.' Soraya shut down his plans to spend some downtime together but at least she would be getting some rest. He would do the same, if his mind would calm sufficiently to let him sleep.

'Okay. I'll give you some space.' Her sister sounded a little put out but thankfully she agreed to Soraya's wishes.

'It's been a long night. Thanks, everyone.' He hung up and escorted Soraya up to her room.

'I want to thank you for everything you did for me tonight,' she said outside her door.

'What? Nearly get you killed in a helicopter crash?' He was only half joking about that, and it would be a long time before he forgave himself for putting her in that situation. It wasn't going to do anything for her fear of flying.

'It wasn't your fault and I don't want you beating yourself up over it. I was talking about the way you protected me.' She smiled at him, her bottom lip quivering, her eyes shimmering with unshed tears. It was clear she needed some time on her own, but he was reluctant to leave her now.

'I just wanted to make sure you were okay. I still do.' He waited for her to say she wanted him to stay, but when she didn't he knew it was time to leave.

After everything they'd been through tonight, the feelings they'd admitted to in the heat of the moment, there was a lot for them to discuss but she obviously wasn't ready for it. If it meant facing the fact that she had to go home because a relationship between them simply wasn't viable, then neither was he.

'You know where I am if you need someone to talk to later,' he said before walking away. He only took a few steps before he had the urge to turn back again. 'You were amazing tonight with Duke and Steve. I hope you know that.'

'Just doing my job,' she said with a smile, but they both knew it was so much more than that.

He knew at the hospital she had a good reputation, that was why he'd wanted her to perform his father's operation and give him the best possible chance of surviving. Being out there tonight in such adverse conditions proved what an amazing woman she was, brave and skilful, and always doing her best for those around her.

Soraya was the only person he could turn to, who understood him at the best of times. After everything they'd gone through tonight, something no one else would be able to comprehend, he could use some time to talk things through with her. To work out what they were going to do about this connection they had between them. They couldn't ignore it when they'd spent the aftermath of the tragedy in each other's arms blocking out the rest of the world.

He didn't know what they were going to do about it when they both had their own lives to go back to once this fake engagement was over and his father was back in his rightful place. But ignoring their feelings wasn't going to make life any easier for them and was storing up trouble for the future. Perhaps they needed to call a halt to the whole thing now before they were in so deep they couldn't walk away without sustaining serious injuries, or maybe they could actually try making a go of this relationship they were alleged to be in already.

If Soraya agreed to a fling for the duration of her stay, before her return home, they might be able to walk away at the end of this without regrets. In his experience so far, she wouldn't want to remain in this environment long term, so he knew an actual relationship was heartache waiting to happen. However, if they embarked on some no-strings time together they could let this chemistry fizz itself out, minus the recriminations at the end of it. They could enjoy the initial passion of that attraction finally sparking to life, and get out before there was nothing left but ashes of the people they once used to be. At least they would both know going into it that 'till death do us part' was never going to be an option. It was lies anyway. Everyone always abandoned him, at least this way he had some control over how and when it would happen.

There was no way of knowing if this was something Soraya would contemplate since she wasn't ready to talk to him. Until then he'd just have to drive himself crazy thinking about her.

The night had started out with such promise and hope, and almost ended in tragedy. He didn't want the same to happen to him and Soraya. Raed hoped she would seek him out at some point. As much for his sake as her own.

Soraya turned on the shower and stepped under the spray, letting the hot water soothe her weary body. The next best thing to having Raed's arms around her.

She'd needed him to hold her tonight, getting used to having him there for her in a crisis. It wasn't something she'd had in her life before, always the one her parents, her sister, and even Frank had turned to when they'd needed support. Usually she ploughed on through life carrying her burdens alone, dealing with them behind the scenes so as not to upset anyone. It was different with Raed. In him she had a confidant she could share her troubles with, or simply lean on when she needed to be held.

She thought of the way he'd wrapped her body up in his as the helicopter had gone down, putting his life on the line to protect her. Frank would never have done anything as selfless as that for her. For the duration of their marriage she was the one who'd taken care of bills so he didn't stress about money, and done everything she could to make his life comfortable. He'd never done the same for her.

She wondered if he'd ever truly loved her, or if she'd simply been a soft touch he'd taken advantage of. Using her generous nature to fund whatever, or whoever, he fancied. He'd never contributed financially and she'd excused it as he'd been working for the greater good of the community. Allegedly. When it had come to their marriage she'd been the one to put the effort in, making their house a home, cooking dinners, or arranging date nights. Looking back, she'd put up with it because she'd been so invested in their relationship, trying to force it to work because she'd thought she'd left it too late to ever find anyone else to love her. Ha!

She would have been better off on her own than being married to a liar and a cheat.

Frank would have avoided her at times like this, unable to deal with any display of emotion, waiting for her to 'get over it'. Not Raed, who was encouraging her to talk to him, letting her know it was okay to feel the way she did. She was so used to holding everything back, to bottling up her emotions to protect everyone else, she was afraid to pop the cork and pour them out.

For all the struggles they'd encountered tonight, the worst of all was that moment of believing she'd lost Raed for ever. He'd brought so much into her life she couldn't bear the thought of no longer having him in it. It was then she realised that she loved him. Despite all the pitfalls that would surely arise, she'd failed to prevent it.

She closed her eyes, dipped her head under the stream of water, and cried out all of her fears, her upset, and all the uncertainty the future held. Her tears mixed with the warm water, cleansing her skin and her soul at the same time.

When she was all cried out, and her skin was beginning to prune, she dried herself off and put her pyjamas on for bed.

Even thoughts of Raed, the way he'd wrapped himself around her, put her needs above his own, wouldn't settle her, because she knew she should be with him now. It was fear keeping her from him, that acting on this attraction would somehow make her life worse. But Raed had helped to pick her back up again after Frank's betrayal and given her security where she'd had none. It mightn't last for ever if they did embark on a relationship, but, as tonight had proved, nothing in this life was guaranteed. She owed it to herself to at least see if there was something worth exploring with Raed, even for a short while. It was time to put her needs first for once.

Raed couldn't sleep. Not when he was worried about how Soraya was coping with everything. The emotional shock that occurred after such a traumatic event wasn't something she should be going through on her own.

It was a relief when he heard the knock on his door and he saw her standing outside.

'Soraya? What's wrong?' He knew there had to be something serious enough to bring her to him at this hour and he could tell by the redness around her eyes that she'd been crying.

She bounced up on her tiptoes and wrapped her arms around his neck. Her mouth demanded a response from his and she got it, his whole body coming alive at the touch of her against him again.

'I thought maybe, you know, we could give this thing a shot. At least until...'

'You have to go home,' he continued, dragging her into his room and kicking the door shut behind her.

Now they were both on the same page that this was a temporary arrangement, that it shouldn't interfere with their lives beyond her stay, it felt as though they were making up for lost time. Their mouths and tongues were seeking each other out, desperate to make that same connection they'd had in the car park that day. The passion hadn't lessened in the interim.

Raed had his hands on her backside as they stumbled into his bedroom, and she was letting hers roam through his hair, down his chest, wherever she could touch him. His whole body was on fire for her, burning with a restlessness to have her completely.

He slipped her robe from her shoulders, kissing the silky skin as he uncovered it, enjoying her gasp when he nibbled the skin at the crook of her neck. Slowly, he slid the spaghetti straps of her camisole down her arms, revealing her full breasts to his hungry gaze and mouth. When he dipped his head to claim her nipple with his mouth, Soraya writhed against him, her hands tugging his hair.

'Is this okay? I don't want to do something you'll regret tomorrow. You've had a shock and I know emotions are running high.' As much as he wanted this, he had to be sure this wasn't some knee-jerk reaction to their near-death experience tonight. He wanted her to do this for all the right reasons, to enjoy this as much as he did.

'Don't. Stop,' she said, her breathy voice heavy with desire, telling him everything he needed to know.

He dropped to his knees and cupped her breasts in his hands, kneading, sucking, worshipping her beautiful body.

'Raed,' she pleaded when he nudged her legs apart and drew her silk shorts torturously slowly down her body, delaying the moment of satisfaction for both of them.

When she was fully exposed to him, he buried his face between her soft thighs and parted her with his tongue. He felt her knees buckle, her fingers tighten in his hair, and heard her groan. All the encouragement he needed to delve deeper inside her.

With his hands firmly planted on her backside, he tasted

and teased that most intimate part of her until they were both fit to burst. Her moans of pleasure gradually increased, her breath ragged, as he brought her to the edge of ecstasy, then tipped her right over. She was clutching at his head, her legs shaking, her cry echoing around the room as she climaxed at the tip of his tongue. Only when the ripples of her orgasm finally subsided, the tension leaving her body, did he relent in his pursuit.

He took her hand and led her towards the bed where they lay side by side, staring into one another's eyes. Her cheeks were flushed, her pupils dark, and her lips swollen. She was beautiful.

'When we're in this room, the outside world doesn't exist, okay?' He didn't want anything to spoil this. Here they could pretend this was all they needed. Each other.

'Fine by me.' She smiled, invitation enough for him to kiss her again.

He was glad she'd come to him of her own volition, that he hadn't had to convince her this was a good idea. It meant she was as powerless to control this thing as he was and now they didn't have to, all bets were off. There was no holding back.

With more time to explore one another, the kisses were long and tender, satisfying and loving.

'I could stay here for ever.' His defences down, the words slipped out. Thankfully Soraya didn't laugh, or freeze, the moment over. Instead, apparently in agreement, she reached for him.

'Tonight will have to do.' She leaned in to kiss him, letting her hand stroke his erection through his boxer briefs.

That light touch was enough to steal his breath and only make him want her more. He pulled off his underwear, eager to feel her hands on him. This time she gripped him tightly, taking possession of him that he willingly gave. She moved her hand up and down his shaft, making it easy for him to relax and let her take control of his body when it felt so good.

Except he wanted more of Soraya, he needed all of her.

He rolled over so his body was pressed firmly against hers, took that sweet pink nipple in his mouth again, and she arched her hips up into his. As tempted as he was to take her there and then, pregnancy was a complication they couldn't afford. That wasn't part of a no-strings deal. So he reached into his nightstand for a condom and sheathed himself quickly.

When he did finally drive into Soraya's warmth, joining them together for the first time, he hoped it wouldn't be the last.

Soraya gasped as Raed filled her, but she was ready for him, ready for this. They wouldn't have this time together for long and she didn't want to waste any more of it. Especially when he was making so much effort to please her.

She sucked in a deep breath as he grazed her nipple with his teeth and thrust inside her again. Her whole body was tingling with arousal and wanting, and she couldn't get enough of him.

Sex with Frank had been perfunctory at best, and infrequent near the end of their marriage. Perhaps that had been the cause of his infidelity, not a result. It didn't excuse any of his behaviour but she was beginning to see their marriage completely differently now, since meeting Raed. They'd never had this passion, this chemistry, this animal lust for one another, and she'd thought that was okay. That she simply wasn't a passionate woman, or someone who inspired it in a man. Frank hadn't been her first, but she hadn't been with anyone else particularly memorable either. She'd assumed her late start in the dating pool meant she'd missed out on the fun part of sex, that she'd been too old to enjoy it. That whatever was wrong in her love life was down to her. Now she realised she simply hadn't been with the right person.

It made all the difference wanting someone so bad she couldn't think straight, and knowing he felt the same made her glow from the inside out. Perhaps it was the holding back that made this all the more explosive and exciting. All the secrecy and lies had been stressful, but being with him tonight felt like the ultimate release. Something that might not be sustained long term, but, given that they'd agreed on a fling, hopefully she could enjoy this level of passion for the duration of her stay at least. It was going to be difficult to leave him, to leave this feeling of absolute ecstasy behind, but at least she would have the memories. And the truth that there was nothing wrong with her. It had taken Raed to show that to her.

When he was kissing her the way he was right now, making love to her so tenderly and passionately, she felt like the only person in the world. As though she were the centre of his world. Even though it might not be true, it was the first time she'd ever felt like that. It was intoxicating, and she wanted him to experience it too.

She tightened her inner muscles around him, heard the hitch in his breath as he fought for restraint, and saw the smile on his lips before he resumed control. He plunged inside her again and again, until she forgot she was supposed to be the one driving him crazy. Carried away on that floaty feeling of bliss, she cried out as she reached nirvana, her orgasm catching her by surprise.

Only when she slowly drifted back into her body again did she blink her eyes open, woozy from her out-of-body experience.

'There you are.' Raed was staring down at her, his expression so full of love and desire for her in that moment it made her want to weep. 'I wondered where you'd gone.'

'You know exactly where I went,' she said with a coy smile.

'Well, I'm glad you're back with me now.' He resumed kissing her neck, moving his hips against hers, and joining them together again.

It wasn't long before he took his own trip to that thought-stealing, brain-scrambling place of wonder as he announced his climax with a caveman-like roar. The sound of him losing control brought a smile of satisfaction to her lips. It matched the one he wore when he came to lie down beside her again on the bed.

'Tell me again why we didn't do this sooner?' he asked through panting breaths as he struggled to recover.

'Er…because you were rude and unreachable when we first met,' she reminded him.

'And broken-hearted, if you remember.'

'Hmm.'

'But I'm over that now.' He reached across and gave her a long, leisurely kiss that her body responded to as though it wasn't completely exhausted by his physical attentions already.

'Me too.' Soraya meant it. Even before tonight, she'd come to terms with what had happened between her and Frank. Raed had been the one to help her move on and she was grateful for the time they had together, even if it wasn't going to last for ever.

'Hey. You disappeared again. Only this time it doesn't look as though it was to a happy place.' Raed tilted her chin up so she had to look at him, no doubt the pain she was feeling at the thought of losing him again written across her face.

'I was just thinking about when I have to leave.'

'It's not for a while yet. Let's just enjoy what we have until then.' He cuddled her close, muffled her worries with his warm body, and kept her distracted for the rest of the night.

Yet, when dawn broke and they had to leave the cocoon they'd made in his bed, it was the only thing she could think of.

CHAPTER ELEVEN

'I'D LIKE TO go and visit Steve and Duke at the hospital. Do you think that's possible?' Soraya asked as they ate breakfast in bed.

The news of their 'engagement' last night in the restaurant, along with tales of their 'heroics' at the crash scene, had been all over the news by the time they'd woken so he hadn't seen any point in smuggling her back to her own room to save face in front of palace staff. As far as the country was concerned they were a real couple so it shouldn't come as any shock that they'd spent the night together.

'Sure. I'll put in a call for the car and security detail while you get ready. As gorgeous as you are naked with bedhead and a post-coital glow, I'm sure it's not the image you want captured the moment we set foot outside the palace.'

Now the palace had made the official announcement to coincide with the leaked pictures from the restaurant last night—someone was definitely getting the sack over that one—Raed knew all hell was about to break loose. Public interest would be through the roof to find out all the details about him and his new fiancée. While that had been the plan all along, to divert attention away from the real story of his father's heart problems, he wasn't looking forward to the press scrum as they fought to get more information, or the next juicy titbit about the couple.

Soraya groaned and threw herself back onto the pillows. 'Could they not give us just one day of rest? Last night was a lot.'

It was clear she shared his dismay about the level of interest people would likely have in them from now on. Aside from recovering from the near fatal crash they'd experienced last night, there were a few personal revelations they had to deal with too. The intensity of the situation had forced their hand and made them face up to the feelings they had for one another and now they'd had one night together he didn't think a fling was going to solve any of their problems.

Far from ending a chapter in his life, last night had opened a new one he was afraid he wouldn't get to explore further.

It seemed their compatibility stretched beyond working together, and their emotional bond, into the bedroom. What they'd experienced last night had been more than just sex. He'd had girlfriends in medical school, enjoyed the freedom of being a single man away from home. Then he'd met Zara and settled down into a long-term relationship. He knew the difference between a fling and something more serious because he felt it. The physical release of finally giving in to their desire for one another had satisfied him temporarily, but it had also awakened a stronger need to have Soraya in his life. She was beautiful, smart, compassionate, supportive, and sexy as hell. Everything he could ever want in a partner. Despite only knowing Soraya for a matter of days he felt a stronger connection to her than he'd ever had with Zara. And soon she would have to leave.

They needed time and privacy to discuss their relationship and that wasn't going to happen with the world watching and waiting to hear what was next.

It wasn't as easy as simply sweeping Soraya up into his arms and walking off into the sunset. Finding the woman of his dreams wasn't a guaranteed happy-ever-after and he didn't want to make the same mistake in giving his heart to someone who couldn't be there when he needed them. Soraya had her job in London, and her sister. He knew how the talk would end when the responsibility she felt for Isolde would never let her leave England for him. It wouldn't be fair to even ask her. Raed knew what he had to do. He just didn't have to like it. Nor did he have to do it right now.

'We might not have all day, but we do have this morning,' he said, voice husky as he reached for her.

Soraya gave a squeal of delight as he straddled her naked body, sending the tray of empty breakfast dishes tumbling to the floor. If he did have to let her go, he wanted to make more memories to keep him company at night.

'I'm glad you're finally back with us,' Raed joked with Duke at his hospital bedside.

'All thanks to you two, apparently,' he said with a weak smile.

'It was Soraya who did all the hard work. She was the one who probably saved your life.'

Soraya blushed at Raed's praise, even though she knew she deserved it. Although if she hadn't carried out the needle decompression to release the trapped air in Duke's pleural cavity, she was sure Raed was more than capable of doing it himself.

'How are you feeling now, Duke?' She diverted the attention back to the patient who, though his skin looked a better shade than it had last night, was still pale.

'Still in a bit of pain but I'm managing it with the medication they gave me.' He grimaced, but his discomfort was to be expected, not only because of the procedure, but also the after-effects of his crash injuries.

'Hopefully, after a couple of weeks' rest you'll be as good as new.' Thankfully there hadn't been any complications as a result of the needle decompression, so he should heal quite soon as long as he did as instructed by the medical staff on his release from hospital.

'That's what I've been told. Again, thank you. I also hear congratulations are in order for you two.'

Soraya glanced at Raed, who looked as uncomfortable as she felt as he mumbled, 'Thanks.'

'We should go and let you get some rest. Steve's on the mend too. They managed to save his foot but he's another one who needs to take it easy for a while. We just wanted to check in on you both to see how you were. You're both looking much better than the last time we saw you,' she joked, drawing a grin from Duke.

'That wouldn't have been hard. Apparently I was a very becoming shade of blue.'

'The same colour as Soraya's eyes.' Raed had meant it as a joke but it made her think back to this morning when they'd been lying in his bed staring into one another's eyes, without a care in the world.

An unexpected pebble of emotion seemed to lodge in her throat, bringing tears to her eyes. Soraya knew it was because that subject of where they were going next in their relationship still had to be addressed. They weren't hiding in bed any more and sooner or later they had to address the future. A conversation she knew was going to tear her apart when her loyalties, and heart, would be split between her sister and her lover.

'Anyway, we're glad you're okay and hope to see you on your feet again soon.' She practically stumbled out into the corridor with Raed in pursuit.

'Soraya? What's wrong?' He grabbed her gently by the shoulders and turned her to face him.

It was on the tip of her tongue to tell him she loved him, that she didn't want to go back to England without him. But that wouldn't have been fair on either of them when it hadn't been part of their agreement.

She was prevented from saying anything as they were suddenly accosted by a wave of men carrying phones and cameras rushing towards them.

Raed's face darkened with a frown. 'We need to get out of here,' he said to their new security detail.

Acting as a human shield, Raed once more put his body between hers and danger, bulldozing his way through the throng of press all shouting questions at them as they passed.

'When's the wedding?'

'Are you going to give up your medical career to become a princess, Ms Yarrow?'

'I—I haven't thought about that,' she stuttered. It wasn't something she'd considered, mostly because this was never supposed to have been a real relationship, and certainly not a permanent one.

'You don't have to answer them,' Raed warned, rushing her past as security fended off the few stray reporters in waiting further down the corridor.

'It's a question we should have prepared for. Our future.' It hurt to even think about it, a deep ache inside her chest at the thought of what might or might not come. No matter what happened between them, Soraya knew it was going to cause her pain. Even if they stood some chance of being together it meant giving up the life she had, her work and family, and risking it on another man. After Frank had left her so broken and devastated, she knew all too well the damage Raed could do if he didn't reciprocate the strength of her feelings for him.

Last night had been such an emotional roller coaster with the dinner, engagement, and the crash, but it had ended on a high. Being with Raed had been amazing and not just for the obvious physical reason. Though that would have been enough on its own for her to be distracted today. Raed understood her on a level no one else had ever come close to. Their backgrounds might be vastly different, but they had the same ethics when it came to work and family.

Frank had never grasped the importance of either to her. A spoiled only child, he'd had everything handed to him. One of the differences between him and Raed was that Raed couldn't wait to strike out on his own and support himself. Frank had simply substituted her for his parents to subsidise him. With everything Raed had done for his family, it was obvious he wasn't selfish like her ex-husband. He was willing to sacrifice everything he had in London to save them.

They'd agreed to continue with a short-term fling until Soraya had to leave the country, but she'd be lying if she said that would be enough for her. She was sure they could have something special together given time and wouldn't just walk away without attempting to salvage something of their budding relationship.

After Frank, Soraya hadn't considered the possibility of meeting anyone else, much less trusting her heart again when it had caused her so much pain in the past by loving someone so completely. Perhaps that was why she'd agreed to a short-term fling, in the mistaken belief that it would somehow protect her. The very nature of a fling suggested it was purely physical, no emotions involved. However, deep down she knew she'd been emotionally involved with Raed from the moment he'd broken down in her office.

Now she had to decide if she was going to make the break, or see if Raed was willing to try and make a go of things. One thing was for sure, a fling wasn't going to do her any good. It was showing her what they could have if he didn't have commitments elsewhere. Heartbreak just waiting to happen. She'd believed that a brief romance with Raed was better than nothing, but she knew it would only prolong her pain, make it all the more damaging when she had to say goodbye to him. Yet she couldn't find it in her to break things off now, before they were too involved, too smitten to think about the future and the repercussions of a separation.

Keeping her emotions to herself had been her way of protecting her family. She hadn't wanted her parents, or Isolde, to feel bad about the burden on her young shoulders. So she'd kept her worries and anxieties to herself so as not to worry them, something she'd carried on into adulthood, and her marriage. Even when money had been tight, Frank had been working later every night, and she'd kept her fears to herself so as not to rock the boat. As though her feelings hadn't mattered as long as he'd been happy. It wasn't until the end of their marriage she'd realised he'd never cared about her feelings when he'd run up debt and cheated on her. It had been a one-way relationship. If she wanted the pattern to change, to no longer be walked over as if she were a doormat, she had to make her feelings heard.

Raed's response to that would determine what happened next.

It wasn't until they were safely in the back of the car that Raed spoke again. 'I didn't think we had a future when you're going back to England tomorrow.'

Although he didn't want her to go, that one question from the journalist had jolted him out of his selfish reverie thinking their feelings for one another could solve all of their problems. Soraya had a career and a family at home and it wouldn't be fair to expect her to give them up to be with him. He'd made that mistake with Zara, expecting her to fall into place in his life in Zaki, sacrificing everything in the hope they could make things work.

He'd seen for himself last night just how good Soraya was at her job, how she enjoyed it, and how much she was needed in that medical role. The reason he'd asked her to perform his father's surgery in the first place was because she was the best surgeon for the job. It would be a waste of her skills, not to mention her future prospects, to give it up and trail around the country behind him while he performed his royal role. He didn't want to do it and it was his legacy. She would only grow to resent him the way he had his parents and his life in Zaki.

It wasn't that he didn't want to be with her, quite the contrary, but it was too much to ask of her to be with him. The sort of person Soraya was, she would probably do it too and he couldn't expect that kind of sacrifice on the basis of one amazing night together.

'I was thinking about that. We're good together, Raed, it would be a shame to ignore that fact. I know we agreed to a fling but maybe we could extend things.' That smile and twinkle of hope in her eyes made Raed's heart feel as though it had bottomed out to join his stomach on the floor. In other circumstances he would be over the moon that she was willing to take a risk on him, especially after everything she'd been through with her ex. But it was a fantasy. He knew from experience it wasn't going to work. Despite his attempts to prove otherwise, his fate was to remain in his home country permanently. A life together just wasn't on the cards.

He didn't want to give her excuses, or reasons to think they could still salvage something. It would be better for her to make a clean break now rather than give her false hope that they had a future together.

If he tried to explain his reasoning to call things off, he knew she'd insist she could make her own decisions. The trouble was she wasn't so good at making the best ones for herself. It was time someone did right by her for a change now, even if it didn't seem like it.

'Listen, Soraya, I've been thinking about us...' His stomach plummeted with the task he'd set himself. 'I don't think it's going to work.'

'But—but...last night...'

Raed could see the pain in her eyes and hated himself for putting it there. He could only hope that if he ended things now she would forget about him quicker instead of his prolonging the hurt letting her think they ever stood a chance as a couple.

'It was great, but let's face it, Soraya, we'd just been through a lot. We found comfort in one another at a time when we were both emotionally fragile. It was an intense situation and we gave in to an attraction, but that's not the basis for any relationship, certainly not a long-distance one.'

They both knew their night together had been a lot more than that but admitting it left an opening for hope he couldn't afford. Soraya had spent her whole life putting other people's feelings before her own and now he was doing this for her. He'd tried so hard to avoid his legacy but embracing it now would help so many. At least he'd had a chance at putting himself first for a while, and now it was time to do something selfless. Even if it didn't feel like it in the interim.

'Maybe I could take some time off work and give us a chance to get to know each other a little better at least.'

The wavering in her voice and the glassy sheen in her eyes brought a lump to his throat and Raed had to cough to clear it before he spoke. 'What's the point, Soraya? I'm a prince with responsibilities to my country and my family. You knew this from the start and that's why we agreed to a fling. So things didn't get messy.'

The minute she'd been a listening ear and let him unburden himself of his worries that morning in his office, he'd known somewhere on a subconscious level that things were always going to get messy. Not least when he'd asked her to be his fake fiancée for the cameras. He'd known then he was attracted to her, there was a connection between them, and it was never just going to be a simple ruse. The pretence otherwise hadn't only been for the press. If he'd admitted to himself that there was something between them he would have tried harder to keep his distance and replace her with a stranger he would never have feelings for. But all of that was too late and now he had to pay the price.

'The point is we could have something special together if we only try. I'm not saying it's going to be easy—'

'And if I don't want to try? We scratched that itch, Soraya.' The bluntness of his words was a direct result of Soraya's attempts to salvage a relationship, but she would be the one expected to make all the sacrifices in the process and he wasn't prepared to let her do that.

He watched her swallow hard and blink back the tears threatening to fall, despising himself for every second he was putting her through this. The only way he could get through it was to remind himself she would be better off without him, or his family's problems, holding her back. She deserved the quiet, anonymous life he'd been denied.

'Okay. I misunderstood the situation.' As the car finally came to a standstill outside the palace, Soraya opened the door and got out.

When she had to reach out her hand to steady herself on the door before she walked away, Raed's heart ached even more for her, but he remained stoic. Even when she turned back to face him.

'What about the engagement? The press? Has all this been for nothing?'

It was hard to look her in the eye but he did so in case she was in any doubt that this was over. 'We can just say things didn't work out and you're missing home. That should be enough of a story to cover my father's absence for a while longer. You can keep the ring. Use it as a down payment on your own house. You shouldn't be sleeping in anyone's spare room.'

'You have it all figured out, don't you?' she said with more than a hint of understandable bitterness.

'I appreciate everything you've done for me and my family, Soraya. I never meant to hurt you.' His words fell flat as she walked away, unwilling to listen to his attempt at a too-late apology.

Raed waited until she disappeared inside, then he dropped his head into his hands, weary of all of the pretence. The pain in his chest was a just punishment for the hurt he'd caused one of the most amazing women he'd ever met in his life. Someone he knew he could never replace.

CHAPTER TWELVE

SORAYA WAS STILL reeling from Raed's abrupt dismissal two weeks later. She'd tried to put it out of her head and get on with the life she'd had before he'd crashed into her office that morning, but it was easier said than done. Even if she didn't still have press doorstepping her for an interview, thoughts of Raed and their night together haunted her. She yearned for the few days they'd had getting to know each other more than she'd ever done for her failed marriage.

'Will you stop mooning over that ring? Either sell it or put it away in a drawer where you can't see it.' Isolde snatched the emerald engagement ring from Soraya and shoved it in her pocket.

'It's not like I wear it. I just like to look at it sometimes and be reminded of Raed.' She pouted. It was all she had left of him now and sometimes it was better to recall the good memories than the pain and humiliation she'd felt when he'd ended things between them.

His actions had brought all her fears bubbling back to the surface that she was never going to be enough for the people in her life. From her parents' inadvertent neglect to Frank's cheating, no one had ever put her feelings first. She'd thought Raed was different, that he understood what she'd been through, that he would never hurt her. But he'd done just that in the most brutal fashion possible. Waiting until they'd spent the night together, until she'd trusted him with her heart and body and begun to believe they could have a future. In the end he'd been just like everyone else. Tossing her feelings aside for more important matters.

Okay, so protecting the royal family and running a country weren't trifling matters, but it hurt all the same. More so in this case because she'd been willing to take a chance on Raed after all she'd been through.

'I'll only give it back when you do as he suggested and put a deposit on a house with it. You can't live in my spare room for ever.'

'I'm sorry I ever told you about that...'

Isolde had made it clear that Soraya was suffocating her with her overprotective sister routine, and she suspected she'd outstayed her welcome at the flat. Isolde needed her space, and she was right, it was ridiculous that her big sister was still in residence, but she couldn't bring herself to sell the ring. Despite the circumstances around the engagement, she liked the idea he had been thinking about her when he'd chosen it. That there was some meaning behind the gesture other than a cover story.

'Raed did us both a favour by making sure you had enough gems to set up a new life. No offence, sis, but I enjoyed our time apart. I mean, I've loved having you live here but you can be a little...suffocating.'

Isolde wasn't telling her anything she didn't already know.

'I know, I'm sorry. I told myself I was moving in to save you. In truth, I think it was the other way around. I wanted to be needed.'

'I still need you, but not every minute of every day. I love you, and I appreciate everything you've done for me, but I can look after myself. It's about time you had a life of your own again.' Isolde gave her a soft smile and Soraya knew her words weren't intended to hurt her, even if they were hard to stomach right now. She'd thought she could have a life with Raed but he hadn't wanted her either.

'I suppose I can help out at the centre now it's up and running.'

Raed's cash injection for the charity had likely been his way of salving his conscience, but it only made her think about how his kind-hearted actions were a stark contrast to the cold words he'd spat at her that last day in the car. Almost as though he'd been putting on a front for her, the way he'd done for the press, and his family. Being who anyone needed him to be in that moment.

'Raed wasn't all bad. Even if we're not allowed to talk about him these days…'

'You've changed your tune. If I remember correctly you wanted to chop off certain parts of him at the time and post them back to his home country one by one because he'd broken my heart.' The level of her sister's ire on her behalf had amused Soraya at a time when she'd been too devastated to think of such cold-hearted revenge herself. It appeared she wasn't the only protective one of the two sisters and it had given her a glow knowing she was loved by someone at least.

'Yes, well, the interview in the paper might have given me a different perspective on his behaviour.' Isolde lobbed the morning paper at her opened at a black and white grainy image of Soraya and Raed in the hospital that last fateful day in Zaki.

It was a special kind of pain seeing the image of him wrapped around her like her personal bodyguard, protecting her from the world. Soraya couldn't marry that selfless behaviour with his cruel parting words to her.

The headline—*Heartbroken Prince Puts Duty Before Love*—was accompanied by a posed picture of Raed, as handsome as ever but she thought he looked a little drawn. It was probably wishful thinking imagining he was pining for her the way she was for him.

"'When asked why his engagement had ended so quickly, Prince Raed would only say that his fiancée had a successful medical career in London and he had responsibilities at home. Although he wouldn't be pushed on the matter, it seems this distance proved a defining factor in the break-up, which has obviously left our beloved Crown Prince heartbroken…'" Soraya read aloud. The article went on to talk about his most recent public engagements, his new social initiatives, and praised him for his return home. She supposed playing the role of heartbroken beloved prince was gaining him some sympathy, and had taken the focus off his parents' absence after all.

Yet she couldn't quite believe it was all an act. It was the first time she'd heard mention of her career in the decision for their break-up…

Suddenly everything began to slot into place. He'd become distant right after that journalist had asked if she was going to give up her career for him.

'He got me to leave because he didn't want to make me choose between you and my job or him.'

'Of course he did.' Isolde rolled her eyes as though Soraya was the last person to understand his real motives.

Now she understood why he'd said those horrible things to her. He'd wanted her to despise him so she wouldn't stay in Zaki, knowing she'd be torn between wanting to be with him, and needing to stay for her sister. Not to mention her career. But it hadn't been his decision to make. If she hadn't been so consumed by self-pity, wallowing in the unfairness of sharing her life with the most selfish of people, she might have realised how out of character he'd been that day.

She'd simply believed he'd been following the pattern of everyone else in her life, had believed the worst of him and taken him at his word, when all along he'd committed to the most selfless act. Sacrificing everything, not only to save his family, but ultimately to protect her too. Without her even having to say the words he'd known she'd fallen for him and made the decision to walk away before things became serious between them. Raed hadn't realised it was too late, and her feelings for him had been cemented when he'd shown her that night just how much he cared for her.

'Why would he speak to the press about such personal issues when he works so hard to keep his feelings private?'

'Because he wants you to see it and realise he's missing you as much as you're missing him?' Isolde offered. 'You're very alike, you know, you and Raed.'

'How so?' Soraya had wanted to believe that, but when he'd gone back to take charge of his country she'd had to face the reality that they had nothing at all in common.

'You're both overprotective siblings who put other people's happiness over your own. It seems to me as though you look after family, and everyone else, because you never had anyone to do that for you. For once in your life someone was trying to do the right thing by you, even if he was being an idiot about it.' Isolde's smile said everything about her new understanding behind Raed's motives.

He'd gone the wrong way about everything, obviously, when it was Soraya he should have spoken to. Then she

would have told him to stop trying to be so damn noble.
That it was her happiness he was sacrificing along with
his own.

'Then I guess it's down to me to tell him that.' For
the first time in her life Soraya decided she was going to
do something for herself and not worry about the consequences. It was time she concentrated on her own happiness, and she needed Raed to find it.

Raed's mouth was dry as he faced the bank of microphones
and reporters gathered in the palace press room to greet
him. He could've put out a statement through one of their
public relations officers or done a one-to-one interview,
but in the end he'd decided he should be responsible for answering the difficult questions so many people had about
him and his family. With their consent he was going to
put the record straight once and for all.

He took a sip of water and prepared to unburden his
soul.

'Thank you all for coming today, and for your patience
in waiting until I reacclimatised from the London weather.'

A polite titter emanated around the room. His return to
Zaki had caused a stir, but he hadn't been able to face the
public until now. A broken heart wasn't something easy
to move past, even more so when he'd caused it himself.
So he'd spent the past two weeks mooning around the palace like a lost soul haunting the corridors, not quite wail-
ing over the loss of his love, but beating himself up over
it nonetheless.

He'd thought time and distance, not to mention a whole
new way of life, would have distracted him from his loss,
but here on his own, save for the staff, he'd felt more alone

than ever. The whole idea of getting Soraya to leave had been to lessen the pain of a long drawn-out goodbye later when things inevitably didn't work out. But by ending the relationship before it had even had a chance to flourish he was beginning to think he'd made a big mistake. The idea that his sacrifice would somehow make her life better, so she didn't have to adjust her life to fit around his, had spectacularly backfired, according to his brother. She wasn't happy with him, and Isolde apparently wanted to do unmentionable things to essential parts of his anatomy for hurting her sister. Understandable. He wasn't his own greatest fan at present either for making himself miserable in the process.

Raed cleared his throat. The sooner he did this, the sooner he could get back to the palace, which didn't give him the anonymity he missed, but was vast enough to hide away in.

'Several weeks ago my father, the King, suffered a massive heart attack while visiting family in London.' He ignored the collective gasp in the room and the flash of cameras, to continue. 'With subsequent surgery he is expected to make a full recovery. Until then, and with the consent of my entire family, I'm going to take over many of his public duties here. Are there any questions?'

The sea of hands in the air was expected but still overwhelming. He'd had the relevant media training for subjects he should avoid talking about, but he wanted to be as open and honest as he could be after all the deception and lies. It was exhausting just being here, never mind having to keep up the pretence. Especially when he didn't have Soraya's support, which had got him through some of the toughest days of his life.

'Yes, man at the front.' Raed picked out a familiar face who he knew had liaised with the palace in the past.

'Why was the news about the King's health kept from us?'

If Raed had hoped the journalists were going to go easy on him, the reality was beginning to set in. This reporter spoke for the whole country who wanted answers.

'We didn't want to panic the population. At that stage we didn't know if he was going to survive, and as a family it was more important to us to concentrate on his survival. As you know, both myself and my brother, Amir, have been living in England. With my father so ill we knew one of us would have to return, but neither of us wanted to leave the family at such a time, especially given the fact that we've already suffered great tragedy and loss. I'm sorry if our actions have offended or upset anyone. That wasn't our intention. We're human and it was concern for our father's well-being that was uppermost in our minds at the time.'

'Will you be returning to London once the King has recovered?' A slightly easier question from the woman in the knitted blue twinset he picked next.

'No. I'm staying here to take up my rightful place as next in line to the throne.' A ripple of murmurs in the crowd was accompanied by a stronger show of hands.

'Yes. The hand at the back of the room.' He couldn't quite see the journalist in question but the hand was bobbing up and down enthusiastically in the crowd.

'What about the rumours of your engagement?'

The question stirred more excitement in the room, including his. He wasn't sure if he was imagining the voice asking it.

'Unfortunately, that didn't work out.'

'Oh, really? Well, I have the ring to prove otherwise.' The hand waggled the large emerald ring he'd so carefully chosen with Soraya in mind, even though it was never supposed to have been anything more than a prop.

'Soraya?' He stood up to try and see better. The crowd, bemused by the interaction, began to part, leaving a straight path towards the woman he'd convinced himself he'd never see again.

'I left without saying goodbye.' She was smiling as she walked towards him, so that was a good thing.

'Well, long-distance relationships never work anyway.'

'Not if you don't even try.'

'I was trying to protect you.' He slid his arms around her waist, needing that physical connection to reassure him he hadn't conjured her up out of his mind in the midst of his crisis.

'I didn't ask you to.' She grinned at him.

Raed wanted so desperately to kiss her, to beg her for another chance, but he was aware they were surrounded by the press and he had something of his reputation left to hold onto.

'Then maybe we need to talk in private.'

The groan from the now invested assembled press reverberated around the room, making Raed laugh for the first time since Soraya had left him. Perhaps he'd be forgiven for his past mistakes if they got a new royal romance to focus on, but he wasn't going to take anything for granted this time.

'Thank you everyone for your questions and your understanding but I need to talk to my fiancée in private.'

He ushered Soraya to his private rooms, leaving his security team to disperse the reporters, hopeful that they had everything they needed for now.

'I hope that wasn't too presumptuous of me. To describe you as my fiancée, I mean.'

'It depends how things go, doesn't it? I don't even know if you want me to stay. I did turn up uninvited.'

'Of course I want you to stay. How did you get in anyway? Do I need to have a word with security?' He was only half joking. As much as he wanted Soraya here, he didn't want her safety jeopardised by lax security. Only pre-approved visitors should be admitted to the grounds, especially with a member of the royal family in residence.

'Your parents pulled a few strings for me. I told them I wanted to surprise you and I did save your father's life after all…'

'You've been talking about me?' He was surprised, but it also showed the bond she'd forged with his family that they felt comfortable enough, not only to discuss their relationship, but to give her security clearance without his knowledge. They must have been pretty confident he needed her with him to have agreed.

'Yeah, about how sad and lonely you are without me,' she said nonchalantly.

'They're not wrong.' Despite all the privileges and luxury available to him out here, none of it had made him happy. Only seeing Soraya again had done that.

'If it's any consolation, I was exactly the same.' She rested her forehead against his.

'I'm sorry. I thought it was for the best.'

'Again, something you should have consulted me on before coming to your own conclusion.'

'I thought by making that decision for you, it was saving you from having to decide between your life in England with Isolde, or one here with me. I know what it's like to be in that position and I didn't want to put you in it.

I didn't want to be responsible for taking you away from your own family.'

'Again, my decision, and, as Isolde has reminded me, she's a grown-up. I don't have to put my life on hold to look after her any more.'

Raed raised an eyebrow at that, disbelieving that either of them would ever stop worrying about their siblings.

'I know, I know, but I'm trying. The thought of losing you made me realise I want a life of my own too. Preferably one with you in it.'

Hearing that made his heart sing, though he was careful not to get too carried away again. 'But our circumstances haven't changed. My life is going to be here from now on, yours is in London. The logistics of a relationship are going to be tricky. Especially when I don't know what kind of schedule I'll have yet. In taking over Father's role in the interim I'll have public engagements and trips abroad to contend with. We might never get to see each other.'

'I'm taking indefinite leave from work. I'm dedicated to giving us a chance if you are. If we get sick of each other in a couple of weeks, I'll go home and back to work and put it down to an extended holiday. However, if we are as great together as I imagine, then I'm willing to move out here to be with you, Raed.'

She couldn't have stunned him more if she'd hit him over the head with a ten-pound mallet. It had never occurred to him that she would be willing to give everything up to be with him, because no one else in his life ever had.

'There's nothing that I would want more, Soraya, but it's a different lifestyle. I'm a prince, there are expectations, and the likelihood is I won't be able to return to my career as a surgeon. If we were serious, the same would apply to you. I couldn't ask you to give up your work for me.'

'You aren't, but you mean more to me than any job, Raed. I know the implications of getting involved with you—we've been there before, remember? But I'm willing to give us a shot if you are. If and when I move out here permanently, perhaps we can still do some consulting work or fund the next generation of surgeons. I'll do whatever it takes to make this work. Just give us a chance, Raed.' She was watching him with her big blue eyes, waiting for his answer. As though it had ever been in question.

If he'd ever been in doubt about his feelings for Soraya, the moment he'd seen her in that press room he'd known he was in love with her. Judging by the lengths she'd gone to, the risks she was willing to take for him, she felt the same. Finally someone loved him for everything he was, and he didn't want to let that slip through his fingers again.

'In that case, Soraya Yarrow, would you do me the honour of going on a real date with me? I figure we can't have a real engagement until we've had a real relationship.' And a real proposal. One that wouldn't be tainted by lies and pretence.

'I'd love to go on a date with you, Raed. I love you. Or is that too pushy for a first date? I wouldn't want to put you off.' She was joking to cover the nerves she undoubtedly had over saying those words because he had them too.

'Not at all. I love you too, Soraya.' He kissed her, long and hard, trying to express just how much.

Her hands crept around his waist to hold him close as she kissed him back and Raed had never felt more like a prince in a fairy tale.

EPILOGUE

'WHO KNEW A life of luxury could be so exhausting?' Soraya laid her head on Raed's chest as they finally relaxed on the back seat of the limo.

He stifled a yawn. 'I did warn you.'

'Yes, you did.' From the time she'd first made her surprise appearance at his press conference he'd been asking her if she knew what she was getting herself into. The truth was that she hadn't realised how intense their life here would be, thrown into the spotlight because of his return as the Crown Prince, and their unconventional romance. However, his position had given them some fantastic opportunities to make a difference to the people here.

It had been only a couple of months since she'd decided to move over permanently to be with him and she didn't regret a moment of it. Yes, she missed her sister, but they spoke every night on the phone and she hoped Isolde would come over for a visit at some point. In Soraya's absence she was helping with the community centre project and relishing every moment of it. Soraya was so proud of her little sister, who had matured so much recently. Or maybe it had happened a long time ago and Soraya had been too busy trying to protect her from the world that she hadn't realised. Whatever the reason, they both seemed happier than ever.

'No regrets?' he asked, cuddling her closer.

'Definitely not.' In Raed's arms, his warmth enveloping her, there was nowhere else she'd rather be. 'I mean, living in a palace is a terrible hardship.'

His chest rose and fell as he laughed. 'We all had to make sacrifices. Seriously though, is this life going to be enough for you?'

He looked at her with such worried eyes that she knew the real question he was asking was if *he* could be enough for her. When all the while she was wondering the same about herself. She wasn't a princess, or from family of any note, but she loved him with all her heart. Whether he was living in a palace or a tiny flat, she knew without all doubt she wanted to be with him.

Raed was the most kind-hearted, loyal man she'd ever met and she considered herself a lucky woman that he'd ever asked her to be his fake fiancée. Even if the circumstances had been less than ideal at the time, it had given them the opportunity to spend time together getting to know one another and help each other move past the relationships that had caused them so much pain. Raed was everything she needed.

She sat up to face him so he could see for himself just how much she loved him and wanted to be with him. 'I know we've had to leave our medical careers behind in England for now, but we've already accomplished so much out here.'

His mother and father were back in the country now too, his father recovering well, but Raed was still undertaking the majority of royal duties for now. He'd become a popular figure with his new initiatives. Not only were they working on a centre for young carers here too, but he was also still in talks for a charity horse show to raise more tourism revenue. Even now they were just returning from a new food bank set up to help families struggling with the cost of living. Soraya was keen to set up a women's health centre too, where she hoped she could resume some medical duties when needed. They were still managing to help lots of people even if they were no longer working in a hospital environment.

'And if I didn't have the resources to make all of these things happen?'

She understood why he was so cautious, not knowing for sure whether his family status had influenced her decision to be with him because of his experience with his ex.

Soraya took his head in her hands. 'I love you, Raed. I don't care if you're a prince, or a surgeon, or a paper boy. I want to be with you.'

He nodded. 'So you'll marry me, then?'

The question shocked her. They hadn't talked about marriage again since she'd moved over, and she'd thought it was something he would only consider further down the line when their future out here was more secure.

'I mean, I considered the full romance package for the proposal, roses, champagne, down on one knee…but we did all that and it didn't work out so well first time around.'

'Yes.' The answer slipped easily from her lips. 'I'll marry you, Raed. Right now if we could. I love you.'

'I love you too, Princess.'

He smiled and it was better than anything money could buy. He was right. They didn't need all the bells and whistles to prove their love for one another, they just needed each other.

Money and status didn't mean anything as long as they had love.

* * * * *

A MOTHER FOR HIS LITTLE PRINCESS

KARIN BAINE

MILLS & BOON

For Charlotte, who helped me achieve so much. xx

CHAPTER ONE

'I THOUGHT I was the princess in the family,' Isolde Yarrow teased her sister over their video call.

She'd taken the opportunity between her physiotherapy patients to phone Soraya and see how the wedding preparations were going. In just a few weeks Soraya was going to be marrying Raed Ayad, Crown Prince of Zaki, an island in the Persian Gulf, to become royalty herself.

It was a long way from the life they'd had growing up when Soraya had worked hard to put food on the table for them both after their parents died, and Isolde was thrilled that her big sis finally had someone to look out for her for a change. Though it didn't mean she wasn't missing her now that she'd moved halfway across the world to take up her new role in the royal family.

'You will always be my little princess, Isolde, though I'm not sure it's a role I'll ever get used to.' Soraya sighed but Isolde could hear the happiness in her voice.

'I'm sure you'll get used to a life of luxury and people waiting on you hand and foot,' she joked, though her sister deserved every second of it after the sacrifices she'd made for her over the years.

'I admit, there are plenty of perks, but we're certainly not letting the grass grow under our feet. We mightn't be able to work in the health service any more, but we're still trying to make a difference. I can't wait until you come over and see all of the charity projects we're working on.'

It was a complete change of lifestyle for her sister, moving abroad to marry a prince, and leaving her career as a cardiac surgeon behind, but Isolde knew she wouldn't have done it unless she loved Raed very much. Something that was entirely reciprocated. Isolde had seen for herself how quickly they'd fallen in love, even though it was supposed to have been a fake romance to divert attention away from the King's ill health at the time.

Raed was a vast improvement on Soraya's ex-husband, Frank, who had taken advantage of her kind nature, cheating on her and running up huge debt, which had led to her sleeping in Isolde's spare room for months after the divorce. Isolde too had been going through a break-up at the time, which had left her sceptical about the whole idea of romance. But Soraya and Raed were now making her question that vow she'd made not to get involved with another man again, given how happy they were together. Though she doubted she'd dip her toes into the commitment pool ever again.

When Isolde was just ten years old, Soraya eighteen, their father had died of lung cancer. Followed less than a year later by their mother. Years of heavy smoking and working in smoky clubs had taken its toll and left Soraya to take care of everything and everyone. Seeing the burden of responsibility left upon her sibling's shoulders, Isolde had decided life was for living. She wasn't going to get tied down with no life to call her own. Instead she'd drifted from one job to another, sofa-surfed, and made sure never to get bogged down in a serious relationship. Then Olly had come into her life and she'd lost all sense when it came to her heart, and the very definition of who she was.

She'd fallen hard for the earnest schoolteacher. He'd convinced her to get some qualifications so she had a better career path than waitressing and bartending, and she'd trained as a physiotherapist and got a full time position at the London Central Hospital, where she'd been working for the last three years. The same hospital Soraya had transferred to when her marriage had fallen apart and she'd wanted a new start.

Isolde's life with Olly had been comfortable, but he'd had to go and spoil it all by talking about the future. Marriage hadn't seemed like a huge step forward when they'd already been living together for so long, but the family bombshell had proved too much for their relationship. Too much of an ask for Isolde.

He'd wanted children, expected her to put her new career on hold to have babies. It had seemed to her in that moment that she was the one being expected to make all the compromises in the relationship, and having a family she didn't want wasn't going to be good for anyone. Not least the innocent lives Olly wanted to bring into the world. She'd seen the toll it had taken on Soraya raising a family she hadn't been fully prepared for and didn't want that life for herself.

In the end neither she nor Olly had wanted to back down, and, with very different ideas of how their future should be, they'd parted ways. Isolde hadn't had the heart to even date since, but she was pleased that Soraya had seemingly found her happy ever after with a handsome prince. Although if she was allowed to have a selfish moan about the situation it would be that she'd been left on her own since her housemate had moved out. She should be enjoying having her own space again, but this was the first time in her life she didn't have her sister around to support her. It was going to take some getting used to.

'I'm counting the days, sis.' Literally. Isolde had been crossing off the days until the wedding on her calendar until she could see her sister again.

'Amir and Farah will be coming too. Oh, it seems so long since we saw everyone. I'm as excited about your visit as the wedding.' Soraya laughed, and Isolde's heart ached a little more. She longed to be with her having fun and putting the world to rights over cocktails and dinner, but she couldn't tell her and put a dampener on her mood. It was about time Soraya had some happiness for herself and Isolde wouldn't do anything to spoil that for her.

'I'm just about to catch up with him. I've got an appointment with one of his patients.' Amir, Raed's younger brother, was a thoracic surgeon in the hospital so their paths crossed often. More so this last year since she'd started treating his daughter, nine-year-old Farah, who'd suffered a spinal injury in the car crash that had also taken her mother away from her.

Now Amir and Isolde's siblings were getting married, and they had no other family here in England with them, they'd been seeing a lot of one another. In a strictly professional capacity only, of course.

'Say hello from us, and we'll see you all soon.' Soraya blew a kiss and waved goodbye.

'Love you, sis.' Isolde swallowed down the lump in her throat before she made a fool of herself in the middle of the rehab unit, or, worse, upset any of her patients by bursting into tears. Instead she plastered on a smile and gave a thumbs up pretending she didn't feel completely lost without her big sister who had always been there, protecting her, and supporting her financially and emotionally over the years. It was time she grew up and stood on her own two feet and there was nothing to be gained from upsetting Soraya when she was enjoying her new life.

Isolde took a deep breath and tried to compose herself, only for the feel of someone's hand on her back to make her jump.

'What the hell—?' She turned around sharply to see who had invaded her personal space and found tall, dark and handsome Amir standing there with his hands in the air as though waiting for the firing squad to take aim.

'Sorry. I didn't mean to startle you. I've been calling out to you the whole way since I saw you walk through Reception, but I think you were on the phone.'

'Yeah, I was talking to Soraya, sorry. She said to say hi, by the way.' Isolde offered him a smile, and though Amir smiled back, she recognised the pain behind it. 'Have you spoken to Raed?'

Amir shook his head. 'Not recently. I know he's busy with the wedding.'

Not so long ago Raed had rebelled against the idea of returning to Zaki to take up his rightful position as heir to the throne. He'd been ready to step aside in favour of

Amir taking over but circumstances had changed everything. The car accident and their father's heart problems some months later had meant Raed had to be the face of the monarchy so the country didn't fall apart in the King's absence. Taken ill while visiting in London, their father had had to have his heart bypass and post-op rehab there before he was fit enough to return home. Soraya had been Raed's fake fiancée, giving the media a cover story to detract from what was really going on with the family. Except they'd fallen for each other and started a new life in Zaki in their royal roles.

It seemed Raed and Soraya had moved on quickly from the lives they'd had back in England for better things, but it wasn't so easy for those of them left behind who didn't have royal roles and a luxurious lifestyle to fill the void of missing family members. Amir's parents had returned home once his father had recovered from his heart bypass, so he no longer had anyone supporting him here in the midst of his grief and Farah's struggle to walk again.

Her incomplete spinal injury had caused some paralysis through her body and, though she had recovered movement in her upper body and no longer had breathing difficulties, she couldn't walk. She'd had surgery to reduce muscle inflammation and swelling, and muscle control came and went in her lower limbs, but her mobility remained limited.

It had been over a year now since Amir had lost his wife and Farah's mother. Isolde knew something about that kind of loss. Except she'd had Soraya to pick up the pieces and put her back together again. Amir's family were at a distance, no longer part of his daily existence and she knew how difficult that was when she'd relied on Soraya her entire life. It was like another bereavement of sorts, mourning that tangible support and having to move on without it.

'Soraya said they've been setting up all sorts of charity initiatives too. No doubt we'll find out all about it when we're over for the wedding. I'm sure Farah is excited about being a bridesmaid.' Isolde was trying to put a positive spin on it all, regardless of feeling as heartbroken as Amir looked.

'She's more worried than anything. It's going to put a spotlight on her, and with being in the wheelchair…she's not looking forward to all of the attention. I know Raed and Soraya have fostered a good relationship with the media because of the charity work and public engagements they're carrying out, but I'm not sure I want to be part of that with Farah the way she is.' It was apparent in the set of Amir's jaw and the frown furrowing his forehead that it was weighing heavily on his mind too. No doubt he was caught between doing what was right for his daughter and his family.

'I understand your concerns. She'll have all of us to look after her though, and if she wants we can put some extra time in together on her exercises, or go dress shopping, or bling out her wheelchair. Whatever would make her more comfortable on the day.' Isolde was sure that in all of the excitement Soraya and Raed had overlooked the fact his niece might be wary of her very public appearance when she was still struggling to come to terms with her life-changing injuries. She would talk to Soraya later and convey any concerns Amir and Farah had about the event and her place in the wedding party. At least she'd managed to make him smile with the idea of pimping out Farah's ride for the big day.

'She'd probably like that.'

It was nice to see Amir relax a little. He was always so tense, concerned with everyone else's welfare. If it wasn't his daughter he was fretting over, it was his patients. Although he'd been through a lot in recent times, Isolde wondered if he ever let loose once in a while.

'I'm going to work on some strengthening exercises with your pneumonia patient now, but I'll call in on Farah later if you're about?'

'Mr Douglas? I'm heading that way myself. I just wanted to check on his chest drain, if you don't mind me crashing in on your physio session?'

'Not at all. It'll be good to have you on hand in case he needs any extra pain relief.'

'Why, are you planning on torturing him today?' Amir asked with a twinkle of mischief glinting in his chocolate-brown eyes.

'No, I did that yesterday,' Isolde answered with just as much sass. 'However, I will be pushing him to get as mobile as possible to fast-track his recovery so we need to make sure his analgesia is adequate to compensate for the effort.'

In low-risk patients who hadn't encountered any complications it was necessary to mobilise them after thoracic surgery, not only to strengthen the limbs, but to prevent any circulatory problems from occurring. Mr Douglas, who'd been admitted for surgery after pneumonia had caused a build-up of fluid on the lungs and breathing dif-

ficulties, should only need three or four days of physiotherapy before he was able to return home. If he followed
Isolde's instruction.

'I will be on hand if he needs anything extra and I'll
check his heart rate and blood pressure before he under-
takes any exercise.'

Isolde knew with post-operative patients it was necessary to keep an eye on them at all stages of their sessions when complications could arise at any second and
she was glad Amir took such a keen interest in his patients' welfare.

Just before they approached the man's bedside Amir
touched her arm and said, 'I know how important physiotherapy is to my patients' recovery. Thank you for everything you do.'

And just like that, he walked away, leaving Isolde
speechless. There were few surgeons who took time to
acknowledge her part in the team that worked with the
patients long after the surgery was over. She counted herself lucky to work with someone so generous, as well as
skilled. All of his patients only ever had good things to
say about him, checking in with them as he did until they
were discharged from the hospital. It was just a shame
such a good man had had truly awful things happen to
him in his personal life.

'Mr Douglas, how are we today?' Amir asked, checking the chart hanging on the end of the bed.

'Good, Doctor. A little sore.'

'That's to be expected but I can increase the pain relief if you're too uncomfortable. Ms Yarrow is here for
your physiotherapy session but I thought I'd check in on

you too.' Amir stood aside to let Isolde do her job and she appreciated that he deferred to her so easily. Ego was not a problem around him, even though as a successful surgeon, and a prince, he would have every right to act superior.

'Hello, Mr Douglas. We're just going to move you into the chair to do a few exercises to start off with today. If you're in any pain at all let us know. Mr Ayad, could you help me move Mr Douglas off the bed?' Although she was capable of transferring patients herself, it would be churlish not to take advantage of an extra pair of hands where she could. Like Amir, she wasn't too proud to ask for help, or appreciate it when it was given.

'Of course.' He came around to the side of the bed and helped to position the patient so his feet were hanging over the edge.

Thoracic surgery was known to be painful and in this instance Amir would have had to go through the chest to evacuate the infection, leaving chest tubes in place to drain the fluid collected around the lungs. She had to be careful when assisting Mr Douglas out of bed to support the incision and drain sites with firm but gentle pressure, avoiding direct pressure on the areas. With one hand on the front of his chest, the other at the back, and her forearms stabilising the entire chest as much as possible, she worked with Amir to move him over onto the chair.

'Okay?' she asked the patient, while nodding her thanks to Amir for his assistance.

'Yes,' Mr Douglas confirmed, a little breathless, like herself.

'We're just going to take five minutes to do a few exercises to minimise any circulatory problems and prevent any restrictions in your chest. With your hands behind your neck I want you to move your head back, slowly extending your spine and using the back of the chair for support.' She sat on the edge of the bed and demonstrated the movement.

Mr Douglas slowly copied the action without too much trouble.

'Good. I need you to do that five times.'

She watched him carefully as he repeated the motion.

'That's it. Now if you can fold your arms across your chest and turn slowly as if you're looking one way, then another, that would be great. We'll repeat that five times too. And then if you can put your hands behind your neck again for me, we're going to bend the trunk carefully from side to side.' She watched as the man followed her instructions wincing every now and then but generally without complaint.

Amir sat quietly to one side observing as she followed with a few leg and arm exercises and she knew if there was any discomfort he would've jumped in to offer his assistance. Although it was a tad intimidating to have the surgeon watching her work, it was also reassuring that he had an interest in her work and was there should she need him. Thankfully, other than helping get Mr Douglas get back into bed again, she didn't.

'You get some sleep now. I think you deserve it,' Amir counselled as they prepared to leave.

'I'll be back again tomorrow and we'll see about getting you on your feet for a little walk about.' Isolde knew this was only the beginning of his recovery and wanted him to be prepared.

'No rest for the wicked,' Mr Douglas joshed as he laid his head back on the pillow. He was snoring before Isolde and Amir had even left the ward.

'How on earth do you manage moving these patients on your own?' Amir queried as they walked out into the corridor.

'With these.' Isolde flexed her biceps, drawing a rarely heard laugh from the surgeon. 'And a lot of patience.'

'It's a more physically demanding job than I realised.'

'Sometimes. It just depends on the patient and the circumstances. I have a good mix. I'm off now to work with a young amputee who is very feisty and independent. I'll probably have my work cut out trying to get him to let me help with anything.'

'You work very hard. I'm finished for the day but why don't you come by the house later? Maybe we can get some takeaway. I know Farah would enjoy the company. I think evenings with her dad in front of the television have lost the novelty appeal and she doesn't have many friends who want to come over much any more. I think they're having trouble adjusting to her new circumstances too.'

'That's awful. I'd love to come over and see her, but don't you think that's blurring the lines a little bit? I mean, we're colleagues, Farah's my patient...' Isolde knew there was nothing more in the invitation than providing his daughter with some female company to lift her spirits, with some dinner thrown in, but she didn't want either of them to get into trouble at work.

Amir screwed up his nose. 'We're going to be family

soon anyway. I think lines have been blurred for a long time. Officially you probably won't be treating Farah much longer, and I won't tell anyone if you won't. But, if you'd rather not I understand.'

'It's fine. We'll work something out. I'm not one for rules anyway. I'll see you at eight. Text me your address,' she shouted behind her as she made her way onto the ward.

He was right, theirs was a complicated situation now because of their siblings' relationship, but Isolde didn't see the harm in spending time with Amir and Farah on a personal level. They were going to be family soon enough and neither she nor Amir were likely to confuse a take-away at his house for anything romantic.

Amir believed Isolde when she said they would work something out. They had to. Farah was his world and he would give anything to make her happy again. It was his fault she'd lost her mother, and that she was confined to a wheelchair, so the least he could do was find a way to make her comfortable.

He was happy that his brother and Soraya had found love and were getting married, though it hadn't worked out so well for him. After spending a lifetime growing up in his brother's shadow, trying to prove that he was worthy of his position in the family to his parents too, Amir had done his best to be the perfect son. He'd studied hard, carved out a successful career, and when Raed had decided he no longer wanted to be next in line to the throne, he'd been ready to step up, willing to take on that responsibility.

Even his marriage had been a way to show his parents he was more than just the second son, the back-up plan for the real Crown Prince. He'd married the right woman from the right family, making them a true Zaki power couple. Shula's parents, wealthy aristocrats who had strong government connections, had encouraged the match, as had Amir's family. And, once Farah had come along, they had seemed like the perfect little family.

Except nothing he'd ever done had seemed to be good enough for his wife. It was only now that she was gone he could admit love had never been a strong factor in their marriage. A good match on paper keeping their respective families happy, perhaps, but in the end it hadn't been sufficient to sustain a long-lasting relationship. Until eventually Shula had told him she didn't love him and wanted a divorce so she was free to pursue other men in the hope of finding what Amir apparently couldn't give her. They'd rowed because he hadn't been able to face giving up on his marriage and admitting defeat to the world at not being able to make his wife happy. He'd wanted counselling, another chance to prove himself, but Shula hadn't and had left home in a frustrated rage.

That was the night she'd had the car accident and he'd been holding onto the guilt ever since. No one knew their marriage had been all but over. Everyone saw him as the grieving husband who'd lost the love of his life. Yes, it was still a great loss, but she'd hurt him, made it clear he'd lost her already that night. He was too embarrassed, too proud, too protective of his daughter to make that information public knowledge. So he'd kept the secret to himself, swallowed down the primal urge to scream every time someone offered their sympathy and added it to the burden of guilt he carried knowing he'd failed as a husband and father. If it took the rest of his life he would try his best to make it up to Farah.

If she wasn't comfortable being part of the royal wedding, it was up to him to find a way to help her, or remove her from the equation altogether if she didn't want to be involved. He didn't blame her. In today's society any difference in abilities was often picked apart in the press and social media and he wouldn't subject his daughter to that if he could help it. Especially when she was already experiencing some alienation from her young friends. It was only natural, he supposed, that with all of her appointments and time spent at the hospital she would get left behind, not being involved in the usual social activities of nine-year-old girls. However, he did hope that some day she would catch up and be that happy, fun-loving little girl he knew and loved again.

The doorbell sounded throughout the house and Amir's stomach did a half-flip. It was silly really. He knew it was Isolde and she was only here because he'd invited her, but she would be the only woman who'd set foot in the house since his wife died. The only reason he'd felt comfortable enough asking her over, apart from Farah needing her help, was the knowledge she wasn't likely to misinterpret this get-together as anything romantic. They were practically family and she was a part of their lives because of her close bond working with Farah. Today he'd seen first-hand how hard she worked and knew, now that her sister had moved away, she'd be returning to an empty house. He'd only thought to offer company to her, as well as himself.

So why was his pulse racing and a cold sweat breaking out on his top lip as though he were on a first date?

'Papa, aren't you going to open the door?' Farah appeared at his side looking up at him with a mixture of confusion and irritation. He knew she'd been looking forward to this since he'd told her they'd be having Isolde's company tonight.

Amir blinked, realising he'd been staring at the door as though he were about to walk into the lion's den, and finally moved to open it.

'Grab these quick before I drop them,' Isolde commanded, her blonde head bobbing up from behind a small stack of pizza boxes as she thrust them forward.

Amir's quick reflexes kicked into action and he managed to take hold of her burden before they toppled to the floor.

'Thanks,' she said, stumbling through the door carrying takeout bags in both hands. 'I didn't know what you liked so I got a selection. There's pizza, chicken wings and fries.'

'I thought we were just going to order in. I didn't expect you to bring dinner with you.' He'd planned on treating her, having something special delivered to the door, since she was a guest. This display of generosity was unexpected.

Isolde closed the door and paused in the hallway. 'No offence, Amir, but I imagined your idea of fast food was some raw sushi couriered over from a top-class restaurant. I'm more a greasy pepperoni kind of girl. Now, where's the kitchen?'

'Through here.' Farah's face lit up the minute she saw her friend and she quickly spun her wheelchair around so Isolde could follow her.

'I hope you like pizza, Farah. I got barbecue chicken, pepperoni and a tomato and cheese just in case.' Isolde shook off her coat one arm at a time as she walked through the house and casually hung it on the back of a chair in the kitchen, making herself at home.

'I've never tried it.' Farah's eyes were as wide as the pizza boxes that he slid onto the kitchen worktop as if she were about to discover some long-lost treasure.

Isolde fixed him with her piercing blue eyes and pursed her lips. 'Amir Ayad, how have you denied your daughter the greatest-tasting junk food for all this time?'

What could he do but smile and shrug as she unboxed the doughy delights?

As Isolde set to work plating the rest of their meal while he poured out the fizzy drinks she'd brought it occurred to him that she fitted so easily into their life she'd really been a blessing. Especially since his parents had returned home after Soraya and Raed, leaving him and Farah on their own in England. Although his father had recovered well, he was taking more of a back seat these days when it came to public engagements, with Raed and Soraya picking up the slack. He couldn't help but feel left out. Especially when he was the one who had been preparing to take over when the time came. Although he didn't need the extra pressure or stress at the minute, it seemed like another area that he'd failed in by not being able to fulfil his royal duties.

Isolde took a bite out of her pepperoni slice and smiled at him, seemingly unfazed by the barbecue sauce smeared around her mouth. There were no airs and graces with her, and Amir didn't feel as though he had to be on his best behaviour when he was around her. It was probably the most comfortable he'd ever been with another person other than Farah.

It was then Amir knew he'd made a big mistake inviting her into their home.

CHAPTER TWO

ISOLDE HOPED SHE hadn't overstepped the mark but she'd wanted to keep this a casual affair. If she was going to any other friend's house for a takeaway, picking up a pizza on the way wouldn't have been a big deal. She could never have known pizza wasn't on a list of permitted foods for Amir's little princess. Although, to be fair to him, he hadn't made it an issue. He'd even tucked in too.

Sitting at his breakfast bar tucking into pizza from takeaway boxes was a long way from the fancy afternoon tea they'd shared months ago with his mother, Raed and Soraya at a five-star hotel to discuss how they would publicly deal with the King's health. It was where they'd first introduced the idea of Soraya pretending to be Raed's fake fiancée to detract attention away from his family's extended stay in England. Thank goodness everything had worked out for them in the end and Raed hadn't taken Isolde up on her offer of playing the role of his future wife!

It had seemed like something exciting and fun to take on at first. The sort of madcap scheme the old Isolde would've been involved in before she'd been tamed. Although she hadn't really known Raed at the time, she'd worked with Amir, had been having physiotherapy sessions with Farah. She knew the family had been through a lot and had wanted to help when she and Soraya had been privy to their conversation over afternoon tea about the damage it could do to their country if the King's ill health was to become common knowledge. They'd needed a distraction, at least one member of the family to return home, and that had ended up being Raed.

It certainly wouldn't have helped Amir to have been under any pressure to go home when he still had Farah to worry about. She was glad Soraya had agreed to accompany Raed and everything had worked out in the end. In hindsight, she wouldn't have wanted the commitment of being in another relationship, even a fake one, never mind the responsibility to a whole nation that her sister had taken on.

'I don't think I could eat another bite,' Amir said eventually, breaking the comfortable silence that had descended as they enjoyed their meal.

'I'm done too,' Farah announced, setting down her half-eaten slice of pizza, though she was wearing a great big tomato-sauce smile on her face.

'Well, what's the verdict?' she asked the pair who were leaning back patting their full bellies in appreciation.

'Yummy!'

'Okay as an occasional treat.' Amir countered his daughter's enthusiasm to remind them both that fast food wasn't a diet staple.

Something that Isolde needed to remember, since she'd done very little cooking for herself lately. She'd become so used to her big sister being the domestic goddess providing her with home-cooked meals it was difficult to get into the routine of making her own. Especially when she was the only one in the flat now and she'd been eating out rather than coming home to an empty place in the evenings. Although her sister had been a tad overbearing since her divorce and moving in, Isolde was missing her lately. Farah wasn't the only one who needed some company.

'And this was my treat,' she said brightly, justifying the feast they'd just enjoyed. Although, as Soraya's chief bridesmaid she didn't want to put on weight now so close to the wedding when the eyes of the world would be watching. She was beginning to understand Farah's anxiety around her appearance when they would all be under close scrutiny in the press.

'Next time, I'll cook,' Amir offered and coming here again, sharing her evening with him and Farah, was something she was already looking forward to.

'I didn't think princes had any need to do that. Don't you have an entourage to cater to your every whim?' Isolde knew he didn't employ any such team of staff or any of the other perks she imagined came with his title. Despite his being a prince, his daughter a princess, they didn't insist anyone used their titles in England. Probably so they could be afforded a relatively normal life here. However, she still enjoyed teasing him about the differences in their social classes.

He fixed her with an intense stare before rolling his brown eyes. 'You know I don't, but if you're volunteering for the position…'

Okay, so he could give as much as he got, but that was what made being around him so easy. They had fun and she never had to worry at what point he was going to hurt her because they were friends, nothing more.

'I'm not. I'm going to have my hands full being Farah's personal wedding stylist.' Isolde turned her attention to the real reason she was here tonight.

The young girl sat up in her chair, alert at the mention of her name. 'You are?'

Isolde began collecting the empty boxes and wrappers from the kitchen worktops and Amir wrapped up the leftovers. 'Yes. I'll just clear this away so we can sit down and brainstorm.'

'No, you won't,' Amir said sternly, the sight of his dark frown stopping Isolde in her tracks. She really had crossed the line this time. Isolde was always telling her she acted without thinking and now she'd somehow managed to cause offence by turning up at Amir's house and taking over.

'Sorry, I just thought…'

'You're our guest. I wouldn't expect you to stay in my kitchen all night. There's a perfectly good sofa in the lounge you can sit on.' He broke into a grin, a telltale sign that he was getting his own back for her earlier tease.

'Thank you, Your Highness.' Isolde gave him a mock curtsey before following him and Farah into the living room.

Although the décor was very high end compared to her budget flat-pack furniture and cheap wallpaper, it still didn't look like the home of a prince. There was no ostentatious display of wealth painted in gold on the walls—the matt grey walls lined with candid family pictures made it look like any normal family's home. Especially with

Farah's artwork and some hand-painted aeroplane models
dotted around that she suspected Amir had constructed
himself. If she'd expected diamond-encrusted thrones
she'd have been disappointed in the comfortable corner
sofa dominating the space, but everything was modest
and tasteful. Just like Amir.

She waited until everyone got comfortable, including
herself, as she kicked off her shoes and tucked her legs
beneath her on the sofa. As if to say he was fine with her
making herself at home, Amir followed suit.

'So what is it we're doing, Isolde?' Unable to contain
her excitement and curiosity any longer, Farah wheeled
herself across the room and positioned her chair directly
in front of Isolde.

'Well, I've had a talk with Soraya. I know we've both
had some dress fittings for the wedding and it hasn't
been easy co-ordinating everything with her when she's
on the other side of the world. So…she's given us the go-
ahead to organise our own dresses.' It hadn't taken much
to persuade Soraya to change her plans for the bridal
party last minute, because she was the kind of sister, the
kind of person, who would rather see everyone happy
than concentrate on what she wanted. She'd insisted she
wasn't giving up her childhood dreams of how her wedding should look and all that mattered was that Isolde and
Raed's family were there and comfortable in their roles.
Although Isolde had to promise that their outfits would
be tasteful and hers in particular would not contravene
any decency laws.

'I can choose my own dress?'

'Better than that. We're going to design them. I'm quite

handy with a sewing machine. We're free to accessorise how we want, and that includes your wheelchair. The only caveat is that we don't upstage the bride.'

Both Isolde and Soraya thought that if Farah was more involved in deciding what to wear she might be more relaxed about the whole affair. Isolde knew Amir wouldn't be happy about Farah being part of the ceremony if she was upset so it was important to get him on side too. After all, Isolde didn't want to be there on her own as the outsider she was. At least when she was with Amir and Farah she felt part of a family again. Something she hadn't realised she needed until Soraya moved away.

'Do I get to design my suit too?' Amir asked, apparently on board with the scheme.

Isolde clicked her tongue against her teeth. 'I'm afraid not. Soraya didn't trust you not to turn up in a purple velvet suit and top hat.'

Amir nodded. 'She knows me too well. We both know I would only show up the groom if I truly let my light shine.'

'Yeah, you're in a sackcloth and ashes. Whereas I and Miss Farah will be resplendent in chiffon.' Isolde took Farah by the hand and twirled her around in her wheelchair, the little girl's smile telling her it would all be worth the effort.

It was going to take some work to make dresses good enough to stand up to scrutiny at a royal wedding but she knew she could do it. With money tight when they were growing up, she'd been the one able to mend their clothes or customise stuff they'd found in second-hand shops. Her quirky sense of style had been part of what made her…her. It was being with Olly, conforming to his ideas of how she should look and behave that had stolen away that part of her identity. Since working full-time at the hospital she hadn't had much chance to break free from her conventional work clothes. It might be nice to rediscover that creative side of her again.

'I've brought some magazines, paper and pencils so we can get cracking any time you're ready, Farah.' Isolde fetched the shoulder bag she'd brought with her from the kitchen but she looked to Amir before she produced the contents, looking for his approval.

His response was to swipe everything off the coffee table and pull it closer to Farah. He was an exceptional father, and it wasn't lost on Isolde that he was content to let her be exactly who she was without trying to temper her behaviour either. She hadn't believed men like that existed. If she'd known perhaps she wouldn't have wasted years of her life on someone who needed to change her. It was just as well Amir came with more baggage and responsibilities than a bohemian spirit like her could ever be comfortable with, or else her vow off men might be in jeopardy.

Amir sat back and watched as Isolde and Farah let their imaginations run loose. It was nice to see his daughter engaged again and having fun. Too much of her young life recently had been spent dealing with things no child should ever have to go through. The trauma of the accident, losing her mother, and her subsequent struggle to walk again had robbed her of her childhood. Isolde seemed to understand what Farah needed, both inside and outside the hospital. She was the only health professional his daughter had really bonded with, who didn't patronise her or push her further than she was ready to go. Isolde took things at Farah's pace and he was grateful for it. Especially now seeing her having fun and laughing again.

'I think fairy wings might be pushing it a little bit, Farah,' he said, peering over her shoulder at the sketch she'd made, still aware that this was Soraya and Raed's day and an important one for their country. There was a fine line between keeping his daughter happy and not wishing to embarrass the family. Anything too over the top ran the risk of drawing the kind of negative attention they were all hoping to protect Farah from in the first place. It was only the crestfallen look on her face, erasing the smile Isolde had managed to put there, that made him regret saying anything.

Isolde lifted the drawing Farah had made and held it up, tilting her head to one side as she studied it. 'You know, I think this would look good at the evening reception. Some glitter and sequins and you're ready to party. Plus, there won't be any cameras there so we can wear what we like.'

She gave Amir a pointed look. He wasn't sure if it was a signal for him to back off out of this project, or to let him know she had it all in hand. Either way he was happy to let her take the lead when the spark was so evidently back in Farah's eyes.

'Maybe I'll get that purple velvet suit for that,' he jested, doing his best to get back into everyone's good books after inadvertently putting a dampener on their fun.

'Or we could design you a Farah and Isolde original,'

Isolde suggested, but that mischievous twinkle in her blue eyes offered a challenge he knew he wasn't prepared to meet.

'I don't think I'm ready for that. I think one maverick in the family is more than enough. Concentrate on Farah's outfit, and yours, and I'll be content to blend into the background.' He could only imagine the horrors Isolde and his daughter would come up with for him if left to their own devices, and wasn't brave enough to be styled by either of them for this very public event. It would be his first official appearance since his wife's death and he didn't particularly want to draw any more attention than was necessary from the press.

'Spoilsport. Though I suppose it gives us more time to concentrate on our fabulous outfits, doesn't it, Farah?'

Farah nodded in agreement and Amir was reminded of the days when his wife and daughter used to team up to get their own way. It seemed such a long time ago now since they'd taken family votes on important issues such as what ice-cream flavour to buy, or whether or not Farah got to stay up late. All of which had been pointless anyway because his daughter had usually got her own way, but he knew that by getting her mother's support it had given her a sense of solidarity, and the feeling that she was getting one over on her father.

These days it was difficult to get her engaged in anything and he'd had to make all the decisions for her. Isolde was giving her back that sense of control in her life. It might only be over something as small as designing her own dress, but taking an interest in something again meant so much. They both had Isolde to thank for that when she'd obviously gone to great lengths to make this happen. He was sure it hadn't been easy to convince a bride to hand over the decision-making on the bridesmaids' outfits. The Yarrow sisters really were remarkable women.

'I'm sure you'll both look beautiful and have all the men falling at your feet.'

Isolde gave a brittle laugh. 'No, thanks. The last thing I need in my life is another man. Although I think I need to remind my darling sister of that too. My invitation came with a plus one. She must think that because she found love after her dud of an ex, the same will happen for me.'

Amir wondered who had put her off the idea of ever finding love and what horrible thing he'd done to Isolde to make her think she was better off alone. Especially when she was so full of love herself. He'd had his troubles with his wife later in the marriage but at least he'd experienced what it was to be part of a couple and a family. Although he wasn't in the market for a relationship again—his focus was on Farah's recovery— he didn't think he wanted to be on his own for ever. He was already feeling the loss of his brother and parents since they'd returned home, and once Farah was old enough to strike out on her own he knew he'd be lonely. Although they were close and she was his whole world, there was nothing he wanted more than for her to have her independence and a life that didn't revolve around her injury.

'Ah, they were more tactful with my invitation. Mine was for myself and Farah only. They mustn't think there's any hope for me finding love again at all.' His laugh was as humourless as Isolde's had been. Neither of them happy with their current situation. It wasn't that he was actively looking for another romantic partner, but he wasn't going to rule out the possibility.

Of course he missed his wife, was devastated by her death and the impact her loss had upon the family, but he wasn't grieving to the extent his brother seemed to think he was. He couldn't tell him otherwise. It seemed like a terrible betrayal to tell anyone that his marriage had been on the rocks at the time of his wife's death. He wanted people to remember her fondly. Yet he felt like a fraud because he hadn't been in love with her the way everyone thought when she died. And although there had been little love to keep him warm at night, he hadn't wanted the scandal of a divorce to rock his family. He'd been prepared to sacrifice his happiness to protect the monarchy, to keep up that front of stability. She hadn't.

It was something he could never share, in order to protect her memory, and Farah's feelings. Not to mention the whole family. That didn't mean he wasn't consumed by guilt over the lies, and the secret he knew he had to keep.

'I'm sure that's not the case. They probably didn't want to upset you, that's all. Hey, if we're both minus significant others why don't we go together? I'll get Soraya to make sure we're seated together so we don't have to make awkward small talk with random toffs. No offence,' she added, obviously including him in that description of the distinguished wedding guests.

'Some taken,' he said with a smile as Farah cheered the idea that Isolde should accompany them.

It was clear that Isolde had some qualms about the day too, though she would likely never admit that she was worried about being out of place. Amir could see why she might have some reservations when she wasn't used to the kind of lifestyle, and the kind of people that would be in attendance. As someone who didn't always appear to follow the usual social niceties, she might stand out in the crowd, though that made her exactly who she was, and why he liked her. Isolde was honest and forthright, qualities he appreciated, in a world where people constantly seemed to be trying to be something they weren't. Him included. It had taken him a long time to realise he couldn't please everyone all of the time, and he didn't want her to think she had to start.

'It's not quite the proposal your brother offered my sister. I don't want us to fake a romance or anything. Maybe we can just go together, as friends.' Isolde was clarifying the situation so there was no doubt that their relationship was probably for Farah's benefit as much as his. He knew how much she liked Isolde so it wouldn't be fair to let her think anything else was going on between them, or that Isolde was a replacement for her mother. When she put it so plainly he didn't see a problem. They were company for each other. All three of them.

'Just friends. I think we can manage that. We seem to be doing okay so far.'

Isolde leaned her head briefly against his shoulder in a gesture of said friendship. It was settled, they would be attending the royal wedding as a strictly platonic couple.

Now all he had to do was reconcile that idea with his treacherous body, which had reacted to her touch as a lot more than just a friend.

CHAPTER THREE

'THIS LOOKS LIKE PARADISE,' Isolde commented, not for the first time. It had been three weeks since the video call with Soraya. They'd kept in touch with texts and emails about the dresses, but she was glad she was here in Zaki to finally see her in person.

From the moment the turquoise water, golden sands and swaying palm trees of Zaki had come into view, she'd felt as though she were in another world. Even the air was different—it smelled clean and fresh, and felt warm on her skin.

'I suppose it does compared to the city, though we're kind of used to it. Before the accident we often travelled over from London as a family. We had always planned to move back here permanently. I just wanted Farah to have a taste of normal life before the madness kicked in and we took up our royal duties. She was supposed to have an education in England first, a childhood not blighted by media intrusion, or responsibility to an entire country. Things didn't work out that way...' Amir's voice trailed off and she could tell he was disappearing back into that abyss of grief that had robbed him and Farah of so much.

'I know, and I'm sorry. Thank you for doing this with me. I'm so out of my comfort zone.' She tried to get him to refocus on the present, not only for Raed and Soraya's sake, but for his and Farah's too. They needed a break from all the heartache and pain they'd gone through in London, and, though they'd be returning to continue Farah's treatment, father and daughter deserved a holiday of sorts.

'You'll be fine,' Amir assured her. 'You're a VIP now. Enjoy it.'

'That's easier said than done when you're not used to this pampered lifestyle.' There wasn't a lot Isolde wasn't willing to tackle—a product of an upbringing by a fierce older sister—but this change of pace was a lot for her to take.

After their long—first-class—flight, where she'd been treated like royalty along with her travelling companions, they were now in the back of a limousine rushing towards the royal palace. She was beginning to wish she hadn't indulged in the complimentary champagne quite so much.

It was easy to forget this was the life her sister was now part of when they lived so far apart. She'd only had a very small taste of the family's importance when they'd been trying so hard to protect the King from press intrusion after his heart attack. It made her wonder, not for the first time, about what Amir and Farah had gone through after the car accident that had taken his wife, Farah's mother, from them.

Even now, over a year later, Farah had been hesitant about travelling in the car. Something that must be a daily occurrence. Amir had gently coaxed her in, reminding her that he was with her and promising to keep her safe.

Isolde had only heard snippets about what had happened from Farah during their physio sessions, and a little of what Soraya knew, but it would have been unprofessional and immoral to ask her any more about it. The little girl had understandably been traumatised, her mother apparently dying upon impact, leaving Farah scared, in pain and alone until the paramedics and fire brigade had arrived on scene to remove her from the vehicle. Given the lengths Raed had gone to—faking an engagement to her sister to put the press off the scent of a story during their father's illness—she could only imagine how intrusive they'd been in the aftermath of the crash.

Amir was fiercely protective of his daughter, and rightly so when she only had one parent looking out for her now. Isolde had been that lost and frightened little girl once when she'd lost both parents and she knew having one strong role model made all the difference. It couldn't have been easy for them to come back here either, knowing there would be talk about them in the press and attention drawn to Farah's condition, but Amir would never let anything happen to Farah when she'd already been through so much. Isolde was simply hanging onto his coat-tails, hoping he would protect her too.

She knew she wasn't everyone's cup of tea, and, though Amir's family had been lovely, not everyone would have time for a commoner like her. While it didn't usually bother her, she didn't want to show Soraya up, or her new family.

Even thinking of Raed and his parents as Soraya's new family made her tear up. It was silly when they were both grown women, and she'd been the one to tell Soraya to go after Raed when he'd gone home to take up his royal role again and left his life in London behind. She wanted her big sister to be happy, but she'd also never been without her support and she couldn't help but feel the same abandonment she'd gone through after her parents had died. At least she was going to see Soraya soon. She was tempted to hug her and never let her go.

As the fairy-tale vision of the palace appeared before them, all arches and columns, tiles and intricate sculpture, the wealth divide was more apparent than ever. Isolde took a deep, shaky breath.

'We're here. Relax, you've met the family before, and Farah and I will be around if you need us.' Amir reached across the back seat to give her hand a squeeze.

'I'm scared too,' Farah admitted as they entered through the golden gates of the palace grounds. They drove into a courtyard, dominated by a huge octagonal water feature, surrounded by perfectly manicured shrubbery.

Amir took her hand too. 'I know it's been a while since you've been here too, and circumstances are different. Just remember this is your family home and you're entitled to be here.

'You too,' he said to Isolde as she opened her mouth to comment otherwise.

She knew this had to be difficult for him too, but she supposed this was a joyous occasion for their siblings. Soraya deserved happiness and Isolde knew if Soraya thought for a second that her little sister wasn't happy she would focus on that rather than her own wedding day. After a lifetime of letting her big sister look after her, it was time for Isolde to reverse their roles.

'I think we should probably keep all of this to ourselves. Raed and Soraya don't need to know we're worried about everything. They've enough to deal with. I say we make a pact that all three of us face whatever is to come, together, and if there are any problems we discuss it with the group rather than take it to the happy couple. Deal?' She looked at Amir and Farah in turn for their support.

'Deal.'

'Deal.'

They each joined hands in solidarity and Isolde knew they'd get through this if they all stayed together. It was once the wedding was over and they were back in England, back to their own lives, that she'd have to worry about getting too close. Until then, she needed her team together.

'Isolde!' Soraya swamped her in a hug before she'd barely set foot onto the marble floor of the palace. The familiar warmth and scent of her big sister was something she'd missed for so long. Isolde let herself be completely immersed in that feeling of unconditional love that she'd been without for six months.

'Brother.' Raed walked over to Amir and gave him a quick hug in a more reserved display of affection.

'Fa-Fa!' Raed turned his attention to his niece, giving her a bear hug before taking off running with her down the hallway, her squeals of delight echoing around the walls.

It made Isolde feel less self-conscious about clinging

onto Soraya for so long. Clearly family was a big deal here too.

'It's so lovely to see you all.' The Queen came to greet them, looking resplendent in yellow silk, and once more Isolde was torn about whether or not to curtsey. The last time they'd met she'd made a botched job of it and been told it wasn't necessary. She supposed they were going to be family soon enough and she couldn't go around curt-seying to everyone all the time or her knees would soon give up. Instead, she reached out and shook her hand, fi-nally leaving go of Soraya.

'Thank you for having me, Djamila.' Amir and Farah had every right to be here but Isolde couldn't help but feel as though she was imposing on the family's gener-ous hospitality.

'I'm sure you're all exhausted after the journey. We've given you rooms together if you'd like to get settled in.'

'Thank you.'

'I can show you up,' Soraya offered, holding tightly to Isolde's arms. 'I can't wait to tell you about all of the work we're doing out here.'

Isolde had heard all about their charity projects on the numerous telephone calls they'd shared since Soraya left the country, but Soraya's excitement at actually getting to show Isolde the work they'd done was tangible. She was proud of her big sis, but at the same time it was a reminder that she had a life away from her. Excitement and glamour Isolde could only dream about. She went to work and came home to her empty flat. The only ex-citement had been the pizza night at Amir's house weeks ago, and that had been to make sure Farah was comfortable with her role in the wedding.

Although they'd achieved their objective, it had given Isolde a ton of work to do on the dresses, which Soraya still had to approve. It was a lot of pressure to keep everyone happy and she was beginning to realise the burden of responsibility her sister had been carrying all these years. She deserved every bit of luxury provided to her by her new family circumstances out here, though Soraya would never be someone who would simply sit back while others struggled. Which no doubt Isolde would see for herself later on.

Amir and Farah had disappeared into the room next door, led by Raed, and Soraya opened the door to Isolde's room. It was bigger than her entire flat.

'Not too shabby,' she said, taking in the sight. 'I might need a map to find my way around though.'

'Isn't it amazing? Apparently Amir specifically asked Raed to save this room for you because it has the best view.' Soraya moved to the double window and opened it up onto a balcony.

'It's beautiful.' For the first time in her life Isolde was truly awestruck. She had a clear view, not only of the palace gardens, but also of the stunning hills in the distance. It was a little paradise, and the wrought-iron table and chairs would be perfect for her to come and chill out day or night. She was already imagining having breakfast out here listening to the birds in the trees tomorrow morning. Different from the sounds of traffic and construction work on the streets of London. Another reminder that she and Soraya now lived in completely different worlds.

'I think this used to be Amir's room before he moved to England. Not that there's any sign of him in it. I wonder if they redecorated it after he left.' Soraya looked around as though she was seeing it for the first time too, picking up one of the dozens of scatter cushions lined up on the huge bed.

Isolde glanced around and saw the framed photograph of Amir and Raed in pride of place on the nightstand, and the handmade aeroplane models dotted around the bookcase, and knew exactly whose room this had been. 'I can see his fingerprints all over it. It's just like his living room.'

Soraya arched an eyebrow at her. 'You've been at his house?'

Isolde got the impression Soraya and Raed had been trying to matchmake ever since that afternoon tea they'd shared together, simply because she and Amir had an easy, comfortable relationship. Mostly because they were friends and knew there was no more to it than that when they both had so much baggage. They didn't need complicated romantic entanglements when they were both struggling to move on from their last partners, but they did enjoy one another's company. It wasn't so easy trying to get that point across to anyone else.

'Yes. I've been working with Farah on getting these dresses ready for the wedding, remember?' She wouldn't mention being invited over for dinner. That was asking for trouble.

'Uh-huh. You two seem to be spending a lot of time together recently, and now he's your plus one?'

'Listen, sis, I get you want me to have my own happy

ever after, but you're seriously looking at the wrong girl if you think I'm going to give up my life to play stepmother to someone else's kid. You know that just isn't me. I'm done being the little housewife and enjoying being foot-loose and fancy free.'

Well, she would, if she had any kind of social life. Un-fortunately when she'd settled down with Olly she'd lost touch with her more…bohemian friends. Now if she was lucky it was a quick drink after work with her colleagues, or a takeaway at a friend's house.

Soraya snorted. 'I'm not sure you were ever the little housewife.'

Isolde lifted one of the silk cushions off the bed and threw it at her. 'You know what I mean. Olly wanted someone to conform to society's rules and settle down with a couple of kids. I'm just not the maternal type.'

'Really? You seem to be doing a pretty good job with Farah, as far as I can see.'

'That's different. She's a patient, and only family by your marriage, not mine. So stop trying to make something out of nothing.' She grabbed another cushion and launched it, then another, until Soraya began to fight back, and the floor became littered with the debris of their childish fight.

Eventually they both collapsed onto the mattress, breathless and smiling. 'I've missed you, Isolde.'

'I've missed you too.'

'But don't think I'm giving up on this. After all, Amir sacrificed his room for you.'

Isolde reached across for the last remaining cushion and batted it onto Soraya's face. 'Enough.'

She was touched by the gesture, that he'd allowed her to encroach on such a personal space so she could enjoy the view better. No doubt his way of saying thank you for helping him with Farah, not that she expected anything for it. She enjoyed her time with the little girl; it gave her a chance to indulge her inner child, although Soraya might say she'd never really grown up. That might have been true at one time but since Soraya had moved here with Raed, Isolde had had no choice but to grow up. It wasn't all it was cracked up to be. Although helping out with Farah had given her a peek at what life might have been like if she had decided to settle down and have kids with Olly.

She saw the worrying Amir did over his daughter, and the responsibility he took in trying to make her happy, because Isolde had been living it with him during these wedding preparations. But the reward of seeing Farah smile made it all worthwhile. Isolde knew because she'd been working towards the same goal. What they all wanted more than anything was to see her walk again, to have her childhood back, and not to have to have physiotherapy or surgery. Unfortunately, there was still a long way to go for that to happen, but that didn't stop Isolde from trying to get her there.

She was close to all her young patients, all of them special to her in different ways, and she did her best to improve their quality of life through their sessions. However, Farah held a bigger piece of her heart. Even before the family connection, when Soraya had stepped in to be Raed's fake fiancée, Isolde had had a real bond with Farah. Perhaps it was the loss of her parents at such a young age that made her relate to that lost, frightened little girl who'd come through the trauma of a crash that took her mother from her.

She knew what it was like to have her whole world upended like that, not knowing what the future held without a mother to turn to. It was scary, and that was without the added stress of not being able to walk. Farah was brave and strong, just like her father.

Isolde had to admit that she had a soft spot for him too. Amir had a quiet strength and seemed to just get on with everything that fate threw at him. He reminded her a little of Soraya that way. He'd been dealt a very difficult hand but ploughed on trying to do his best for everyone. She was sure it wasn't easy when he was grieving the loss of his wife and he had his daughter's troubles to worry about. It gave Isolde a new perspective on having grown up expecting Soraya to simply deal with everything that came along because she was so capable. She could see now the strength of character it took to do that in the face of so many challenges, and she'd let Isolde sail through life without a care in the world, oblivious to her own emotional struggles. Exactly what Amir was trying to do now for Farah.

Isolde wasn't the girl's mother, but she felt a responsibility to try and make her happy too. Even if that came in the form of her dressmaking skills, rather than her medical ones for now.

'I just want you to be happy, Isolde.' Soraya rolled over onto her side and fixed her with her 'serious big sister' look.

'I am,' she lied. It wasn't that she was sad about anything in particular, she simply hadn't found anything in her life that made her happy the way Soraya was out here. And she was lonely. She didn't know what she would do if she didn't have Amir and Farah to call on every now and then. Although once the wedding was over she wouldn't have that to use as an excuse to see them any more. Perhaps she needed to spread her wings and go travelling. She'd never wanted to settle down, so maybe keeping on the move was the way forward.

'Welcome to our Home from Home centre. A place where young carers can hang out and have fun. We've got counsellors on hand for anyone who needs a chat, and we're currently offering cooking lessons for families on a budget.'

It was clear Soraya was very excited about their new venture as Amir and Isolde struggled to keep up with her on their way into the new building.

'This must have taken some planning,' he said to Raed, who had hung back and let his fiancée take the lead in showing them around. Farah was tired and had remained at the palace with his parents, while Amir and Isolde tagged along on the tour.

'We just transferred the idea from the London branch. All Soraya's idea of course, but we both come here when we can to help out.' Raed had contributed heavily to the funding of the UK project in an attempt to get Soraya on board with the fake-fiancée ruse at the time. Amir had since learned that the cause was one very close to her heart because of the time she'd spent caring for her parents before they died, and afterwards raising Isolde

on her own. She was a good influence on the family, reminding them how privileged they were in their position,
and that they could make a difference. Amir was glad
his brother and soon-to-be sister-in-law were still able to
make such a huge difference to people's lives out here.
One of the reasons they'd all gone into the medical field
was to help people and this way Raed and Soraya got to
continue their good work.

'How are you funding it?' he asked, curious to find
out how they kept it maintained now that it was up and
running.

'I mean, we have all sorts of financial managers involved, but we've also got lots of donations and sponsor-
ship secured. As long as we keep the profile raised in the
press, we should be good.' Raed was a man of his word
and Amir knew he wouldn't simply walk away from a
project when he tired of it.

Although he'd resisted coming back here to take up
his royal duties again, when the time had come, he'd
stepped up. With their father ill at the time, and Amir
unable to return because of Farah, Raed had left the life
he had built for himself in London to do the right thing
by everyone else. He'd been willing to sacrifice his own
happiness for that of the country. Thank goodness he'd
met Soraya, who'd been willing to stand by him. They
deserved all the happiness they'd found together.

'We'd like you to meet some of our young people.'
Soraya walked them past the bank of computer games
and a pool table, waving at the groups of teens congre-
gated, chatting and laughing.

It was a bright modern space littered with oversized

beanbags to sit on and plenty of activities to take part in. Soraya pointed to a couple of doors off to the side, which were apparently off limits to them at present.

'That's our counsellor's office, and next door is the quiet space where kids can come and do their homework. Not all the children have a place at home where they can study so they come here.' It was clear Soraya had tried to cover all the needs of their young carers, probably because she'd been the child who'd needed a space to hang out, to study without interruption, and free from responsibility.

Isolde had told him everything Soraya had done for her growing up, a very different childhood from the one he and Raed had experienced. Though it hadn't been easy because of the pressures they'd been under as young children to be well behaved in the public spotlight, Amir was thankful for the material things they'd never had to worry about. Emotionally, however, it could be argued that their needs had been as neglected as these young children. That was part of the reason he'd wanted Farah's early schooling to take place in England, out of the spotlight, and where he was able to devote more time to her than his parents ever had to him.

'Is there somewhere for little sisters who are oblivious to all the grown-up struggles their siblings are going through to go so they don't feel left out?' Isolde took her sister's hand and it was obvious she understood things now in a different light. He knew how much she was struggling without her family, the same way he was, but she was putting Soraya's feelings before her own. Showing a real maturity for someone who often said she'd never grown up.

'Come here and I'll show you.' Soraya took her by the hand and led her to a long table where the kids were getting stuck into arts and crafts, glitter and glue everywhere.

'Hi,' Isolde said and immediately took a seat to see what everyone was making while Soraya and Raed spoke to some of the adult leaders.

Spotting the empty seat beside Isolde, Amir sat down too, wishing they had brought Farah along and tried to get her involved too. He'd seen how engaged she'd been with Isolde over the whole dress-designing sessions, clearly a creative soul like her mentor.

'So, what are you making here?' Isolde took a fresh sheet of paper from the pile in the middle of the table and glanced at the work the young boy next to her was doing, his tongue sticking out in concentration.

'We're making pictures showing our wishes,' he said, grabbing a glue stick and some pipe cleaners.

'I've made a unicorn,' the little girl on the other side of Isolde said, proudly showing off her drawing, which was little more than a squiggle saturated with silver glitter and glue, but which she was clearly very proud of.

'That's an excellent unicorn,' Isolde said, giving her a thumbs up for her efforts. 'I think I'll do a beach scene.'

'Is that where you wish you were?' Amir asked, curious about the things Isolde wanted in life because she never discussed her needs, only everyone else's. It struck him that since they'd first met, she'd always been working towards improving other people's lives. Not only her patients'. He knew she was missing her sister as much as he was missing his family, but Isolde hadn't told Soraya lest she upset her. She'd never once voiced dissatisfaction with her lot, but he couldn't help but feel she needed more.

'Some days,' she said on a wistful sigh.

'Maybe we should gatecrash the honeymoon,' he suggested, only half joking.

'I think I'd prefer something more low-key.'

'A desert island perhaps?'

'Definitely.'

It had been a long time since he and Farah had been on a holiday, or had any time out from their recent stresses. This trip didn't count, since they would be under a spotlight for the whole duration, and had a duty not to mess up in the eyes of the world's press. A nice quiet break on an isolated beach in the sun actually sounded like heaven. He was sure Farah would enjoy it too. Though he suspected asking Isolde to join them might be pushing the boundaries of their friendship a little far, he couldn't imagine going on such a trip without her now.

She brought him such peace simply by being around he didn't know what he was going to do once the wedding was over and there was no longer any excuse for them to hang out. He supposed they'd still see each other at work, and any family occasions, but it wouldn't be the same as eating pizza in his kitchen.

The trouble was he didn't know how to tell her he wanted her to stay in his life without making things weird between them. She'd made it clear she didn't want to settle down, or have family of her own, so he knew that ruled him out even if he had held any romantic notions that they might end up as more than just friends. That was primarily what had held him back from looking at her as anything else, along with his need to protect Farah. She needed stability, not her father introducing women into her life that weren't going to be around for ever. Perhaps it was time they both got used to that idea before he got as attached to Isolde as Farah.

'What are you making, Amir? A picture of you in a pilot uniform?' she asked with a wink.

'I see you've discovered my penchant for all things aeronautical. Yes, in different circumstances perhaps I might've entertained the idea of becoming a pilot. Though I'm afraid I simply went for a sunny day in the park.' He put forward his efforts of a crayoned sun and tissue-paper grass illustrating his simple dream to a chorus of titters from unimpressed children around him. Clearly he wasn't the artistic one around here.

'Thanks for the room, by the way. It was very kind of you to give it up for me.' Isolde went off topic to acknowledge the gesture he'd made in an attempt to make her feel more at home.

'It was no problem. I thought you might enjoy the view.' Amir knew what it was like feeling like an outsider in that vast mansion, and he was part of the family. His role had always been to stay in the background, supporting his older brother, like everyone else. He didn't resent Raed, he'd always admired him, but his parents tended to forget they had another child when they had spent their lives prepping Raed to be King. With the wedding coming up he didn't wish for Isolde to get lost in the noise too. At least if she had a quiet place to retreat to, a space to call her own, it might help to shield her from the pressures of royal life.

'I do. Much better than the one I have now,' she said, squinting at his picture. 'Although, if that's your big dream I think we're both in need of a sunny holiday.'

For a moment the idea that there might be a chance they would get to go on their dream vacation together seemed to hover in the air, at least as far as Amir was concerned. Then Isolde turned away, focusing on the children's artwork again, and the moment passed.

'So, what's your big dream?' he asked the little boy who was studiously sketching away next to him. This was why they were here, to interact with these children, not to get carried away with pipe dreams and what ifs.

'This is me in the hospital.' The boy pointed to the macabre stick figure stretched out on what he supposed to be a hospital bed, the strange vision causing Amir to furrow his brow. He was contemplating whether or not he should speak to one of the counsellors on the child's behalf when Raed walked over.

'Ah, I see you've met Fahid. Good.' Raed rested his hand on the child's back like a proud parent. 'This little man is not only caring for his sick, widowed mother, but he's also waiting for a lobectomy. He has benign tumours all over his lungs.'

As a thoracic surgeon, Amir knew what a lobectomy was, and he suspected that was why he was really here. He gave Raed the side-eye but his brother simply smiled and shrugged.

'Call it a working holiday,' he said, placing Fahid's drawing in front of him. Now he knew exactly what it depicted, Amir couldn't help but be affected. This child's dream was something he could help to achieve.

'How long's the waiting list?'

Raed held his gaze, communicating the importance of his participation in this scenario. 'Too long and his mother is worried sick because she can't do anything to help him. He lost his father a few years ago and they only have each other.'

'When I have my surgery I can play football with my friends again.' Fahid, seemingly oblivious to the background shenanigans, continued to colour, adding in a faceless surgeon he was likely hoping would miraculously cure him.

Amir thought of Farah, of the things she could no longer do, and how he wished he were in a position to change that. Now here he was able to make a difference to another child's life and he knew he couldn't go back home until he'd done his part.

'Send me his files,' he said gruffly to Raed, ticked off that he'd been manipulated in such an obvious way.

'It was lovely to meet you, Fahid, and everyone else.' He scraped back his chair and left the table.

'All you had to do was ask,' he hissed at Raed as he walked by, suddenly needing some air and time out from his brother's charity project.

'I'm sorry, brother—'

'Amir?'

He heard the concern in Raed and Isolde's voices behind him but he couldn't stop, he couldn't talk, because he was afraid of all that pain and emotion he'd been holding back since the aftermath of the accident.

It wasn't the idea of performing the routine procedure on Fahid that was causing him distress, or even the underhanded way his brother had gone about things. No, it was the fact no one, not even a surgeon as skilled as he, could fix his daughter so easily. He would do anything if Farah could have her life back with one simple operation. It didn't matter that her injuries were beyond anyone's capabilities, he still felt like a failure. As a father, and as a surgeon. It was his job to take care of Farah, to improve lives, and if anyone should be able to help her it should be him. If he was going to change a child's life, it should be his own.

He'd already failed his family when his wife had wanted a divorce. It was his fault she'd driven off in such a state that night because he wouldn't agree to it, that she'd crashed the car, and injured Farah, that she'd died. The only thing he could do to try and make things right was to help his daughter walk again and he couldn't even do that.

Seeing Fahid, the struggles he was having, and knowing that one operation could turn his life around, had brought all that guilt to the fore. He'd been trying to keep it at bay, focusing on Farah's recovery, afraid that he'd fall apart. She needed him to be strong. It was all he could do.

Right now he needed some space to get those defences back in place. He was already vulnerable, away from home, he and Farah in the spotlight for the first time since the accident, and battling this increasing need for Isolde in his life. The last thing he needed was a public emotional breakdown.

* * *

'I'll go.' Isolde touched Raed's arm, silently asking him not to go after his brother. She'd witnessed the exchange, seen the pained expression on Amir's face as he'd left, and knew he needed some space from everyone pressuring him. She hoped that didn't include her.

'Raed? What happened?' Soraya arrived on the scene having missed the exchange but Isolde was sure she knew what had Amir so riled. She doubted there was anything that went on in this centre that her sister wasn't aware of.

'I think hearing Fahid's story has probably made him think about Farah and wish he could make her life better with one simple procedure. Give him a moment. I'll go and check on him.' Isolde said her goodbyes to the kids and made her way towards the back door, which Amir had disappeared through only moments ago, hoping she wouldn't be intruding too much.

Given the scene she'd just witnessed, she figured the last thing he'd want was his brother following him, but she considered herself neutral in this sibling battle. She knew Raed and Soraya had meant well with this whole set-up, but she also knew how much Amir beat himself up every day about not being able to help Farah. It must have been hard for him to be rendered powerless when it came to his own daughter's health issues. Never more so than when he was reminded of the difference he could make to the quality of another child's life.

He was pacing up and down the car park at the back, his body so tense she was sure he was ready to snap in half at any given moment.

'Hey,' she said, tapping him on the shoulder to let him know she was there.

He whirled around, poised and ready for combat. Then he saw her and she watched as all the fight left him, his shoulders falling and his fists unclenching. 'Sorry. I didn't realise it was you, Isolde.'

'I come in peace.' She held her hands up in surrender, finding some satisfaction in the half-smile she managed to raise.

'It's not your fault. It's not anyone's fault. Except mine,' he said cryptically, scrubbing his hands over his scalp.

'You can talk to me, Amir. I know there are things that are bothering us that we can't say to family, but we can confide in each other. We're both kind of floundering in the deep end at the moment.'

'It's not that I begrudge helping anyone on my time off, and not even that Raed tricked me into agreeing to do the surgery. Which, by the way, I would have done anyway if he'd asked.'

'I know that, and he knows that. Perhaps they simply wanted you to meet Fahid for yourself and understand the impact you could have on his life.'

'I guess so. It's just a reminder that I can't do anything for my own daughter. A few hours in an operating theatre with other people's children and I can give them their childhood back. Fahid's already lost his father, he's grieving and scared. Just like my Farah. I understand his mother's feelings of inadequacy but at least I can do something for their family. It doesn't matter how much time I devote to Farah, I can't do the same for her. I can't make her wish come true.' The pain was so obvious in his words, in his eyes, that it hurt to even watch him go through it. Isolde felt every bit as powerless as he did right now.

'You have done everything you possibly could, Amir, but you can't work miracles. I've seen you together and you are the best father that little girl could ever ask for.' She worked with a lot of families and not every parent was as present and involved as Amir in their child's treatment. But some things simply couldn't be fixed by sheer determination.

'You don't understand. All of this is my fault.' He threw up his hands and walked away. For a moment she thought he was going to leave the grounds altogether, away from the conversation. Instead, he moved over to the bench just outside the centre's doors.

Isolde followed him over and sat down, realising he wanted, needed, someone to talk to about whatever he'd been holding onto for all these months. She traced her fingers over the letters carved into the back of the seat.

'"Reflection." Couldn't be more apt, could it?'

'I don't know… *Guilt* might be more apt.' Amir leaned forward and rested his head in his hands and it was all she could do not to hug him. He looked like the loneliest man in the world and she wanted to remind him he wasn't. That she was here for him.

'What happened to Farah wasn't your fault. From what I heard you weren't even in the car that night.' It was natural for a parent to blame themselves when a child was hurt; she'd seen enough of that at the hospital. That level of responsibility was the reason she couldn't imagine ever having children of her own. It was heartbreaking to watch and she didn't think she could ever be the parent a child deserved. Watching Amir's guilt was proof of that. If a man who devoted his whole life to his daughter's well-being couldn't get things right, what hope did she have?

He lifted his head and turned his dark, sorrowful eyes onto her. 'I caused the accident. It's my fault Farah can't walk and that her mother's no longer around.'

'That's not—'

Amir interrupted another attempt to placate him with a bombshell that left Isolde temporarily speechless.

'She told me she wanted a divorce. I said I would never agree. It would cause too much of a scandal to my family. That's why she drove away with Farah, why she was so distracted. I was willing to force us both to stay in a loveless marriage, one where I obviously wasn't enough, to save face. It cost me everything. All I had to do was be brave and agree. Instead, I sent her to her death.'

By all accounts, including from his own family, he'd had the perfect marriage. She'd seen how devastated he'd been by the loss of his wife and she would never have guessed there had been any problems. Which explained why he felt as though he couldn't talk to anyone about it. She'd been around the royal family enough to know they didn't like to present anything other than a perfect front to the world. Apparently that extended to each other too, if he hadn't been able to reach out to his brother during all of this turmoil. It was clear by the way Raed had talked about the tragic loss of his sister-in-law in the past that he wasn't aware that their marriage had been in difficulty.

She supposed the same could have been said about the secrecy between her and Soraya when it came to their personal lives. Both had been going through their own relationship struggles and had neglected to turn to one another for support through fear of upsetting each other. Perhaps if they had they wouldn't have stayed in toxic relationships for as long as they had. If she'd known half of what Frank had been up to she wouldn't have hesitated in dragging her sister away from him. As it was she hadn't known until it was too late, until he'd taken everything from Soraya, and left her with nowhere to go except Isolde's spare room.

It was easy to get lost in a relationship, as if it were the only important thing in the world, making it difficult to let go. She'd lost her sense of self when she'd been with Olly, and would've done almost anything to keep him happy. Except have a family. It was only when he'd pushed that point that she'd realised how much of herself she'd compromised and finally woken up.

She supposed Amir hadn't reached that point, admitting things hadn't been good. Perhaps with a little time he would have, which was what made this all the more difficult. Now he never would, forever holding onto the fact his wife hadn't been happy. Afraid to tell anyone and taint her memory. Still, it didn't make him accountable for what had happened.

'You weren't the one driving, Amir,' she said softly. Feeling some level of guilt over the situation was understandable but it didn't make it justified. In the circumstances she would likely have felt the same way when she'd blamed herself for the end of her relationship with Olly, even though he'd known who she was when they'd got together. It must have been harder for Amir when he hadn't been able to vent to anyone about what had happened, how hurt he was. At least until now.

'I may as well have been. Although my driving was just one more thing she criticised.' When he talked about his wife now she could hear the hint of bitterness mixed with his grief. On the occasions when he had mentioned her, Isolde had always taken that faraway look as a longing for the life they'd had together. Now she thought it might be more about regret. The kind she experienced in moments of vulnerability that made her think about the time she'd wasted with Olly, and the wish that things could somehow have worked out differently. Simply because sometimes being on her own had seemed harder than staying in a troubled relationship.

'I'm sorry you weren't on good terms when she died. I think it's conflicted your emotions over what happened. Really, your marriage ending and the crash are two different events.' And she suspected that neither were his fault.

'I should have just put on my happy face the way I'm supposed to and agreed, then she would never have driven off like that in such a rage. That's what the royal family are supposed to do, we just grit our teeth and bear whatever life throws at us. It's what I did my whole childhood.'

'That's not healthy either, Amir.' Isolde thought of Soraya, the way she'd dealt with everything from their parents' ill health, to working non-stop to provide for the family without complaint. It was noble, but ultimately had led her to believe that her feelings didn't matter. That she should keep everything to herself and concentrate on making other people happy. Something Isolde realised she'd tried to emulate with Olly. It was time someone broke out of this self-sacrificing cycle because, in the end, no one was happy.

'Yeah, I don't want Farah to grow up thinking that way, believing she can't be who she wants to be through fear of upsetting anyone. I let a toxic relationship go on too long, fostering the same kind of atmosphere I had growing up in my own house. I had to be the best son to keep my parents happy because they were so focused on Raed they didn't need me causing them any trouble. That carried over into my marriage, trying not only to be the best son, but to be the best husband too. I thought that meant clinging onto a marriage that wasn't good for any of us. It caused Farah irreparable damage.'

His voice broke then, his daughter his apparent kryptonite. Yet Isolde knew he'd done the right thing. She hoped with time he'd realise that too.

'You didn't do anything wrong. It's easy to blame ourselves for things going wrong. Believe me, I did the same thing in my relationship. I was so used to having Soraya protecting me and looking after me I guess I was afraid to be on my own. So, when she married Frank, and I met Olly, I tried to be everything he wanted. I didn't want anyone else to leave me, so I tried to be what he needed. I gave up a transient life, living in the moment, to settle down with a steady job. Now, ironically, it's that stable life that's my safety net. The security of my career and home was all I could rely on once Olly was out of my life. Then Soraya's marriage ended and she needed somewhere to go. For once I was able to do something for her. So I stayed put, stayed still, and tried to be the responsible adult she needed me to be.'

She believed now her young carefree years, which she realised now had come at the expense of her sister's freedom, had been a direct response to her parents' deaths. A child who'd seen how short and fragile life was at first hand and had wanted to enjoy every second of it. She missed that naïve existence, although it had left Soraya to carry the burden of responsibility alone, and she didn't think she could be that selfish any more.

'I can't imagine anyone trying to tell you what to do.' Amir smiled at her and she wished she'd always been the person he apparently thought her to be—strong, independent, and nobody's fool. It would've saved her a lot of heartache.

'Yes, well, I was young, naïve, and eager to please. Thank goodness I saw the error of my ways.' It was her turn to smile, trying to lighten the mood when discussing a dark period in her past. It seemed only fair when Amir had been so open with her on a subject that had not only been causing him untold pain, but was also something he hadn't shared even with family.

She was privileged he trusted her with the information and it only went to prove how close they'd become in such a short span of time. If it weren't for the upcoming wedding, and her need to be around someone who understood her, she would have heeded the warning signs. As it was, she didn't want to see or hear them at a time when she needed all the friends she could get.

'What was the wake-up call for you?'

'That would be when he wanted me to give up my new job and have his babies. That was one thing I wasn't prepared to compromise on. Soraya and I went through a lot as kids and I think some of that could've been prevented. My parents refused to give up smoking even though they knew it was killing them, that lung cancer would take them away from their two young daughters. Okay, so the damage had been done long before we arrived, but they might have been able to buy some extra time if they'd thought of us. It might seem selfish to some, but I don't want to be responsible for bringing more lives into the world only to let them down like that.'

'That's not selfish, that's self-preservation. I think the things we've done, the way we've acted, has been out of a need for survival when we didn't have anyone else to protect us. Have you ever told Soraya any of this?'

She shook her head. 'I was enough of a burden to her growing up without adding my orphan issues to her load.'

Her shaky smile wasn't enough to convince him to drop the subject.

'Well, I'm here, and I know what a wonderful, generous, loving person you are. I'm sure you'd be an amazing mother, and yeah, we make mistakes as parents, but our children love us unconditionally. Thank goodness.'

Isolde looked into Amir's eyes and saw that same feeling of loneliness and fear she'd been living with since she lost her parents. He'd been through a lot after his loss too, because of the secrets he'd been forced to keep, and the front he'd had to adopt for Farah's sake.

It brought back those memories of whispered voices and people crying, no one willing to tell her what was going on because she was 'too young to understand'. Only to be told later that her parent had gone, leaving her more confused. She'd been through that twice in barely a year, left with just her big sister to comfort her and take care of her. Yet she'd never been able to voice the impact the loss of her parents had on her until now because she'd known Soraya had been through much worse, having to deal with everything left behind. This was the first time she'd been allowed to express that fear, and have it validated. Amir understood and it opened the floodgates for all of the confusing emotions she'd felt at that time to come flooding to the fore, finally grieving for her parents and the loss of a future with them. To her horror, her eyes began to fill with tears and her bottom lip started to wobble.

'I wish I'd known you back then,' she said on a sob.

Amir reached out and brushed his thumb across her trembling bottom lip. 'You have me now.'

When he leaned in and pressed his mouth against hers it felt like the most natural thing in the world. His kiss, so tender and comforting, was somewhere she wanted to stay for ever. She wanted to believe that she did have him, that this could last for ever. It was the first time since Soraya had moved away that she didn't feel alone.

Then Amir stood up and walked away, reminding her that any sense of security was only fleeting. In the end, everyone left her.

CHAPTER FOUR

IDIOT. AMIR WAS still chastising himself days later for crossing the line with Isolde and kissing her. Every time he saw her he remembered feeling her soft lips against his, the taste of her, and felt the need to kiss her all over again. It had been an error of judgement in a moment of weakness, when they'd both been vulnerable and in need of some emotional support. A mistake because nothing could come of it.

Even if he weren't a widower with a young daughter he needed to focus on, or a member of the royal family Isolde's sister was about to marry into, a relationship wasn't something he should even be considering. Not with someone like Isolde, who'd made it clear settling down with a family was not something the future held for her. He and Farah were a ready-made family and, like Isolde, he wasn't about to compromise that status for anything. First and foremost he was a father and wouldn't jeopardise that for any romantic interlude. He was never going to be the type of man to embark on a fling, and he wouldn't bring just any woman into his daughter's life. Isolde especially made things difficult when she was already such a big part of Farah's life. There was no point in starting something when she'd been very clear she didn't want the responsibility that came with being part of a family unit. Yet he didn't want to lose her out of their lives altogether.

He didn't know if it was too late to make amends when she hadn't shown up at the hospital for Fahid's operation. Raed was here supporting them both, as was Soraya, though she'd gone to get some refreshments while they waited for the time slot in the operating theatre.

'I'm sorry again, Amir. I didn't mean to upset you. I should have gone about things differently.' Raed apologised for the umpteenth time since the day in the centre.

'It's all right. I suppose I'm still trying to get used to the fact I'm not superhuman, and I can't fix everything, or everybody. Fahid reminded me of Farah, having lost a parent, and I simply yearned to be able to make a difference to my daughter's life in the same way. I should be grateful for the things I can do. Now you're back in the arms of the family, carrying out the role I couldn't, it's just as well I have a medical career to fall back on.'

He was only partly joking. Although as the eldest son, Raed was always meant to be next in line to the throne, Amir had been preparing himself to take over for a while. When his brother had first voiced his plans to surrender his position in the royal family, Amir had thought it was his time to shine, to prove to his parents and his wife that he was worthy of his position in the family too. More than a spare son should anything happen to the heir. He guessed he was wrong. Although, with Farah's future uncertain, he supposed it relieved some of the pressure that otherwise would have fallen on his shoulders.

'I'm sorry, brother. With everything that happened, I

never thought to ask how you felt about anything, or what your long-term plans are.'

It was true, they hadn't had an honest conversation about the situation as a family since the afternoon they'd come up with the 'fake fiancée' cover story, inveigling Soraya into their mess. Amir supposed because no one wanted to upset their father, who, though much stronger than he had been, was still recovering from his heart attack and subsequent operation.

Although the rest of his family were living in a different country, Amir liked to think that everything that had happened had brought them closer. All were concerned about him and Farah checking in regularly with them, and asking about his work along with her progress. Perhaps the chasm had been all in his head growing up, and he'd been the one constantly comparing himself to his elder brother. They hadn't been particularly close when they'd both lived in London, busy with their own lives and futures. Now it seemed the losses, and near losses, they'd suffered had made every one of them realise how lucky they were to have one another.

He knew he'd always have a family home to return to, a lifestyle that meant never having to worry about money, if he ever decided to return and look after Farah full-time. His family would be supportive of whatever he chose, he knew that, and it was a comfort to him on the days when he did feel alone and powerless.

'I'm not sure myself. I don't want to uproot Farah when she's still receiving treatment so I guess life in London goes on as usual for now. Long term, I might come back to Zaki. That was always the plan, and now, with everyone else back here, life is kind of lonely.'

It was the first time he'd admitted that to his brother, always wanting to be seen as strong and capable by his family. Something that didn't really seem to matter any more. He'd failed in his duty as a son, a prince, a husband, and as a father. The best he could do now was be there for his daughter, come what may.

'I'm sorry we're not there for you, Amir. You know you and Farah are always welcome to come home. I'm sure Mother and Father would be glad to have us all here. But you do what you have to do.' Raed wasn't one to say things he didn't mean and it meant a lot to Amir that his brother would happily welcome him back.

He'd always looked up to his older brother. When he'd seen the difference Raed had been making in the medical field, he'd followed him into the profession. It had seemed to him then that if he wasn't going to be an important figurehead in the family, a medical career could be as rewarding, and it had been. He'd even been able to work in Zaki for a time, making a difference to many patients and their families, before Farah had been born.

The news of Raed's intended surrender of his position had given him a renewed sense of purpose and he'd been preparing to take the role himself. Deep down he had hoped it would help save his marriage, that returning to their home country in prominent roles would make his wife look more favourably upon him. But it hadn't been enough. Then the crash and his father's ill health had changed all their lives and made them reassess everything. He'd become a little more sensitive in the interim, it would seem.

'As long as you don't spring any more surprises on me...'

'Don't worry, I've had very strong words with my husband about being tactful in the future. We had discussed the possibility of getting you involved, but I certainly wasn't part of the ambush.' Soraya appeared beside them carrying coffee. She'd been mortified by the events of that day at the centre, apologising for both of them every day since, even though she hadn't been present at the time.

When it came down to it, Amir knew his brother wasn't guilty of being deceitful or conniving, simply oblivious to the parallels between the young boy and Farah, and why it hurt so much. Fahid was a child whose life had been turned upside down by ill health and the loss of a parent too. It simply didn't seem fair that Amir could turn things around for that family when he couldn't do the same for his own.

Though he'd have to get used to that, he supposed, such was the nature of his job. Treating a child wasn't anything new to him, and, whether the circumstances were close to his daughter's or not, he had a duty of care. Somehow he was going to have to find a way to separate his personal life and feelings from his work.

To be fair to Raed, he was one of the few people who treated Farah the same way he always had, as though he didn't see her wheelchair. Day-to-day life for Amir, however, was a constant reminder of all the things his daughter could no longer do. The only one who knew the struggles they faced on a practical level was Isolde, someone else who never talked down to Farah, or ever saw her as anything other than a capable young girl.

'Isolde! I thought you weren't coming. Djamila said you weren't feeling well.' It was Soraya who alerted him to her arrival and he immediately felt better. If she harboured any resentment for him kissing her, surely she wouldn't have bothered coming to see him before the surgery to wish him luck like all the others.

'I'm a little better so I thought I should come down for support. You said Fahid wouldn't have any family in with him today?' She was avoiding Amir's eye and letting him know he wasn't the reason she was here after all.

His euphoria deflated. 'No, his mother isn't well enough to come down but she signed all the relevant permission papers to give the go-ahead. I said I'd phone her directly once he's out of Theatre.'

This time she had to look at him as she simply said, 'Good.'

'I've told her Fahid won't be able to do any heavy lifting for a while. Can we get the family some support while he recuperates?' Although the surgery should improve the quality of life, post-surgery the young boy still needed time to recover from the operation. Amir wasn't the sort of man who would simply walk away from his patient once his job was done. He might be in the country only temporarily but he still wanted to make sure the young boy would be taken care of in his absence.

'We've been working with his mother to get her to agree to carers coming in throughout the day to help her and relieve Fahid of some of his duties. She's reluctant to let strangers into the house. I think she's afraid social services will accuse her of neglect and take him away from her. Perhaps we could get some volunteers from the centre to call on her in a less formal arrangement to help out.' Efficient Soraya had obviously already taken a great interest in the boy's case. Unsurprising when she probably saw a lot of herself in the child. Her experiences, along with her natural empathy, were qualities that would make a great asset for the royal family.

'I can do it. At least for as long as I'm here. Fahid is probably going to need some physio too to regain his strength post-op so I'm sure we can make arrangements for me to see him here and at home to keep an eye on things.' Isolde surprised them all with her generous offer. Though Amir supposed he should be used to her altruistic tendencies when she'd gone above and beyond the call of duty for him and Farah. He could only hope no one else would take advantage of her kindness the way he had.

'That's a great idea. You and Amir can work together on this one,' Soraya said, looking at him for confirmation.

Unbeknown to her, it did put him and Isolde in a sticky situation, forcing them closer together when he was trying to keep a professional and personal distance from her. But he couldn't deny it would aid Fahid and his family to have them both on his side.

'If that's okay with Isolde?' He tested the waters before committing himself to anything further.

'Sure,' she said flatly, her lack of enthusiasm saying everything she hadn't about the prospect of working together. 'You must let me know what the surgery entails so I can tailor an exercise plan for him.'

'Like any lung surgery it's a major undertaking as the

organs are so close to the heart and blood vessels. I'll have to go in through the chest and ribs to remove the lobes, so he'll need a chest drain to remove excess fluid.' It was a standard procedure for him, but all surgery carried risks of complication and treatment post-surgery was equally vital to the patient's recovery and quality of life.

'So, standard physio following that type of operation? Deep-breathing and coughing exercises to help lungs re-expand, and aid breathing?' Isolde was very matter-of-fact. He knew this was as commonplace to her as the surgery was to him but having her on board too gave Fahid a better chance to get his life back on track as soon as possible.

'Yes, and, of course, no heavy lifting for a while to prevent strain on the chest muscles and incision site.'

'Of course. I can start gentle exercises with him in the hospital after the op to get him mobile as soon as possible to help his lung capacity as well as his circulation.'

'That would be great, thank you.'

Amir and Raed might have cleared the air but the tension between him and Isolde was still palpable. Although, despite his faux pas, she was still here in support and planning her part in Fahid's recovery. She could easily have stayed away, or minimised her role in the boy's treatment, but, like him, that simply wasn't in her nature. He admired the dedication to her job, but more than that he admired the woman she was.

Since the kiss he'd tried to put a little distance between them, retiring to bed early in the evenings, and making sure to be in a crowd during the day. It had been for their own benefit, but whenever she looked at him there was an unmistakable wounded look in her eyes and she'd been uncharacteristically subdued since the kiss.

He hadn't wanted to cause an awkward atmosphere between them—if anything, by walking away he'd hoped to avoid just that. What he didn't want was for Isolde to blame herself and believe she'd done something wrong. He'd taken advantage when she'd been at her most vulnerable, confiding in him about her ex and the way he'd manipulated her. Now Amir worried he was guilty of the same thing, kissing her when her defences were at an all-time low.

Despite everything, she was the one he most wanted to see now before going into the operating theatre. He didn't get nervous before surgery but he thought he'd be able to concentrate better knowing things were okay between them. He needed that peace of mind.

'I'm going to go and see Fahid before we go into the surgery. Isolde, perhaps you'd like to walk down with me?' He knew he was playing with fire putting her on the spot this way, but avoiding each other wasn't helping the awkwardness between them.

Isolde contemplated saying no, she wouldn't, but that would only alert Soraya and Raed that something was wrong between them. She'd almost not bothered to come at all today, her conscience getting the better of her at the last minute knowing that little boy was here without any family, probably afraid about what was going to happen to him. They'd only met briefly that day at the centre, but she hoped if he saw a few familiar faces it might give him some comfort. When their parents had been going through their health problems, she and Soraya would've been grateful for friends to support them, and at the end of the day this was what it was all about. Making a difference to a family that were in difficult circumstances, because they didn't want them to struggle the way they had.

When her hesitation over agreeing to accompany Amir began to draw attention from her sister, Isolde gave a hasty, and insincere, 'I'd love to.'

He was the reason it had taken her so long deciding to come after all. That kiss had changed everything between them, and not for the better. It had come out of the blue, but she'd enjoyed it. Lost herself in the moment. She knew she wouldn't have regretted it if he hadn't got up and walked away. Instantly humiliating her, and sullying what had been a beautiful moment. Worse, he'd been avoiding her since, letting her know how sorry he was it had ever happened. It didn't do much for her self-esteem. Especially when she'd laid herself so bare in the moment, shared things with him she'd never told anyone, and left her heart unguarded for a fraction too long.

If she had any self-respect she'd pretend it had never happened too, and carry on as normal instead of being wounded by his subsequent rejection. Or thinking there was a chance they could actually be a couple. When he'd kissed her, all the reasons they shouldn't be together had disappeared. The touch of his lips on hers obliterating all the obstacles she knew they'd have to get over, making them fall away, leaving only her want for him. Without any of the issues that had kept them from moving their friendship on taking up space in her head, she'd had to admit to the attraction and the growing feelings for him.

Now he'd made it clear they weren't reciprocated, she didn't know how to put them back in the box and pretend they'd never existed.

'I'm sorry I put you on the spot, but I thought we should talk about what happened between us.' He kept his eyes trained on the corridor before them, not slowing his pace, as if he wanted this resolved before they reached the doors at the bottom. She wasn't so sure it could all be wrapped up in a few seconds. At least not for her.

The way he spoke about the kiss so casually made her cringe at the significance she'd assigned it. 'It's okay. It doesn't matter.'

Suddenly, faced with the possibility of confronting what had happened, and analysing exactly why he wished he'd never kissed her, Isolde wanted to forget the whole business. This time he did stop, glanced around the corridor and pulled her into an empty cubicle, drawing the curtain around for privacy, but making her feel suffocated by her own embarrassment.

'I'm sorry I kissed you.'

'Yeah, well, I gathered that by the way you left me sitting there then proceeded to ignore me for days on end.' She couldn't keep the sarcasm from her voice, her defence mechanism kicking in as he prepared to spell out exactly why he didn't want her.

Amir visibly flinched. 'I know. I handled things badly.'

Isolde snorted. Handling her was what had got them in this mess in the first place.

'I crossed the line and ruined our friendship. If I've been avoiding you it's because I was embarrassed by my behaviour.'

'Wait, what?' Isolde unfolded her arms from her defensive pose as he presented her with a new scenario.

'You were upset and vulnerable and I took advantage of you. I'm sorry. I don't want to lose you from my life, from Farah's life.'

'Amir, I was well aware of what I was doing, what we were doing. I thought… I thought you regretted kissing me. That that was why you walked away.'

A look of relief transformed Amir's face from a frown into a smile. 'I did, but not in the way you think. You were delicate and I believed I'd acted inappropriately. That's why I left, why I've been too embarrassed to face you.'

Isolde laughed, sharing his relief over their crossed wires. 'In case you're in any doubt, I wanted you to kiss me, Amir. I enjoyed it.'

A deep flush infused his cheeks. 'Okay, then I'm glad we got that sorted.'

For a few seconds they stared at each other in silence with stupid grins on their faces, then reality set in.

'But we can't do it again.' It pained her to say it but the fallout from one little kiss had been too great for them to risk happening again when they were going to be tied together for some time with the wedding, Fahid, and Farah. Their circumstances hadn't changed just because they apparently had some chemistry they'd been suppressing all this time. And what a chemistry. She hadn't been able to put that kiss out of her head since it happened and she doubted she ever would.

Amir nodded his head. 'Agreed. Neither of us are in the right place for anything to happen, and I don't want us to spoil what we've got.'

They stared at each other in silence for a moment, as though in mourning for a relationship they could never have. Yet despite their vow to remain platonic there was still that same tension in the air between them, something waiting to snap. Then it did.

In a sudden frenzy of arms and mouths they were locked in a passionate embrace, kissing harder and with more intensity than the last time their lips had met. Now it was so much more than seeking, and giving, a moment of comfort. A kiss born from that explosion of sexual tension between them, expressing not only that attraction to one another, but feelings they knew they shouldn't be allowing to run amok. And with good reason. This passionate display was intoxicating, all-consuming, and dangerous.

Isolde had been in a relationship before where all common sense went out of the window for the sake of keeping her partner happy. While it was true she was certainly very happy in this very moment, long term she knew it wasn't sustainable. She didn't want to be blinded by her libido. If her past relationship had taught her anything it was that she shouldn't compromise who she was for any man. Amir hadn't tricked her into thinking he was anything but a devoted father so it would be her own fault if she got hurt further down the line when she woke up to the fact he and Farah needed a wife and mother. Roles she'd never wanted and still didn't.

Yet being here in his arms, enveloped in his warmth, his lips on hers, she'd never felt so wanted. Needed. Loved. It was then she realised she had to put a stop to this before it became a habit they couldn't and didn't want to break.

She pulled away from Amir, dizzy from the kiss and the sudden loss of his attentions. When she looked at him, his eyes almost black with desire as he stumbled back, she could see he was as confused and disoriented by the whole situation as she was. This had caught them both by surprise. When he'd asked her to walk with him, to clear the air, she doubted he'd planned on pulling her into a cubicle and kissing them both senseless. It made it all the more dangerous. He didn't have any more control over his emotions than she did, and if one of them didn't call a halt now they'd both end up in trouble. The last thing she wanted was to wreak havoc in his and Farah's lives and hurt them any more, and that was exactly what would happen if they took this any further.

'That's the last time that can happen,' she said, her pulse still racing, her inner wanton screaming, 'No!' at the top of her voice in protest.

The truth was she wanted it to happen again and again, obliterating everything else in the world so all she had to think about were Amir's touch and the taste of him on her lips. That was the problem. Every time he kissed her she forgot the reasons why they shouldn't be doing it and just concentrated on enjoying the moment. Forgetting the fundamental problem that he had a daughter, that he was a man she could never simply entertain a fling with when their lives were so deeply entwined, was pain just waiting to happen.

She didn't want to lose him from her life the way she'd lost everyone else she cared about and that was bound to happen when things inevitably didn't work out. They were too different, their plans for the future on opposite paths. That didn't mean she didn't like him, or wasn't hoping for a miracle that it could all somehow work out. Which was exactly why she had to walk away.

If she couldn't be around him without wanting more than a friendship, then she was going to have to wean herself off him. From now on Amir had to be off limits. No more spontaneous passionate embraces, because the euphoria was always going to give way to the ultimate disappointment when the realisation they couldn't take things any further kicked in. She couldn't carry on waiting for this to happen again, hoping some maternal instinct would take over and she'd feel the need to settle down with a family. But in the end she knew Amir and Farah deserved more than her inevitably letting them down.

When Amir didn't make any move to stop her, she knew he'd likely come to the same conclusion.

CHAPTER FIVE

'OKAY, TEAM. LET'S do this.' Amir rallied everyone in the operating theatre once they knew Fahid was fully under the anaesthetic.

Although, he wasn't feeling as relaxed about the procedure as he'd hoped. Not that he wasn't confident about the surgery—it was something he was very competent and capable in. He had simply hoped that he and Isolde would've cleared the air before he entered the operating theatre. Kissing her again hadn't been in his plans.

Perhaps it was finding out he hadn't crossed the line with her the first time around, that he hadn't misread the situation after all, that had prompted him to do it a second time. It could've been simply that he'd missed her these past days and he'd needed that physical connection to feel whole again. Whatever the reason, he hadn't been able to keep his feelings in check. That overwhelming urge to hold her, to kiss her, to taste her, had consumed him again, and caused him to recklessly act on it.

He wasn't usually the type of person to act on impulse, or in fact to do anything simply because he wanted to. It was in his nature to act appropriately at all times lest he sully the family name, always mulling over the consequences of his actions before he did anything, keeping his reputation as a good son, father, and prince intact. Isolde made him forget all of that, left no time for him to contemplate anything other than his need to have her in his arms. It was his own fault for kissing her in the first place and unleashing all of these feelings, having managed to keep them in check for so long. Now he knew how good it was to kiss her it would be impossible for him to ever erase it from his mind.

It was for the best that it had been Isolde who'd put an end to things because he wasn't sure he would've been capable. When she had come to her senses, he was still lost in the moment and likely would have stayed there for ever if he'd been allowed. Not the actions of a man who was still trying to make it up to his daughter for the last time he'd acted without thinking things through completely. If he'd thought a little more about what a divorce could cost the family and been honest with his wife about how unhappy he was, she would never have driven off with Farah so erratically. He didn't want to make the same mistake again by putting his needs above those of his loved ones.

Farah was more important than any doomed relationship he might hope to pursue with Isolde. He couldn't operate and fix the things preventing her from having a normal life the way he was doing for Fahid, so all he could do was devote himself to making her comfortable. Getting involved with someone she already relied on, a woman who had no desire to be a substitute parent, was not going to improve his daughter's life. If anything, it could make things worse if he took away her ally for his own selfish means.

He looked at Fahid's face, so serene, and totally at his mercy. There was no choice, he supposed, when he was the expert, the one shouldering responsibility for the outcome of this operation.

He made an incision between the boy's ribs and with the aid of a thoracoscope, a small video camera, he was able to remove the lobes. A relatively straightforward procedure for him but one that could change the boy's life dramatically.

It made him think of Farah, the way she relied on him to simply get her through life. Despite all the ways he'd let her down so far.

Amir desperately needed to be the same steady rock for his daughter as he was for this little boy relying on him to make his life better. That wasn't going to happen when he still had eyes on Isolde. It was time for him to back away, to take control of his life the way he did in the operating theatre. Once the wedding was over he needed to get back to a more professional relationship with Isolde. One where Farah's feelings and development were more important than theirs. In the meantime, they had Fahid and the wedding to keep them distracted. Hopefully.

'I know we don't have any of our fancy hospital equipment out here, Farah, but we still need to keep your body strong to maintain what movement you do have.' Isolde had managed to avoid Amir for less than twenty four hours since she had to keep up with Farah's physiotherapy, but at least he'd given them some space today. Putting their personal issues aside so she could focus on her patient.

They had to keep up the strengthening exercises at least so the progress Farah had made so far wouldn't be in vain. With some weight training and aerobic exercises she had at least been able to recover upper-body movement. It was a lot to ask of the young girl every day but to her credit she worked hard, so determined was she to walk again.

'Do you think I could dance at the wedding?' she asked tentatively.

Isolde didn't want to disappoint her but she wanted to be realistic about the chances of that happening. 'Well, you're very adept at your wheelchair now. I think you'll be able to spin and twirl like everyone else on the dance floor.'

'You know what I mean.' Farah watched her through narrowed eyes.

'You won't be able to do anything if you don't do these exercises...'

Farah sighed, but continued with the seated ankle exercises, raising her toes up towards the calf muscles, then relaxing. These days she was able to do more without Isolde's assistance but there was still a long way to go for complete independence of mobility.

She moved on to the marching exercises, starting with both feet on the ground, then lifting up alternate knees. The movement mimicked a walking motion without causing pressure to the joints. Spinal cord injury exercises stimulated the undamaged regions of the spinal cord as well as strengthening the pathways that controlled movement, which was why it was important to stick to the routine.

'Can I try the treadmill?' Farah asked once she'd completed the reps.

'We don't have the harness to support your body weight. I'm not sure it would be such a good idea.' Isolde didn't want any injuries to set back her recovery or upset Amir.

'Can't I try? I'll be careful. I promise.'

Isolde knew it was the one time Farah felt as though she were actually walking again and she didn't want to do anything that might upset her. 'I suppose we could keep it on the lowest setting and I could walk behind you.'

The little girl's smile was the incentive to make it work. Even if they only managed a couple of steps she knew it would please Farah and give her a sense of achievement. If she stumbled at all Isolde would switch off the machine.

She helped Farah out of her chair, grateful that the arm exercises had given the girl the strength to support her body weight on the hand rails. Isolde positioned herself directly behind Farah, hoping they wouldn't both end up in a heap on the floor. She turned on the treadmill and made sure it was at the lowest, slowest setting. For the first few steps she nudged the backs of Farah's knees with hers to promote the walking movement but in no time at all Farah managed to do it on her own.

'I'm doing it!' she cried out, the excitement and effort present in every trembling limb.

'You're amazing, Farah.' She was a truly remarkable little girl who'd put in more work than a lot of Isolde's older patients to achieve these spectacular results.

When she could see Farah starting to tire, her shaky

steps not quite keeping pace with the machine, she decided to call it a day.

'I'm going to turn the treadmill off now, Farah, okay. We can do some more tomorrow.'

When Farah didn't argue she knew this new milestone had taken an extra effort. Isolde took her time transferring her back into her wheelchair even though she was bubbling with excitement.

'I can't wait to tell your father. He's going to be so proud.' She could only imagine how happy it would make Amir to see his little girl walk again. Even though it was baby steps at the moment, it augured well for the future. She knew all he wanted was for his daughter to be happy again, and hopefully it would alleviate some of that unnecessary guilt he was carrying.

Although things between them were complicated, Isolde still cared about Amir, and wanted only the best for him and his daughter. The lapses of judgement that kept finding them falling onto one another's mouths was an inconvenience, a consequence of spending so much time with someone she admired so greatly. They really needed to be careful before one, or both, of them got hurt. It wasn't as though they were young, free and single to carry on how they liked. They had complications and weighty baggage, which made anything long term impossible. For now, however, they had to maintain a united front for the family's sake and she wasn't sure how keeping secrets would impact on their already unstable relationship.

'Can't we keep it a secret? I want to surprise him at the wedding.'

'I don't know, Farah, it doesn't seem right to keep this from him.'

Isolde could see why she would want to surprise him but she wasn't comfortable with the idea of keeping secrets from Amir when it came to his daughter. He was fiercely protective and invested in Farah's recovery and he might see it as a betrayal of trust for her physiotherapist to keep this information from him. There was also the manner in which Farah intended to reveal the news to him. Doing it in a very public environment added extra pressure on her to replicate those few precious independent steps and Isolde didn't want the little girl to end up embarrassed or hurt if things didn't go to plan. Certainly that was something Amir would never forgive her for.

'Please, Isolde.' Those familiar big brown eyes, so much like her father's, were able to persuade Isolde to do anything.

That was how she knew she was in so much mess already.

'I need you to cough for me, Fahid. If we can't keep your airways clear it can lead to infection,' Isolde told the boy, trying once more to coax him into his exercises. He'd been co-operative at the hospital but now, four days later, he was home, and a little more resistant.

'It hurts…'

'Now, Fahid, you know Isolde and I only want you to get better. If you do these exercises now, you'll be back on your feet in no time. It's all to help you breathe easier so you can be active for longer periods of time.' Amir sat down beside him on the sofa so he was at eye level, speaking to the boy as a friend rather than his surgeon or an authoritative adult figure. He had a way with children, and all of his patients. Isolde too at times.

He made it seem as though they were very much a team when they were working together in situations like this. Often her job could be isolating, when she worked independently from the doctors and nurses. Of course she had to liaise with medical teams to get an overall view of a patient's treatment, and sometimes it took another colleague to help her with certain patients, but mostly she worked alone. It was nice to have someone to play off against to get a patient's co-operation, and to get a clearer picture of a patient's journey.

She usually focused on the aftercare, but having Amir to explain what Fahid had gone through in surgery gave her a greater insight into what he'd gone through thus far. As well as reminding her of the incredible job Amir did on a daily basis. Carrying out major surgery on such a young patient should not be something taken for granted and it was only treated as unremarkable because of the effortless, efficient way Amir carried out these life-enhancing, sometimes life-saving procedures.

Since Olly, she'd strived for a greater independence, afraid of anyone else trying to change who she was. Even living with Soraya had been challenging at times, regardless that her sister had cooked and cleaned for her like old times. She'd got used to being on her own, and she'd had to once Soraya had moved to Zaki. Now she was beginning to see the benefits of having someone else around.

Amir never tried to take over, only ever to assist, to try and make things easier for her. He didn't attempt to change her or threaten her independence. Instead, he showed her what a difference a supportive partner could make. Even if it was only in a professional capacity.

Perhaps some day she would even venture to share her personal life with someone again if they could show the same kind of respect for her that Amir did. It was a shame being with him in particular would mean compromising who she was and what she wanted all over again.

'Okay, Fahid, I want you to take a big deep breath slowly in through your nose. Hold for two seconds then breath slowly out through your mouth. We're going to repeat this five times.' Isolde coached him through his breathing exercises, working towards strengthening his lungs to get them functioning at full capacity again.

'It won't be long before you're playing football again,' Amir added, making the boy's smile wider than ever and persuading him it was in his best interests to co-operate.

They'd decided, in order to make him more comfortable, they'd do their follow-up visits at home, where his mother could be present, and his surroundings would be less intimidating. It was best for Fahid and his mother, but awkward for her and Amir given their current circumstances.

After yet another lapse into forbidden territory—Amir's lips—she should have been trying harder than ever to keep her distance from him, but now they simply had more reason to be spending time together. As though fate were conspiring to torture her by repeatedly pushing him into her eyeline.

He looked good today, as always. When visiting Fahid he kept it casual—no tie, shirt collar open and sleeves rolled up over his thick forearms. Total Isolde bait. She supposed it was an attempt to be more laid-back around their young patient, less formal, and therefore less intimidating. Everything Amir did was calculated to maximise the benefit towards others. That was why those spontaneous passionate clinches they kept falling into seemed so out of character for him.

She confessed, the idea that she could inspire such impulsive behaviour in him did little to quell her ardent admiration for him. There was something inherently sexy in making a man lose control like that in his pursuit of her. It was reciprocated, of course, but she had been known in the past for her reckless tendencies. Amir, on the other hand, had apparently lived the life of a saint. His only crime, according to him, was failing to make his marriage work. That made her feel like a wanton hussy, seducing him away from his life of order and best behaviour. Except she hadn't encouraged anything until he'd kissed her. Then all bets were off. How was she supposed to have resisted such undisguised lust from a man she'd apparently been harbouring a secret crush on for the best part of the year?

She didn't know when she'd crossed that line from respecting him at work, admiring his devotion to his daughter, and enjoying his company, to wanting him to kiss her as if they'd just hooked up in the alley behind a dive bar. But it was apparent there was no going back.

Despite their best intentions, trying to remain emotionally and physically distant, except when treating Fahid, it wasn't going to erase the memories or the feelings she had towards him. She hadn't said anything yet through fear

of upsetting anyone before the wedding, but she might
have to pass Farah's care on to someone else when they
got back home. The last thing she wanted to do was upset
the little girl, or set back her recovery in any way. However, she wanted the best for her, and that might have
to be a different physiotherapist. One who wouldn't be
mooning over her father.

The journey here hadn't been the most comfortable,
despite the luxury car they'd travelled in. Making small
talk, trying to keep to the safe topic of their mutual patient, had been stilted and unnatural. Mostly because
there was so much other, personal stuff they had apparently decided they didn't need to discuss. Those kisses,
the unresolved feelings they clearly had for one another,
hung in the air between them. That crackling electricity making it a real possibility that they could suddenly
launch themselves at one another at any given moment
for a repeat performance. Perhaps that was why he'd
squeezed himself into the furthest corner of the car away
from her.

It was this kind of behaviour, this tension, that made
working together long term completely untenable.

'Thanks again for doing this. I feel like a lottery win-
ner having members of the royal family coming into my
home to tend to my boy.' Fahid's mother had been effu-
sive with her gratitude from the moment they'd walked
in the door. This was partially for her benefit too so she
would feel as though she was involved with her son's
treatment and wasn't completely powerless as it all happened around her. Isolde knew something about that.
From the moment her parents had died she didn't think

she'd had much of a say in anything. It had taken until that make-or-break talk with Olly for her to finally stand up and speak her mind, assert her autonomy over her own body, and life, by telling him she didn't want children under any circumstances.

She was sure when Fahid's mother had decided to have a family she hadn't expected it to be this way. There'd been no plan for his father to die and leave her as a single parent, or for her own health problems to impact on her son's life. This was exactly what Isolde wanted to avoid—somehow ending up causing her child the pain she and Soraya had gone through during their childhood. She was making sure she wasn't going to be responsible for inflicting this sort of pain.

It was obvious this woman loved her son, that he was her life. There were happy, smiling photographs of the pair all over the flat, and his toys littered the floor. But it was also apparent that he had the weight of responsibility that no child his age should have to endure. In her haste to welcome Isolde and Amir, Fahid's mother had directed him to make tea, offer them food, and tidy up to make room for them. All of which they'd protested against, of course. This was his life, but it shouldn't have to be.

'Not at all. We're here in our professional capacity,' Amir reminded her, probably trying to avoid the usual bowing and scraping that went on any time he met a member of the public, who all seemed as enamoured with him as Isolde. Almost.

'And strictly speaking I'm not a member of the royal family so there's definitely no need to stand on ceremony for me,' Isolde added.

'Thank you all the same,' Fahid's mother insisted. 'I don't know where I'd be without Fahid.' Her voice wobbled with emotion and Isolde considered how much the woman must've fretted over her son's health problems and the effect it could have had on both of them. He was her lifeline and her link to the outside world. All of the mobility aids dotted around, and the fact she hadn't come to the door to greet them, suggested her movements were limited. Hopefully now Fahid had gone through his surgery and they were working on his recovery, he would find an improvement in his quality of life that would filter through to his mother too.

'My sister said she was trying to get some help for you at home. Have you had anyone contact you?' It was another way of relieving Fahid's burden at home and Isolde knew Soraya was keen to give him the sort of childhood she'd been denied because of her duty to family. If it came to it, Isolde wouldn't be surprised if her sister came out and cooked and cleaned for the family if it meant Fahid had more chance to go out and play, and just be a little boy.

'Yes. We're going to have someone coming out several times a day to help me around the house and cook us some dinner. It's going to make such a difference to both of us.' The gratitude and optimism over the change was apparent in Fahid's mother's smile, and it made Isolde suddenly well up.

It was emotional for Isolde knowing that they'd been able to bring some positive changes to help this little family, and she knew that was all Soraya wanted too.

'I'll let Soraya know. She was very keen to get everyone involved to help you both, as was Raed.' She thought of the initial introduction they'd had to Fahid and the impact it had on Amir. It was bound to be on his mind every time he followed up on Fahid's progress that his own daughter hadn't been so fortunate, that her problems couldn't be solved with a few phone calls and favours. If all she'd needed was a dedicated surgeon and someone who cared she would have been cured a long time ago.

Isolde had been continuing in private with Farah's exercises since they'd flown out while Amir had been dealing with family matters and Fahid. Isolde's first instinct had been to run and fetch Amir to witness that first breakthrough, knowing it was everything he'd been striving for, but Farah had asked her not to. Her continued progress made it harder not to share the news with him.

She got the impression the little girl was afraid to get her father's hopes up in case it didn't happen again. Neither of them had wanted to put her under pressure to 'perform', especially with the wedding coming up. There was the possibility that the 'establishment', the PR managers behind the scenes concerned with the family's appearance, might prefer if she ditched the wheelchair for aesthetic reasons if she could, but it wouldn't have been fair to expect so much from her during such a spectacle. Instead, they had continued working on those first baby steps in private. Today Farah had managed a stilted walk a little farther and both of them had been fit to burst from the excitement.

It felt wrong not to share such a huge development with Amir, but she had to put Farah's needs first. Strictly speaking she wasn't on the work clock so she didn't think it would pose a risk to her job by keeping the information from him. Although there was a moral question. She could only hope things worked out the way Farah wanted and he would be so happy he'd forgive Isolde for her part in the deceit.

'Everything seems to be healing as it should. We'll keep an eye on Fahid while we're in the country, but when we head back to the UK we'll have to hand over his care to another team. Don't worry though, they'll be under strict orders from the royal family to look after him,' Amir joked after he'd finished his examination of Fahid.

Both he and Isolde made their move to leave.

'We'll see ourselves out. Don't get up. It was very nice to meet you.' Isolde shook hands with the woman and Amir followed.

'Thank you for everything. We're so privileged to have had your help this far, and thank your family for all they've done for us. You have no idea how much it means to us.' Fahid's mother shuffled to the edge of the sofa and grabbed them both into a hug.

Isolde knew all too well how much their assistance had changed the lives of this family. It had given them some independence, and hopefully Fahid would get to have more of a childhood. Everything she wished someone had given to her sister when they were younger. Still, she couldn't change history and making a difference to someone else's life was the next best thing.

Once they'd said their goodbyes, she and Amir got back into the car. She slumped onto the back seat and closed her eyes, emotionally drained by the visit.

'Are you okay?'

The sound of Amir's voice filled the back of the car and filtered through the fog in Isolde's head.

'I'm not the one who's just gone through major surgery, or who struggles to do anything without physical help.'

Okay, so she was a little tetchy as they walked away knowing it was probably the last time she'd see them again, their problems no longer hers to worry about. She didn't feel good about walking away even though Fahid and his mother seemed happy enough with the way things had gone. As though her conscience should be salved now she'd done her bit and they were no longer her concern.

How many times had Soraya had visits from do-gooders who'd promised the world only for them never to be heard of again? Too many to mention. She didn't want to be one of those fake people, but there was nothing she could do about it unless she prolonged her stay in the country. Something that would not go down well with her boss or her landlord. The only thing she could do was ask Soraya to keep her up to date on their progress and offer virtual assistance from afar if needed.

'I know, but it's clear it had an effect on you.' Amir spoke softly, gently, as though he were talking to an easily spooked horse, trying to tame her before she lashed out again.

It wasn't his fault that she couldn't handle being reminded of the bad old days left to Soraya to fend for them when their parents had gone, or the fact she had to go home. These past few days feeling as though she had her family back, of being part of something, had been great. She wasn't looking forward to returning home alone.

'Yes, well, I'm a big girl. I'll get over it.' She had to

or she'd end up bitter and twisted, resenting the fact that she couldn't do more for others, or make things work with him.

'It's just…working with Fahid is bringing up a lot of emotional issues for both of us. You were there for me when I had my wobble.' He gave her a coy smile that said he was embarrassed over the whole affair, his emotional outburst at the centre that day having been the catalyst for all the subsequent trouble between them. 'I just want you to know I'm here if you need to talk.'

'Thanks, but I'll be okay,' she said, and forced her face to reverse the frown etched on her forehead so he wouldn't think there was anything wrong.

If there was one thing she didn't need right now it was Amir being nice to her, being sympathetic and showing an understanding of the issues from her past that she was only just coming to terms with herself.

It was becoming clear that the more she was around him, the more reasons she had to like him, which in these circumstances wasn't a good thing. This wedding couldn't come soon enough so she could do her duty as Soraya's sister, celebrate her nuptials, then get the hell out of Amir's orbit before things got completely out of control.

CHAPTER SIX

'Nervous?'

'A bit. Although I'm not sure I'm the one who's supposed to need reassurance today. You have to be the most laid-back bride I've ever seen, Soraya. No one would ever guess you're about to marry into the royal family before the eyes of the world. Are you on drugs?'

Soraya laughed. 'No drugs. I'm just happy to be marrying the love of my life.'

Isolde couldn't believe her sister was this relaxed on her wedding day without some sort of sedative to keep her from flailing around. Worked up about appearing in public, Isolde had already had a breakdown over her wayward locks and smudged mascara, and she was only background crew. Her anxiety over the forthcoming day had caused her stomach to roll so much she hadn't been able to touch the champagne breakfast that had been laid out for them this morning, and she was only the bridesmaid.

Mind you, she had a lot on her mind. Including the prospect of spending the day in Amir's company, something they'd both learned wasn't a good idea these days. Left unsupervised they tended to get a bit carried away. Perhaps it was a blessing in disguise they'd be surrounded by photographers and film crews for most of the day.

Hopefully it should remove that temptation of throwing themselves at one another if there was a danger of someone catching it on camera. They'd have some explaining to do to a lot of people if they were caught in a compromising position.

There was also the matter of Farah's planned surprise. Although it was scheduled to happen during the evening reception, which would be held for family and friends only, away from the press, there was a lot at stake. She didn't want anyone to be embarrassed or disappointed if things didn't work out the way they hoped, especially Amir and Farah. Nor did she want Amir to be mad at her for keeping his daughter's secret. There was a separate anxiety swirling around her body at how Amir was going to react and if she was going to be in the firing line. Given that he was a senior member of the royal family, there was a real possibility she'd committed some sort of treason, and a firing squad might be seen as just punishment for a Jezebel who kept kissing the widowed Prince and was now interfering in family matters.

'I'm so happy for you, sis. You look beautiful.' That happiness she spoke of was radiating out of her every pore, her love for Raed shining brightly on her face.

'Well, I did have a team of stylists.' Soraya screwed up her nose, batting away any compliments, but she couldn't convince Isolde she was anything but stunning today.

Her ivory silk dress clung beautifully to her curves, though preserved her modesty with the lace collar and sleeves. She was every inch the fairy-tale princess.

'We had the same team and I do not even compare. I think I have so many pins in my hair trying to keep it in place they're embedded in my scalp, and I think you mistakenly assigned me a make-up artist who usually works on drag queens.'

They were standing in front of the huge crystal-encrusted mirror in the suite the hotel had given them to get ready in. The team who had brushed and primped and squeezed them into submission had gone now so Isolde assumed it was safe to assert some damage control.

She took a tissue and began to wipe carefully at the heavy dark eye make-up and blusher staining her pale complexion. It was too much, too bold, for someone who usually got by with some lip gloss and face powder.

Soraya gave her a gentle push. 'It's not that bad, but you don't need it.'

She took the tissue and dabbed it on her tongue to wipe away the excess eyeliner, making Isolde grin.

'What's so funny?' Soraya demanded to know.

'This. It's just like being a kid again when I came in covered in dirt from playing outside and you'd take a handkerchief and scrub my face with it.'

Not all the memories of growing up were bad but they tended to fade into the background against the struggles they'd faced. Soraya had been her mother, father and grandmother figure all rolled into one. The one who'd cleaned her up, mopped her tears and baked for her. Doing all she could to give Isolde as normal a childhood as possible despite their circumstances.

Soraya's smile was a little wobbly. 'We did it, didn't we? Despite everything, we made it through. Who would've thought we'd end up hobnobbing with royalty?

I'm proud of you, Isolde, for everything you've become, helping Farah and Fahid. Thank you for being my sister.'

All the emotion Isolde had been trying to hold at bay today was suddenly rushing up to meet Soraya's outpouring, and she gulped in an attempt to keep it away for a little longer.

'Don't start crying! You'll set me off, and we don't want to be walking down that aisle looking like two demented pandas. Raed will run a mile.' Isolde managed to turn Soraya's sentimental sob into a hiccup-laugh.

She cleared her throat and dabbed her eyes. 'You're right. The tears can wait until you have to go home and I'm forced to say goodbye to you.'

Isolde didn't want to think about that. It wasn't going to help stem this tidal wave of sorrow and loss threatening to drown her when she thought how long it might be before she saw her sister again. Of course, there would be visits and family celebrations, but it was never going to be just the two of them again. As selfish as it sounded, and as happy as she was that her sister had found her soulmate, she couldn't help think about where it left her, without her sister to guide her and keep her out of trouble.

'Hey, it's not goodbye, it's *au revoir* for now,' Isolde managed to say through the unshed tears, trying to lighten the mood with some cheese.

'You're such a dork sometimes.' Soraya sniffed through a laugh, but Isolde had successfully helped to avoid another make-up catastrophe.

'Yes, but people love me for it. Now, where is the remaining member of our little girl band?' She and Soraya had got ready together. It had given them some much-needed sister time, which there hadn't been a lot of recently. There wasn't a lot of opportunity for the two of them to be on their own when there was so much going on at the palace, and this made today even more special.

'Farah's with Djamila getting ready. She should be here any minute. I assume Raed and Amir are having their heart-to-heart talk too. I know he's not looking forward to saying goodbye either.' Soraya slipped into her matching ivory silk heels and stood in front of the mirror again as she put her earrings in.

'Yes, I know Amir is missing his family, as is Farah. Wait, I've got something for you.' Isolde rushed off to grab the tatty blue velvet box from her bag, which she'd brought from home, and presented it to her sister.

'Mum's necklace?' Soraya traced her fingers over the pearl necklace nestled in the silky lining.

'You don't have to wear it, but I thought it could be your something borrowed.' They didn't have a lot of keepsakes from their parents. For as long as she could remember they'd been ill, unable to work, with little money coming in to buy nice things. Though they'd always found money for their cigarettes. The necklace had always been precious to Isolde. Despite being the eldest, Soraya had passed it on to her when their mother had died. A selfless gesture she was forever grateful for when it gave her something tangible of her mother. A memory other than sickness. She remembered her mother wearing it, seeing it nestled around her neck when she bent down to kiss Isolde at night. At least now Isolde was able to give a little piece of their mother back on this special occasion.

'Thank you,' Soraya said as she fastened the pearls

around her neck. 'It will feel like I have Mum with me today in some small way.'

Sometimes Isolde forgot how much of an impact their parents' death had had on her older sister beyond the financial difficulties it had left. Isolde had been too young to really comprehend what had happened at the time, and had simply substituted Soraya into that parenting role, even though she'd been barely an adult at eighteen, too young to parent another child. In hindsight it was Soraya who'd perhaps suffered the greater loss, and had to set her grief aside to look after her sibling. Lending her their mother's necklace on her wedding day was the least she could do.

Isolde gave her a hug, careful not to crease her beautiful dress before she made her grand entrance.

'I wish you could stay,' Soraya said on a sigh. 'I mean long term. Amir and Farah too.'

'And give up my amazing flat? Impossible.' Although she wasn't being serious, the dream remained out of reach. As much as she wished they could be one big happy family living the life of luxury out here, it wasn't going to happen. Her time out here had told Isolde one thing and that was she needed to put more distance between her and Amir, not entangle their lives even further.

'Is there something going on with you and Amir?' As always Soraya seemed to see right through her, but this wasn't the time to get into the latest mess she'd got herself into. Even Super Sis couldn't get her out of this one and it wasn't fair to even involve her now, when she should be focusing on getting married. This was her wedding day, not another 'Isolde screws up and I have to fix it' day. They'd both grown up and finally cut those apron strings and it wouldn't be fair to either of them to try and reattach them now.

So she lied.

'No. Not at all. I've just been spending a lot of time at his place getting Farah's input with these dresses. I think the girl really has a future in fashion, you know.' She tried to change the subject but she could see by Soraya's face she wasn't buying it, or willing to move on.

'It's just…there's a bit of an atmosphere between you. Raed's noticed it too. You seemed so relaxed in each other's company at that afternoon tea we had in the hotel, and now… I don't know, it's as if you can't stand to be in the same room as one another now.'

Isolde shrugged. 'You know me, I always outstay my welcome. Perhaps he got fed up with me coming around so often. It doesn't matter now, does it? The dresses are finished so I won't have to go round to his any more.'

'Hmm… Well, whatever it is, I hope it's not influencing your decision not to move out here. You know I'd love to have you stay.'

'Hey, there's only room for one princess in this family and that's you. Now, I think we've kept your husband-to-be waiting long enough. Let's go get your gorgeous flower girl and roll.'

The only thing rolling was Soraya's eyes. 'Just so you know, we're not done with this. I have the small matter of marrying the Crown Prince to take care of, but believe me, Isolde Yarrow, I will get to the bottom of whatever is going on with you.'

'Yes, ma'am.' Isolde gave her a mock salute, treating her promise lightly.

During their childhood Isolde had folded easily under Soraya's interrogation, and always ended up spilling her guts, forced to face the consequences. She suspected the same would be true now, even though they weren't talking about a broken ornament or some stolen sweets she had to confess to. This was about her feelings for Amir, something she wasn't ready to face up to herself yet. The prospect of doing so, and with her sister, should have been terrifying, but Isolde remained relatively calm. Because once the ceremony was over she was going home and leaving the whole royal family behind her. It was the only way to survive.

Amir's hands were sweaty, he was swaying on his feet, and his heart was pounding. Yet he wasn't even the one getting married. He'd been through this before and hadn't felt this nervous. His wedding had been every bit as grand and well attended, with almost the same press interest, but he'd felt in control then. With a life mapped out before him, marrying the right woman and securing his rightful place in the royal family. It was all a lie of course, but he hadn't realised at the time it was all part of trying to be the perfect son and prince. Now he had no idea what the future held for him or Farah.

If anything this past year had helped him understand why Raed had planned to abandon his position once upon a time. It was too much pressure. Especially now he had Farah to think about. There was nothing more important to him than her welfare. That was why he hadn't pursued Isolde any further when she'd pushed him away, even though he'd wanted to. He knew spending time with Fahid was difficult, it was for him too for different reasons. All he'd done was try and reach out to her, to offer some support, but it was clear she didn't want anything to do with him any more. It was probably for the best when anything more between them than Farah's welfare would be sure to end in tears.

'Are they coming yet?' Raed whispered to him, his eyes trained firmly on the front of the church, showing great restraint.

Amir cast a glance over his shoulder as the organ began to play. 'They're beautiful.'

Soraya looked stunning as she made her way towards them, her veil coyly covering her face, her body sheathed in silk. But it was her bridesmaids who'd captured his attention first. Isolde was pushing Farah's wheelchair, which had been wrapped in ribbon and flowers, both wearing full-length pale green dresses that perfectly matched the colour of his tunic. It was the first time he'd been allowed to see what they'd been working so hard on and he was astounded by what they'd produced.

The pair had enjoyed keeping their secrets, giggling and whispering on those evenings when Isolde had come over and shared dinner with them. The only clues he'd garnered were the fabric samples he'd found on occasion, offcuts from where Isolde had altered the dresses after one of their fittings. The surprise was worth the wait. They both looked incredible, and so happy. He knew Farah wanted to keep her legs covered to hide the scars she'd been left with since the accident, but Isolde had opted to wear the same design, probably so she wouldn't feel self-conscious. If he'd thought he wouldn't make a spectacle of himself he'd have run over and hugged them both, he was so proud. Instead, all he could do was smile as they came to stand across the aisle from him and Raed. Isolde smiled back at him.

You look fabulous, he mouthed, managing to refrain from giving a chef's kiss and completely embarrassing everyone in public.

Thank you, she mouthed back, giving a little curtsey.

Seeing Farah so happy, and with the knowledge Isolde hadn't requested a personal exclusion zone so he couldn't be within a hundred feet of her, he was able to relax a little bit. He preferred it when they were able to joke around with one another rather than getting upset and finding excuses to stay away from one another. Sometimes he almost wished they could go back to the time before they'd realised they liked kissing one another.

Soraya turned and handed her bouquet to Isolde, then faced Raed, who lifted her veil. When his brother saw his bride properly for the first time, Amir could see he was about to lose it. He knew the feeling, but he was also aware that the eyes of the world were upon them. Amir placed a hand at his brother's back, silently urging him to hold it together. Raed straightened up, cleared his throat, and Amir hoped the moment had passed for both of them as the ceremony began.

He listened along with the rest of the people there as Raed and Soraya said their vows. It was only when they reached the 'Till death do us part', bit that he got a tad overwhelmed. Those feelings of guilt and regret that always tended to show up when he thought of the accident, and the way his marriage had come to a traumatic end, made him think of his own vows. He'd meant every word when he'd said them, but he didn't think he'd married for the right reasons. Certainly, he didn't remember looking at his wife the way Raed looked at Soraya, as if his whole life depended on being with her.

He felt more like that about Isolde than he ever had about his wife, which was what made the whole situation so difficult. Farah was so fond of her, and she'd done so much to help his daughter rediscover her confidence, he didn't want to lose her, but he also knew that it would be painful to be around her every day knowing they couldn't be together. Isolde was most definitely not the right woman for him, but she was the one he still wanted. As always he'd do whatever was right for his daughter and today he'd simply have to set his own needs aside and enjoy the day. It might be the last time they were all together and it was a celebration of his brother finding his soul mate. Something that didn't always work out for everyone else.

'Doesn't Papa look handsome today?' Farah broke the silence in the car only to make things even more awkward.

Yes, Amir looked handsome enough in his silk tunic and trousers that she could certainly have wished away the entire congregation and dragged him into the cloisters for a snog, but she certainly couldn't say that. Not to Farah, nor her father, if they were all to get through this day unscathed.

'No one is looking at me when they have such beautiful dresses to admire. You both look wonderful and I'm so proud of you.' Amir reached across the back seat to hug his daughter, thus successfully changing the subject so Isolde could avoid being put on the spot.

Isolde thought he deserved to be told how pretty he looked today too. 'Yes, your papa is very handsome, Farah. I'm sure there will be a queue of ladies waiting to add him to their dance card tonight.'

The thought of it made her queasy. Poor, hot widower Amir was having the spotlight shone on him today and she had no doubt it would earn him a new team of admirers who would willingly throw themselves at him in the hope of catching his attention. She'd done it herself on occasion, which was why she'd been using Farah as a barrier between them all day, emotionally and physically. Given their positions in the wedding, spending time together today had been inevitable, but at least they'd had Farah to fuss over and keep them from focusing on the lingering glances they kept throwing one another.

It had been a big day for all of them already with the televised ceremony, the official photographs and the reception. Now they were on their way to the evening reception back at the palace where they could let their hair down away from prying eyes and the pressure to be on their best behaviour would finally be off.

Although she could quite happily just crawl into bed and bypass it altogether she was so exhausted. Perhaps she could sneak off after the happy couple had their first dance. Soraya and Raed were so wrapped up in each other she doubted she'd be missed anyway. Not that she begrudged either of them the joy they'd clearly found in one another when life hadn't been easy up until now, especially for Soraya. However, she'd be lying if she said there wasn't a green-eyed monster waiting in the wings watching them declare their love for one another and wishing for the impossible, wishing someone could love her unconditionally too. Where not wanting to traumatise another generation would be respected, not seen as a fatal flaw in a relationship.

'I'm afraid I'll be booked up all night with my favourite girl.' He hugged Farah a little tighter and went some way to taming Isolde's wild jealousy. Perhaps she wouldn't have to resist a catfight on the dance floor after all.

'I don't mind if you want to dance with Isolde, Papa.' Farah's generous offer to share her father with Isolde was touching, but it also raised more red flags. As if they needed any more.

'That's okay, Farah. I'm not much of a dancer. I wouldn't want to embarrass your dad.' Nor would she want anyone to get the wrong impression. Soraya was already suspicious something was going on and she was sure the two of them slow-dancing would give away just how close they'd become. She was sure she wasn't a good enough actress to pretend being in Amir's arms wasn't exactly where she wanted to be.

'Papa wouldn't be embarrassed, would you, Papa?' There was something in the way Farah looked up at her father, as though she was desperate for the two of them to be together, that really set alarm bells ringing for Isolde.

Amir glanced at her over the top of his daughter's head, a frown deepening across his forehead. He clearly didn't know what had brought this on either. 'Of course

I wouldn't be embarrassed to dance with Isolde but we don't force anyone to do anything they're not comfortable with, do we, sweetheart?'

'Yes, but I know Isolde wants to dance with you, so that's okay.' Farah sat back in her seat, arms folded, very confident in her belief.

Isolde saw her worried expression reflected in Amir's face, both of them clearly wondering how she'd come to that conclusion. Whether Isolde had inadvertently said or done something to indicate that, or Farah had decided she wanted to push them together, it was a concerning development. It felt as though Farah was trying to matchmake between them, and Isolde didn't want to break her heart along with her own when she had to go home and leave them behind. Although it was flattering that the little girl saw her as a romantic interest for her father, it wouldn't do to let her get carried away by the notion.

Things were difficult enough between Isolde and Amir, trying to dodge their own feelings because of the repercussions their actions could have, without figuring Farah's feelings into the equation too. Neither of them would ever dream of hurting her, and that was exactly the reason they'd tried to keep what had happened between them under wraps.

Isolde had even kept the details of their kisses from Soraya though she was fit to burst with the secret, dying to share with someone about how much she'd enjoyed every second. All in vain apparently, if Farah had picked up on the tension between them. They hadn't been as discreet as they'd assumed if everyone around them could sense something was amiss. All the more reason to get some distance between them quick. Once they were back to their own lives, away from the glare of publicity and watchful family members, hopefully all interest in their private feelings would die down. Even if the actual emotions involved might take longer to dissipate, if at all.

They let the matter drop rather than fuel whatever fantasy Farah was harbouring. Isolde prayed that the surprise Farah had in store for her father would take her mind off anything else. If all went to plan everyone would be distracted and maybe that would even be the time for Isolde to slip away undetected.

Suddenly the sound of screeching brakes filled the air and the car lurched forward, pushing all three of them violently forward. Then they were spinning. Isolde grabbed hold of the edge of her seat with one hand, and Farah with the other. Amir too was doing his best to shield her, one arm stretched out across her, trying to keep her back in her seat.

The spinning and the squealing of tyres trying to get purchase on the tarmac seemed to last an eternity, but it was probably only seconds before the car came to a shuddering standstill.

'Are you two okay?' Amir's concern for them both was immediate.

'I'm fine. Farah, are you hurt?' Isolde gave her a brief check over and, while there were no obvious injuries, the little girl was sobbing hard.

Amir undid her seat belt and gathered her up into his arms. 'Shh, sweetheart. Everyone's all right.'

It was then Isolde realised the trauma this must be bringing back to the little girl after the accident that had cost her her mobility and her mother. 'I'll go and see what happened but we're all okay, Farah.'

Amir looked as though he was going to stop her then thought better of it, simply nodding as she tried to get her door open. It took brute force and a shoulder-bump to finally wrench it ajar wide enough to try and shimmy out. The vehicle was wedged up against a tree, the car door taking the brunt of the impact. She managed to wriggle the top half of her body out of the gap and planted her hands on the car roof to lever the rest of her body out. The fabric of her dress ripped as she forced her hips through the gap, and she winced as the jagged metal where the door had been damaged grazed along her skin.

'Isolde, are you okay? Do you need me to come out?' Amir asked, apparently having witnessed her minor injury.

'No. I'm fine. You stay with Farah until I can get some help,' she said through gritted teeth, willing the sharp pain away.

Given the occasion, and the people involved, she was sure it wouldn't be long before help arrived, even though they were out in the country. They'd been in a convoy of cars following the royal carriage containing Soraya and Raed. Quite the spectacle. Whatever had caused the accident she was sure it wouldn't go unnoticed. Especially when they were due at the palace.

Once she managed to squeeze herself free, collapsing in a heap on the grass verge in a very undignified manner, she was able to see something of what had occurred. A motorcycle belonging to one of the police outriders was lying across the road. The glare of a hi-vis jacket lying under the car in front was stomach-churning but explained why their driver had swerved so suddenly, trying to avoid a further accident.

She got to her feet and saw Amir's parents being led over to the side of the road, seemingly uninjured but understandably shaken.

'Are you okay? What about Soraya and Raed?' There was no sign of the other cars or carriage, which had been in front.

'We're okay and I don't think the others even know what's happened, they were so far ahead of us. It's that poor policeman who's been hurt.' Djamila was visibly upset and Isolde guessed that she'd witnessed the accident.

'Amir and Farah are in the back of the car if you want to see them. They're fine but we're trying to keep her calm. I think it's brought back a lot of difficult memories for her. I'll go and see what I can do to help here.' Isolde left them and rushed over to where a small crowd had gathered on the ground around the injured outrider.

'Can I help?' she asked, kneeling down on the road, every speck of gravel digging into the skin on her knees through what was left of her flimsy dress. Not that it mattered. The pain was simply a reminder that she was alive. The shock and whatever other after-effects of the crash were still to manifest would likely show up later once the adrenaline had worn off. For now, however, she was simply glad that all of her loved ones were safe.

'Sweetheart, you'll be safe with your grandparents. I know this is scary but we're all okay. I need to go and help the man that was injured.' Amir didn't want to leave Farah, he knew this was bringing back so many bad memories, but he also knew there was someone out there who needed him more right now. His mother and father had recounted the accident to him and the fact that Isolde was out there dealing with everything on her own.

'In case he has a little girl who needs him too?' Farah asked, her big wide eyes tugging violently on his heartstrings. It was apparent that she was worried some other innocent child was about to lose a parent and have her world turned upside down. Not if he could help it.

'Exactly,' he said, swallowing down all that love he had for his daughter for now so he could provide some assistance. Later, once he knew he'd done everything he could, he might just hug her and never let go.

Farah nodded and went to his mother, freeing him to leave the relative comfort and safety of the car. He found Isolde halfway under the car in front tending to the accident victim.

'What can I do to help?' He ducked his head under the chassis of the car to offer his assistance.

Isolde turned slightly to see him, her face smeared with dirt and grease. 'This is Mike. The front wheels of the car have gone over him. He's conscious, pulse is a little fast, breathing is a little shallow, and he's experiencing serious pain in his chest. He can't move his hand. It looks as though his fingers have been crushed.'

'The paramedics will be able to give you something for that pain when they get here. In the meantime, let's try and make you more comfortable.' Easier said than done given the circumstances as it was difficult to get access to the patient and assess his condition. Crush injuries had a high risk of death if not treated immediately, and, though they were at the mercy of the paramedic's response time, Amir would do what he could.

He called over all the drivers and members of security that had been travelling with the family. 'We need to try and lift the car off Mike. Isolde, before we do that can you make a tourniquet around his wrist?'

With a quick flick of his wrists he undid his tie and passed it to Isolde for a makeshift tourniquet. If blood flow was restricted or impaired for more than fifteen minutes toxins could be released into the bloodstream and cause kidney failure.

'Okay, done.'

'Now I need you to hold his head steady as you can and we'll do our best to make it a clean lift.'

There was no room for mistakes here. They needed to lift the car straight up and over, away from Mike, and without jarring him at all. It was a precarious situation and they didn't know the extent of his injuries. One knock could cause paralysis, but with no idea how long it would take the emergency services to get here Amir thought they had to do something.

'We're ready,' she shouted back so he knew she was in place to watch their patient and make sure they didn't cause him any further injury in their attempt to help him.

'Okay. On the count of three I want everyone to lift. Then we'll shuffle over to the right until we're clear. Ready?' Amir was at the back of the vehicle with some of the others, more positioned around the side of the car, all hands under the chassis, ready to lift. It was said that in extreme circumstances adrenaline could propel a man to lift a car single-handed but he was hoping there were enough of them to manage it without relying on a myth.

'One, two, three…' Using every ounce of effort he possessed verbalised in a grunt, he took the strain along with the others.

'All good,' Isolde shouted up from underneath to let them know it had been a successful operation so far. With her at risk too if they lost their grip and dropped the car, Amir dug deep for his inner bodybuilder. He mightn't have the same bulky physique as the security guys, but he certainly had all the heart.

They shuffled in unison across the road until they were clear of Mike and Isolde on the grass.

'On the count of three, drop and step away.' He didn't want anyone injured by a car falling on them because they were in a rush. They had to do this carefully and methodically.

'One, two, three…' He pulled his hands free and stepped back, watching to make sure everyone else had done the same. Once they were sure it had been a success whoops and hollers filtered into the air along with the back-slaps. Amir didn't wait for congratulations, moving quickly over to the pair left lying in the middle of the road.

'Are you both okay?' he asked, now he could see the couple more clearly. Isolde was stretched out lying on her belly tending to the injured policeman, her beautiful dress now ripped and covered in dirt.

'I'm okay, but Mike has lacerations and contusions

all over.' Now the car had been lifted away Isolde was able to sit up and talk while staying close to the patient.

Amir knelt down to take a preliminary look but it wasn't easy to see the injuries clearly, given the position Mike was lying in and because he was still wearing his protective clothing. 'Mike, I know you're uncomfortable at the minute but we don't want to move you or take your helmet off in case we exacerbate any injuries. What we will do is try and stabilise you so the paramedics can transfer you quickly and safely to the hospital when they get here.'

He stood up again to address those standing around watching. 'Can we get some blankets, water, and if anyone has a first-aid kit to hand it would be helpful.'

The crowd of men dispersed and disappeared back into the convoy of cars to retrieve any useful items. In the meantime Amir took off his jacket and covered the policeman to try and keep him warm. There was a very real chance of his body going into shock and causing all manner of complications.

'Are you hanging in there, Mike?'

'Just tired…' he mumbled in response.

'Please try and stay awake. There's a real chance you could have suffered a concussion when you hit the ground and we need to keep you conscious for now. They'll be able to monitor you better at the hospital. It won't be long until the ambulance gets here.' Amir did his best to keep the man talking. Falling asleep now could mask any complications such as a brain injury. At least in the hospital they would be able to treat any complications.

Some of the drivers and security men returned with

blankets and bottles of water. Amir covered Mike first to try and keep him warm, then handed another blanket and some water to Isolde.

'What do you want to do about that hand?' she asked, taking a swig from the bottle.

'We need to elevate it above the heart to reduce pain and swelling.' Amir was about to do just that when another driver handed him a small first-aid kit. He pulled out a disposable ice treatment pack and some bandages.

'Mike, I'm going to apply an ice pack to these fingers. It might be uncomfortable at first but it should numb the pain in that area.' He broke the ice pack to activate it and wrapped it in the bandages so it wouldn't cause any burns to Mike's skin and gently pressed it against his fingers, which were now beginning to swell and bruise.

The policeman drew a sharp intake of breath but let Amir proceed. He knew there were likely more serious injuries going on, but it was going to take careful handling and X-rays at the hospital to determine the extent of the damage.

'Mike? Stay with us.' Isolde suddenly sounded very concerned and began gently patting the policeman's face, which had turned grey, and he wasn't responding.

Amir checked Mike's pulse and, when he couldn't find it, tore open his clothing to listen to his chest. Nothing. 'He's gone into cardiac arrest. We're going to have to perform CPR.'

As he was a surgeon most of his work was undertaken in the operating theatre, where it was controlled and chock-full of medical equipment for unforeseen situations like this. Unfortunately, there were no defibrillators available out here in the middle of nowhere, so until the ambulance came it was all down to him and Isolde.

'What do you need me to do?' Though emergency medical intervention wasn't her expertise either, he knew she'd see it through with him.

'I'll start chest compressions. On the count of thirty, you do the rescue breaths. Hopefully help will arrive soon.' Without further delay, Amir put the heel of his hand in the middle of Mike's chest, interlocked the fingers of his other hand, and with arms locked began to push down.

'One, two...' He counted with every compression until he reached thirty and paused.

At which point Isolde tilted Mike's head up, pinched his nose, and placed her lips around his open mouth. She blew until his chest rose, then repeated the action. Then it was Amir's turn again. They continued, not knowing if there was any internal bleeding, but determined to get his heart beating again.

His arms were beginning to tire and he was on the brink of asking Isolde to swap over when he saw Mike's chest rise by itself.

'Stop!' he shouted before Isolde gave another rescue breath and leaned down to listen to the man's chest.

'He's breathing.' The sheer relief had him welling up that their efforts hadn't been in vain as he rolled Mike into the recovery position.

'Thank goodness.' Isolde threw her arms around him and hugged him.

He knew it was because she was as relieved as he. It was an act of solidarity and a release from the pressure of having this man's life in their hands. He enjoyed it all the same. Not just the warmth of her in his arms, but having a partner again, someone to share his life experiences with. With an extra helping of guilt, he also realised the reason he enjoyed being with Isolde so much was because she accepted him, appreciated him, co-operated with him. All the things his wife hadn't always been keen to do. When he was around Isolde he felt loved, and it was an intoxicating dilemma always wanting to be around her, yet knowing nothing could come of it.

She was the one to let go first, backing away slowly with a look of regret in her eyes.

'The ambulance is going to be here very soon, Mike,' she soothed their patient, and Amir knew she would wait with him until the last second when they transferred his care over to the paramedics.

He was sure it came as a relief all round when the sirens were heard approaching.

Once Amir had passed on all the details of Mike's condition to the ambulance crew, he focused his attention on Isolde, who was looking a little bit worse for wear. As he was sure he did too.

'You should go and get checked at the hospital too. I know you hurt yourself getting out of the car.' He could see the tears in her dress and the cuts on the exposed skin where she'd struggled to get out of the car in her determination to go and help.

Isolde most definitely was not a pernickety princess afraid of getting her hands, or clothes, dirty. She was courageous, selfless and unbelievably kind. He didn't know why she thought she wouldn't be suited to motherhood when it was clear she was a natural nurturer. The responsibility she claimed she didn't want was there in every action she took to look after others.

Still, it wasn't any of his business when it was clear there couldn't be anything between them, and therefore not an issue. They just had to make sure Farah understood that too. Her earlier comments were concerning and he didn't want her to get ideas in her head that Isolde was going to become part of their little family. If anything, once they were back in England they'd probably have to put more distance between them, at least in their personal lives. He didn't want Farah to be disappointed so he'd probably have to have a word with her later and put her straight on the nature of their relationship. Something they'd had trouble deciphering but now realised had no future as anything other than colleagues.

They'd initially moved to England as a family after Farah was born. He'd had a soft spot for the country since he'd studied there and he wanted her to have the best education. She'd been enrolled in a top private school before she could even talk. In hindsight he'd probably thought it would be a new start for all of them, the cracks already beginning to show in the marriage, but he guessed it, like him, hadn't lived up to his wife's expectations.

She'd wanted glitz and glamour, and to be social climbers. He hadn't. She'd thrown it back at him that night before driving off, telling him he was boring and unambitious. Laughable, when he'd been lined up to take over the throne in Zaki. England had simply been his last chance for a quiet family life before he took up his real duties. So he'd shied away from the society life, following Raed's example. In a way he envied his older brother's anonymous, normal life, though going home had never been in question for Amir. He always did the right thing. Even when it wasn't always what he wanted.

Like now. What he really wanted was to be back with his family with support and company, but he knew Farah was getting the best treatment with Isolde in London. She'd already come so far, he didn't want to set her back by upsetting her routine. However, he would have to be careful she didn't read more into Isolde's presence in their lives than her being Farah's physiotherapist.

'It's just a few cuts. Nothing to worry the health service over. A shower and a change of clothes and I'll be as right as rain. It's just as well Farah and I had designed equally fabulous outfits for the reception.' She looked forlornly at her ruined dress, which he knew had taken a lot of work on her behalf. It said a lot about her that she'd been willing to sacrifice it to help someone else.

'Speaking of whom…' His mother and father were walking towards them pushing Farah in her wheelchair, now that she'd been given the all clear by the emergency services.

'Papa!' Farah threw her arms around his waist and hugged him tight.

'Hey. Everyone is safe,' he said, stroking her hair, grateful that she'd been spared in the accident that had taken her mother, but sorry she'd had to experience the trauma again.

'What…about…the…policeman?' she hiccupped through sobs.

Amir's heart lurched. It was a sign of how much her mother's death had affected her that she was so worried about a stranger's family having to go through the same thing.

'He's going to be all right, Farah. The ambulance is going to take him to hospital and they'll make sure he's okay.' Isolde crouched down at eye level with Farah and did her best to reassure her too. Only to have Farah launch herself at her next, almost knocking her over in the process. He saw Isolde wince when she wrapped her arms around her and squeezed.

'Careful,' Amir warned but Isolde waved away his concern.

'She's fine. I'm fine. We're all fine. So I suggest we make our way to the party before my sister loses her mind completely.' It was only now she'd thought to check her phone, kindly retrieved from the car with her bag by Djamila. The numerous texts, missed calls and voice messages would suggest Soraya had heard about the accident.

'I did tell her none of us were hurt,' Djamila interjected. No doubt she'd had a billion calls too, but Isolde knew nothing would pacify her sister other than seeing for herself. Thankfully they weren't too far from the palace or she was likely to turn that carriage around and race back.

'That's big sis, overprotective and made to worry. I'll just send a quick text to confirm I'm still alive.' Isolde knew Soraya was going to make a great mother some day because she was so good at it already. She'd benefitted from her sister's love and support her entire life, and now it was time to let her have her own life instead of worrying about her all the time.

Tonight had given her a taste of what it was like to feel that kind of fear only a parent could go through when it seemed their child was in danger. Soraya might have been panicking that her little sister might have been injured, but Isolde's first thought had been for Farah's safety, and it hadn't just been in a professional capacity. The line had definitely been blurred between physiotherapist, friend, and something more that involved more emotions than she was prepared to deal with.

Given that the little girl was clinging to her too it was clear it wasn't a one-sided problem. Farah was too attached, figuratively and literally, and she was going to get hurt if Isolde remained in her life giving her false hope that she was somehow going to become a substitute mother figure. That was never going to happen. Better she made the break sooner rather than later instead of stoking the little girl's fantasy.

With one hand still holding onto Farah, Isolde deftly typed a quick message to Soraya with the other to assure her they were all safe and on their way to the palace.

Tonight she would hug her sister, get changed, and celebrate her nuptials. Because tomorrow she'd be gone.

CHAPTER SEVEN

AMIR CHECKED HIS phone for messages and took a note of the time. Farah and Isolde had been an age getting ready and he hoped it wasn't because she didn't want to come down again, or she had some sort of delayed shock after the accident. Farah hadn't wanted anyone but Isolde to help her get changed so he'd showered, put on a suit that didn't look as if it had been in a car wreck, and come down to the reception party. Now he was sitting foot tapping at the table waiting for their big entrance and a sign that his daughter hadn't been retraumatised by today's events.

Soraya and Raed had rushed to meet them the second they'd reached the palace, barely letting them get out of the car before swarming around them to make sure they hadn't downplayed the incident. Once he and Isolde had assured them all they needed was to shower and change they'd finally agreed to go ahead with the reception. Though they'd already apparently told their assembled guests what had happened, extolling their bravery and heroics, they'd insisted on putting the evening on hold until the whole family were together. His mother and father had since made their appearance but they were all listening to the DJ's filler music until the real party started.

He stopped Soraya as she moved between guests, his anxiety getting the better of him. 'Should I go up and see what's keeping them?'

'Listen, if there's one thing my sister hates, it's being rushed. Relax, Amir, they'll be here soon. She would have told you if there had been any problems with Farah. Don't worry. They're just making sure they look good for you.'

The knowing wink she gave him before moving on to mingle with the rest of the guests did nothing to alleviate his restlessness. Things were already difficult without the whole family thinking there was something going on between him and Isolde. Simply wishing it into existence didn't make it work. If anyone knew that, it was him. From the outside it probably seemed so easy for them to be together when they spent so much time in each other's company already, and Farah trusted her, liked her, and more importantly was comfortable around her. It was him who'd messed things up, and now he had to take all of that away from her to protect both of them from more pain long term.

As he fidgeted with the edge of the linen tablecloth he had a sudden urge to look up. The whole room seemed to fall silent and his hands stilled as Isolde and Farah entered the room. His daughter was wearing a pretty baby-blue jumpsuit. She'd been careful to keep her legs covered but the light crepe material, ruffled at the top with puffed sleeves, and embellished with embroidered sparkly butterflies, still made her look like the princess she was. Despite her carefully co-ordinated ivory bag and shoes, crepe bow in her hair, the prettiest accessory she wore was her smile. And of course the fairy wings Isolde had encouraged her to wear.

'I hope we didn't keep everyone waiting too long,' Isolde whispered as she wheeled Farah over to the table.

'It was worth the wait,' Amir said diplomatically, meaning every word. He would have sat here all night just to be rewarded with the utter happiness radiating from his daughter, her earlier distress hopefully now a distant memory.

He kissed Farah on the cheek and it felt only natural to do the same with Isolde. Although the second he made contact that electricity sparked straight back to life, singeing his lips where he'd touched her skin.

'Do I look all right? This wasn't how I started the day...' Isolde glanced around the room, patting her hair into place and tugging at the hem of her dress.

'You look beautiful.' He didn't have to lie to make her feel better when she was as stunning as ever. The hair, which had been scraped back into an elegant updo earlier, was now hanging loose around her shoulders, a little damp at the ends from her rush to join the party. She was back to her minimal make-up, which he personally preferred to the full mask she'd sported for the official photographs, looking more like herself. As for the cobalt-blue dress...it was stunning.

'We fairies try our best.' She twirled around so he could see the wings she was wearing to match Farah's. It didn't matter to her what anyone thought except Farah and he adored her for that.

Amir took a step back as the words his subconscious conjured hit him in the gut as well as the heart. He was glad when the music started and the bride and groom were called to the floor for their first dance as husband and wife, because he didn't think he was capable of speech in that moment. Despite all the soul-searching and promises not to kiss Isolde again, he'd fallen for her anyway, and he didn't know what to do about it.

As he watched the loved-up newly-weds sway together on the floor he envied their uncomplicated relationship. He wished things were as easy for him and Isolde to be together without the spectre of impending doom haunting their every move.

Raed left his dance partner briefly to speak to the DJ and grinned at Amir. It was only when the DJ called for the chief bridesmaid and best man to come to the floor that he realised why. He wasn't going to let his baby brother fade into the background despite his best efforts. There was a round of applause, someone pushed him forward, and Farah urging, 'Dance with Isolde, Papa,' leaving him with no choice.

'May I?' he asked, holding out a hand for Isolde.

'You may.' She took his hand and let him lead her onto the dance floor, leaving Farah with her grandparents watching from the sidelines.

The slow number left them nowhere to hide, their bodies pressed tightly together as they let the music carry them across the dance floor.

'Good to see you enjoying yourself, brother.' Raed nudged him with his elbow as they passed each other.

Amir gave a strained smile. This was not fun, it was torture. Her breath at his ear, her breasts pushed against his chest and the strands of her hair brushing against his cheek were driving him crazy.

'Sorry,' Isolde whispered into his ear, making the hairs on the back of his neck to attention. He felt bad for making it obvious he was uncomfortable.

'You've nothing to be sorry for.' To try and prove the point he pulled her even closer. It wasn't her fault he couldn't get a handle on his emotions when he was in her orbit. Especially when she'd given him a million reasons to be grateful.

'Thank you for everything you've done for Farah today. The outfits were amazing. You're a woman of many talents. I can't remember the last time my daughter looked so happy.' She was sitting singing along to the music with his parents, looking like any other child enjoying the party. Miles away from the frightened young girl who'd first met Isolde, struggling to deal with her life-changing injuries and not even wanting to be seen in public. She'd surprised everyone today with her bravery.

'I can't take all the credit. I think a lot of the changes in her are down to her devoted father too. It just takes time to process everything she's been through. I see it a lot in my line of work.'

He did too but perhaps because this was so close he hadn't seen the changes in her until now. It was a slow transition but gradually she was getting back to the little girl she used to be. He knew Isolde was a lot to do with that even if she was reluctant to accept a starring role.

It also hadn't been lost on him that her first concern when the crash happened had been for Farah, and she'd come to comfort her once they'd dealt with the patient.

He knew why she was reluctant to get close, given her background, he knew why he was afraid of letting her get too embedded into their lives, but he couldn't seem to accept it. Fate seemed to be pushing them together at every turn and his resistance was getting lower by the second. He just wished they didn't have to keep this safety barrier erected between them and could simply enjoy being together.

The slow song ended to a round of applause, followed by a faster pop number, which meant he had to reluctantly loosen his hold on Isolde before it became too obvious he didn't want to let go.

'I think there's someone else who wants to dance with you.' Isolde went to get Farah and wheeled her onto the dance floor as everyone else made their way up to join in.

Amir walked over to meet them, but Isolde quickly dodged around in front of Farah's wheelchair and placed a hand on his chest to stop him. 'Just wait here. Farah has something planned for you both.'

He had no idea what they were up to but they'd clearly been working on something other than dresses behind the closed doors and conspiratorial giggles. Nevertheless, he did as he was told and waited patiently to see what they had in store for him next.

He watched as Isolde kicked away the foot stand on Farah's wheelchair, then proceeded to lift her out. His first instinct was to rush over and grab her before she fell over. They'd been here before, every time a knock to her confidence and setting her recovery back even further. However, he trusted Isolde. She wouldn't do anything to humiliate him or his daughter in public like this, and she'd said it was Farah's idea. If his daughter had plucked up the courage to do something in front of everyone it was a major progression and he wasn't going to stop her. All he could do was be there for her if she needed him.

His heart was in his mouth as Isolde manoeuvred Farah onto her feet and slowly let go until she was standing on her own two feet. Her legs were shaking with the effort but her smile made him want to weep with pride. Then she started to walk and he couldn't hold back the tears. This was everything he and Isolde had been working for and his amazing, brave daughter had chosen tonight to prove the effort had all been worth it.

With Isolde right by her side Farah took a couple of shuffling steps forward, her eyes completely focused on him. It reminded him of when she'd taken her very first steps at just over a year old. She had that same determination to reach him, her body trying to keep up with her will. When she stumbled both he and Isolde rushed to catch her, but her smile was just as bright.

'I did it, Papa,' she said, pride and hope shining in every word that this was only the start and some day she wouldn't need the wheelchair at all.

'Yes, you did, my brave, brilliant girl.' He kissed the top of her head, tears soaking his face.

Amir could hear the gasps of astonishment all around as the guests and wedding party witnessed the miracle along with him. Farah looked tired but he knew his daughter, she wouldn't want to end the moment too early.

'She's been working on this for a while. She wanted to surprise you,' Isolde said with a hint of wariness in her voice. No doubt she'd struggled over not telling him about Farah's progress, but it was more important to him that she'd kept Farah's confidence and provided her with a friend who could be trusted.

'You certainly did that, but I don't want you to overexert yourself too quickly. Isolde, could you help position Farah so she's standing on my feet?' That way he could take the strain and do his best to hold her up without losing the moment.

Isolde went one better. Not only did she get Farah closer to him, she stood behind her, keeping her upright and resting her hands on her hips, so the three of them were ostensibly dancing together. It didn't matter it wasn't in time to the music or particularly energetic, Amir was dancing with his daughter. Something he'd thought he'd never get to do ever again. And suddenly their whole future looked so much brighter with possibilities. He pulled her close, then went in for a full group hug to include Isolde, the three of them doing little more than swaying to the music together but it was perfect.

When the song was over he carried Farah back to her wheelchair, telling her they had to take one step at a time. As soon as she was settled the rest of the family came to hug her and tell her how proud they were of her, tears abounding.

'I should take her up to bed, she's exhausted,' he told everyone when he noticed her yawn.

'Your father and I can settle her and then rejoin the party. We have the room.' His mother's offer was a welcome reminder that as long as they were here he didn't have to do everything on his own. He had support.

'I'm sure she would much rather sleep in her own bed. You want me to come up with you, Farah?'

She shook her head. 'You stay here.'

Her glance flicked between him and Isolde and he could see she hadn't given up on her idea of getting them together. At this moment he didn't want to do anything to burst her bubble.

'You stay and enjoy yourselves,' his mother insisted, collecting his father and Farah before making a gracious exit.

'On a scale of one to ten, how mad at me are you?' Isolde asked as they watched the others leave.

'Zero,' he said honestly. 'Of course I would've wanted to know she was back on her feet, but I wouldn't wish away the smile it put on her face when she surprised me.'

'She's worked hard.'

'As have you. Between making the dresses and helping her to walk again, you've had your work cut out for you.'

'I'm happy if she's happy. That's all I can ask for.' Isolde's words were said by good parents the world over, always wanting the best for their children. Although he could never say that. It would send her running if she thought for one moment anyone saw her as a mother figure. Amir saw her as much more but he knew it was the one role that would scare her away.

'Well, we both thank you.'

He heard her take in a small breath, as though she was about to say something, then without warning she reached up and hugged him. It had been an emotional moment for both of them, but there was something so final in that embrace he didn't want to let go.

'Why don't we both go and get a drink?' Whatever she'd been about to say he knew he wasn't ready to hear it, wanting the euphoria of the evening to continue as long as possible.

Instead of trying to catch the attention of the busy waiters, he made his way to the bar with Isolde in tow.

'You kept that quiet.'

'Such a brave little girl.'

'You should be very proud.'

As they waited for their drinks it seemed everyone who'd witnessed the father-daughter dance wanted to offer their support and congratulations. Although it was very kind, it was also overwhelming. He needed some space to process everything too.

Grabbing the two glasses of champagne that eventually appeared on the bar top and gesturing for Isolde to follow him, he made his way to the French doors at the back of the room. She opened the doors so he didn't spill their drinks in an awkward attempt to do it himself and they stepped out onto the patio away from the crowd.

'I needed some air,' he explained, perching on the top of the steps that led down to the vast manicured gardens.

Isolde sat down beside him and accepted the champagne offered to her. 'Understandable. Today has been a lot.'

'Here's to surviving,' he said, raising his drink in a toast.

Isolde clinked her glass to his. 'I'm sorry for not telling you about Farah, and for...you know, hugging you.'

'Will you stop apologising? It was a big moment. I lost serious man points back there by blubbing over my baby.'

'We were all in tears, Amir. It would've looked kinda weird if you hadn't been moved. I think Farah did it on purpose to make a show of you in public.'

He knew she was joking but so was he. When Farah had taken those first wobbly steps towards him he hadn't cared about anyone else in the room, except perhaps for Isolde who was very much part of it all.

'I didn't think Soraya and Raed had eyes for anyone other than each other. I'm surprised they noticed.'

Isolde slapped him playfully on the arm. 'Don't be mean. They're happy.'

'Yeah, it's sickening, isn't it?' He tossed back the champagne, swallowing the bubbles before they had time to go up his nose.

'No, it's lovely.' She laughed, refusing to get drawn into his pity party.

'I know. I'm just jealous that they get to be together and we can't.' Perhaps it was the events of the day that had worn down his defences, the glass of champagne helping him to say what he was feeling without overthinking the consequences.

'We're here now.' Isolde bumped affectionately against him but it only made Amir want more than a glancing touch between them.

He set his glass on the step, took Isolde's and did the same with hers, before taking her hands in his. 'You know what I mean, Isolde. We like each other, I don't think that's in doubt, and apparently our mouths are magnetised or something since they always seem to be drawn together.'

'Amir...we've been through this. There's Farah to think

about, and us. We both know how this ends.' She rested her forehead against his.

'Why do we have to think about anything? Why can't we just enjoy ourselves like everyone else here? For weeks we've been doing the right thing and setting aside what we want. When do we get to have some fun? Why can't we just have a drink and a dance without the weight of everyone else's expectations dragging us down?'

Amir got to his feet and pulled Isolde up with him. He'd had his fill of trying to be perfect and tempering his actions to be mindful of other people's feelings. Just for once he wanted to be himself, to do what he wanted, and feel without limits.

He began to dance, twirling Isolde around before pulling her back into hold, one hand resting on her back, the other clasping her hand between their bodies. She gasped and laughed at the impulsive move, only making him want to do it more. He dipped her back, her eyes staring up at him with such vulnerability and trust that made her parted lips too irresistible.

The kiss happened because he wanted it to and because he knew she wanted it too. The soft touch of her mouth against his was his reward for braving a step out of his comfort zone but it was over too quickly when Isolde broke it off and pushed up on his chest. He'd got it wrong again.

'I'm sorry—'

'Let's not go through this again. When it comes to kissing you I am a very willing participant,' she said with a smile that managed to soothe his guilty conscience before it overwhelmed him again.

'But it can't happen again. I get it.'

Isolde faced him with her hands on her hips. 'Will you please stop answering for me? What I was going to say was if we're going to…indulge ourselves, I'd rather not do it in public. If this is going to be a one-off we don't need witnesses who'll read too much into it. Right?'

'Right.' Amir was reeling from her reaction, trying to understand what was happening.

She took him by the hand, leading him back inside.

'Where are we going?'

Isolde didn't answer him until they'd ducked through to the other side of the busy room and out into the hall-way. 'I think the best man and bridesmaid are expected to get it on at a wedding, then never speak about it again.'

'You mean…one night together?' He didn't dare believe that was what she was suggesting in case he'd read everything wrong again.

'If that's what you want?' Isolde's earlier display of confidence wavered as she bit her lip waiting for him to respond.

'I want,' he said, unable to stop himself reaching for her, holding her face in his hands so he could kiss her without restraint.

If one night was all they were going to get, he would take it. It was better to show her how he felt for a limited time than to never get the chance. No one had to know, would force their expectations for what happened next between them, or had to suffer the consequences of things not working out. It would be their secret. Their time together. Though he wanted longer, more than one night, just maybe it could be enough to persuade her they had a future together.

Now all bets were off Isolde knew they were in danger of getting carried away. It was as though they'd finally unleashed everything they'd been feeling for one another, everything they'd been trying to keep under wraps, in that one kiss.

'I think we should go to my room before there are rumours of another royal wedding happening.' She was only partly joking. As much as she was enjoying finally getting to have Amir without the guilt of her actions making things difficult, she could do without Soraya, or anyone else, seeing them making out and getting the wrong idea. She doubted the explanation that they were embarking on a one-night stand together because she couldn't commit would do either of their reputations any good.

'You're right. We shouldn't take any unnecessary risks.' Amir grabbed hold of her hand and practically sprinted to the top of the stairs in his haste to get to her room. In the end she had to kick off her heels to catch up with him, running barefoot, her shoes dangling from her fingers as they ran through the palace corridors like two horny teenagers.

When he'd confessed to wanting a brief respite from all of his worry and responsibility to his family, Isolde had been able to relate. It was nice to have the opportunity to be reckless and impulsive again even for a short while, not having to be on her guard. The chemistry between her and Amir had always been there, occasionally boiling over into a passionate encounter. Until now they'd been fearful about acting upon it, guilty when they had. She was looking forward to that freedom to display her emotion and do what she wanted with Amir. The very thought sent shivers of delight along her spine.

He'd surprised her with the idea that they should get a little reckless, and she'd taken that idea and run with it, until they were heading towards a night together. Heaven. She'd had a little wobble of confidence when she thought about what this represented to Amir. Although she wasn't privy to all the details of his personal life, she was pretty sure this was the first time he'd been with anyone since his wife had died. That was a huge step for him and something they hadn't talked about in this sudden rush to be together. It was a milestone for him, one that he might not have even considered yet. What she didn't want was for him to assign any more significance to this than a one-night stand, because the idea of this was to avoid any hurt, not make things worse.

Before she opened her bedroom door she paused to make sure this was genuinely what he wanted, that he wasn't going to confuse this for something other than a physical release. They couldn't afford to get involved in anything emotional, which was why turning this into a meaningless fling was the only way to make it work.

'Amir, I really want this, I do, but are you sure? I mean, are you ready to move on, albeit temporarily?' She traced her fingers over the exposed skin at his throat where he'd opened his top button and loosened his shirt, trying to keep things flirty, despite the seriousness of the question.

Amir stopped her wandering fingers with one hand, his brown eyes holding her captive. 'I'm sure.'

He didn't get into the details of why he was so sure, and if she was honest it did niggle a bit that he wasn't going to explain so they both knew why he was so certain. However, as he backed her against the door and kissed her hard, letting his hands skim along her body, all her worries fled. She was already turned on but as he stroked the bare skin of her thighs she went into meltdown.

It had been a while for her too. Perhaps that was why she wanted to make sure they didn't assign more significance than a hook-up. If she thought about it too much she might realise it was a bad idea because Amir was the furthest thing from being a meaningless hook-up. Her sister had just married into his family, they were colleagues, she was treating his daughter...there were so many emotional connections. And that didn't even include the feelings she knew she already had for him. Then he slid his hand under her dress, into her panties, and she didn't care any more.

They stumbled into her room and she dropped her shoes onto the floor to leave her hands free to undress him. Amidst a frenzy of kisses and trembling fingers she eventually managed to strip him of his shirt so she could slide her hands over the hard planes of his torso, mapping every muscle to memory. Amir unzipped her dress, the sensation of his fingers tracing the line of her spine making her skin tingle with arousal. Her dress fell to the ground leaving her standing there in just her underwear. She should have felt vulnerable, exposed, but the hungry look in his eyes and his clearly physical reaction to seeing her half naked were enough to embolden her.

Isolde undid her bra and let it fall away. Her heart was racing with a mixture of anxiety and exhilaration about baring herself so completely to him, but he made her feel so sexy just with one look it wasn't long before her panties followed the rest of her clothes. She took a lot of satisfaction in seeing his Adam's apple bob as he swallowed hard watching her. Even more when he grabbed hold of her backside and pulled her close, crushing her against his hard body in his haste to kiss her again.

Isolde fumbled with the rest of his clothes, undoing his belt, opening his fly, and pushing away the last barrier between their naked bodies. The feel of his solid manhood pressed intimately against her made her breathless and slick with need.

Amir lifted her off the ground, hooking her legs around his hips, and backed her against the wall. She clung to him, her arms around his neck, her mouth clashing with his. It was the most intense, passionate display of mutual desire she could ever remember. The fact that they'd been holding back for so long was probably the reason it had exploded so spectacularly into this animalistic need for one another.

He palmed her breast and took her nipple into his mouth, sucking on the tip so hard she was teetering on the brink between pleasure and pain. She bucked against him with a gasp, not wanting him to stop as the sensitive nub grazed the roof of his mouth. Arousal swept over her until nothing else mattered except her need for him, her mind and body so attuned to what he was doing with his mouth that she ached for all of him.

It briefly crossed her mind that the reason it was so

intense, so all-consuming, was because they had feelings for one another they were afraid to explore. This was always going to be more than a casual thing when there were emotions involved, real enough for her to try and run away from them. She knew that, but for tonight she didn't want to acknowledge it. There would be time for tears and self-recrimination another day. Now they were going to simply live in the moment.

'I need you,' she gasped at his ear, feeling him tighten against her in response.

'Now?' He searched her face, looking for confirmation she was ready despite every part of her body telling him so.

'Now,' she said, wriggling against him until he was the one gasping with need.

Amir filled her with one thrust, taking their breath away, and making them smile at one another as though they'd just won the lottery. As her body adjusted to accommodate his thick erection she thought she had.

She buried her head against his neck, completely surrendering her body to him.

'You okay?' he asked, tilting her chin up so he could see her face.

'Yeah. More than okay,' she assured him, fighting the unexpected tears threatening to ruin the moment, reminding herself there were no emotions allowed. Apart from absolute euphoria, of course.

He kissed her again, this time a softer, more tender perusal of her lips, slowing the pace and giving them time to breathe again. It didn't make her want him any less and she ground her hips to his to deepen their connection further. Amir braced one hand on the wall, the other on the curve of her backside, as he drove into her, slowly filling her to satiate that need.

Sparks fired in her brain, all her nerve endings stimulated at once, overloading her body with sensation and making her quiver. He thrust again, grunting with effort into her ear. The sound was enough on its own to start that building pressure inside her searching for that final release.

She loved hearing those primal noises coming from a man so usually in control. It showed how much he wanted her, how much he needed this, and how passionate he was about her. As he carried her over to the bed she couldn't help but wonder how it would feel to have this every night to come home to. Knowing that this feeling of completeness was something Soraya and Raed had to look forward to for the rest of their lives, and she and Amir didn't.

It wasn't fair, but life never had been for either of them. All they could do was grab this moment of happiness with both hands and have the memory to cherish long after they'd parted ways. The problem was everything Amir was doing to her, making her feel, could never be replicated. It was the first and last time she'd ever get to experience it. If it was punishment for her decision to remain child-free she was certainly going to make sure she enjoyed her freedom first.

If this was the only time they'd have together to explore those feelings they were both afraid to admit to, Amir wanted to make it last longer than a quick pounding against a wall. Regardless of his body insisting otherwise, a combination of his want for Isolde and because of how long it had been since he'd had this kind of release. She was everything he'd imagined and feared. Beautiful, sexy and energetic. The kind of partner in the bedroom every man wanted but only he was lucky enough to have. For tonight.

Something had changed between them then, the frantic urge to join together overtaken by something more meaningful. This was supposed to be a one-time thing, something to forget once they'd got it out of their systems. Yet as he looked at Isolde, feeling what he was feeling, this was no longer simply sex. He was making love to her. He wanted Isolde to know how he felt about her without actually saying the words and forcing her to run. As if continuing to pretend this was purely physical would protect them.

He knew all the reasons they shouldn't be together past tonight, but it didn't stop him from wishing for more. Now more than ever. If only Isolde could see herself the way he saw her, as a loving, caring woman who'd been burned in the past, she might be able to see a future for them. There was no telling if it would work out for them long term, but Amir was willing to try rather than lose her altogether.

Apparently sensing his mood change, Isolde kissed his neck, sliding her hand between their bodies to stroke the most intimate part of him so he couldn't think too deeply any more, that animal part of him coming back to the fore. Tomorrow he would try and talk to her. Tonight was about actions, not words.

He pulled away and flipped Isolde so she was on her hands and knees, facing away, presenting her sweet backside towards him. Amir gripped her hips and slid easily inside her wet channel. Her little satisfied groans and the sexy look she cast him over her shoulder stole the last of his control. As he thrust forward, she pushed back, and they rode that final peak together until the room echoed with their cries of ecstasy. He was thankful the other rooms were a considerable distance away, given that they were supposed to be keeping this rendezvous secret, not announcing it to the world. His head was spinning, his body trembling as his climax hit. He lay down beside a smiling Isolde and reached over to give her a glancing kiss on the lips.

'Are you okay?'

'Better than okay,' she replied through panting breath, stroking her hand across his chest.

Even now, his body thoroughly sated, that simple contact was able to thrill him. He didn't think he'd ever tire of touching her, of being touched by her. It was just a shame it would end all too soon.

'I need a drink.' On unsteady legs he padded towards the mini fridge they kept stocked up in the rooms for guests and grabbed a bottle of water, his throat parched, lips dry. The refreshing ice-cold liquid went some way to aid his recovery from his exertions.

He climbed back onto the bed and passed the bottle to Isolde. She let out a sharp gasp as she spilled some onto her chest when she took a drink. A wicked idea began to form in Amir's head that he couldn't resist. He took a swig of the water, enough to cool his mouth completely, before leaning down and sucking Isolde's nipple into his mouth.

'Amir!' she gasped with the shock, though she was clearly loving it.

He licked the puckered tip, making her writhe beneath him, something he was getting way too addicted to already. With devilish glee he tipped a little more of the water out over her other nipple and watched it tighten with her squeal. Amir lapped the water dripping over her breast, teased her taut flesh with the tip of his tongue until it and he were hard. He simply couldn't get enough of her. So he was going to make sure they made enough memories tonight to last a lifetime.

Isolde woke to the sound of the shower running, and an empty bed. If she'd thought she could move she would've joined Amir under the water for some more passionate acrobatics. However, her body was refusing to co-operate, thoroughly sated and pleasantly numb from all their previous exhaustive antics. Instead she snuggled under the covers against the pillows, which now smelled of his cologne, never wanting to leave.

'Morning.'

The sound of his voice forced her eyes open and she was rewarded with the sight of him walking, naked and wet, towards her. He dropped the towel he'd been using to dry his hair and slid in next to her. Regardless of her weariness she wanted him all over again. If she were lying on her deathbed she knew she'd still reach for him. Amir had made her feel things last night she'd never experienced before, a deep emotional connection that terrified but also made for out-of-this-world sex. She didn't want to leave this bed because she knew once she did it was all over, that she'd never get to have any of this— would never get Amir—ever again.

'Morning.' The thought that this could be the first and last time she got to wake up next to him made her bottom lip quiver a little so she covered it up by kissing him. A move that only made the moment even more bittersweet when he stroked her hair and kissed her tenderly in return.

'I've been thinking...'

She could see the excitement in the tension of his body and the shine in his eyes that he was building up to something and it didn't take much to guess what that was. Mistaking one night for the beginning of a relationship was exactly what she'd feared and warned him about from the start. They were supposed to part on reasonably good terms because they'd known going into this it was a one-time thing. She didn't want arguments and recriminations to be the lasting memory she had of their time together.

'Amir, don't. I know what you're going to say but sleeping together doesn't change anything.' Not their circumstances, but deep down she knew it had changed everything for her. No one else would ever come close to how he'd made her feel last night, and she knew no one could ever replace him in her affections. Her love life, if she ever deigned to have one again, would never recover.

'Are you honestly telling me you wouldn't want to do this again?' He was grinning at her, probably because he knew the answer to that question by her reluctance to leave the bed or tell him to go.

She narrowed her eyes at him. 'You know I would, but that wasn't the deal.'

It was that safety guard that had finally given her the excuse to act on her feelings. She hoped she wouldn't come to regret it when their time together had been even more than she could possibly have imagined.

Amir shuffled up into a sitting position. 'Hear me out. Soraya and Raed might be going on honeymoon but we're not due back at work until the end of the week. Why don't we stay here?'

'As much as I really, really enjoyed last night, I don't think I could survive on a diet of pure sex if we locked ourselves in for the next few days. Plus, your family might start to think something was wrong...' She had an idea of where he was going with this, but she didn't know if it was a good idea and tried to deflect the subject with humour.

It didn't work.

'I'm serious, Isolde. Although we don't have to be. I'm proposing to extend our casual arrangement for the duration of our stay here.'

'I don't want Farah to get hurt.'

'No one will have to know if you don't want. We managed to sneak away last night without causing a scandal. I'm sure we can do it again. I'll just ask Mother if Farah can stay in their rooms for an extra couple of nights so I can have some time to myself. Let's face it, it doesn't happen very often.'

'And this indecent proposal, would it have the same boundaries as last night? No complications, or expectations?' It was tempting to take him up on the offer of having a little more time together, the best of both worlds if they could continue exploring this amazing sexual chemistry without having to worry about anything long term. But she worried it was too good to be true.

'Listen, Isolde, if I thought there was a chance we could all live happily together for ever I'd take it. But we both know life isn't like that. You've made your feelings clear. Neither me, nor Farah, are in your long-term future.'

Isolde flinched at the bluntness of his words, and hoped that wasn't how it had come across when she'd tried to explain her reasons for not wanting anything serious with him. It was the only way she thought she could protect them all when she knew she could never measure up to the woman they both deserved in their lives.

'It's nothing personal, Amir. I'm just not cut out for the domesticity of family life. Ask my sister, she's still looking after me. What kind of mother would I be when I can't take care of myself?'

He was frowning at her now, all signs of his mischievous smile gone. 'I wish you wouldn't put yourself down like that. Yes, Soraya took care of you growing up because you were orphans, and she was your big sister. I know you were hurt in the past and perhaps that's clouding your view, but I see you, Isolde. You're a caring, responsible adult, whether you like it or not. If you don't want children that's entirely your prerogative, but don't put yourself down like that. There's no need to justify your feelings to me by denigrating yourself.'

Feeling thoroughly chastised now, Isolde whispered, 'Sorry.'

Amir caught her under the chin and tilted her face up to him.

'You don't have to say sorry to me for anything. You helped my daughter to walk again, for goodness' sake.' His light laugh told of his relief as well as his gratitude and Soraya suspected as soon as Farah opened her eyes he'd be checking in on her after last night's milestone.

'That's work though. I'm not so good with the emotional stuff.' She shrugged.

'I don't agree with you on that, but I guess that brings us back to where we started. If this is the only way I can have you, no strings, I'll take it. Even if it's only for a few more days. What do you say? Shall we upgrade from a one-night stand to a fling?'

He turned around so quickly from telling her she was a better person than she believed herself, to validating that idea she was only good for a good time, that her head was spinning trying to figure out who she was to him.

'Is that what you want, Amir?'

'It's all you're able to give me, isn't it?'

'Yes…yes, it is,' she reminded them both in case there was any future confusion. It wasn't going to do either of them any good wishing for the impossible. Instead they had to settle for reality. Or at least a version of it that would hopefully hurt less in the long run, and let them pretend they were getting this thing between them out of their systems.

As she reached for Amir again, her body coming alive again, hungry for more of him, she knew they were just fooling themselves that this could ever be enough. They were simply prolonging the inevitable, but she was too weak, too invested in what they did have to just walk away. Like every addict she had to wean herself off her

particular drug of choice slowly, because going cold tur-
key would be too much of a shock to the system after the
good time she was quickly getting used to.

CHAPTER EIGHT

'WHAT WOULD YOU like to do today, Princess?' Amir asked Farah as he poured himself a glass of orange juice.

He'd left Isolde to shower and dress and come down to breakfast with the rest of the family partly to avoid suspicion by appearing separately but also because he was famished. Last night, and this morning, had used up a lot of calories.

Not that he was complaining and he had to stifle a broad smile every time he thought of Isolde lying up there naked in his arms. He wished they were the ones jetting off on an exotic holiday together looking forward to sun, sea and lots of sex, leaving the rest of the world behind, instead of the happy couple making moon eyes at each other over the breakfast cereal. Neither he nor Isolde were ready for a honeymoon, but that time spent together in isolation sounded like bliss. He was lucky she'd agreed on another couple of days with him at least. It was probably the closest they'd get and he intended to enjoy every moment they had in private, but he wasn't going to neglect his daughter in the process.

'We're spending it together?' Her happy little face made the bite of toast he'd just taken feel like lead in his stomach. Even without last night's development with

Isolde he'd spent more time away from her these past few days dealing with Fahid than he had in an entire year.

'Yes. It's your day, you get to choose what we do. I think you deserve it after all your hard work, even though it was naughty to keep secrets from your father.' He gave her a fake scowl, which didn't fool her in the slightest, probably because he'd sobbed like a baby over how proud of her he was last night.

'I wanted to surprise you, and I did,' she said casually, spooning her cereal into her mouth.

'You surprised us all, Farah,' Soraya added, making her grin at the notion it was more than her father she'd left flabbergasted.

'We're all very proud of you,' his father announced from the top of the table. He wasn't a man who often showed any affection, or praised anyone, so the comment did leave them all stunned for a moment.

Amir wondered if his near-death experience in England after his heart attack had made him appreciate his family more. Especially when they'd all worked so hard to keep things running during his illness and recuperation. If he'd ever told Amir he was proud of him, had made him feel good enough for the family he'd been born into, he might not have spent his whole life trying to prove himself worthy, or married someone he thought would impress them rather than someone he loved. It was too late to make amends with Farah's mother, but he hoped to end the toxic parent-child relationship that seemed to have plagued the royal family for years.

'So, what do you want to do? Manicures and mocktails, or rides at the amusement park?' That one might be a bit more difficult to pull off last minute, getting security in place for somewhere so public, but he reckoned he owed Farah some time, and a reward for all of her hard work. It would give her the incentive to keep going and hopefully progress even more. Although it was early days and he didn't want to put any pressure on her, he knew they were all hoping that some day she'd have full mobility back. That in the future they'd be able to look back on this time as a nightmare they survived.

The only good thing to come out of it all was meeting Isolde, and he knew even that time with her was limited.

'Morning.' She breezed into the dining room, washed, dressed, and not a hair out of place. As beautiful as she looked, he couldn't help think he preferred her naked with her hair in disarray, the way he'd left her in bed.

'Morning...' A chorus went up from around the table but he hoped the smile in response was solely for his benefit.

'I'm afraid we're nearly finished our breakfast and I have to go and finish packing, but we'll come and see you before we leave,' Soraya said, setting down her cup and getting up from the table just as Isolde sat down.

'Sorry, I slept in.' Isolde yawned.

'I didn't think you stayed that late last night. You'd disappeared before everyone left.'

Amir wondered if his absence had been noted too, or if it was considered anything other than a coincidence, but Soraya didn't as much as glance in his direction. The same couldn't be said for Isolde, who was watching him as she dug her spoon into her grapefruit, the juice spraying everywhere.

'I think it was all the excitement that kept me awake half the night.'

Amir almost choked on his toast and had to wash it down with more orange juice. So much for keeping things secret. He could feel his face flush with heat, imagining them all staring at him knowing full well why Isolde was exhausted. Though when he did look up the only person watching him was Isolde with that coy smile on her face that made him want to take her straight back up to bed again.

'The wedding, or our amazing girl?' Soraya asked, resting her hands on Farah's shoulders.

'Both. It's not easy keeping secrets, you know.' Isolde was playing with fire and someone was going to get burned if she wasn't careful. It was her idea to keep things quiet but it wouldn't take much for the others to catch on that she was talking about him, not Farah.

'We're going to do something special to celebrate today, aren't we, Farah?' He turned the conversation back to safer territory, and prayed Isolde would take the hint to stop teasing him.

'Oh, have you planned something nice?' Thankfully she turned her attention to Farah so he could breathe again.

His daughter thought for a moment before answering. 'I'd like to go to the beach.'

It was a simple request but one that surprised him. The beach was somewhere they'd liked to go as a family but since the crash he hadn't been able to persuade her to go. She'd been quite the water baby until the accident and hopefully this was a further turning point in her confidence.

'Anything you want, Princess.'

'I'm sure the kitchen will prepare you a hamper if you'd like,' his mother offered.

'Sounds great. Farah, why don't you go and write a list of all your favourites and we'll see if Chef can accommodate them for you?' Amir thought she deserved an extra-special treat for the courage with which she continually surprised him.

'Can Isolde come with us? To the beach, I mean?' His daughter's plea was so heartfelt that he didn't think he could decline her request without seeming petty. It wasn't that he didn't want to spend time with Isolde, or that he didn't want her intruding on his family time, but he wondered how he was going to manage to keep his burgeoning feelings for her under wraps.

It was one thing behind closed doors where they were free to explore those fresh emotions, but, as this breakfast had proved, hiding them around others was becoming increasingly difficult. Something they were going to have to resolve before they completely screwed the family dynamics. It would be difficult to treat this as a fling if everyone knew and expected more, and awkward once they returned to normal, meeting up at family gatherings with everyone party to their history. This would be a good test of their restraint.

'I'm sure your father would like to have you all to himself. I can stay here.' It was Isolde who provided the escape, declining the invitation so he didn't have to upset his daughter. Her empathy was one of the many things about her he appreciated. Though she often talked about being too selfish, he'd seen her put other people's feelings, especially Farah's, before her own.

'Nonsense. You haven't much time left, go and enjoy yourself. We won't be here as we have a prior engagement, and with Soraya and Raed heading off on their honeymoon it wouldn't be polite to leave you here on your own.'

'I'm sure I can find something to keep me occupied in a palace—' Isolde tried to appease his mother, who was concerned that their guest should be left alone, but Amir knew it was a wasted exercise.

'I won't hear another word. You've done so much for my granddaughter, and my son, it's the least we can do.' His mother rose from the table, matter settled as far as she was concerned. A continued rejection would be deemed an insult now and he was grateful Isolde seemed to realise that.

'In that case, thank you. I'd be delighted to go to the beach with you and your father, Farah.'

Amir saw the apology in Isolde's eyes when she looked at him and he acknowledged it with a smile, trying to reassure her it was okay. It wasn't her fault. Besides, getting to spend more time with Isolde was something to look forward to. It was the days when she wouldn't be there that he was dreading.

As the sea came into view through the car window Isolde didn't know who was more excited, Farah or her. It had been a long time since she'd had a beach holiday and working in London wasn't conducive to days at the seaside. She supposed it was the same for Amir and Farah, who'd been practically living at the hospital for the past year. They probably all needed a break and a chance to soak up some vitamin D. Although she hadn't originally been part of Amir's plan.

She didn't mind. After all, she'd monopolised him for most of the night and this morning, and he needed to spend time with his daughter. She suspected he'd also tried to make a clear distinction between his family life and their secret fling, which she appreciated since she didn't want the complication of anyone else finding out. Okay, so she'd had a little fun teasing him at breakfast, but only because she'd enjoyed seeing him get hot under the collar when she'd reminded him of their incredible night together. She knew she had to rein it in today around Farah. That didn't mean she hadn't chosen to wear an awesome bathing suit beneath her coverall that would totally rock his world.

'Looks like we're here. This is a spot the family owns so we shouldn't be disturbed.' As the car came to a standstill Amir unbuckled his belt and got out to retrieve Farah's wheelchair.

Isolde loved that he still did that even though they had people willing to do the heavy lifting for him. She knew it was because he was the kind of father who wanted to do everything he could for his daughter. The very reason they couldn't have more than a casual fling. Not only was she the wrong woman for his little family, but being with her would compromise the time he had with his daughter. She didn't want to do anything that could jeopardise the bond he had with Farah, especially when she wasn't going to be a long-term prospect for him.

Isolde helped unbuckle Farah and get her into the wheelchair. Although they'd made some progress she wasn't able to sustain her balance and mobility just yet and still needed some assistance. As frustrating as it was for Farah not to be back to her old self straight away, it was going to take more time and hard work. With her father's help, Isolde knew the little girl would get there. She couldn't help but wonder if she'd still be around to see it.

It wasn't a vast stretch of beach, but the little alcove had beautiful golden sand and a bank of surrounding trees making it private. Amir was able to ask security to keep a distance as no one could disturb them without being seen, and the party of three made their way onto the beach via a little wooden ramp she suspected had been added especially for Farah's use. The sunloungers and parasol awaited their arrival but Isolde couldn't wait to feel the sand beneath her toes and whipped off her sandals to paddle at the edge of the sea.

The cool water was refreshing and she scooped some up over her neck to try and lower her body temperature in the midday heat. When she turned back Amir was watching her intently, his jaw clenched, and she just knew he was thinking about last night. Now she was too, and counting the hours until she was back in his arms again. So much for cooling down.

'Would you like some pink lemonade, Isolde?' Farah had set out the contents of the picnic hamper they'd been given by the kitchen for their day out. She could get used to this level of pampering. Going back to her one-bed flat alone was going to be so difficult for a multitude of reasons.

'Yes, thank you.' She came to join them at the table positioned between the sunloungers and helped herself to some of the salad and cold meats spread out on platters.

Farah dutifully poured them all some of the home-made pink lemonade, which they drank greedily. Once she'd had her fill, Isolde made herself comfy on her sunbed, with Farah doing the same on hers. It was only Amir who was sitting awkwardly on the edge of his not looking relaxed in the least.

'Aren't you too warm, Amir? At least take your shoes and jacket off.' Isolde stripped off her loose floral cover-all to reveal her red two-piece bikini and felt Amir's eyes burning on every exposed part of her skin.

'I'm fine,' he insisted gruffly.

Isolde took out the bottle of suncream and applied it to Farah first so her shoulders didn't get burned. Then she began rubbing it into her own skin, smoothing it over her legs and arms, before squirting it onto her chest.

'I'm going for a swim,' Amir announced, hastily tugging off his T-shirt, kicking off his trainers, and heading off barefoot towards the edge of the sea.

Once he'd waded out waist-deep he dived in and swam away, his powerful strokes taking him further and further from the shore. Her little show, which she'd hoped would keep his interest stoked until they were able to be together in private later, had backfired. Now he was further away than ever.

'Will Papa be all right out there?' Farah asked anxiously and Isolde inwardly chastised herself again for crossing the line. There was something about Amir that made her walk that dangerous line even though they were supposed to be discreet. She couldn't seem to help herself when she was around him and that wasn't in keeping with the rules she had made in the first place.

'He looks like a very good swimmer but I'm sure he won't go far,' Isolde assured her, trying to convince herself too.

'I'd like to go in the water too,' Farah pronounced.

'Are you sure? Do you want to wait for your father to come back first?'

Farah shook her head displaying the same determination as her father. Isolde supposed the water would be good for her, taking the pressure off her limbs and giving her a sense of freedom.

'Okay. Put your arms around my neck and hold on tight.' Isolde decided it would be easier to carry her down to the water and she wasn't heavy.

With Farah in her arms she waded out, the cool water taking their breath away at first, but they soon acclimatised. In the distance Amir had turned around, perhaps seeing them in the water, and had begun swimming back. She was relieved, as was Farah apparently as she waved frantically, causing Isolde to nearly drop her in the process.

'I'm in the sea, Papa,' she shouted, though he was still too far away to hear.

Isolde manoeuvred her around, holding Farah under the arms and letting the water take the weight of her legs so she was essentially floating on the surface.

'You two look like you're having fun,' Amir said when

he swam up to join them. His hair was slicked back with water, droplets beaded on his long dark eyelashes, and she'd had a nice view of his taut chest from the moment he'd peeled off his shirt. He was a beautiful man.

Farah beamed. 'I wanted to swim like you, Papa.'

Isolde saw the look of concern on Amir's face that she was expecting too much. 'The buoyancy of the water is good for taking the pressure off her limbs. You could try and kick, Farah, if you want? It'll help strengthen your muscles.'

'I don't know if I can…'

'Try and come to me.' Amir reached out, encouraging Farah to close the small distance between them. It was all the encouragement she needed.

She launched herself at him, grabbing for his hands, splashing everyone in the process.

'Good girl. Now try kicking your legs out behind you.' Isolde moved to support her in case she couldn't manage to stay afloat. The last thing they wanted was for her to struggle and get swamped by the water, putting off any further attempts.

She could see the same determination on Farah's face as she had when they were working in secret to surprise her father. Whether Amir knew it or not his little girl idolised him and wanted to do it all to make him proud. When Isolde thought of her childhood and how little her parents were involved in it because of their illness, she realised exactly what she'd missed out on.

There were few memories of her father except for coughing and sickness, hospital appointments and whispering behind closed doors. He hadn't been well enough to attend school plays or cheer her on during sports days. She had a vague recollection of her mum at a nativity play when she'd been an angel, but neither of them had been around during the high-school years. That had been Soraya.

Her parents hadn't been around and she didn't want the same for Farah. Today had proved she and Amir were incapable of separating their so-called 'no-strings fling' from his family life. They didn't need her screwing things up for them. She would be as guilty as her parents if she hung around knowing she wasn't capable of being the mother figure Farah needed, or the wife Amir deserved. Soraya might have been the best big sister anyone could have asked for, but they hadn't had the greatest role models. Isolde wouldn't know where to begin looking after a family, whereas Soraya had been doing it for most of her life. She wasn't about to do to Farah what her parents had done to them.

Farah had a devoted father and it wasn't fair of Isolde to take him away from her simply because she wanted him. That wasn't going to last for ever, as her last relationship proved all too well. Eventually Amir would see who she really was, once the rose-tinted glasses fell away, and leave her anyway. Everyone always did.

Staying here, lying to them both that no one would get hurt if they kept anything serious off the cards, was selfish and destructive. She'd had her fun and she didn't want to outstay her welcome. But this wasn't the time for that conversation. Not when Farah was on the brink of another revelation.

* * *

'That's it. Keep your head up, Farah, and kick those feet.' Amir bounced back another few feet to encourage her to go a little bit further, his heart about ready to burst with pride.

She'd come on so well these past months, fighting so hard to get her mobility back, and it was beginning to pay dividends. A year ago, when his life had seemed to be over, he could never have imagined her taking a few steps in front of a crowd, or trying to swim to him. Nor would he have believed he'd meet someone who accepted him for who he was without all his royal connections, or that he'd want to be with. Isolde was at the heart of the big changes that had happened in their lives for the better. He'd resisted the idea of a relationship because he didn't want to detract any attention from Farah, who'd needed him so badly, but Isolde was there for her just as much as he was.

Yes, she was clearly afraid of that level of commitment that came from being with someone who already had a child, but she was everything Farah needed too. The attraction between him and Isolde wasn't in question after last night, and the fact she'd agreed to continue their clandestine fling for a while longer told him she was interested in more than a normal one-night stand. He hoped, just maybe, by the end of this trip she would be as ready to take a risk on them as he was.

Farah threw herself forward again, unbothered by any water going up her nose in the race to reach him. He reached out his arms and took her hands but kept walking back, pulling her along with him. With every little kick of her feet she sent a shower of water up over Isolde, but she was just as excited as Amir to see her progress and wasn't fazed at all by being splashed.

'You're doing brilliantly, Farah, keep going,' Isolde encouraged, keeping up pace alongside to make sure she was safe.

Amir could see for himself how much Isolde cared for his daughter, even if she was afraid to admit it. It was this commitment, this certainty that she wanted only the best for Farah too, that convinced him they should try and make things work as a couple, maybe even as a family. He would have to tread carefully, not frighten her off before they had a chance to be a couple, by putting the 'f' word out there. It was scary for him too, opening up their lives to include someone else when he and Farah were used to being a duo. Even though Isolde had been a part of their world for a while, making that transition from colleague and friend to something more was a big step for all of them.

In a way it had been easier when it was just the two of them. Apart from Farah's struggle to walk again, and the guilt and grief that had plagued him. But at least he hadn't had to answer to anyone else. He hadn't had to walk on eggshells, or moderate his behaviour or emotions through fear of upsetting a partner. All he'd had to do was focus on getting his daughter better. Now Farah was making progress he was beginning to look to the future. He didn't want to be on his own for ever, and though he hadn't wanted to be with someone who clearly thought he wasn't good enough, he knew Isolde wasn't that person.

When Farah grew tired he scooped her up and carried her back to the lounger. Isolde followed them out of the water and once more he was tormented by the sight of her in that barely there bikini, knowing he couldn't touch her until they were safe behind closed doors later tonight.

'Amir, can I have a word?' Isolde waited until he had Farah settled with her tablet and earphones watching her favourite video clips on the Internet.

It would give them a chance for a serious private conversation about the future without their raging libidos getting in the way. Thankfully she pulled her coverall back over her head, at least giving the illusion of wearing clothes that would hopefully prevent him being distracted so he could focus on the things he had to say to Isolde. The question he had to ask her.

She waited for him at the edge of the water and they walked a little together, far enough that Farah couldn't hear them, but where they could still keep an eye on her.

'I wanted to speak to you as well. I think we should—'

'This isn't going to work,' Isolde interrupted him.

'I know, it's obvious that we're together. Maybe we should try and cool things while we're out here but I thought once we're home we should try and make a go of it. As a couple,' he clarified.

Isolde blinked at him. 'You know I can't do that.'

'I know you're wary, especially with Farah involved, but I think it's worth taking the chance, don't you?' Amir rested his hands on her shoulders, desperately wanting to gather her into his arms and kiss her as he'd been able to this morning pre-breakfast. He'd be able to resist if he thought it was only a matter of time before they could be together all the time.

When Isolde shook her head he thought his heart had been ripped out of his chest.

'No. I told you I didn't want this. Farah's getting too attached and I, I can't promise either of you what you want, what you need. It wouldn't be fair on any of us. I have to go.' She walked away before he even had the chance to react, collecting her things from the lounger and putting her shoes back on.

'Now? Wait until we can get back to the palace and we can talk about this some more in private.' Of course she was going to have a wobble when it was everything she'd told him she was afraid of, getting involved with a single father, but he knew they had something good together. If only he could get her to look past her fears and concentrate on the present, they could have a chance.

'It's over, Amir. There's no point in living in dream land any more. I'll walk back to the palace.'

'You don't have to do that, Isolde. Don't put yourself in danger. Just get in the car. Please.'

He knew they'd put her under pressure to be a part of their day, and perhaps it had been too much to expect when she'd asked for space. Amir chastised himself for rushing her to a place she wasn't ready to go just yet. Hopefully there was still time to undo any damage before they went back to England. He didn't want to lose her now.

'No. I'll go on foot, thanks. I need the space.' Clutching her belongings, Isolde turned her back on him and started walking.

Amir had a horrible feeling it was the last time he was going to see her again, but as much as he wanted to go after her, he couldn't leave Farah. He was torn, and that was the problem.

Isolde's heart was cracking right down the centre. It was painful and debilitating, and all her own fault. Despite knowing all the risks of getting involved with Amir, she'd pushed and pushed the boundaries until her emotions were well and truly unlocked. Now she had to suffer the pain of her heart breaking as a consequence.

She'd fallen for Amir, and Farah, wanted nothing more than to be part of their family, but she wasn't what they needed. He'd realise that soon enough. Better he did that now than when she'd damaged his relationship with his daughter beyond repair. At least she only had herself to worry about. Amir would have to find an explanation for Farah for her sudden retreat from their lives, but it was for her own good in the long run.

Today had brought all of her fears to life about getting involved with Amir. Not only had she realised how in-grained she was becoming into their lives, but the chance of disrupting their father/daughter relationship was very real. They were both coming to rely on a person who'd never taken responsibility for anything in her life. Even now she couldn't face her own emotions, knowing she cared very deeply for the pair, but walking away none-theless. Proving the point to everyone involved that she was a bad bet.

Since Amir wasn't racing after her, or forcing the chauffeur to follow her journey, Isolde had to assume he'd come to that conclusion in the end too. He'd stayed with his daughter, and that was the right decision. Even if she felt lonelier than ever.

Warm salty tears streaked her face as she walked along the rough dirt track back towards the palace. Her discomfort as the stones penetrated the thin soles of her beach sandals felt like a just punishment for her stupidity but she needed the space from Amir and Farah to think clearly. Something she clearly hadn't been doing since the wedding. Their time together had been amazing, but a mistake. One she couldn't afford to repeat.

To avoid another lapse she was going to pack her bags and book the first flight out. Hopefully now Farah was making progress, Amir would be too caught up with his daughter to make a scene over her departure.

With Soraya and Raed on honeymoon too she could slip away without any fuss. Now the celebrations were over she was merely a guest in danger of outstaying her welcome anyway. A simple note of thanks to her generous hosts would have to suffice because she couldn't bear to say her goodbyes. They were more painful than she could ever have imagined.

CHAPTER NINE

'It's so good to hear your voice, Isolde. I still find it odd not speaking to you every day.' Soraya sighed on the other end of the phone.

'You were the one who went and got married,' she teased. 'We've both been busy but I'm sure we'll catch up with each other at some point.'

Isolde felt that familiar twinge of guilt and sadness she always got when reminded that she was very much on her own these days. Not only had she left Amir, Farah, and the rest of the family back there, but she'd handed in her notice at the hospital, doing her best to avoid the Ayads in her last weeks of work. Unable to face seeing them again, she'd got another physio to help with Farah and made sure she was working different shifts from Amir. She had thought a trip away touring Europe whilst she decided on her next step would give her the time and distance to get over her heartbreak. Yet it hadn't satisfied her the way she'd hoped. When she got back she planned starting afresh at a new job, meeting new people, but the closer her return date, the more she was dreading going back to a life without Amir, Farah and Soraya. A life without her family.

It had been a lovely trip but it hadn't solved anything.

She'd expected to revel in her freedom, not having responsibilities to family or work. Being the Isolde she used to be. Walking around the Louvre in Paris and visiting chocolate shops in Belgium on her own hadn't been as much fun as she'd expected. It had only made her realise how much she was missing her loved ones.

'I...er...have something to tell you...' Soraya said ominously.

Isolde would've assumed she was about to announce a honeymoon baby was on the way, except her sister's hesitant tone suggested it wasn't good news she was about to impart.

'What is it? Is everything all right?' During her trip away, she'd kept contact to a minimum. Partly because she didn't want to be reminded of everything she'd left behind. Namely Amir. She hadn't heard a word about him, changing the subject any time Soraya mentioned him in a call, and had successfully avoided him at work by leaving. Hopefully one day she'd be back in the job she loved. She might even meet someone who'd make her forget Amir, but right now it didn't feel possible.

Soraya took a deep breath. 'Amir and Farah have moved back with us.'

Silence descended as Isolde processed that. Isolde only realised it had gone on too long when Soraya came on the line again. 'Isolde? Can you hear me? Are you there?'

Then she had to respond. Regardless of her world having just been upended all over again. 'Yes. I heard you.'

'He decided he wanted to have his family around him again. I guess to support him and Farah while she works on her mobility. What happened between you two anyway? You seemed so close to him and Farah at the wedding, then the next thing I heard you'd gone home without them.'

Isolde didn't like keeping secrets from her sister but she didn't want to make things any more awkward in the family. Especially if Amir was living over there now too. 'What has he said?'

'Nothing. He doesn't say much any more unless he's talking about Farah. It's as though the light has gone out of his eyes. Raed said he hasn't seen him like this since the accident. What happened, Isolde? I saw you together. I know something was going on.'

Even from this distance it seemed she couldn't keep anything from her big sister.

'One night, Soraya. That's all it was.'

'Oh, Isolde.' The sound of despair and disappointment in her sibling's voice made Isolde wince.

'He wanted more than I could give him,' she said quietly, the pain starting all over again.

'What were you thinking, Isolde? He and Farah have been through so much already.'

'Why do you think I ended it? They both need someone who can take on the responsibility of being a parent. We all know that's not me. I'm too selfish.'

Soraya tutted. 'That's nonsense. I've seen how you are with Farah, and Amir for that matter. I know it's scary making that sort of commitment. Believe me, I had a wobble before Raed and I finally got together, but it's worth taking the risk. If I thought you didn't love them

I'd say fine, move on, enjoy your travels, but I can hear in your voice that you're not happy. Why else would you be phoning me when you're in one of the most romantic cities in the world?'

'For company...' Isolde looked up at the Eiffel Tower twinkling in the evening light and knew she'd do anything to see Farah's face, to be with Amir. In the back of her mind she'd chosen Paris thinking some handsome Frenchman might sweep her off her feet and kiss her until she forgot all about Amir. Except he was the only man she wanted kissing her.

She'd made a big mistake. Huge.

Her fear of causing the same sort of trauma she and Soraya had gone through as children had prevented her from committing to Amir, but she hadn't taken her own feelings into account. How much she missed him and Farah, or that she'd fallen in love with him. It was difficult to admit that to herself.

Perhaps that was even what she'd been running away from. If there was one thing that defined her move into the world of maturity it was acknowledging her feelings. She hadn't been ready when Amir had asked her to commit to more than a fling, but now not having him in her life at all seemed a worse fate. Quitting her job, flying off on a whim, doing all of those things that she associated with her younger, carefree self simply weren't that fun any more. The last time she'd had that was the day on the beach with Amir and Farah, watching her swim to her proud father. Before she'd freaked out about having actual feelings for someone and run away.

'So, do you want me to tell him you're on your way or…?'

Isolde hated that her sister knew her so well. Better than she even knew herself.

'Hey, Fa-Fa, you want to come with us to the centre today?' Raed came to join Amir and Farah in the garden.

Amir had taken her out for some fresh air after her morning's physio session. She was still in her wheelchair for most of the time but she was making progress. The only problem now was the transition from Isolde to the new physio. It wasn't that Sam wasn't good at his job. He was patient and enthusiastic. He just wasn't Isolde. Farah wasn't responding to him the way she did with Isolde and Amir couldn't blame her when he felt the same. No one could replace Isolde.

'Can I, Papa?'

'Well, I thought we were going to have lunch out here today, together?'

'We do that every day, Papa,' she said, rolling her eyes.

It would be an understatement to say that things hadn't worked out the way he'd planned. After Isolde had left he'd tried to carry on as normal, looking after Farah and working at the hospital when they'd returned to London. Except he'd just been going through the motions. Farah had been upset and confused, as he had been too when he'd discovered Isolde had left the hospital altogether. He'd messed things up for all of them.

Moving here was supposed to be a new start where they had family to support them and help them settle down. Farrah had started a new private school and made some friends, but he was finding it harder to adjust. Raed and Soraya had got him involved at the centre but he was missing the dynamic atmosphere of the hospital. More than that, he missed Isolde.

He'd left everything of her behind, but the memories of their time together burned brightly still in his mind. According to Soraya she was travelling, currently in Paris, living her best life. It felt as though she was trying to prove to him how unsuitable she was as a long-term partner by quitting her job and taking off on a whim, but he wasn't quite buying it. He knew how much she loved her job, and Farah. There was even a sneaking suspicion that she had feelings for him that went beyond the bedroom, and that was why she'd got on the first flight home as soon as he'd suggested moving their relationship to something more serious.

Soraya had hinted at the same, though she hadn't elaborated. He knew they'd been in contact recently but all she'd said was that she didn't believe her sister was happy. It didn't do anything to make him feel better. He hadn't chased her back to London, or even sought her out when he had returned, because he'd thought that was what she wanted. If she wasn't any happier he wondered if the sacrifice had been worth it. They could've had something special but they'd thrown it away in the attempt to prevent each other from being hurt, to make them happy. Well, he was hurt and he certainly wasn't happy.

'Maybe I could come with you? I'm sure there's something I can find to keep me busy.' If Fahid wasn't there for him to check in with, he was sure there was something to keep him busier there than here. The gardener wasn't keen on him 'helping' with the pruning, weeding, or any-thing else he'd tried to do to keep his mind off Isolde and who she might be with in Paris. He didn't want to think of her walking arm in arm along the Champs-Élysées with a handsome stranger, stopping for dinner and a bottle of wine in some quaint bistro… Yeah, he'd been thinking about that way too much.

'Er… I think you'd be better staying here. There's a delivery coming today,' Soraya told him as she arrived on the scene.

'Can't the staff take it in?' He didn't understand why she was using such a lame excuse to get rid of him when they all knew collecting the mail was not something the royal family dirtied their hands with when living at the palace.

'No…er…this is one you're going to want to be here for yourself.' Apparently it was Raed's turn to fob him off. Amir didn't miss the shifty look he shot Soraya. Something was going on and they clearly didn't want him at the centre.

'Fine. Go do your secret stuff and I'll wait here.' He threw his hands up, not wanting to stand in the way if they'd planned something special with Farah today. They were very good at including her in things. That at least justified his reasons for uprooting them to come out here.

'Yeah, we need to leave. Amir, no offence but you might want to have a shave and change your clothes, bro.' Raed checked his watch and made a gesture to Soraya that Amir wasn't sure he was supposed to have seen.

'It's that special a delivery, huh?' he asked no one in

particular as the troublesome trio were already hightailing it out of the gardens.

A glimpse of himself in the windows of the summer house told him perhaps his brother was right. He was beginning to look as bad as he felt.

Isolde's arrival into the country was an altogether different experience when she wasn't travelling as part of the royal family. Soraya and Raed had wanted to pull out all the stops for her but that kind of went against the idea of her low-key visit. She didn't want fanfares and golden carriages heralding her arrival in case Amir didn't want her. In which case she'd be leaving with her tail firmly between her legs and her dignity trailing on the ground behind her.

However, the crowded economy seats on the plane, the overly hot, bumpy bus journey and the racing driver currently masquerading as her taxi transfer were making her rethink returning to her civilian status here so quickly.

Turning up at the palace gates completely unannounced would not have guaranteed her entry, so Soraya and Raed had made arrangements ahead of her arrival. It didn't make the security any less intimidating on the way in.

She wanted to slip in to shower and change after her journey, before she went to find Amir. Soraya had texted to say they'd taken Farah out for the day. Though she was sorry not to see her again, Isolde was glad she and Amir would hopefully have privacy to talk. Despite her sister's assurance that he was missing her, she couldn't be one hundred per cent certain he'd be happy to see her, never mind want to pick up where they'd left off. It had been a big step for him to invite her into his life, and Farah's, and she'd thrown it back in his face. There was no way of knowing if he'd forgive her for that, or indeed, with some time and distance, realise he'd had a lucky escape.

Now it was her turn to show her hand, to tell him she'd made a mistake, and that she loved him, wanted him back. Then it was down to Amir to decide if there was any chance of a future together. If he said no she was on a plane back to England. There was no way she could stay if he didn't want her. In fact any family get-togethers were going to be off limits because she couldn't stand the humiliation and heartache of seeing him, perhaps even with a new partner.

The thought alone made her queasy. It was becoming clear to her she was only here because of her assumption he still wanted her in his life. If she'd missed her chance to be with him, she didn't think she'd ever recover from it.

Instead of heading into the palace she found herself veering off into the gardens for some fresh air to stop her head spinning, and somewhere to sit before her legs gave way.

'Isolde? What are you doing here?' Amir appeared before her, the sun shining behind his head to give him an ethereal look that made her wonder if she'd conjured him up in her imagination.

Then he took her hand in his and she knew he was real. 'Are you okay? You don't look well.'

'This wasn't how it was supposed to be...' She hadn't meant to say it aloud, but this was all wrong. In all the plans she'd made, all the scenarios she'd dreamed, she looked so ravishing he couldn't resist. Not so tired and dishevelled he thought she needed an ambulance.

'What's happened, Isolde? I thought you were in Paris?' He sat down beside her, still clutching her hand, but Isolde figured that was out of concern rather than his desperate need to touch her again.

'I was. I left. I came back.'

'So I see.' His smile was as beautiful as she remembered and she wondered how she'd ever found the strength to leave him, and why.

'I had some time to think, and I, I wanted to see you again.' She was struggling to find the words she knew she needed to say to make this journey worth it, but she was afraid they weren't enough to get the result she wanted.

'Oh? Are you the special delivery I'm supposed to be waiting for?' he asked with a smirk. At least he didn't seem disappointed or angry with her. It was a start.

'I guess so. I'm sorry how we left things. How I left things.' It was entirely her fault and she accepted that.

He was frowning now, the memory of the last time they'd seen each other clearly not a happy one for either of them. 'By the time we came back to the palace that day you'd already gone. Farah was so upset. As was I.'

Hearing it didn't make what she had to say any easier. Okay, so he'd wanted her to stay, but she hadn't, and it was bound to have affected how he felt about her. Especially when she'd caused distress to his daughter too by leaving without another word.

'I'm sorry. I handled things badly. But I was afraid if I stayed you'd change my mind.'

At that, Amir stopped scowling, his eyes wide with

surprise at the knowledge that he'd had the power to make her stay all along. 'You seemed so dead set on leaving. I didn't think you wanted to be with us. With me.'

His words reached in and squeezed Isolde's heart. Knowing she'd hurt him enough to feel that way was devastating.

'It was all I wanted but I thought I was being selfish. That you needed a real grown-up.' She smiled at that. If her time away had taught her anything it was that she was an adult with real, grown-up emotions that couldn't be silenced by last-minute holidays drinking wine on her own.

'And now?'

Isolde swallowed the anxiety creeping up and threatening to overwhelm her with thoughts that this wasn't the right thing to do, that opening up her heart to him was only going to cause more heartache for both of them. But what choice did she have? If she went home now without even trying, she would be back at square one, unsettled, unhappy, and uncertain that she'd done the right thing.

She took a deep breath. 'I've had feelings for you for a long time, Amir. That night together…it awakened something stronger that frightened me. I'm no use at long-term relationships, and I can't guarantee I'll make a good partner to you, or role model for Farah. I don't want to hurt either of you. I never did. But I thought I should at least tell you how I feel.'

'You haven't put a name to it yet. I mean, I understand you're frightened about getting into something serious. So am I. The only way we'll hurt each other is by keeping things to ourselves. We need to be honest, and that includes how we feel about one another. I moved out here with Farah because I couldn't bear life back in London without you. So, in case you're in any doubt, Isolde Yarrow, I'm in love with you.'

A choir of angels sang out her relief as he put her out of her misery by saying the words first so she knew she was safe to say them too. 'I love you too, Amir. I was just afraid to admit it, even to myself.'

The moment the words left her lips he caught them in a kiss. Her sigh of contentment filled the air.

Being with Amir again, feeling that security of his arms around her, was everything she'd been searching for. She just hadn't realised it.

EPILOGUE

'THIS IS THE LIFE.' Isolde lay back on the lounger and let the sun warm her face.

'We need to make the most of the peace and quiet,' Amir said as he lay down beside her.

Isolde instinctively put a hand on her swollen belly, thinking about the chaos that would descend in just a couple of months' time. A baby hadn't been on their agenda at all, but theirs had been conceived on the night of the wedding at the palace.

Although she'd never expected to be a mother, finding out she was expecting Amir's baby had made her feel complete. She had Amir, Farah, her sister, and the rest of the royal family around her, but finally she knew she'd found her role. The idea of being a parent had always terrified her—she'd thought she would screw it up as badly as her parents had—but being around Farah had shown her she was capable of taking on that responsibility and love for a child. Isolde was lucky Amir and Farah had come into her life. She'd never known such love.

'Farah is going to make a wonderful big sister.' The little girl was working so hard to get back on her feet so she'd be able to play with her new brother or sister it was heart-warming. She'd been over the moon when Isolde and Amir had officially become a couple, and hearing there was a baby on the way had made her cry as many happy tears as her father when he'd found out.

'And cousin. There are big changes coming.' Amir grinned.

Not long after her positive pregnancy test, Soraya had announced she and Raed were having a honeymoon baby too. All working together at the centre and living together at the palace had finally given her a true sense of family. Everything was going so well for them both she was afraid to believe it was real.

She reached out a hand to take Amir's. 'Thank you. I can't remember ever being this happy.'

He smiled at her and her heart grew two sizes. She loved him so much she couldn't believe she'd ever been afraid to acknowledge it.

Amir swung his legs around so he was sitting on the edge of his sunbed and rummaged in the bag they'd brought with them to the beach.

'What are you looking for?' she asked, sitting up to see if she could help, but he didn't answer.

Instead he got up off the lounger and knelt in the sand between their two beds.

'What are you doing? You'll burn yourself on the sand.'

Amir held out a small box and opened it to reveal a diamond and platinum ring sparkling so much in the sun it nearly blinded Isolde. 'This is the happiest I've ever been too, but I want to make things official. Isolde Yarrow, would you do me the honour of being my wife?'

She could see the uncertainty on his face and understood his reservations about asking her when she'd protested against any sort of commitment for so long. But affirming their love for one another in a ceremony made him hers as much as the other way around and she didn't want to be without him ever again.

'Yes. There's nothing I'd love more than to be your wife, Amir.' Isolde held her hand out and watched as he slipped the ring on her finger before pulling her into an embrace.

Their family was getting bigger by the day and she couldn't be happier about it.

* * * * *

COMING SOON!

We really hope you enjoyed reading this book.
If you're looking for more romance
be sure to head to the shops when
new books are available on

Thursday 18th January

To see which titles are coming soon, please visit
millsandboon.co.uk/nextmonth

MILLS & BOON

afterglow BOOKS

Introducing our newest series, Afterglow.

From showing up to glowing up, Afterglow characters are on the path to leading their best lives and finding romance along the way – with a dash of sizzling spice!

Follow characters from all walks of life as they chase their dreams and find that true love is only the beginning...

Two stories published every month. Launching January 2024

millsandboon.co.uk

MILLS & BOON®

Coming next month

ER DOC'S LAS VEGAS REUNION
Denise N. Wheatley

'Do you have a minute?' Brandi asked. 'I'd like for you to meet someone.'

As the men walked toward them, Eva's entire body went numb.

'Nooo,' she whispered. 'It can't be...'

'I'm sorry?' Brandi asked her.

'That's—that's Dr *who*?'

'Dr Malone. Dr Clark Malone to be exact. He's one of our emergency room physicians, so you two will be working very closely together.'

Eva's knees gave way. She leaned against the wall, her racing heart palpitating inside her throat as she struggled to grasp Brandi's words.

Clark Malone...

He and Eva shared a tumultuous past that she'd buried deep in the corners of her mind. Up until now. Because as he approached, a whirlwind of memories came racing to the forefront, the first being that he was no longer a handsome yet wiry young medical student. Clark had matured into a full blown, broad shouldered, extremely fine-looking man.

They'd met during their first year of medical school. Despite the undeniable chemistry between them, Eva and Clark had formed a tight platonic bond. Together they'd helped one another adjust to a new city, an extremely challenging course load and a rigorous schedule. While free time was sparse, they'd sneak off on occasion to Cedar Rapids, Iowa's Black Sheep Social Club for live jazz music, or Pub 217 for veggie black bean burgers. The friendship they'd built was solid, inimitable even. But all that had changed one night during their third year.

Losing Clark as a friend had hurt her deeply. But Eva's aspirations had taken precedence over her emotions – she'd worked too hard to risk getting distracted. But she'd thought about him many times over the years—particularly that one steamy night they'd shared. While it had been amazing, Eva couldn't help but regret how it led to the demise of their friendship. She'd contemplated contacting Clark on numerous occasions but had always talked herself out of it. After the emotional rollercoaster ride they'd endured, she didn't think he would want to hear from her. Since he'd never reached out to her either, Eva had figured he'd moved on and decided to do the same.

Now here he was, standing before her at Fremont General Hospital of all places.

What were the odds?

Continue reading
ER DOC'S LAS VEGAS REUNION
Denise N. Wheatley

Available next month
millsandboon.co.uk

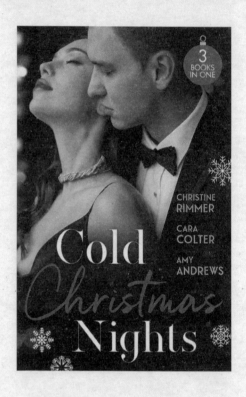

LET'S TALK

Romance

For exclusive extracts, competitions and special offers, find us online:

- **f** MillsandBoon
- **X** @MillsandBoon
- **◎** @MillsandBoonUK
- **♪** @MillsandBoonUK

Get in touch on 01413 063 232

MILLS & BOON

THE HEART OF ROMANCE

A ROMANCE FOR EVERY READER

MODERN
Prepare to be swept off your feet by sophisticated, sexy and seductive heroes, in some of the world's most glamourous and romantic locations, where power and passion collide.

HISTORICAL
Escape with historical heroes from time gone by. Whether your passion is for wicked Regency Rakes, muscled Vikings or rugged Highlanders, awaken the romance of the past.

MEDICAL
Set your pulse racing with dedicated, delectable doctors in the high-pressure world of medicine, where emotions run high and passion, comfort and love are the best medicine.

True Love
Celebrate true love with tender stories of heartfelt romance, from the rush of falling in love to the joy a new baby can bring, and a focus on the emotional heart of a relationship.

Desire
Indulge in secrets and scandal, intense drama and sizzling hot action with heroes who have it all: wealth, status, good looks... everything but the right woman.

HEROES
The excitement of a gripping thriller, with intense romance at its heart. Resourceful, true-to-life women and strong, fearless men face danger and desire - a killer combination!

To see which titles are coming soon, please visit

millsandboon.co.uk/nextmonth